Håkan Magnusson

AN APOCALYPSE STORY

David L. Parrott

Green Barn Workshop Press

Green Barn Workshop Press
29 Parrot Road
DuBois, Pennsylvania 15801 (USA)
www.greenbarnworkshop.com

Publisher's Note: This is a work of fiction. Names, characters, places, and incidents are a product of the author's imagination. Locales and public names are sometimes used for atmospheric purposes. Any resemblance to actual people, living or dead, or to businesses, companies, events, institutions, or locales is completely coincidental.

Book Layout © 2016 BookDesignTemplates.com

Håkan Magnusson/ David L. Parrott. -- 1st ed.
ISBN 979-8-9904153-0-0

But as the days of Noah were, so shall also the coming of the Son of man be.

For as in the days that were before the flood they were eating and drinking, marrying and giving in marriage, until the day that Noah entered into the ark,

And knew not until the flood came, and took them all away;

So shall also the coming of the <u>Son of Man</u> be.

CHAPTER ONE

Stefan Andersson, 90 miles north of the Arctic Circle, near the city of Kiruna, Sweden

It was a glorious first day of spring – the first such in three and a half years. Stefan blamed *that* for what he did that day. Spring fever, cabin fever, the effect of the warmth of the sunshine on his upturned face, the scent of thawing ground, and moldering leaves in his nostrils. That was what caused him to abandon caution and act so foolishly, the "frisky winds of spring" as an old Swedish folk song put it

.

Vårvindar friska leka	*Spring breezes weave and whisper,*
Och viska lunderna kring	*All through the trees, now green,*
Likt älskande par.	*As young lovers be.*
Strömarna ila,	*Streams flow in a hurry,*
Finna ej vila	*No rest or worry*
Förrän I havet störtvågen far.	*Until their foam meets the sea.*
Klaga mitt hjärta,	*Cry out my heart.*
Klaga och hör	*Cry out and hear*
Vallhornets klang	*The herdsman's horn*
Bland klipporna dör.	*Now echo, then pale.*
Strömkarlen spelar,	*River sprites playing,*
Sorgerna delar	*Sorrows dismaying*
Vakan kring berg och dal.	*They wake in hill and dale.*

He pulled his truck just out of the woods so he could see the train arrive at the Kiruna Work Camp and begin unloading its human cargo and other goods.

That was when he first saw her. She was in the line with all the others, the guards were shouting and prodding the workers, and then suddenly she was running.

Right towards him.

This is nuts, he said to himself, I should leave.

But ... she was beautiful, and he was lonely.

He pulled his truck forward out of the trees so she could see him.

One of the Russian guards raised his Kalashnikov and swung it in her direction. One quick burst and she'd be gone. But then something strange happened. Something Stefan had not seen in any of his previous clandestine visits. The prisoners turned on the guards, knocking them down, and wrestling with them for their weapons.

Stefan still sat immobilized in the truck, slack-jawed, amazed. There were gunshots, and one old man fell suddenly. Beside him Björn stirred and yelped, looking at him anxiously as if to say *"Master, do something!"*

So, he did.

He floored it and raced down the hill, mud and thawing snow flying from the tires of his truck.

He spun the truck in the muddy field beside her just as a guard turned his attention to them and raised his rifle. "Get in!" he shouted as he whipped the door open and jumped out.

She hesitated. Her dark eyes met his, and Stefan could see bits of mud on her face and clothes, and tiny droplets of sweat on her brow. Her eyebrows were furrowed in concentration, her deep brown eyes studying him, the truck, the dog. A line of bullets arced up beside her, and one of them struck the bottom of the truck door opening, another struck Björn sitting beside him and he let out a single yelp, and a third smashed through the vent window on the far side of the truck. The girl dove in the truck.

Stefan climbed back in beside her as another round of

bullets tore up the ground beneath him.

He floored the accelerator again and the truck roared up the hill toward a line of pine trees and away.

CHAPTER TWO

Once they crested the hill and were deep in the forest, Stefan slowed the truck down. The road had narrowed and become more rutted and as they moved slowly through the trees he introduced himself, *"Jag heter Stefan."*

"Miko," the girl responded, and then switched to English, no doubt because from his accent she could tell he wasn't *actually* Swedish. "Your dog is bleeding." She nodded downward. Stefan glanced down and saw a dark spot on the old rug he used as a seat cover. Before he could say anything else, the girl had grabbed a rag from the floor of the truck and begun squeezing the dog's foot.

Stefan slowed down his truck even more. He could feel Björn's breath coming in raspy huffs. He looked sideways at him and saw Björn's nervous look and squinting eyes. He didn't whimper, but he was in pain. Stefan wondered if he should stop the truck and tend to him further. But no sooner did that thought cross his mind than something buzzed over the truck and wheeled towards them. A drone. Shit!

"Take the wheel!" Stefan yelled to the girl.

She shook her head "No."

"They'll catch us! Take the damn wheel!" Stefan said, slowing the truck and swinging the door open.

The drone circled behind them and came in closer. Stefan stepped onto the running board as the truck continued forward and saw the girl reluctantly grab the wheel to keep the truck from crashing into the woods. He stood on the running board, reached into a toolbox mounted in the truck bed, and quickly pulled out a shotgun, as the drone swung back down out of the trees. He blasted it out of the sky. He swung back into the cab, out of breath from the sudden exertion.

She gave him a dirty look, which Stefan didn't know how to interpret.

"Why did you hesitate? Do you want to go back to the camps?" He asked her.

She looked away, "Yeah, sure, take me back. I'm missing dinner."

Stefan shook his head. Why the hostility? "A little gratitude wouldn't kill you."

"I figured that's what you expected. A little gratitude. That's what the guards at the camp wanted too. A little gratitude." She looked away, out the window.

Stefan slowed the truck to a stop at a bend and turned towards her. Which was useless, because she was concentrating hard on a stand of white birch trees out the passenger side window.

He turned off the truck engine, and it was suddenly still in the truck. The wind blew gently, swaying the tree branches near them. It also seemed much darker. The sun had dipped below the tree line, and now the darkness began to roll over them like a wave.

In a quiet voice, Stefan said, "There are sled dog trails right there in the woods. About a hundred yards or so up that trail are some *Korvakota* – old Sami teepees that they used at night for the tourist trips. I think you'll find a few provisions still left, canned food, stuff to make a fire."

Still no response. He waited. Björn huffed and puffed and whimpered slightly, and Stefan ruffled the thick white fur on his head. The girl continued looking out the window, avoiding his gaze. But he noticed a wetness on her chin, a single drop of water poised to fall.

"They..." she started to say, and her hand raised to her nose as she became choked up. "They..."

Stefan reached past Björn and popped open the glove box of the truck. He had some napkins from the diner in Kuuravaara – with the logo of that now long-gone enterprise. She reached in, took one, and blew her nose loudly.

Stefan wanted to say "They hurt you. But I never will. I'm a good man. A gentleman." But when had that ever been true?

He ruffled Björn's fur again, and gave him his favorite rub, pushing a knuckle inside his warm soft, and furry ear. Björn responded by leaning towards him, a warm and comforting weight.

Miko wiped her eyes, blew her nose, and glanced at him, her face blotchy and reddish. "Your dog is hurt. Shouldn't we get him somewhere?"

Stefan started the truck and headed further into the deep forest. A flash of green appeared across a meadow – the northern lights came into view wherever there was a break in the woods.

CHAPTER THREE

Miko Nakama

Therefore prophesy and say unto them, Thus saith the Lord GOD; Behold, O my people, I will open your graves, and cause you to come up out of your graves, and bring you into the land of Israel. And ye shall know that I am the LORD, when I have opened your graves, O my people, and brought you up out of your graves, And shall put my spirit in you, and ye shall live, and I shall place you in your own land: then shall ye know that I the LORD have spoken it, and performed it, saith the LORD.

Two hours later they arrived at Stefan's hideaway. Miko could tell they were getting close because the dog Björn started sniffing the air, his nose pointed upwards, glancing from side to side and whimpering with excitement. When they turned into the drive he started barking – so loudly that it made Miko's ears ring, and Stefan reached up a hand and squeezed the big dog's mouth shut to silence him. Some reindeer were grazing on some exposed grass that ignored them, their sad eyes shining red in the lights of the truck as they slowly stepped off the rutted old road.

The truck pulled deeper into the woods, near what looked like a fallen down mining shed, and everything was illuminated with the pale green light of the aurora sky above.

"Not much of a house," Miko said to Stefan who had been silent for some time.

"That's not my house. It's my workshop."

He got out, stretched stiffly, and groaned. He opened a rickety door on the shop and pulled the truck inside a dark musty building. The dog raced around excitedly, with one foot held up in the air, still wrapped in a rag and duct tape. He was off barking at the reindeer and herding them away from the clearing into the woods.

Stefan started walking towards what looked like a root cellar, fumbling in his pocket for a key. In the dim light, Miko made out a door recessed into the hillside.

"You live in a hobbit hole!" she said.

He responded with a dirty look, stepped in turned on a flashlight, and then seemed to disappear sideways. She heard an engine starting up, and then the lights came on.

"It's a mineshaft," she said. "You live in an old coal mine?"

He looked at her askance, as if she were a dolt. "Old iron ore mine."

It made sense to her now. How he had managed to live hidden away since the holocaust.

"I didn't expect any guests to my 'man cave'," he said, apologetically, kicking aside some clothes. Miko wondered if he knew how appropriate that term was for what she was seeing – a literal "caveman" in his natural habitat.

More lights came on. He began fumbling with what looked like a wood stove made out of a steel drum. He took out blackened wood chunks and put them in another metal container. He put a pan of water on the heater to warm and whistled for the dog, who came limping up. Miko held him while Stefan gently cleaned and wrapped his paw, after which the dog headed for a pile of pillows that was his favorite spot.

"Why did you take wood *out* of your wood stove?"

"It's charcoal now," he said - as if that explained anything. Miko shook her head.

He pointed back towards the door, "provides heat, makes charcoal, which I use to power the generator and my truck."

"Seems like a lot of work," Miko said.

"Seen any gas stations open lately?" Stefan said, meeting her gaze. She noticed how blue his eyes were, the gaunt lines on his face. How old was he? Or was he just weathered, like an American Indian?

"You're a prepper! I've heard about your kind."

"I've lived like this for five years," Stefan said.

"Why?" Miko said.

His gaze returned to her. It was intense, unsettling, and direct. "I had a feeling something bad was going to happen."

"Just a feeling – so you moved into a cave?"

He shrugged, and met her eyes again, as if weighing what he might say next, "I had dreams. Dreams about things turning bad. I learned not to talk about them with other people."

"You became a hermit!" Miko said, and then regretted it. Why was she grilling him, Christ, he had just saved her from the goddamn camps.

"I had friends, a car repair business. I used to go to a church in Kiruna. Those people are all gone or working in the camps now." He had moved on to a different section of his tunnel or whatever you might call it that appeared to be a makeshift kitchen and was rummaging around for food.

"You haven't talked to anyone in four years?" she said, pulling up a stool at a thick wooden counter. She noticed there was only a single stool.

"I have a couple of Sami friends still around a bit further north. They leave them alone. They live off the reindeer as their grandparents used to." He disappeared down a side shaft she hadn't even noticed, and came back with a clear glass jug, and what looked like a bag of frozen vegetables and something else wrapped in paper. He noticed her looking somewhat incredulously at the bag of vegetables and added, "Root cellar. All permafrost up here, you know…"

She shook her head. He was the strangest man she had ever met.

"Cider? I also have some coffee squirreled away if you like that?"

"Cider," she said. He got two glasses from a cupboard. They were weathered and cloudy, but clean. She also noticed there were no dirty dishes in the sink, but a few clean ones drying in a rack beside it. He poured her a tall glass of cider, which she found a bit bitter but refreshing after the long ride. She watched as he put wood in an old enameled stove, like something you'd see in the Skansen Museum in Stockholm

He unwrapped two pieces of meat, added some lard to a black cast iron frying pan, and then put the meat in.

"Hey, what's in this cider? Did you spike it?"

He laughed, and she noted how his eyes crinkled up. "Just apples, and yeast. It's kind of like cheap beer."

"More like *Strong* beer." Was he trying to get her drunk? Odd, though, because he seemed more concerned about getting her food. She noticed the dog had also limped off his pillow in the corner and was sitting beside her, hopeful of a meal.

He was slicing leeks and mushrooms to add to the meat. He got a bottle of something that looked like a rosé wine out of his cold storage area, uncorked it, and added a dash of it to the frying pan. "If you think the cider is strong, taste this… He poured a bit into her glass for her to try.

It was not rosé. It had an odd flavor. Definitely not wine.

Maybe he was trying to get her drunk, but if so, why hadn't he filled her glass?

"Lingonberry mead," he said. "Fermented honey with lingonberries to add flavoring. My honey and lingonberries from Kuarravaara, more?"

She nodded yes, and their eyes met again as he leaned forward to fill her glass. What an odd man. He sounded like a teacher, but he looked like a lumberjack. A warmth seemed to settle over her. When was the last time she had shared a meal with a man? What was this sensation she was feeling? - - no, she knew. It was freedom.

Later, she justified what happened afterward for that. After four years of bondage, he had set her free. Almost, dare she think it, like a white knight coming to her rescue?

She awoke in the middle of the night from a dream. She was being chased, and in her terror had thrashed around and fallen partway off the couch he had made up for her in what passed for his living room. He was sleeping on an Ikea futon bed down the tunnel, near the stove. It was warmer there, and she stood near the fire and warmed herself, it had gotten chilly over by the couch which was right against the cold stone wall. She saw his face illuminated by the glow of the wood stove and went and squeezed in beside him. He was soundly asleep, but he stirred, wrapped an arm around her, and pulled her to him.

That was when all hell broke loose.

.

CHAPTER FOUR

Stefan Andersson

Stefan dreamt that he was running. He was in the woods, and behind him, there was someone, or perhaps more accurately, *something* chasing him. It crashed through the deep pine forest behind him. He dared not look back. Up ahead, was the lake, and the road around the lake was off to his left. The water glittered in the crisp fall sunshine. The sky was a deep, deep blue. He reached a small valley in the forest, and that is when he noticed the rushing water. It was sunny and clear, yet the forest was flooding, the lake was overflowing and beginning to rush towards him. Clear cold water rushed towards him - but he could look down and see the forest floor through the rippling water. He had never seen anything like it. It was very striking and odd and something he would not forget, even when he awoke.

He stepped into the water that was rising in the woods and continued to try to race ahead, but his steps came slower, and now behind him he heard the breath of the beast. It was almost like he was in slow motion, paralyzed. There was rising water ahead and the beast chasing him from behind. He could feel it closing in on him, its breath husky and loud. It was in his ear now, warm and insistent. He felt a hand on his shoulder, but he didn't want to turn and look. It squeezed him tighter. It was turning him around, and his heart raced.

Stefan woke up with a start and almost screamed. Someone was on top of him! He was being attacked!

Wait, no. Not attacked. It was the girl. She had slipped

into his bed. Her head was beside his, and her breath was warm and insistent.

"I was cold," she said, simply.

He calmed down, tried to shake off the images from the dream, and came back to reality. The strange flood in the pine forest, being chased by a monster, *that* was just a dream, *this* was real.

He felt the pleasing weight of her on him and reached down to draw her even closer. Her breath and her scent were intoxicating. His hand on her lower back felt the raised edge of her t-shirt and the soft skin below it. He could feel tiny soft hairs, and skin as smooth as a baby's cheek. He felt how soft and yet firm she was as he pressed her even harder against him. He drew his hand up to her shoulder blades, pressing her against him, becoming fully aroused.

She sighed as his hand slid back down lower.

And that was when he found it, and shouted, "Stop!"

"What? What?"

"Your chip. They've chipped you!"

"I didn't know! I swear I didn't know! It's where I can't reach or feel it!" she said. She bolted upright, pulling the blanket with her to cover herself.

Stefan reached over and turned on the light. Miko sat with her face in her hands, shaking her head.

"Yeah, right," Stefan said, disgusted. He reached to the end of the bed to his jeans and pulled them on.

"Cut the chip out then you son of a bitch!"

He nodded, calmer. "OK, I can do that..."

"What? No, I was being sarcastic!"

"I cut mine out. I numbed it up with Novocain and popped it out."

He was up off the bed, reaching for a t-shirt on a shelf beside the bed.

Less than an hour later Stefan was back in the truck, heading slowly North along a forest road in the rough direction of Kurravaara. He didn't turn his headlights on, instead, he drove by the flickering of the Northern lights. Small shrubs and baby trees brushed up on the underside of his truck because even these roads were reverting to nature. It was a strange time to be awake. He was so used to his structured schedule that to be up and about at four in the morning was an odd sensation. His senses were keener, his impressions of his surroundings stronger. He felt oddly light-headed and almost giddy.

His mind returned to the task he had just completed; to the image of Miko lying face-down on his bed, her eyes closed. He had lifted her shirt slightly to reveal her lower back. Her skin was milky white. Her slanted eyes and raven hair had made him think she was a Saami girl, but her skin was too pale. Thai? Japanese? Her name sounded Japanese. There was a smattering of freckles leading down to the swell of her hips, now covered with his blanket, but only with that. He sighed. He wouldn't be able to get that image out of his mind anytime soon.

North of Lake Nukutusjarvi there were meadows. Ages ago the Saami kept herds here, and he knew some reindeer had returned. Hopefully, they wouldn't remember him coming to hunt them a few months ago.

He stopped the truck when he saw their dark shadows against the hillside. From his pocket he took out some apple slices he had thawed, and approached the reindeer slowly; years without human contact had made them much less tame than before. He held out the apple slices, and one of the older reindeer spotted them in his hand and approached.

It remembered people and came forward to take an apple slice and nuzzled his hand. Its nose sought out his pocket for more, and when it did Stefan slipped the old dog collar over its neck. He patted its head and it shook itself — a shared moment of pleasure between man and beast.

Finding the rest of the apples in his pocket, the reindeer greedily ate them, while Stefan stroked its soft fur. Its warm and trusting eyes searched his face — Stefan wondered if it was remembering an old friend. Which was silly, reindeer are not very bright. Then he turned away and returned to the truck which seemed oddly empty without Björn riding along. He took out his shotgun from the toolbox once again and fired it into the air. The reindeer all leaped up at once and took off, including the one with the collar which had the chip firmly duct-taped to it. Stefan got back into his truck and headed home.

At the Ångström Supercomputing Laboratory in Uppsala, a red dot appeared on a screen. The technician announced, "Miko's moving again. Running actually, through the woods."

Dr. Bob spoke to the avatar of Håkan on the screen, "She's heading north now, into the forest. Probably heading to Kuuravaara with our target - maybe on skis?"

Håkan, who was always awake, acknowledged his comment, today choosing a female voice that sounded like a British TV personality. The chip provided speed telemetry, heart rate, temperature, and other data, Håkan studied it for a moment as it moved on one of the many screens in the room.

"*Fucking* Stefan," Håkan said.

"What do you mean?" Dr. Bob asked.

"He's done something with the chip, and the girl must be with him somewhere else. Those idiots at the camp shouldn't have wasted their only drone flying so close to him – God knows where he and the girl will be now…

In the deep snow of the northern forest, Stefan turned the truck to head for home. He saw some clouds sneaking in from the west. It had gotten chillier in the long arctic night. As he headed back to his place it began to snow. Springtime was over, at least for the moment. He hoped it wouldn't take 4 more years for it to return again.

CHAPTER FIVE

When he returned to his place, she was sleeping soundly. Not wanting to disturb her, Stefan began to make breakfast. In his underground freezer, tucked in the back of his mine and cooled by permafrost, he had some egg whites and yolks, frozen separately. They were from his last visit to Duvnik's farm. Thinking of him sparked an idea of what they might do next.

Stefan also brought out some dark coffee beans, kept for special occasions, and began brewing coffee. He started making *Rågpannkakor* – rye pancakes, with flour, and canned milk. In another frying pan, he used some bear lard to oil the pan and then began cooking some reindeer sausage. Miko began stirring, and rose, with a blanket wrapped around her. She came and sat at his kitchen counter.

"Oh my god, that smells good." She said, lifting a cup of coffee that he had placed before her. "I haven't seen a meal like this cooked at home in years."

Stefan noticed her smile – something he had not seen before, it lit up the room like a sunrise. Unsure just how to broach the subject, he dove in, "Could be some time before we eat like this again. I want to leave after breakfast."

Her face fell. "I was hoping to hide out here for a while."

He pursed his lips, "The chip…"

"But you got rid of it."

"What I did last night might slow them down. But not for long."

He slid a plate before her. Scrambled eggs, pancakes, and sausage. He added a slice of *Vörtlimpa* - rye bread he had made with grain leftover from brewing beer. "Oh god, this is good." She said, eating with a strong appetite. "I guess I should enjoy this while it lasts."

Their eyes met over the brim of her coffee cup. He wondered how much to tell her of what he thought lay ahead. At the very least they needed to get far deeper into the tundra – beyond the easy range of snow machines and troops from the mining camp. But for this moment, her dark eyes were merry...

After this remarkably pleasant *frukost*, they cleaned the dishes and began to close up his place. He couldn't help but wonder if he would ever return here. He didn't know if it made him happy or sad; it seemed to make him both at once. He loved solitude. He loved the quiet of the forest, the evenings reading a book with Björn sitting beside him, leaning warmly into him. He loved the physicality of chopping wood to make charcoal, making repairs to his truck, and long afternoons skiing on old logging trails. But at times it had been too quiet, too peaceful, too removed from life with others. At times the solitude had overwhelmed him and he had longed for a companion. It was ironic that now that he seemed to have found someone this time of solitude must end.

Reluctantly, they put on their outdoor clothes and went to his shop. He readied a sleigh to carry some supplies, added a thermos that contained the very last of his brewed coffee to his pack, and locked the door. He found skis and boots that fit her, and they set off.

The sun was at its highest point of the day when they approached Duvnik's farm. Björn had begun limping badly an hour before, and Stefan had lifted him onto the pile of blankets on the sleigh and sternly told him to lay still. Miko skied beside him, her face pink from the cold, with a determined look. She had struggled at first to keep up, but after an hour or so she began to find her stride. Despite her stoic look, though, Stefan worried that her borrowed ski boots were chafing her feet and he was glad their ski tour was nearly finished for the day. But only a moment later he saw the snowmobile tracks angling in from the south and knew they were in trouble. For the Russians to have used some of their precious remaining gasoline meant that this was the highest of priorities for them.

Stefan reached out and tapped Miko's shoulder. She turned to him and he held a finger to his lips. Björn stirred uneasily on the sleigh, a low growl came from his throat, and then in an instant, he was off the sled, racing up the snowmobile track toward the farm, the fur on his back standing up.

Stefan had a hunting rifle on his back, he pulled it off his shoulder chambered a round, and then raced forward to try to catch up to Björn.

Smoke was coming from the chimney of the low stone house. Reindeer were milling around and they were startled by Björn's loud and frantic barking as he raced back and forth, his nose to the scent on the ground. Björn raced off towards the trees, back to the South when Stefan reached the house. From all of this activity, Stefan concluded that there must have been dogs here just moments before and that Björn was defending this territory against them. He saw that Miko was approaching, pulling the sled with one hand, her face screwed up with exertion. She was a trooper.

Stefan saw the front door was ajar and used the butt of his rifle to tap it open. He immediately saw Duvnik lying dead inside. But he wasn't alone. Just inside the door were two other dead men. They wore the uniform of the mining security force. Russians, probably. They must have been the first of his assailants in the door. Duvnik had died fighting whoever followed them in, so it had probably been four men against one.

But at least he died fighting, Stefan thought. Unlike the rest of humanity, those who died in the pandemic…

"Ravna!" Stefan called out. He still held the rifle forward but used his foot to kick open their bedroom door. "Ravna!" he yelled out again. Silence.

Miko poked her head in the doorway, and Stefan was so keyed up with adrenaline that he swung the rifle toward her without even thinking. That was when he saw something else that made his heart sink into his shoes. Duvnik's reindeer herd was standing just behind her. The reindeer had come to the yard for their feeding time, expecting Duvnik to give them their daily treat of rye and oats. Standing prominently among them was one pure white reindeer that Stefan knew only too well – the one that wore the collar he had put on her last night, the collar with the chip.

He sank to his knees and buried his face in his hands. Oh God, he thought, I led them right here!

He saw Miko's ski boots through his fingers, she stood before him, "I'm sorry about your friend!" she said. "Did something happen to his wife, too?"

Stefan felt tears come to his eyes. "That's not all. That reindeer – he pointed behind her - the one with the collar. That is where I put your chip."

"Oh no," Miko said, shaking her head, "No, no, no!"

"I thought the reindeer would lead them away. I should have known. I should have known! So Stupid!"

"Do you think they killed his wife also?"

"Oh, they killed her all right. Three years ago. But his daughter Ravna hid from them. She's about 15 years old now ."

Miko's face grew pale in the waning sunlight. She knew what that meant for the guards – a new girl, barely a teenager.

Stefan stood up and dusted off the snow from his knees. "I'm going after them. I swear to God – I'm getting her back if I have to kill every Goddamn Russian in Kiruna to do it."

CHAPTER SIX

Ravna Duvniksdottir

"One death is a tragedy.
A million deaths,
a statistic."
Joseph Stalin

"Viehkat! Niibi!" "Run!...Knife!"

That is what her father yelled when they heard the roar of the snowmobiles. She had been tending the reindeer near her father's work shed. Ravna took off towards the reindeer standing frightened at the edge of the tundra. She grabbed an extra *puuko* knife and thrust it in her fur boot top, and then swung onto the back of Aggi, her favorite reindeer, and galloped towards the meadow.

She heard shouting, and men screaming, but not her father screaming. Then there were gunshots, and then silence. She leaned forward and coaxed Aggi forward, heading for a stand of stunted fir trees across the tundra. She had escaped the Russians this way before...

Aggi galloped for the woods, sensing her fear. But then she heard the snow machine starting up and looked over her shoulder. Two men had run out of the cabin and were mounting their snow machines again. Neither one was her father. Her heart sank. She leaned her head forward and felt Aggi's warm fur, his musky tundra scent, and she saw that his eyes too were wide with fear.

She was barely in the woods when they caught up to her. One of them raised his rifle and there was a deafening bang, and then she and Aggi fell together as she cried out *"NO!"*

They marched her back to her father's shop and found a small sleigh and some rope. One Russian had a broken front tooth and dark hair. The other was fair, with blue eyes, and was thinner, better looking. They talked quickly in Russian and laughed, and her mind raced with what horrible things they had in mind. They opened her coat, looking for weapons, she supposed, but it seemed more like they were just leering at her. She felt her face color, and one of them pointed at her and said something in Russian, and they laughed again.

They tied her to the sled and hooked it to the back of their snowmobile. She noticed how poorly "Gap Tooth" tied knots. They started to pull her down the trail back to Kiruna, but the knotted rope came apart, and there was what sounded like some cursing, and then the blond man tied it differently. While they did this, Ravna saw her father's black and white herding dog Čalmmo howling on the porch. Čalmmo had white dots of fur above its eyes, which could see the spirit world. She bowed her head and wished the spirit of her father peace on his journey.

By the time this all was done, the temperature had dropped again, and the sun was setting in the southwest sky. The lights of the snowmobiles came on, and they seemed to speed up. Ravna wondered if they would travel most of the night to the Kiruna mining camp and train station, but perhaps halfway there the blond Russian raised his hand and pointed, and they headed to a cabin just off the trail. Gap Tooth kicked the door in and while Blondie led her, still bound, to a musty couch. The Russians fumbled around making a fire. They must be city boys, she thought; they are so inept. It took a long time for the fire to start, and then it was so smoky that she wondered if birds had nested in the flue. Eventually, it began to warm up in the cabin, and the years-old damp and musty smells began to clear away.

Gap Tooth produced a flask from his coat and the two began drinking. This made Ravna even more nervous, for she could easily imagine the terrible things that would happen next. But she hoped it would also cloud their thinking and make them careless. In this, she was right because soon they began to show the effects of the spirits. They stumbled around, with Gap Tooth talking louder and louder, and now gesturing at her to remove her coat. She pretended to be compliant and held her hands out for him to untie, her ankles were still bound together.

The blond man shouted something at Gap Tooth when she had her coat off and he was starting to remove her tunic as well. He stopped, his face angry, and retied her wrists — but again, he had no skills, and she immediately began to work her wrists and fingers to get free. Gap Tooth was hooting and hollering as he got her top off and began fondling her, looking back at his friend with glee. But also hurrying, excited.

He yanked her trousers down and exposed her nakedness, and now he was on her, thrusting. She held her tied hands to her right - away from the side where the blonde man sat watching. She soon made progress getting one hand free and used that to distract herself from what was going on with the drunken oaf overshadowing her. She made a show of screaming at the same time as Gap Tooth tried to press himself into her. But now her hand was free, and she clutched the *Puuko* and as he pressed into her, she sharply swung it up and into his side, and then pressed it sideways as hard as she could, hoping to find his heart.

She succeeded.

He bellowed like a reindeer she had once seen taken by a wolf and rolled off her. And instantly Blonde Man was on top of her, struggling to get the knife from her hand. They thrashed together onto the floor on top of Gap Tooth who writhed and screamed in his death throes. She saw sparks fly up in a cloud from the fire as Gap tooth's hand landed in the flames, and he winced and with his last movement pulled it back. Just then the Blonde Man finally yanked the knife free from her hand and tossed it away. His face flushed red, he shoved her back onto the couch, and now he jumped on her, his face suffused with lust.

While he used both hands to push his pants down again, her hand found the other *Puuko* that she had in her boot. When he attempted to press into her, she wrapped her arms around his back in an embrace, but it was a deadly one. In her left hand, she had the L-shaped antler handle of the second knife, and it gave her a strong grip to push the blade deep into his back. His face, which had been flushed with pleasure suddenly turned black with pain and he leaped off her. He only took two stumbling steps away from her when he collapsed face-first onto the floor and began kicking. In just moments the men were both still on the floor. Ravna pulled her clothes, now soiled with blood, back on. The fire was dying out, but embers were smoldering on the floorboards.

"You two idiots would have burned this place down," she said, but her voice sounded hollow and eerie in the silence of the cabin. She stomped out the burning patches on the floor and dragged the men off into the darkness of a small kitchen area in the back. She built the fire, and though she had never had a drink before in her life, she picked up the tipped-over whiskey flask and took a sip. It tasted awful, like medicine. She found some drier lumber in a bin that the Russians had overlooked and built a decent fire.

When it was roaring up in the hearth, she slid the couch closer to the fire and sat and drank the rest of the bottle. It wasn't much, but it spread a warm glow into her sore belly and groin where the Russians had pushed into her. When there was just a tiny sip left in the bottle, she raised it to the fire, "I toast you father, *verisurman saaneiden vainajala* — may your journey through the sky bring you peace denied you at your blood-death."

As if in answer, she saw the flicker of red aurora borealis through the smudged window. A single tear flowed down her cheek, and she lay back into her coat on the couch before the fire and slept.

Stefan Andersson

The sun was setting when Stefan and Miko headed down the trail made by the snowmobiles. They traveled through the night, which was lit by a full moon, and by ever clearer Northern Lights as they continued over the snow. From time to time they would pause, and Stefan would sit with Miko on the sleigh, pulled by one of the more docile reindeer from Duvnik's her. They were sharing strong, hot, black coffee from a big thermos that had the word *Duvnik* inked on the side — another gift from his farm.

Late at night, the Northern Lights turned red, and Stefan stared at it, shaking his head.

"What is it?" Miko asked, twisting her toes in her boots to try to warm them.

"The Saami think that a blood aurora means death. That seems true tonight, with what happened to Duvnik," Stefan said, but inwardly he was thinking of Ravna. Was she already dead at the hands of her captors? It was the most likely possibility he thought sadly, but said nothing.

"My feet are freezing, we must find somewhere to stop," Miko said.

Stefan met her eyes, which glowed with reflected light, "I think there is a cabin not too far ahead. It is rough, but we can take a break there. It shouldn't take long." He got back on the runners of his sleigh and flicked the reins. The reindeer shook his antlers and grudgingly began pulling ahead.

Stefan was wrong. It was much longer than he thought to the cabin when they finally made it, the sky had begun to lighten with the spring dawn. Worse than that, there were two snowmobiles parked in front of the cabin, one with a crudely fastened sled tied to it. Ravna! He thought.

He noticed a wisp of smoke coming from the chimney, a fire that had burned out. The front door was just slightly ajar. He held a finger to his lips to silence Miko and waved her away. He gently cocked his rifle and holding it at waist level prodded the door open. Immediately, he saw Ravna lying on the couch, and his heart sank. She was covered in dried blood. Oh God, no, he thought.

But she opened her eyes and stared at him. She was alive!

He swung the rifle to and fro, expecting at any second to be jumped by the Russians. Ravna smiled a tired smile at him and sat up, but he motioned frantically for her to stay down. Then she laughed.

"Hello *Herr* Stefan," she said, using the formal greeting as a joke. She often called him Herr Stefan or Uncle Stefan in jest at the times when he came to visit her father

It was then that he spotted the soles two pairs of large black boots facing him from the small kitchen area in the back. He looked back at Ravna.

"They're dead," she said.

Over his shoulder, he felt rather than saw Miko enter. He stepped forward to Ravna, and put his hands on her shoulders, looking in her eyes he said, "How badly are you hurt?"

"I am not hurt," she smiled again. "Father said to take two knives. I used both of them."

In the gathering light, he saw the bony antler handle of a *Puuko* sticking out of the back of a blond man closest to them. Miko now had stepped closer, looking from Ravna to the Russians to Stefan with her mouth open.

"All this blood?" Stefan asked.

"None of it is mine," Ravna said. "But it is smelly. Can we build a fire in the stove and warm some water so I can wash it off?"

CHAPTER SEVEN

Ulf Johansson, Visby, Gotland

Ulf Johansson had been given a task, and *by god!* he was going to complete it if it was the last thing he did in this life.

On the day of the invasion, Ulf's phone lit up with Red Alerts. It was late fall, and he was sailing in the archipelago north of Stockholm with Kalle and Patrik. By the time his phone rang from the chopper base at Gävle, the garrison at Visby had already been overrun.

"Life Guard Regiment, report to base immediately!"

He knew even then that it was too late. But they raced to the chopper base as fast as they could anyway. In the early fall darkness, the seven of them were dropped on the rocky shore north of Visby. His orders were simple: ***"Clear Russian forces from Gotland."***

Simple. No problem. Fifty Russian special forces troops with all the best equipment in the world, vs. the seven of them with odds and ends they had thrown together at Gävle before boarding the chopper. And now, nearly four years later, they were still fighting.

The seven of them were now only three: him, Kalle (whose real name was Karl-Erik), and Patrik. Two others, Magnus and Henrik caught the virus that killed almost everyone on the island. Ole and Mattias were shot on bombing missions that went awry. Now it was just him, Kalle, and Patrik.

And... one last Russian.

They were high in the abandoned church tower that overlooked the main village square in Visby. It had taken a long time to climb up the broken stairs and ascend a makeshift wooden ladder they had erected for the last stage of the climb. The ladder was rickety and dangerous, but once in the tower, they had a view of the town they had never had before.

Patrik had a stolen Russian sniper rifle, having run out of bullets for his Swedish-issue weapon three years ago. They had taken it from the dead blue hands of the Russian who had killed Ole a year ago.

"How does it feel to be hunted down like a wild dog?" Ulf whispered as they saw the Russian poke his head out of a door and look both ways before he left the shelter of an old stone yarn shop a couple of hundred yards away.

"Same way it felt to us, no doubt," Kalle said from beside him.

Thinking himself safe, the Russian poked his head out of the doorway once again and took a tentative step out. The tower was silent, and time seemed to slow down. A wren landed on the sill of the broken-out window, a twig in her mouth, and cocked her head sideways in puzzlement at the humans invading her nesting area. She had wet feet and her eyes were watery from the cold. Ulf watched Patrik take a breath in, and then slowly release it, and then his trigger finger gently moved. There was a deafening bang in the church tower that made Ulf's ears ring, and then far away a misty spray of orange barely visible and the Russian fell forward on the slush of the gray cobbled square. The wren flew around frantically for a moment and then back out the window where she had come from.

"Take that, *Motherfucker!*" Kalle shouted and high-fived Ulf. "Last one! Last Russian!" He danced a little jig around the cold and dark tower.

Ulf was shocked, Kalle never swore. But he hugged him

and slapped his back, "Good work men. It's been a long time coming!"

"Great shot Patrik! You finally got the last of them!" Ulf said over his shoulder.

He turned back to hug Patrik, to congratulate him on *Mission Accomplished*. But Patrik wasn't celebrating. Tears were streaming down his face.

Kalle observed Patrik also, his boisterous demeanor now changed.

Ulf was sobered as well, as he saw Patrik take a cloth from his pocket and wipe his eyes and his face from tears. Both of them turned to Ulf, their eyebrows raised. As always, they looked to him. He looked out the church window, over the red tile roofs of the small medieval town, out to the deep blue Baltic Sea that separated them from the mainland. They had no idea what was going on over there...

He paused for a moment, feeling their eyes on him, feeling the weight of being the leader, the one who had to make the difficult decisions.

"Our mission was to liberate Gotland from the invaders," Ulf said, he paused again, letting his words sink in. "I would think there are still some on the mainland. Perhaps we should go sailing."

Kalle also looked out to sea, as did Patrik.

Ulf knew what they were thinking because he felt the same way. Four years of fighting. Four years of sleepless nights and tension, of cold, poor rations. Four years of winter – when it seemed even the Baltic might completely freeze over, which was something no one in living memory had ever seen.

"Yeah," Kalle said, "I'm sure it's a target-rich environment." He paused, still looking to the west, to the sea,

"I suppose we could find a boat somewhere. We could liberate that first…"

"We might get slaughtered before we even land," Patrik said, regaining his composure, and finding his voice.

"The weather does seem to be improving, though," Ulf offered.

There was a pause. No one said anything. Ulf saw the tension in their faces. He couldn't demand that they follow him. Not anymore. They had completed their mission. This would be a new mission. One that they took on themselves.

Kalle didn't turn to him, but he spoke again, to the open blue sea. "I had a girl in Uppsala, a former student."

Patrik moved closer and leaned one grubby hand against the broken window frame. "My parents, and *Mormor*, and *Morfar*, they live near there, on our old family farm, just south of Sandviken."

Ulf didn't want to say what he was thinking. That the chances of any of these people being alive were about zero. He didn't want them to see that he was tired of fighting. That though they had finally killed the invaders here, he had no desire to die fighting over there.

But they didn't know what lay on the other side of the sea. There had been nothing but silence from there for nearly four years. No radio, no phone messages, no television broadcasts; pure silence.

"I haven't had a good cup of coffee in three years. I bet there is still some coffee left at the Gevalia coffee roasting factory in Gävle," Ulf said.

"You're an idiot," Patrik said, shaking his head. But he hadn't taken his gaze from the sea.

Kalle nodded.

"OK. I'll drink it by myself. Perhaps find a frozen *Pepparkaka* or two that we could unthaw to go with it."

Patrik turned and looked at him, and blinked. As if that motion might make him disappear, Ulf thought.

By this time the few remaining people who were still alive in Visby had realized what had happened.

They came out of homes and shops where they either had been living or hiding, depending on how you looked at it. Ulf saw how shabby they were, how threadbare their clothes, how dirty and no doubt smelly. They wore a hodgepodge of hats and gloves, mismatched boots, torn trousers, stained skirts, and sweaters. There were at most a dozen.

One older man pointed up at the tower where Ulf, Patrik, and Kalle stood in the window. He smiled and even this far away Ulf could see his broken teeth. The Gotlanders around him squinted into the bright afternoon sunshine, and a woman said something, and all the others nodded, and then they took off their gloves and mittens and began clapping. And hooting, and hollering, and raising their hands in the air.

From this far away, Ulf couldn't make out the words. But the sentiment was clear. They were free. They could start over now, and, for the first time in years, a warm sun was shining.

CHAPTER EIGHT

Ulf thought that when they saw the coast of Sweden it would be a happy day. But he was wrong. It was a sad day – a bitter disappointment.

They had left around 3 a.m., an hour before dawn on what they figured must be about the last day of May. Three years after the holocaust, no one knew what day or time it was anymore.

They were on a small sailing boat that they had liberated from the wrecked boatyard that lay near the Uppsala University Gotland campus by the ferry dock. There were several intact boats to choose from that had been trapped in the ice at the dock for several years. The weather was warmer, but it had been nearly a month since they killed the last Russian. In that time the ice from the harbor had finally retreated. It appeared to be safe to make the crossing, finally. They were going home! At last, they were going home...

They sailed out of Visby harbor in the darkness – the new darkness that had descended on Europe since the electrical systems had all been destroyed or simply run out of fuel.

"What if we hit an iceberg in the dark, like the Titanic," Ulf asked Kalle as the sailboat heeled into a southerly breeze offshore.

"We die," Kalle said simply.

Patrik's head snapped around, he'd been dozing a bit while Ulf and Kalle had been preparing the boat to sail.

"Just like the Titanic?" Patrik said.

Kalle, ever the intellectual, answered like the professor he had once been. "Yes. One would expect at most half an hour or so before hypothermia sets in. Even the less salty Baltic is below freezing – probably about 30 degrees. So, 30 degrees,

30 minutes, roughly."

"Oh," Patrik said.

"Yeah, so keep watch," Ulf said, turning in his seat to scan the horizon. In the far north, they could see the glimmer of red northern lights – a rare event, which filled him with a sense of foreboding.

Eventually, the sun rose, and the ice was less prevalent away from the shore, making it easier and safer to sail.

It would be a long day, a long, long Swedish spring day – nearly 20 hours. They sailed all day, and when the sun began to set, Ulf's faith in Kalle was beginning to wane. They still seemed to be far out at sea, and would most likely have to sleep on open water, taking turns watching for icebergs or rocks.

"Look!" Patrik said, standing and holding the mast, they all stood to see the dark shadow of the shore in the distance. "Kalle! You did it! You got us home."

"Well, not home, per se," Kalle replied. "But somewhere, I hope, on the coast of Sweden, not Poland or Russia."

Patrik looked at him nervously, his mouth slightly agape.

"The sun has been to our North all day," Ulf said, "I'm no navigator, but even I can tell we're heading west towards Stockholm. We can't be all that far from home."

They sailed on, for almost two hours, in the strange northern twilight. Around the barrier islands, of Södra Stegholmen and Bedarön, which Patrik identified using their binoculars. They could have tied up there, but they continued into the protected harbor, away from any possible storms or ice floes.

"Nynäshamn," Kalle said simply, as they got within clear sight of the port.

"Wow," Ulf said, "You got us right to the ferry port. Just

like being on a cruise ship."

They all stood and silently surveyed the landscape. It was a mess. Sunk in the middle of the harbor was the giant modern ferry with the big red words "Destination Gotland" stenciled on the side. But it was tilted down to the sea, and rocking gently in the ebb tide. Rust had started to form at the water line, birds were nesting on the railings and flying in and out of the broken cab windows, and seaweed clung to the sides.

Ulf noticed that Patrik looked away, trying to hide the tears in his eyes.

There were other sunken Russian landing boats, and what looked like the bow of a Swedish submarine sticking out of the water to the south. There were crashed and rusted hulks of helicopters partway out of the water. This must have been one of the places where the Russians first came ashore.

"Let's head slightly north, and tie up for the night."

"I want to go on shore. I want to be back in Sweden. It will feel like we're home." Patrik said.

As always, Patrik wanted to be first in. Impulsive. Cocksure. Stubborn, all those words came to Ulf's mind…

"There are probably border patrols. Do you feel like getting in a firefight with trigger-happy Russians, or cooking some dinner and resting? It's been a long day."

"We might find some beer!" Patrik replied. "That would help us sleep better!"

Kalle had already swung the beam of the ship North, and turned the rudder, heading away from Nynäshamn. "If we did find beer, it would be flat and skanky, like when we liberated the *Gotlands Bryggeri.*"

"Perhaps we can find another distillery," Patrik said. "One that does whiskey. Whiskey keeps better than beer!"

"There's a big distillery between Gävle and Sandviken,"

Ulf said. "We'll liberate that one. Maybe the Russians didn't get that far north."

He saw Kalle was looking at him with narrowed eyes. Of course, the Russians got that far north. They most likely took over the whole damn country – as revenge for their failures in Ukraine and revenge against Sweden for joining NATO. But any victory the Russians might have had was overwhelmed by the death and destruction of the pandemic. Ulf was pretty sure they had unleashed that too – to pave the way for their latest military debacle.

But Kalle, oblivious to Ulf's brooding thoughts, said nothing. He just kept steering the boat into the darkness, looking for a safe place to tie up for the night that was sheltered and safe.

"But it could take days to get that far north," Patrik said, not willing to let the subject go.

"Yes. Which means we will live for another week if we don't get hasty and tip off a Russian patrol."

"If there are any Russian patrols," Patrik said, his voice betraying his discouragement.

Kalle had Ulf toss the anchor near a sandy outcrop away from the detritus of the wrecked port town. The hulks of burned town buildings could be seen, as well as some that had escaped damage. It was probably close to midnight, and the sun finally faded somewhere into the northwest sky.

"No lights in the town," Ulf said.

"So, no Russian patrols," Patrik said, still with an edge to his voice.

"Probably. But go ahead and scout the town for us to make sure. We'll warm up some food while you get a six-pack of cold beer for us," Ulf said.

Patrik swore under his breath. It had been a long day.

They had found their way back to their homeland, but it looked about as devastated as Visby, so far. It had been a long and ultimately discouraging day. There would be no hero's welcome for them here, Ulf thought, as they ate cold rations and tucked into cold sleeping bags in the cabin of the small sailboat.

CHAPTER NINE

*And I saw when the Lamb opened one of the seals,
and I heard, as it were the noise of thunder, one of the
four beasts saying, Come and see.
[2] And I saw, and behold a white horse:
and he that sat on him had a bow;
and a crown was given unto him:
and he went forth conquering, and to conquer.*

They sailed north, around the archipelago. Ulf would have liked to have landed at Stockholm, and so did Patrik and Kalle, to complete the circle from where they had received the call to battle four years ago.

"We should stop at my Farmor's *stuga* and check on it," Patrik said.

"I don't want to see that cottage. Not yet," Kalle said. This was a surprise to Ulf. He would have thought Kalle would have wanted to stop in and see what remained.

"Maybe later," Kalle said, squinting into the late evening sun to the south and west. "Not sure I want to see that."

Ulf knew what he meant. They had already seen outlying *stugor* with bleached bones or half-frozen corpses on porches, in yards, in cars. Who would want to see their grandparents like that? Kalle kept the bow of their sailboat pointed north, to enter the still colder and darker Gulf of Bothnia, through the rough and choppy Sea of Åland. Ulf spread a navigation map out on the roof of the cabin.

"We'll head here," he pointed, "near the harbor called Ålands hav" - it's remote, and protected from storms. We'll find a way through the protected channel to the mainland."

Patrik made a face at him, "Why are you still in charge?

The fight is over."

"Maybe because he kept us alive for four years?" Kalle offered, squaring up to Patrik, "Or have you forgotten that?"

Patrik shrugged, he would not take the bait. "Seems like the war is over. Nobody won. Why still fight?"

"We don't have to fight," Ulf said, trying to smooth things over. "We can look for a cold beer frozen in a snowbank somewhere."

"The snow is melting," Patrik said, still in a glum mood.

"My father had a saying," Ulf responded, "Why be difficult? With a little effort, you could be impossible!"

Kalle snorted a laugh and slapped Patrik on the shoulder. "Come on. Let's get going. Who knows what we will find?"

They sailed slowly through the maze of islands and bays and found a place to dock late in the day. According to Ulf's nautical chart, they should be somewhere near a tiny spot on the map called Kvarngärdet. The weather had turned gloomy. The sun would break through the clouds and it seemed like it would clear off and be nice, but shortly thereafter more clouds would appear and a cold wind would blow from the frozen interior, and it would start to spit rain.

It seemed to Ulf that the weather mirrored his internal state. One moment sunny and hopeful, the next dark and gloomy. He wondered if it was PTSD. They had been schooled on the signs of the disorder back in training camp, and now that the fighting in Gotland was over, he was seeing some of those signs in himself: for the first time he was not sleeping well. He would wake up thrashing and all sweaty. Then he would lie awake, with panicky thoughts.

It started on Gotland when they were in the final stages of mopping up the last few Russian invaders. His panicky thoughts back then had to do with the threat of being killed by the last of the Russians. He would hear a noise in the night and wonder if it was the footsteps of someone sneaking in to kill them.

He would get up quietly, hoping to not wake the others. He would stare out into the darkness, his gun at his side, looking for enemies. After a while, he would realize that the threat was all in his head and return to his cot to try to get back to sleep. But he could feel his pulse beating in his head, his heart still racing from the tension and fear. His mind would race also.

What seemed like minor problems during the day would loom large in the night: Where will we find food? What if our ammo runs out? What if some of the villagers are secretly plotting with the Russians to kill us?

But it went deeper than that, Ulf thought as he sat on the bow of the boat watching the sun set into the clouds in the north. Patrik and Kalle had taken the skiff and gone ashore, looking for food and drink. Ulf sat alone with his thoughts.

It was a feeling of hopelessness – that all the things he might have hoped for in life were now gone, never to return. Some were simple things, like looking forward to being with his parents and his sister Agneta for the holidays. But others were deeper. No home, no family, no children. Life no longer made any sense to him. What could he possibly look forward to?

He was snapped out of his reverie by shouting from Patrik and Kalle. "Hoo hoo!" Patrik shouted when the skiff was in sight coming back from their mission to visit the closest *stuga* near the shore.

"Whiskey, vodka, and tinned herring!" Kalle said, he too was in a jovial mood, no doubt because they had already "tested" the drink to see if it was not spoiled.

"And a nice jar of lingonberry jam! Hoo hoo!" Patrik said as they tossed Ulf a line and climbed excitedly back on board.

Their enthusiasm was contagious as they dumped a tattered old IKEA mesh bag full of treasures on the deck of the ship and passed the bottle of whiskey to Ulf. He found his coffee cup and poured himself a healthy (unhealthy?) portion. He tilted it up and quaffed it in a large gulp, feeling the warmth spread to his stomach.

He saw the sun dip below the horizon, heading north to circle the Arctic for the night. His mind returned to the gloomy thoughts he had pondered while they were away.

Hope? Perhaps the best one could hope for now was a drink, a meal, and living for yet another day.

Another sunrise - another sunset. *Var så god...*

In the morning they sailed a bit further and tied the boat up at the dock of the small port town of Östhammars Hamn and walked through the deserted streets. The shops were empty, stripped clean long ago. There were abandoned cars, which Ulf had learned sometimes contained decomposed stiffs and were not good to open. There was still snow lingering in places where the bright sun hadn't penetrated. They walked past an abandoned restaurant which was surrounded by slushy melted snow. Near the entrance was a chalkboard, with a barely visible invitation to partake of the *dagens lunch* special for the day.

"We could try to find more food..." Patrik said, somewhat hopefully.

"Let's head to the countryside and see what we can find. I am pretty sure there are farms nearby," Kalle responded. Ulf nodded his assent, and they turned and headed east on Edsgaten.

They traveled out of town, crossing Highway 76 carefully, not knowing if they might be seen or not. Soon they were in ancient Uppland farm country, with geology that featured flatlands interspersed with hilly raised mounds that looked like islands in the sea, because that's what they were after the high ocean receded.

At one of the first farms they came to, and to Ulf's surprise, they found horses. It looked to Ulf like a whole herd of wild horses.

"Those are North Swedish Horses," Kalle offered, his face lighting up with pleasure. He was the only horse enthusiast among them. "We could ride them."

"What?" Ulf said, taken aback. He was not afraid of many things, but horses made him nervous.

"We can become Cowboys!" Patrik said, joining in.

"These are like *Dole* Horses," Kalle said, his eyes still open wide with obvious enjoyment at this unexpected find.

"*Dalahästar*? I thought those were just tourist trinkets made of wood?" Ulf said.

Kalle looked at him and shook his head at his stupidity. "No, no, this is an old Swedish breed. Very hardy. Probably why there are still some alive."

The horses were running around in circles, when they crossed a patch of snow they started walking slowly, lifting their feet almost comically.

"Look, they know how to walk in the snow. We should catch some and ride them." Patrik said, catching some of Kalle's enthusiasm.

"Too dangerous," Ulf said. "They might bite."

"We thought you were our fearless leader," Kalle said, smiling.

"Not in this..." Ulf said, but in watching the horses he realized that maybe Kalle was right. They wouldn't have to find a working vehicle and hope to find unspoiled gasoline. They had given up on that on Gotland two years ago, it was just a waste of time. And today it had taken them hours just to walk through the abandoned port town and out into the countryside,

Pointing at the horses, Ulf said, "How would we catch them and harness them?"

"I'll show you..." Kalle said, climbing over a wooden fence and into the pasture where the horses grazed.

Once again, he showed Ulf why he was such a valuable team member. He wasn't the toughest physically. But he was smart. *He knew stuff...*

It took the whole day to befriend the horses. Patrik had found a small stash of carrots that had been left in a barrel in the abandoned barn where the horses had been living. They were still encased in ice and had to be chipped out with a chisel.

Ulf was scared to do it, but eventually, he coaxed one of the smaller horses to him with a carrot and had it eating out of his hand. To his relief, it didn't mistake his fingers for carrots.

Ulf noticed something else that was odd. The way the horse met his eyes with its gaze. As if remembering, wondering, "Where have you been human? Why were you gone so long?" He patted its head, dusting some mud out of the scraggly mane, and to Ulf's great surprise, it leaned into him, resting its head against him, nuzzling him.

"You've made a friend," Kalle said. "That horse likes you."

Ulf shrugged. He was surprised too...

"Probably because you smell like horse manure..." Patrik said, laughing.

They slept in the barn and then rode north the next day. At times there were cold showers that almost felt like it was snowing. Typical late May weather, Ulf thought, not sure if it *was* the month of May or not, but it seemed like it was. It would drizzle for two hours, and then rain hard for five minutes, and then clear off and the sun would come out. They would ride in glorious sunshine for an hour or more, but then it would cloud up again and the whole process would repeat itself. Twice they retreated to barns to get out of the rain near the hamlet of Sandika. Stopping and starting, it took all day to get from Östhammar to Forsmark, a journey of less than 20 kilometers.

"We're the Four Horsemen of the Apocalypse, well, three actually," Patrik joked as the sky turned dark once again as they approached Forsmark.

Ulf knew what he was talking about – War, Famine, Pestilence, and Death. But since Ole and Karl had died fighting alongside them on Gotland, he couldn't feel the humor in this.

Near Forsmark they heard the noise of a convoy of vehicles coming, so they ducked into a copse of white birch and Norway maple trees when they saw a truck approaching. The horses backed into the woods, their eyes wide with fear and their nostrils dilated. Kalle caught Ulf's eye and leaned forward to his horse, speaking it soothingly to calm it down. Ulf and Patrik did the same, to quiet their horses.

Neither the men nor the horses had seen a vehicle drive past in more than three years. Leading the way was a *Pansarterrängbil* armored personal carrier. No one seemed to be manning the machine gun on the top, though the lid was open and it appeared ready to use. It was followed by a big diesel truck with the title and logo *"Vattenfall"* (the name of the big Swedish electrical company) emblazoned on the side. To Ulf's relief, the men driving the truck were not in Russian uniforms, and they didn't spot them in the trees. But they also were not in Swedish military *Life Guards' Dragoon* uniforms either.

Ulf did not recognize anyone he could see from any of the regiments he was familiar with before. The lorry trundled through the small village square and headed off to the coast, towards the nuclear plant, Ulf assumed.

"Where do you suppose they are getting fuel?" Patrik said, in amazement.

"Beats me," Ulf said.

"They didn't look like Russkies," Kalle said as the truck receded into the distance.

"They don't look like they are part of any Swedish regiments, either."

"Then who's in charge of Sweden now?" Patrik asked.

"I don't know. But I doubt if they would appreciate us...." Ulf said, gesturing towards their military garb. "We should change our clothes."

"We would need a story to go with them..." Kalle said.

"We're Gotland farmers, off to see the mainland!" Patrik said.

"Probably not a good idea to keep these Kalashnikov rifles strapped to our backs, unless we think we can win any firefight we get into," Ulf said, partially ignoring Patrik's suggestion.

"We're traveling Stockholm dentists, off on a holiday!" Patrik persisted.

"Shut up," Ulf said.

Ulf led them into the town of Forsmark itself, which was never very big. Having a nearby nuclear power plant that might melt down or explode at any moment probably hadn't done much to foster growth over the past few decades, Ulf thought. The doors to some houses swung open and creaked in the breeze, others they had to kick in.

On Gotland, they had learned that you could give houses what Kalle called "The Sniff Test." You opened the door and put your head inside. The first good sniff lets you know whether or not there were "stiffs" inside. They avoided those houses.

After visiting half a dozen houses they had new clothes on. "See," Patrik said, turning in a circle like a fashion model, "Stockholm dentists, out for a saunter."

They also managed to find some more booze, which was good, and some canned goods that hadn't burst. They put them in their packs and continued. Their only remaining weapons were small automatic pistols, now – easier to hide, but still lethal. Ulf hoped they wouldn't run into real Russian Army regulars or Spetnatz special forces and be out-gunned.

"We do need a plausible cover story," Ulf said, once they were back on their horses and heading north again, "And Stockholm Dentists on Holiday doesn't cut it."

"We are Gotlanders, who were running out of food and had to leave the island," Kalle said. "Who would know what happened to the Russians there? There has been no communication with the mainland for over three years…"

Ulf nodded, that seemed as good a story as any.

That night Ulf slept fitfully. Seeing the convoy of Army trucks had unnerved him.

They were sleeping in a small barn with the horses, and Ulf climbed down from the hayloft and went outside to pee. He saw a figure crouched on a log-splitting stump nearby. It was Kalle, smoking a cigar they had liberated from someone's home in Forsmark along with their new clothes.

"The lights are on at the Forsmark nuclear plant, you can see it lighting up the sky over. What are they doing there?" Kalle said, gesturing with the tip of his cigar.

"Who are they?" Ulf said.

"That's what I'm asking also, who are they?" Kalle said. "Who the hell was on the road today, and how did they keep Forsmark going when everything else blew up or stopped working?"

"Maybe we should head that way and investigate?"

"I don't know, boss. If it's an important installation, and they have power, cameras, drones…"

"Right. We'd never get near there without being seen. I'd like to have some assurance they are friendly before we go waltzing in there."

Kalle nodded, stubbed out his cigar, and headed back to their sleeping loft. Ulf noted it was easy to see the nuclear plant even though it was miles away – the only man-made light on this part of the planet. To the east toward the power plant it was sometime in the 21st century, but when he turned back towards the barn the sky with a billion stars arching above him was from The Dark Ages – no lights, no planes, no smoke rising from chimneys.

Jesus, what a world, he thought.

He lay down on the green wool army blanket he had spread on the hay, but sleep eluded him. Someone new was in charge of this part of Sweden. He still felt the weight of the lives of his friends' well-being that he had carried with him. Should they surrender? Join whatever new army was running the show?

In Gotland, he had known who his enemy was. It was simple. They were Russian invaders. But apparently, that invasion had collapsed on the mainland, and some other group had risen and seized power, and now they were "running the show." Could Ulf keep his crew alive long enough to find out if they were friend or foe?

What weighed him down in this was losing Karl and Ove.

The guilt of it. Feeling that there could have been more he might have done if he was smarter, more careful; a better leader. How many nights after each death had he woken up, and ruminated on every decision he had made? It still haunted him. If they found alcohol and drank it in the evening, it was worse. He would wake up sweating and thrashing around, with panicky thoughts of conflict in his mind. Thoughts like — *If only I was a better leader, they might still be alive!*

He wasn't sure if it was PTSD, or just feeling like he was inadequate. He had some training in leading men, but despite that, he had failed. He didn't want to fail again. To wake up for years in the future mulling over some mistake that took two seconds to make in real time.

"You lead a charmed life," his mother, Ingrid used to say when he was little. But after nearly four years of fighting, it didn't seem so charmed anymore. He had heard somewhere that that was really what PTSD was all about- that most normal people had a feeling of invincibility, that they couldn't die, that they lived a charmed life. And PTSD was losing that feeling. Feeling instead that at any moment, at any second, one mistake or bit of bad luck could take it all away. And once you lost that confidence, you lived with fear and regret — nightmares of all the things that both could and would go wrong.

It was living under the tyranny of Murphy's Law. *What could go wrong, would go wrong.* That was what happened at Gotland, he thought. The Russians were fighting for their life just like he was. That was what everyone seemed to be doing now, just trying to stay alive.

Still not sleepy, he shifted to the other side, tried to calm his mind, and let sleep come. He thought again of the night sky, bright toward Forsmark where some atomic glow was keeping things lit, black towards the east. What was left of the world? Were they back to the Dark Ages, or was it even more primordial than that? Back to Homo Sapiens vs. Neanderthals?.

CHAPTER TEN

Gorm Gorannson, Gävle Sweden

"Gorm" Gorannson had given up on life in general when his wife and daughter died from the flu. Or Plague, or Pestilence, or whatever the hell they called it. Given up caring about pretty much everything. He gave up on most people he knew – at least the few who survived. That's how he justified it. Working for them, that is. The Russkies.

Hell, the Russians were just the remnants of old Swedish Vikings anyway. The *"rödingarna"* – "the Reds – red salmon fish." Also known as the *ryssarna,* "Russians," Any good Viking historian would know that, and Gorm was one, even if he was just an amateur enthusiast. That's why he went by the name of the old Viking king Gorm even though his real name was Goran.

He buried her. And he carved a stone with Runes in her honor, just like his namesake. Two days later he added another stone, for his daughter. They reminded him of an old stone he had seen in Denmark, the runes on that stone said:

Kurmur, Kunukr
Karthi Kubl-Thus
Aft Thurui Kun Sina
Tanmarkar Bot

Gorm, King,
Carved this Stone
In Memory of his Wife
Danmark's ornament

He buried them in a mound in his backyard, not in one of the mass graves outside Gävle in the forest. He told Svein that if he succumbed to the pandemic bury him with them, if it came to that. If Svein was still alive…

Svein was his Viking Re-enactor friend from their local club. He had adopted the name Svein after Svein Knuttson, the prince and son of "Cnut the Great," who once upon a time was king of Denmark, Norway, and England.

That was why Gorm went to work for the Russians. Because he no longer cared. Russians, Danes, Swedes, it was all the same. At least he could still work. The only thing that gave him pleasure now *was* his work. He drove the steam train on the old *Inlandsbanen* rail line from stations in Uppland and Dalarna to the far north Iron mines of Kiruna.

He drove the old Swedish locomotives that they had rescued from the railway museum of the Svenska Jarnvag Museum in Gävle and the old Gefle-Dalarna railway museum in Falun. They had been mothballed way back in World War Two for just this sort of a scenario – and even though some of these standard Swedish locomotives were a hundred years old, they were in surprisingly good shape because they had been maintained in good running order until the late 1990s and in museum collections since.

He loved driving the steam train. It was a dream come true. But stopping at the camps, that bothered him. Seeing the human cargo, bothered him.

Like the day before, when he had been at Kiruna making a delivery of goods and people. He had noticed the pretty Japanese girl when she boarded, and Svein as usual had boasted that he would have her.

"Now there's a ripe one. I'll be visiting her cabin, *Jah,* for sure," Svein had said.

Gorm held his piece, watching the pretty girl and others milling about on the platform. He was the first to spot the person in the truck hiding in the woods, probably because the *Lok* cab was so high in the air that he could see further than anyone.

"Yes, I'll be stopping by her cabin on our next layover trip. I'll bring some of that fresh Absolut vodka we found in Östersund."

Gorm looked at him, and shook his head, "OK, you've talked about sex and drinking, now on to your other topic, bodybuilding."

Svein looked aggrieved, "If I was not so jacked, who would shovel all the coal that keeps this machine running? Answer me that."

Gorm snorted. It was a standing joke – a story that Svein liked to use to impress the women at the camps, that his big muscles and his ability to shovel coal were the reason that they were able to move the giant locomotive. In reality, it had a mechanical coal feeder – rescued from the old steam engine in Arvidsjaur that was one of their backup engines if things went wrong on the railway up in the north, in Norbottens Län.

"I hope you haven't gotten a callous on your hand pulling the lever on the trip up here. Or broken a fingernail." Gorm said.

But Svein wasn't paying attention. There was a commotion on the platform. Then something Gorm had never seen, a fight with the workers. Not only that, but the guards were lifting their long rifles to stop it.

"She's running!" Svein said and leaned forward to join the fray. He began to step off the cab platform, but Gorm horse-collared him, holding him back.

"Hey!"

"No. They'll shoot you. Stay!"

Svein turned his head angrily back at him, to protest, but then the gunfire erupted, and all hell broke loose. People screaming, and men shouting. Someone dove for the shooter and wrestled him for his gun. And out of the distance came the strange pickup truck, which was a sight to behold. It had giant tires, and a crazy-looking *Saami* backwoodsman at the wheel. Beside the *Saami* guy was a big white sled dog leaning forward and barking. With mud and snow flying he somehow scooped up the girl in an instant and roared away, as the Russians shouted and swore and tried to shoot it, apparently missing because in a moment the truck, the driver, and the pretty girl disappeared into the brush and low trees on the hillside.

"Damn him!" Svein shouted, shaking himself free. *"Skit!"* Svein swore, *"Skit! Skit! Skit!!"* He shook his fist at the departing truck and the girl inside. "I wanted her!"

Gorm thought about that the next day on the long journey back to the south, and eventually to Uppsala. He loved running the steam engine, but this part of the trip was always the worst. The old Inlandsbanan track, with its rickety ties and decaying iron rail, forced them to keep the speed low. So did the herds of *elg* and *ren.* Either of them could derail the train if he hit a whole herd on the track. He had to keep the speed low all the way down to Östersund – and at best it was a very long day, but often they had to stop for the night at one of the abandoned villages along the way and rest.

Miles and miles of scrubby pine forest, rocky hillsides, small lakes, and bridges would pass – and if he was not careful or rested enough, his eyes would begin to close, and if they rounded a bend without slowing or raced out onto one of the old bridges the train could derail and he would be to blame. The Russian commander at the end of the line in Uppsala had told him when he was given this job, "*Very simple, you wreck train, we wreck you.*"

He had seen enough examples of their brand of discipline to know that the Russian wasn't kidding. It had been common enough in occupied parts of Ukraine when their military was there – and he knew that if he made a big mistake there would be big consequences. He was happy today that their destination was just a few hours south at Malmberget to pick up other supplies from the work camp destined for Uppsala. Supplies which sometimes included people – and increasingly other strange things they were fabricating in the camps, like the creepy worker bots they were making.

Even though today's journey was just a few hours across the northern tundra, he still had time to reflect on the events of the day before.

He was still trying to wrap his head around what he had seen – it was nothing like he had seen at the work camp in Kiruna before. A man with his vehicle, racing about the tundra saving pretty girls. He hadn't seen someone in a private vehicle in three years. Where in the hell did he get the fuel? Amazing!

"Some *caveman* stole my girl," Svein said later, sharing his thoughts while they took on water at Kiruna rail yard, the big train hissing and wheezing behind them, preparing for the next long run.

"Why would you call him a caveman?" Gorm said. "He seemed pretty sophisticated to me. He somehow has managed to keep a vehicle going through 4 years of nuclear winter." He paused and poured some coffee from his thermos and thought about it some more. Beside his coffee cup, there was a fresh *kanelbulle* (cinnamon roll) warming on one of the hot pipes snaking out of the boiler. The aroma of the coffee and cinnamon together warmed his heart. He saw Svein give him a dirty look for contradicting him.

"You know damn well that the guards would have kept that one for themselves." Gorm continued. Inwardly he smiled, this was a good topic of conversation, something they could talk about for the next two days as they chugged their way down to Östersund.

Svein took the bait…"I have a case of Absolut Vodka. It would buy anything from the guards."

Gorm shook his head. Svein was probably right, which was sad. But you would have had to give up your whole case of vodka for that one, he thought. He would save this topic for later – it was worthy of further discussion when things got boring. Instead, he said, "Did you notice the weather yesterday?"

"Yes," Svein said. "It was very warm. It seems the endless winter is finally over."

Gorm shrugged. "First really spring-like weather I can remember." He looked out at the cabins and factory area – to the LKAB mines and beyond it the Badjelánnda – the Higher Land – Saami fishing and grazing grounds, all bleak and white.

"They might have to fix the fence, and put guards in the towers again if it keeps up," Gorm said, pointing to the elevated gun platforms that overlooked the fence, now drifted deep with snow.

Svein shook his head, "Where would they go?"

Gorm shrugged, but he was thinking of the man with the truck, the dog, and the pretty girl. Out there, somewhere. Loose. Free. Living on his own terms.

CHAPTER ELEVEN

Gorm was driving the Lok the next day when he spotted Richard lying like a heap of old clothes in the snow beside the tracks. He thought he was going to run right over him – he hit the brakes, sparks flew from the drive wheels and the giant machine bucked and squealed, like a pig on its way to the slaughter. Still, it took over a hundred yards for the Lok to stop, if he hadn't been going slowly uphill it might have taken half a mile to stop.

Svein reached Richard first and got him upright. Their eyes met, and Svein shook his head slowly with the clear message – *"inte så bra..."* - not good."

"Richard!" Gorm called out. He climbed from the locomotive cab down to where he lay and began shaking him. Richard was trying to speak. But his lips were cracked and bloody. His face was black with frostbite.

"I tried," Richard whispered and Gorm leaned closer. Richard's breath came in raspy huffs. Gorm had heard that sound before – a death rattle. He had heard it when his *"farfar"* "father's father" – that is, his grandfather, had died.

"I tried to stop you last time you drove by," Richard said. "You didn't see..."

Gorm's heart sank. That was three days ago. There was a bloody trail in the snow from the snowbank just yards away. Richard had been waiting for him, and he hadn't seen him.

Gorm felt tears welling up in his eyes. He held Richard close to him. God, he was cold. He was so Goddamn cold...

"Help me lift him. We can get him to the cab," Gorm said to Svein.

Svein just looked at him. Shook his head just in the slightest to say "No."

Gorm was about to raise his voice. He had about had it with Svein lately!

But then he looked down. Richards's eyes were still open but fixed. He was gone.

"Three days. He's been laying in the snow waiting for us three days," Gorm said.

"I'll help you bury him," Svein said, willfully ignoring his last statement.

Svein helped him pull Richard up and over a hillock away from the train track. Svein used his coal shovel from the locomotive to dig a depression in the snow. Gorm went to gather pine and birch branches to lay over Richard and cover him up. When they had placed Richard in the grave they bowed their heads for a moment of silence, though neither of them knew what a priest or religious person would say for such an occasion. Svein began covering Richard up with snow, and Gorm put pine branches over him, hoping that it would keep the wolves and wild dogs from getting to him.

"Why would Richard try to escape?" Svein asked, even though he knew Gorm had no way of knowing, "He had to have known there was no food or shelter for 100 miles – everyone knew that."

"Probably just couldn't take it anymore," Gorm said, but not with any conviction. Richard had been enthusiastic about their work at the robot factory. "Maybe the warm weather made him think they could escape."

Svein looked north, across the forbidding landscape of tundra and forest, he shook his head in disbelief.

"We have to stop at the camp for coal and water. We can ask some of the other engineers." But something nagged at Gorm's subconscious. Something gave him an uneasy feeling that they were missing some piece of the puzzle.

"We better go," Svein said. "They will want to know why

it took so long to get there."

"Just a few more branches..." Gorm said, and headed in a different direction this time, up another slight rise to the east where there were more pine trees with lower branches. He crested the small hill and his heart sank. From here he could see almost as far as the camp. The snow was littered with what looked like clumps of old clothes. But that's not what they were. Turning back, he raised his voice, "SVEIN!"

The younger man was already trudging through the snow back to the Big Lok. But something in Gorm's voice arrested him, he dropped his shovel and ran to Gorm.

Gorm pointed to the bodies lying in the snow across the tundra, in the distance they could see one of the towers of the camp fence

"Something terrible must have happened at the camp. All the workers ran away and died here..." Gorm said, but still, that nagging feeling, that unease that he was missing a clue. Something was not right.

"We should go. Now," he said to Svein, who stood speechless beside him, staring away. Svein nodded, and they walked as quickly as they could across the crunchy snow. A mist surrounded the giant train and they climbed on board, unsure of what awaited them at the camp station just ahead.

*   *   *   *   *   *   *   *

Dr. Bob

In the first-floor conference hall, Ångström Laboratoriet, Uppsala Sweden:

Dr. Bob walked to one of the large monitors that covered the wall and looked at the inputs from the cameras and sensors. He saw the view from the forward-facing camera from Lok 1105, formerly of Arvisjaur, and could tell that the scenery of the tundra was beginning to move once again. In the cab camera, he could see the engineer Göransson and his coal tender/fireman Svensson were back to work.

"They're moving again," the chief biological engineer Hans Von Linné said to him. "No sign of any problems in the telemetry of the locomotive. It's functioning normally. Why did they stop the train?"

"Don't you have body cameras on them?" Dr. Bob asked, then realized it was a foolish question. They were locomotive drivers, not soldiers or security forces. He paused for a moment, thinking. What would Håkan want him to do? Gorm Göransson was an important part of their logistical system — or he would be until they could complete getting the rest of the Forsmark nuclear reactors back online. It was the only nuclear facility that hadn't either melted down or gone completely offline during the breakdown 4 years ago.

Hans looked at him, askance.

"I know. Dumb question," Dr. Bob said. Hans said nothing, he was concentrating on the computer screen. He pulled a flexible controller device out of his pocket and slid his thumb across the screen. The movie film backed up and replayed to a point where Gorm had applied the brakes and the giant locomotive wheezed and bucked to a halt. Just visible to the left of the tracks, as the train passed by, was a pathetic figure waving at Gorm as the train stopped.

"Who's that?" Dr. Bob said, suddenly interested.

"One of the engineers at the Robot Camp. His name was Richard Halvarsson."

"What's he doing lying outside in the snow."

Hans shook his head. Their eyes met.

Dr. Bob then knew. It was all part of the plan... Håkan's plan.

Malmberget Forced Labor Camp-Malmberget/Gällivare Sweden

Gorm spotted Nijinsky and Kovalev on the platform and immediately knew he was in trouble. They never came out in uniform, with their weapons, to greet the supply train.

The train squealed and wheezed to a halt, like a tired draft horse after a long journey, panting and dripping with sweat.

Gorm had spent enough time with both of them to know their background – stories shared over a fire in an oil barrel while sipping their homemade vodka. Nijinsky was a Tatar from somewhere in the wilds of Siberia – Muslim, dark, fine-featured – no doubt he had been a heartthrob for the young ladies in Novosibirsk or whatever God-forsaken town he hailed from. Anton Kovalev was a St. Petersburg bureaucrat, short and pudgy, with a doughy face already showing the signs of too much vodka, too many boiled potatoes, and cabbage. Gorm wasn't sure which of them was the more dangerous. He noticed Svein tensing beside him, something in his shoulders and neck seemed to tighten up, like a boxer bracing for a blow to the midsection

The locomotive continued past them so that they would have access to the materials from Kiruna in the cars behind the coal tender. Svein and Gorm climbed down.

"You're late!" Kovalev said to Gorm when he stepped down from the locomotive cab.

"Nice to see you also," Gorm replied. Svein shot him a glance, catching the sarcasm.

"Why did you stop the train in the woods back there?"

"I had to take a dump," Gorm said, approaching Kovalev,

using his advantage in size over the bureaucrat. "I stepped into the woods away from your camera because I didn't want my FAT ASS broadcast live on your TV network." He noticed Svein had not moved forward with him, but Nijiinsky had moved forward, tightening his grip on his Kalashnikov and bringing it up slightly.

"Planning on shooting me for a potty break? Are those against the rules now too?" Gorm said, now confronting Nijiinsky.

To his surprise, he saw him raise the gun higher. As if he was contemplating just that, shooting him. He glanced back at Kovalev, his face was sweaty. "Go ahead and shoot." He tilted his head toward the locomotive, "I guess you can have one of your new bots drive this thing, right? They can do anything." Through the window, he could see some of the bots milling around in the factory. It reminded him of Richard, and his ire rose.

"Okay, I lied," Gorm said. "I stopped and talked to Richard, who was dying along the train tracks because you forced him and the other engineers out onto the tundra without any provisions." He added, with his voice rising, "Like kicking a dog out into the arctic cold on a snowy night."

"*Vänd tillbaka,*" he heard Svein whisper behind him.

"No, I won't come back," he said over his shoulder. "I want an answer. Which of you bastards gave the order to send those people out into the cold."

"We had orders from above," Nijinsky said, pointing the Kalashnikov at Gorm's chest.

"Their work here was done," Kovalev added. "They were free to go."

Gorm stepped closer to him and stared down into his pudgy face. "Free to go, or free to die now that you didn't need them."

"It was them or us," Nijinsky said.

"Haven't you noticed?" Kovalev said in a less confrontational tone. "What you have been delivering? Or, should I say, not delivering?"

"Food," Svein said from behind him. "We haven't delivered any food in a month."

"Not just food," Kovalev said.

"No mechanical parts, either," Nijinsky said, also more quietly, his Russian accent more noticeable to Gorm.

That was when Gorm noticed. Kovalev was scared, not of him, but of something else. He wasn't sweating because a big Swede was towering over him, he was sweating because something had changed at the robot factory.

Gorm glanced up and saw one of the cameras tracking him, its evil eye narrowing to view his face more closely. It dawned on him suddenly. The clues had been there for months, he just hadn't been paying attention. His mouth went dry.

"We didn't mean to do anything to harm Richard's team," Kovalev said, smiling a nervous smile and lifting his pudgy little hand in supplication. "It is getting warmer, you know. We thought they might find a new life here in the north, in Lappland."

Gorm stepped back, and for the sake of the cameras, he nodded. "You are right. The weather is getting much warmer. Spring may finally come." He didn't add what he was thinking, that it would be coming too late to save Richard and his team. And that it had still been bitterly cold at night, which was why Richard's face had been black with frostbite.

Svein stepped forward, "While the weather is nice, I think we need to get some supplies unloaded."

Gorm looked at him, and their eyes met. He nodded, "Svein's right. There is a refrigerator car full of supplies for you. Not sure why they didn't have us deliver it on the way up." Gorm said, but now he knew why. They didn't want him and Svein here when Richard's team was being pushed out.

They began unloading the supplies. Nijinsky brought the baggage lorry forward and they began stacking boxes on it. Each box was neatly labeled with one word in English, "Bio-Hazard."

It should have been evident to Gorm on the last couple of visits that things had changed. How stupid I am to not have noticed before, Gorm thought. One glance through the windows confirmed this suspicion, and what he saw made the hair on the back of his neck rise. They didn't need engineers anymore, because they weren't building mechanical robots anymore.

They were growing them, or 3D printing them, or putting them together in NanoAssemblers or some other crazy technology Håkan and its creepy biology department had come up with. He had met Dr. Hans Von Linne when he got his latest shipment loaded in Uppsala, and there was something about him and his boxes of raw materials that gave Gorm the willys.

At the Swedish Missionskykan, Hudiksvall Sweden: 3 and ½ Years Earlier

Blessed are they which are persecuted for righteousness sake: for theirs is the kingdom of heaven.
Blessed are ye, when men shall revile you, and persecute you, and shall say all manner of evil against you falsely, for my sake.
Rejoice, and be exceeding glad: for great is your reward in heaven: for so persecuted they the prophets which were before you.

Rachel Sjöblom knew she'd be raped, and she wasn't wrong about that fact. But she was wrong about pretty much everything else about the event.

Of course, she'd be raped. She was a single young woman. She was the town preacher, and umpteen thousand Russians had come ashore at Stockholm, Gävle, and even here, her hometown of Hudiksvall.

Plus, she was a student of history. OK, *church history*, but she had studied all the other stuff too, particularly the *first* holocaust, the one that happened to the Jews. She knew what happened when the Russians "liberated" Europe from the Nazis. What they did in Ukraine, even though Russian internet trolls worked tirelessly to suppress that information.

As a student of history, she also knew more than most people about the *rysshärjningarna* "the Russian Pillage" when the Russians invaded Sweden in 1719 and burned all the Baltic coastal towns. All that had remained in Gävle then was the big Lutheran Church. Everything else was destroyed.

The chronicles of that war didn't mention all the rapes of that event, but Rachel knew they had happened. It was hard to miss the fact that there were a lot more dark-haired Swedes on the coast than in the interior towns that were spared.

So, Rachel knew what was coming. Like Jesus, at Gethsemane, she had prayed the night before *"Let this cup of suffering pass from me. But not my will but thine be done."*

Still, that didn't make it any easier when they came to burn her church. She couldn't understand what they were saying, but she could tell what the intent was. All of the soldiers who broke into the church wanted to rape her, that was clear. They wanted it to happen in the sanctuary at the altar, and they dragged her there. The words, *"like a sheep, led to the slaughter"* came to mind.

They had started to tear her clothes off when there was the deafening roar of a Kalashnikov machine gun firing and the men dove to the ground.

Standing in the doorway she saw an officer. Something was shouted in Russian by this man with a better uniform than the rest. She could see it angered the men who still held her. They snarled like dogs, which as far as Rachel was concerned, was what they were acting like, a pack of wild dogs.

"Come, mine," the officer said, grabbing her away from the others with one hand, while the gun was cradled against his hip with his finger on the trigger, *"Sozhgi eto"* he shouted to them as he dragged her away, across the street, kicking in a door with one foot.

She didn't know what that meant, but they began pulling out lighters and tearing up hymnals to start a fire. By the time she had been dragged out of the church's front door, she could smell the fire and hear the wood starting to crackle. Her captor shoved her onto the floor of the nearest house and began raping her savagely.

"Lord Forgive Them, For They Know Not What They Do!"
"Lord Forgive Them, For They Know Not What They Do!"
"Lord Forgive Them, For They Know Not What They Do!"

She prayed out loud while it was going on. Shouted it.

"Lord Forgive Them, For They Know Not What They Do!"
"Lord Forgive Them, For They Know Not What They Do!"
"Lord Forgive Them, For They Know Not What They Do!"

"Shut up!" he yelled at her as he was on top of her, and in her. "Shut Up! Shut Up!" and he swung his fist at her and hit her mouth. She felt her lip split open, bleed, and start to swell.

She turned her head and prayed in silence instead. She noticed his breath was raspy and labored, and then he stopped. She could feel the wet warmth of it. He had succeeded in doing what he wanted to do.

Which she would have thought would have made him happy. But it didn't. He lay like a heavy weight over her, collapsed from his exertions, his bristly black face pressing against her neck.

And then something unexpected. She felt another wetness, against her neck, onto her bare chest. He was weeping.

Forgive him. She felt like the Lord was saying that, to her. *Forgive him, he doesn't know what he is doing.*

She argued with that voice, in her mind. "Could've fooled me. He sure looked like he had done this before."

Forgive him.

That would be like a dog, licking the boots of the evil master who had kicked him.

Forgive him.

"What is your name?"

"Evgeny," he said to her, lifting his head so that their eyes met.

"My name is Rachel, Pastor Rachel," she said, though it was hard to speak with a split lip that was swelling up. One tooth on that side felt a bit loose also.

He rolled off her, went and stood, and watched the church burn across the street.

The mob of soldiers had moved on. She could hear shouts and screams from others they were attacking nearby. She could smell the smoke from the *Missionskyrkan* as the last ten years of her life went up in flames.

"The Lord giveth, and the Lord taketh away. Blessed is the name of the Lord."

Rachel assumed that the only reason she survived those first weeks was because she became what she thought of as an "ISIS bride." She was one of the lucky ones, she thought. She had a <u>single </u>husband and wasn't shared by other men like some of *the Brides* were.

Also, Evgeny spoke some English – though it was pretty crude, like a toddler or preschool child speaking. Like most of the Swedes her age, she had grown up learning English and it was almost as common as Swedish in Hudiksvall.

"Why are we getting new chips?"

"Boss Lady says so," he said.

"All the Brides?"

"No, we don't have many. You special."

God only knew what that meant, Rachel thought – to be "special" in Evgeny's book probably didn't count for much. You get to stay alive, eat, and provide me with sex, whenever, wherever and however I feel like it.

But that very day it became pretty much a moot point because everyone around them suddenly started dying. At first, she thought it was something the Russians were doing. As usual, everyone blamed the Americans the Jews, or the Chinese, but in the final analysis, what did it matter? It seemed to be some sort of "uber-flu" — a stuffy head, congestion, a high fever. And then, trouble breathing, and then, sensitivity to light, and within hours, death.

Children and old people got it first, then teens, young adults, and people who had "never been sick a day in their life." Going, going, gone.

Except, Rachel noticed, people who had gotten "the new chips." *None* of them got sick.

While there was still electricity, Rachel could catch news feeds from around the world showing that it was everywhere. She saw an American doctor from their CDC, saying that the best they could figure was that it had spread worldwide via the airlines, then somehow "mutated and turned on." Also, it had probably been created in a lab, *weaponized* by biological warfare experts, and perhaps even accidentally released. Before he could finish his explanation, he started coughing.

There was still enough electricity for the first day or two for them to find out that it was worldwide, and everyone was blaming everyone else. Then someone set off some nukes, thankfully none landed in Sweden, and then all hell broke loose.

"I go north!" Evgeny told her the last time she saw him.

"Have fun," she said, and he raised the back of his hand to strike her. But paused.

"You good woman. Sorry. Everyone dead, I go north."

He put her hand on her shoulder and stared at her with his dark mournful eyes. She would remember those eyes, when her daughter was born, those same dark and mournful eyes.

CHAPTER FOURTEEN

She sat with Rabbi David on the train ride north. There was no end to the devastation, but at least they didn't have to wear masks to protect themselves from radiation like they did at Gävle.

"How can there be a good God, and still be evil?" she asked him, as they paused at the train station in Östersund, a city that was heavy with the smell of death from the plague.

"You're asking me?"

"No, I'm praying out loud to Saint fucking Augustine."

"Hmmph."

"What do you mean, Hmmph! Don't you have anything more to say on the subject!"

"I've written three books on the subject. Thought I covered it pretty well…"

"But this situation is new!"

"*There is nothing new under the sun,*" he responded.

"Well, thank you, *O wise Solomon,*" she responded, but she could hear the tone of her voice. She was grouchy. Even grouchier than her normal monthly period. And she suspected why – she had woken up nauseous and thrown up. At first, she panicked and thought this might be a sign that she too had gotten the plague. But that was supposed to be mostly a respiratory thing. no, it was even worse than that. Much worse, as it dawned on her what was going on.

How could she bring a child into this world?

Rabbi David was looking at her, oddly, his eyes squinting slightly - which was what she knew he did when he was trying to figure something out. He tilted his head back.

"Grouchy this morning…Are you feeling OK?" He started, and the blood drained from his face.

"I think so. Pretty funny, huh, just like Sarah. Or should I say, Hagar?"

He shook his head, still not completely getting it.

"Abraham's wife for one, and his concubine for another." she said, *"Shall I have pleasure in my old age!"*

"There you go, quoting the Bible at me again," he said.

"Torah."

"OK, *The Torah.*"

His eyes met hers. He extended his hand and placed it on her hand on the seat of the train coach, and it was only then that she noticed it was shaking.

"Ta det lugnt, det löser sig"

"No, No! I won't take it easy, and it won't be OK," she responded in English. "I can't bring a child into this world. Not like this! Not like this! Not in a fucked-up world like this…"

Part Two: The Journey to Uppsala

Old Norse oath:

"May you have peace,

as long as the falcon flies,

the pine grows,

the river flows to the sea,

and the Saami are skiing."

At the cabin in the forest near Kiruna

Miko and I set out to save Ravna, but that is not how things turned out, Stefan thought as they skied through the frozen forest to the south. They had discussed this before they set out, and before they realized they were being followed.

"We can't linger here for long," Stefan had said. "They will be expecting the guards back this morning." He said that, but what he felt was something different. There was a tiredness in his bones that made him want to spend the day by the fire, napping. But he knew that would be deadly.

"We can head north, into the forest, to take the girl back to her people?" Miko asked.

Ravna grinned and nodded, "Uncle Gáktu is alive. He's in the mountains of Norway near Abisko."

Stefan tilted his head, considering the idea. "The nearest village is Kurravaara, but no one survived there. That is straight north. We could ski on the frozen streams and lakes. Continue on up to Salmi. Perhaps there are Saami villagers alive there? Abisko is east, along the rail line and highway."

"Why did so many Saami people survive the plague?" Miko asked, her eyes meeting Stefan's

"They live in isolation on the tundra. Just us showing up in a village even now could still wipe it out."

In response, Miko pouted. Stefan caught her expression and had to shift his gaze away from her, she was pretty darned good to look at.

"So, on to Uncle Gáktu's then?" Ravna asked, her bright

white teeth shining in the dim room. Stefan noticed that she was the perkiest of the three of them - the resilience of youth.

"Too dangerous," Stefan said. "There are still occasional patrols on the highway. God knows where they get the fuel to waste on *Terrängbilar*. But they drive them every now and then, with the machine guns mounted on the roof. I've seen them mowing down reindeer just for fun."

Ravna's face clouded. "I don't want to go north to Salmi. I don't know any of those villagers."

Stefan shook his head, caught Miko's eye again, "You are Saami, and you killed two of the Russian guards. They will look for you in the north," he hated to have to say it, but he knew it was true, "there will be reprisals. They won't believe the villagers who say they didn't see you."

Ravna's eyes misted and she blushed with shame. Stefan wasn't sure how old she was, but she was old enough to understand that because she killed the guards, some of her people might now pay a heavy price.

As if reading his mind, Miko asked, "How old are you?"

"Fourteen and a half," Ravna said, and Stefan noticed a note of defiance in her tone.

"She could go to Malmberget. We all could. In the forest, outside the camp, there are survivors, resistors, some have escaped from the old iron mine and the camp - as I did," Miko said.

"But," Ravna protested, "I don't want to live with *The Others*. I want to live with Saami people."

Stefan held up his hand, like a traffic cop, to silence her, "Miko is right. If we find other Sami people, we would be bringing them nothing but trouble. Either disease or death or both. Is that what you want?"

Ravna didn't answer, she looked angrily from Stefan to

Miko, and back. "You're not my father! You can't tell me what to do!"

Stefan considered raising his voice and protesting in anger, but where would that get him? Instead, he said in a quiet voice, "You are right. No one can replace your father. But I do have an obligation to him and to you to keep you safe."

"I don't need your help!" Ravna said but with a touch less anger and conviction than before.

"This whole situation began with what I did yesterday. It's become my responsibility. I was the one who put Miko's chip on the reindeer. That is what brought the guards to your house. It is my fault. This is my mess."

He saw Ravna's eyes widen, with disbelief, and then understanding. "You got him killed!" she cried. "It was your fault."

She turned to Miko, "Both of you. It's your fault too."

Stefan's heart sank, "Of course, you are right. We caused this. Miko ran away from the camps with a chip under her skin. I cut it out and got the idea to put it on a reindeer that would wander in the forest and lead them astray, but that led the guards to you and your father."

He paused and allowed Ravna to compose herself, her eyes were wet, but no tears fell.

"We can't tell you what to do. But none of us can stay here, now." For a moment, this gave him a sense of dismay. What if this hadn't happened? He thought of Miko at his place the night before – in those brief hours before he found the chip. What might have happened between the two of them? Could they have made a new life here in the north, away from the camps? He had to press that idea away and come back to the present. "We all have to go somewhere, and quickly. They will be looking for these two snow machine riders to return right now."

Ravna looked from him to Miko and back again, listening.

"I'm not your father. You can ski off to be with your Uncle Gáktu if you wish. But I think it will be bringing death to his house. I have done that once. I will not do it again. I say head south with us, to the resistance. Start over. Don't let the camp guards who killed your father win."

From the woods nearby there was a bark. It was Čalmmo. He had followed their scent and caught up to them at the cabin. Björn gave an excited bar, knocked the door open, and chased Čalmmo around in circles by the cabin porch, forgetting his injured paw for the moment.

Čalmmo rushed to Ravna and put his paws on her chest, licking her face in greeting. "Looks like I have one companion," Ravna said. "We need to get the reindeer back in harness and go, then."

Björn trotted along behind the sled in the snow. Pat, pat, pat, ouch. Pat, pat, pat, ouch.

He looked up at Stefan, whose face was red with exertion and panted. *Faddar, my foot is hurted.*

Stefan reached out a hand and patted his head, "Good boy. Not much longer, then we rest."

He is a good, good faddar. Soon he will give me a puppy biscuit for I am a hungry boy.

But it was a very long time.

To Björn, it seemed a very long, long time.

Pat, pat, pat, *ouch*

The Winter Soldier

Stefan started the journey south feeling hopeful. Ecstatic, even. The sunlight and late winter warmth were invigorating, and it seemed like it would be a quick jaunt to their destination.

At first, they skied on the snowmobile tracks that led towards the camp at Kiruna. That was wonderful – the snow was packed down and the reindeer could make great headway with the sleds. They had two sleds for all their gear and food – as Ravna had found another reindeer from her herd to join them. On the second sled, there was room for a person to sit, and Miko took a break from skiing from time to time - - she couldn't ski all day like Stefan and Ravna, who had lived on the tundra for years.

At the rate they started, they could have made it to Malmberget by sunset – and it was a long spring sunset, not one of the short days of winter. They would have ten hours of daylight for skiing. It would be a breeze, Stefan thought.

But things didn't turn out that way. They had only skied a few kilometers down the trail when Stefan saw Ravna stiffen and lift her head to look about. That was when he heard the snowmobiles in the distance. "Off the path!" he shouted, and they steered the sleds into the muskeg and did their best to get out of sight in a thicket of bushes and dwarf northern trees. Stefan held Björn close to him with one arm and shushed him. Ravna did likewise with Čalmmo. In his other arm, tucked into his side, he held the Kalashnikov rifle that they had taken from one of the dead Russian guards at the cabin. He could see the tension in the eyes of Ravna and Miko as they huddled close to the trunks of nearby scrub spruce trees for cover

He felt a sense of relief when the snowmobiles blasted past them at high speed. But no sooner had they passed than the engine sound changed, and the machines turned abruptly and headed back to their tracks. They had seen their tracks but didn't know that they were hiding in the muskeg. They would know in just a few seconds because there was no way to hide their assembled group of dogs, reindeer, and people.

There was no time to think through options. Stefan had one moment to make a decision. He saw they were wearing camp guard uniforms, and that was all he needed to see. He clicked off the safety on the Kalashnikov. They spotted him at the same time he saw them, shifting on their sleds to turn and try to avoid him. He stood in the clear on the ski trail with his weapon, he held it firmly to his hip and sprayed them with bullets as they came ever closer to him. It sounded like a machine gun on a battlefield – something Stefan had only seen in movies, not real life.

The drivers fell from all three machines at once, and the snow machines hurtled out of control and then crashed into the thick muskeg brush. As the flying machines rolled past him, kicking up clouds of snow spray which flew into the air and then fell like a shower of snow. As if someone had tossed handfuls of glitter into the air at a party.

The engines of the snowmobiles went silent, shut off by dead-man switches which for once was an accurate description of their function. His ears were still ringing from the deafening sound of the roaring snow machines, and the sound of the machine gun, and then there was an eerie silence as the snow drifted back down on the ground, muffling the world around them.

One of the search party was still moving, and before Stefan could even say anything, Ravna drew a pistol from his coat and shot him. He jerked once more, in his death throes, so she shot him again, her face cold and impassive. She raised her gun towards the other camp guards, and Stefan reached across and grabbed her wrist, "Enough. It is done." Over his shoulder, he saw Miko's face blanched white with fear or revulsion.

"Why?" Miko mouthed to him, looking at the party of searchers. Two were men, and one was a woman, though she was swarthy and thickly built. None of them wore uniforms like the Russians they had killed yesterday.

Stefan shrugged and shook his head. "No time to consider options. If they were soldiers, we might all be dead right now, instead of them. They had to have been from the camp, and they would have either killed us or taken us there."

He didn't have to add what that would mean for her and Ravna. But his words did little to console her, her eyes filled with tears and she turned away to hide her face.

"We must cover them up. Hide the bodies." Stefan said.

Ravna helped Stefan drag the bodies into the thick undergrowth of the nearby spruce trees. They covered them with spruce branches and kicked snow over them. Miko did not participate, but held the dogs and watched, her face blotchy with distress. Then Stephan approached the tipped-over and silent snowmobiles.

"Can we take the snow machines?" Ravna asked, apparently unmoved by the sight of the three dead searchers. "We could be in Malmberget by noon."

"Same answer as yesterday. I doubt they have enough

fuel to get us to Malmberget. They can easily be spotted by drones because of their noise and heat, and we can't see or hear anyone while riding them. Too risky..."

Once the snowmobiles were also covered with branches and snow, they headed south towards Malmberget. Stefan would have liked to use a GPS device, like his old phone, which he had used at times over the past few years, to find a path across the muskeg. But he figured that if he was connected to that network, there might be a way of tracking him. He didn't bother digging it out of his pack. Instead, he went old school and pulled out a compass.

"What's that?" Miko said, seeing him holding it.

"You've never seen a compass?" Stefan said.

"Only in books or old movies. Never saw someone actually use one."

"My grandfather used them when we drove the herds, back in the day," Ravna said.

"Thanks for making me feel ancient," Stefan said. He held it up and sighted across it to a stand of white birch in the distance. "We'll head that way. It's almost due South. We should be able to locate the rail line outside of town and follow it to Malmberget."

"Isn't that dangerous?" Miko said.

Stefan saw the tension in her face and body. She had just escaped from the concentration camp train and probably wanted little to do with it. "We'll stay well away from the rail line itself. I'm sure they've got cameras and drones near it. I don't want to be spotted from the train, either."

They skied on, soon they were circling to the east of the Kiruna Flygplats. The hanger doors were off their hinges, most likely from scavengers seeking fuel in the early days of the Holocaust. Now the whole place just looked like any of the other derelict buildings of the old town. The late-day sun had broken through and the snow was dripping from the eaves as they slowly made their way past the abandoned buildings. There were no tracks in the snow to show that anyone had been there for ages.

Over the thickly wooded hills, they went and Ravna spotted the train line ahead. The reindeer struggled through the thick snow to pull the sleds. Stefan had them take turns breaking the trail. Even Miko, though she glared at him when he motioned with his mitten for her to take the lead. That way the animals could at least have a bit of a break.

Late in the day, they heard the muted roar of the train coming from the north and they slipped behind the nearby trees. He noticed Miko shaking beside him and reached clumsily with his mitten and ski pole to put a hand on her shoulder, but she shrugged him off, her dark eyes flashing again. Stefan noticed that the train had an old passenger car, what looked like a couple of tanker cars of some sort, and then the usual string of ore cars. Someone was still making steel somewhere in the south. It was also odd that they were running the train down the Inlandsbanan. The tracks were better and the route shorter along the coast. Why go through mid-Sweden and not along the much more civilized Baltic route?

As with many things since the troubles began, he had no answers and no way to find out. They were back in the Stone Age.

After the train passed, Miko spoke out again when the noise of the train had passed, "I'll need to stop soon. My feet are getting blisters, and if we are going to do this again tomorrow, they will need to heal a bit."

Stefan nodded. "We're near the old Kalixfors army airfield. Maybe we can find some cover there – it shouldn't be that long."

That night Stefan had one of his dreams. He was in California at the time of The Great Fire. They were in a house on a hillside near Victorville, and people were panicking because a wall of fire was coming over the mountain divide and heading their way. Miko was there, and there were others. He was holding a baby boy, while others were shouting and throwing possessions into cars and vans.

There was a great roaring sound, and descending the hill behind them was a fire tornado. The house was filling with smoke, and the men were shouting and the women were screaming for everyone to leave. He heard Miko crying out "Boy-San! Boy San!" which was the name of the baby he was holding. But a man had Miko's arm at the elbow and was stuffing her in a car, even as she reached back to another man who was carrying the little boy, racing for another car that was further away.

"To Denver! We will meet in Denver!" someone was shouting, "To Denver!"

The door to the car slammed shut, and it roared away. As it did so Stefan could smell the burning rubber of the tires clearly. He made it out the door to the house just as the spinning cone of fire hit it and the house blew up just as if a bomb had gone off. The next car that they had pulled up to rescue them was already on fire, even though others from the house were climbing in. He hesitated, while they held the door open for him to enter. Instead, he ran behind it, towards the last remaining house in the subdivision. Over the top of the car, he could see Miko with her head out the window screaming something, which he thought was the phrase "Boy-San!" But then the car with the other occupants already inside exploded too as the fire tornado spun over it, igniting the gas tank into yet another bomb.

He felt a searing pain in his back as he was blown off his feet into the nearby ditch. It was a drainage ditch, with brackish red water and mud. He crawled, dragging the boy with him, into an open culvert just a yard away, as the flames roared over them like a jet taking off. He pushed further into the pipe, put his hand over the boy's mouth, and pressed him down into the layer of muck in the pipe, burying his face in there also. The heat was like being in an oven, and the sound roared in his ears, but after holding his breath for a couple of minutes at least, he heard the roar lessen and the tornado continued down the hill to claim its next victims.

He and Boy-San stayed in that culvert all night, while the fire lit the sky and all the houses and trees burned to the ground around them. At dawn he crawled back out into a fire-blasted war zone – it looked like he had landed on another planet, a land of fire and smoldering black rubble. Just yards away there were the dead people hanging half out of the car, blown and burned into gruesome shapes. He reached his hand to cover the boys' eyes, but the boy saw through his fingers and let out a piteous wail. It must have been his mother's friends and family, the boys' relatives, that lay charred and burned in the wreckage. On smoldering shoes, he set off to go try to find some other survivors, and some source of water to ease his parched and burned throat. The boy whimpered and clung to him down the hill to the highway of charred vehicles on the road below, the road back to what might be left of civilization.

Stefan woke up, sweating despite the cold night – as if he had been in fiery California, not snowy Kiruna all night. It was not yet dawn, and he tried to get back to sleep. He knew why his sleep was troubled, it was because of the events of the past few days. Not just the journey south, but what he chose to do yesterday in killing the Russian guards out on the tundra. He was not hardened to kill like a soldier in a war, even though he had been living in what was basically a war zone for the last four years. Only by venturing out of his safe place, his comfort zone, had he come into a place of life or death struggle where he lived now. He knew sleep was impossible, so he tried to just close his eyes and rest, and await the morning.

*   *   *   *   *   *   *   *   *   *   *

In the morning they drank stale three-year-old coffee from a large bean can that Ravna had fashioned into a crude coffeepot. It tasted delicious.

"Your eyes are red. Did you not sleep last night?" Ravna said to him, handing him a cup of steaming coffee.

"Oh, I slept. Just had one of my bad dreams," he said.

"What about? Wolves?" Ravna said, in a perky voice. No one should be this perky in the morning, Stefan thought, wondering again at the resilience of youth.

"No, only Saami people have nightmares of wolves," Stefan said, trying to make a joke, but not succeeding well. He now regretted having said anything.

"What then?" Miko said, her pretty eyes meeting his over the rim of the small vegetable can that they had made into a cup after dinner. "You are worried about our journey. Did you dream we were captured?"

"No," he hesitated, "it was from the earlier time. From the Great Fire of California."

"I was there," Miko said, and her face fell. "Were you there also? It was horrific."

Ravna was looking from one of them to the other.

"I wasn't there. Just heard about it, as everyone did."

"I barely survived," Miko said and looked away. "Made it to Denver eventually and lived in the refugee camps for a year."

"I know," Stefan said and realized he shouldn't have said that.

"How do you know?" Ravna said, rounding on him with a rising note of emotion in her voice. "Were you lovers!"

"Pfff!" Miko snorted from beside her. "Fat chance."

"How did you know then? I thought you two just met?"

Stefan saw them staring at him, eyes agape. *Fuck it,* it doesn't much matter anymore. "I have dreams of true things."

"Bull!" Miko said. "Lots of people say that. Scientists have proven that dreams are just random brain waves or something. I read that somewhere."

"Then who was Boy-San?" Stefan said, for some reason losing his patience. I must be more tired than I thought I was, he reflected, not controlling my impulses.

Ravna turned to Miko and Stefan saw tears welling up in Miko's eyes. She was shaking her head, "No one... No one knows..."

Ravna got a flabbergasted look on her face and practically shouted at Stefan, "What the *hell*!"

"I get dreams of things. They are either of things that happened or dreams of things that will happen. That's all."

"So who was Boy-San?" Ravna said, reaching a hand to touch Miko's arm. It was a gesture more of a mother reaching out to a daughter than a teen reaching out to an elder. That surprised Stefan.

Miko snuffled wiped her nose on her sleeve, and looked down as she said, "Boy-San was my son. He died in the fire with a man from Hawaii - My Uncle Walter Wauke. His nickname was Dr. Wu – not sure how he got that name."

"Part of that is right," Stefan said.

"Which part?" Ravna said.

"The part about him being her uncle. I sensed that, though I can't say why. But they didn't die in the fire."

"WHAT!" Miko half-shouted, half-screamed.

"They didn't die, and they didn't make it to Denver," Stefan answered in a calm voice, thinking over the scenario of the dream, meeting Ravna's eyes, noticing her mouth hanging open in astonishment. He turned back to Miko, "There was a culvert in front of the house, a big pipe that had a small amount of muddy water in it. When the second car blew up Boy-San and Wu fell into that and spent the night underground in the mud. The next day they wandered down to the highway. Route 395, right? There was a burned road sign that I could still read."

Miko stared at him incredulously, and then a river of tears began pouring down her face, but through her tears, she asked, *"Is he alive? Can you tell me that? Is he alive?"*

Stefan could only   shake his head, "No." Now he regretted having said anything at all, seeing how upset Miko was. It was not a good start to the day...

CHAPTER EIGHTEEN

Stefan's goal for the day was to make it past Sjisjka to one of the other little railroad towns, like Kaitum or Fjällåsen. Stefan had seen these little towns while riding the train south in the past and knew they were there. They could find shelter and maybe some old canned food at one or the other of them. That was the plan, but no sooner had they started skiing than things went awry.

He should have known from the scent of the air that a storm was coming, but he ignored the obvious signs. They were barely down the trail from Kalixfors when it hit them. He stopped with his hands on his ski poles and paused. The two reindeer pulling their sleighs caught up to him and stopped. Stefan had nicknamed the reindeer *Crag* and *Tundra* after the reindeer in the children's story *The Wild Christmas Reindeer* by Jan Brett.

"Feels like some heavy snow is coming," Stefan said. Pausing and petting Crag's snowy mane.

Crag nuzzled him, snuffling around his pockets for a treat. All he had were "puppy biscuits" in his pockets, and those were reserved for his favorite, Björn.

"Pretty big storm," Ravna said, lifting her nose in the air like a hunting dog and sniffing. "I bet we get at least a meter of *Habllek*."

"What?" Miko shouted.

"I said, at least a meter of *Habllek!*" Ravna shouted back over the rising wind in a petulant tone. "You know, Snow that Falls!"

Despite the impending trouble, Stefan had to laugh, "The Saami have lots of words for snow!" But Miko was not laughing, she had been silent and brooding since their discussion of her lost son.

"Not True!" Ravna said. "Only a few words for snow. Lots of words for what the snow is like *Slievar, skabrram, and rido* – and that up ahead, *Åppås* untouched winter snow without tracks."

Stefan noticed she still had her saucy teenage tone. She was lecturing them like they were dolts. "It all looks like *Åppås* to me," but his voice was drowned out by the rising wind. He realized further discussion was futile, "Should we go back? It's getting bad."

Miko nodded yes. Ravna shook her head no. Stefan looked into the snow ahead, his cheeks were getting stung by the cold hard flakes. There was no food back at Kalixfors...

"Shouldn't be far to the Kaitum," Stefan said. "Let's press on."

"Let's go back!" he heard Miko shout.

"Trust me!" Stefan said and pushed his ski poles into the soft snow to break the trail ahead. One of the problems was that there was no real road here – just old trails across the muskeg that had been used to build the railway and then were sometimes used by people on snow machines.

He covered his face with a scarf so that only his eyes would have been visible to others. They skied on, with Stefan leading and trying to keep them on the trail as best he could. But unlike the day before, the driving snow kept him from easily seeing the trail, and by mid-day, he was no longer sure they were heading in the right direction.

They were making slow progress and Stefan was beginning to think he had made the right decision to press until heard a growl and a loud bark. It was Čalmmo. He was in the lead and had caught the scent of a wolf or wolf pack, in the driving snow Stefan couldn't tell which. Čalmmo bolted forward, with Björn running with him, and then the reindeer reared up and bolted off the trail in fear. One was pulling the sleigh carrying Miko.

Stefan raced ahead, hearing the dogs barking excitedly as they gave chase, and then, from off the trail he heard Miko scream. The reindeer pulling the sled had turned from the trail into the muskeg.

He raced as fast as he could following the trail of the sleigh runners into the thick brush. He could barely see the runner tracks in the driving snow, and he glanced behind him to see Ravna gamely trying to keep up with him. He had to duck under willow branches and push through scraggly spruce trees to reach Miko and the sleigh, which was turned over up ahead in a thicket. He heard her crying out in pain and rushed to her side. She was tangled in the lines of the sled, face up in the snow. She had stopped crying out and was lying very still, her eyes open, staring straight up at the sky.

For just the briefest instant, he thought she had broken her neck and was dead. "I think I've broken my leg," she said, just as Ravna arrived out of breath with exertion. Stefan's heart sank.

Stefan knelt in the snow, sinking in up to his waist because it was so thick here in the shelter of the bushes. He felt along Miko's lower leg and she cried out. If there *was* a break at least the bone was not sticking out.

"This has not been a very good day for me," Miko said. "First news of my son, and then this."

Ravna met his eyes. She was young, but she knew how serious this was. Both the two dogs and the reindeer were gone, and the sled and Miko's leg were now broken, and it was snowing even harder. What more could go wrong?

CHAPTER NINETEEN

The *Stuga*

They got Miko covered up with the blankets on the sleigh, but already the hard-driving snow was drifting over her.

Ravna met his eyes, and neither of them moved for a few tense moments. Stefan pondered what to do next, blaming himself for pressing on into this cold and miserable weather.

Stefan could see the toll that the cold and her injured leg were having on her.

"How are you?" Ravna asked her after she and Stefan had struggled for a few minutes to get the sled back from the tangle of bushes and onto the trail.

"I can't feel my legs…" Miko said. "The good news is that I also can't feel the pain from my ankle as much."

"We have to get you somewhere warm as soon as possible," Stefan said. Without saying it, he was worried that that shock was setting in, or that she also had a broken back and was paralyzed…

Ravna was able to call for the reindeer, who fortunately had not gone too far into the muskeg. She coaxed Crag back into the traces of the sleigh.

"We might have a difficult time catching the dogs again. They are chasing a wolf, but hopefully, not a whole pack that might turn on them and fight. We'll just have to hope for the best…but for now, it's important to get you to some shelter as fast as we can."

He saw Ravna's concern in her eyes, and that she worked to tuck the blankets under Miko's legs in the hopes that they weren't totally frozen. Soon they were off again down the trail, but they were racing against the cold and the setting sun.

It wasn't long before they came to the small hamlet of Kaitum. The railway station looked like a two-stall outhouse, with faded Falun red batten siding, and an equally faded green door. A large sign above on the front of the tiny station said "KAITUM" in large white letters on a black background. The station looked more like a rotting shack rather than a train station. No covered platform, no waiting room, nothing but a faded train schedule board. But there was a path through the woods to an old stuga, and they headed that way.

The cottage was an old log structure, off by itself. The snow was still piled high on the roof, and nearly up to the windows. The door was locked, which was a good sign. It meant that this house had not been pilfered. Stefan used the butt of his rifle to tap the door open by hitting the lock, trying to be careful not to break the door window glass nearby.

Stefan leaned in and gave it "the sniff test." The sniff test was also "the stiff test" – to check and see if there were any victims of the Pandemic who had died here when it swept through. Stefan also kept his weapon at the ready in case it had become the home of any wild animals. He heard what might have been the scuttling of voles running away, but he wasn't sure. The sun was now below the horizon.

"It seems safe," he yelled over his shoulder to Ravna and Miko.

He went in and rooted around the cabin. He found a candle and some matches he could light. There was a rime of frost on everything and a sprinkling of mouse or vole droppings, but no sign of any people.

Whoever lived here had left in a hurry, but not before the power had been cut off because there was a kerosene lantern on the table. But unlike most places, this one had not been looted by survivors of the holocaust. This was likely due to there being so few people in this tiny village that they all either quickly died or left when the plague hit.

Stefan worked with Ravna to get Miko in. She was able to move at least one leg, the other she kept held up but yelped with pain whenever they bumped it on anything. It appeared that at least she wasn't paralyzed or she wouldn't be crying out in pain.

"Nice open concept!" Miko said looking around at the dimly lit cabin with a wry grin.

They trundled her into the cabin and got her to a couch. But as they leaned down together to place her on the couch he felt a tremor in his lower back, a spasm, and he gasped and let go of Miko, who sort of dropped the last foot or two onto the couch. *Oh Shit! This is not good!* Stefan thought.

Ravna gave him a dirty look until she saw that he was wincing in pain and pressing his palms against his lower back.

"Your back, huh," Ravna said. "My grandpa had that problem!"

"Thanks for the comparison," Stefan said, slowly getting completely vertical. "I'll be OK, you'll see. I just overdid it a bit today."

Ravna looked at him skeptically.

Miko said, "I'd say we all overdid it today, almost dying out in the wilderness. I guess that's why they haven't been too worried about people escaping from the camps..."

"Yeah, they would most likely either freeze or starve to death," then he noticed Ravna tilting her head in disagreement. He said to her, "Not everyone can live on the tundra. It helps if your family has been doing it for a few thousand years."

Ravna grinned at the off-handed compliment, and added,

"Speaking of starving, I am. I'm going to look for food."

Stefan meanwhile started a fire in the stove. It was a well-worn, heavy, antique enameled stove of the kind often found in old Swedish farmhouses. He moved gingerly not to aggravate his back any further, but it slowed him down. The owners of the stuga had left behind wood, matches, and kindling. It was obvious that the task of building a fire in the stove would have been a daily activity for them in the winter.

Meanwhile, Ravna had grabbed a stepstool and was exploring what was in the pantry cupboard. The sight of mouse droppings everywhere there had been dry food did not bother her in the least, Stefan noticed.

"OK, I've found beans and vegetables in some cans which haven't burst. Also, a bunch of cans of corned beef hash!"

"Great!" Stefan said, but winced when he spoke loudly, "The hash will have both meat and potatoes. Are there any bulges in the cans? That would mean they have gone bad and shouldn't use them. Also, we'll need to either melt snow or get some water from the stream outside to boil the vegetables."

Ravna was still rooting around in the cupboards. But Stefan noticed that now when she breathed, he couldn't see her breath. The fireplace in the stove was starting to warm up the stuga.

"Hey, look what I found," Ravna said and pulled out a bottle of Vodka from the top cupboard. "Oh, and this too!" She held up a bottle of whiskey.

"Surprising that didn't freeze and break. This house must have been insulated enough to keep it relatively warm, above 25 below," Stefan said.

"Toasty," Miko said with sarcasm from the couch. "Give me some of that. I could use a painkiller."

"It has to warm up first. It can burn your throat badly if

it's too cold. This feels like it's below freezing. I'll warm it on the stove."

Stefan found two coffee cups in the cupboard and placed them on the stove. He put a hefty dose of the whiskey in each and moved them onto the burner. There was a plastic jar of honey shaped like a bear, and he put that in some melting snow in a pan that Ravna had fetched.

Soon he had a hot toddy to share with Miko, and he began finally feeling warm.

"Hey, I want one of those. I like whiskey!" Ravna said, eyeing him and sipping his hot drink.

"You're only fourteen," Stefan responded, "when have you ever had whiskey."

"Two nights ago. I pried the bottle from a dead Russian's hand." She paused, and added, "And I'm fifteen, nearly sixteen."

Really, Stefan thought, trying to remember how old she had been the time before when he had seen her with Duvnik. He thought she had been twelve then, and that it was two years ago... Sixteen, that is about the age of consent, he thought, meeting her eyes over the brim of her cup as he poured a generous portion into the cup. It seemed her eyes opened up to him – as if she was inviting him in. He'd had that feeling before with women. He was never sure if it was his imagination or something real that he sensed.

"Hey, my leg is feeling better. I'd like another of those," Miko said.

Stefan nodded. He poured her one, and himself another. His shot was about twice what he gave Miko. He could use a bit of a painkiller himself. It had been a hell of a day.

Ravna opened the cans of hash and beans and put them in a large frying pan. The dogs had curled up near the stove, but when the food was opened, they sat up, hoping for some too. Stefan knew they had burned plenty of calories hauling the sled. When Ravna gave them each a can of hash they gobbled it up greedily and looked for more. Stefan made a mental note to look for more unspoiled food in the nearby village before they left tomorrow, both for themselves and the dogs.

While Ravna stirred the food on the stove, Stefan took the kerosene lantern over to Miko and knelt in front of her.

"We've got to get these boots off and see what your ankle looks like."

Miko stared at him and bit her lip. She took a sip of her whiskey to steel herself against what was coming next.

Stefan unlaced her boots and tried to remove them as gently as possible. The left boot was no problem, but the right ankle bulged out about the boot top – it was already quite swollen. While Miko looked away he pulled the sides of the boot as far apart as he could and then jerked the boot off her ankle backward.

Miko screamed, and Ravna jumped with alarm at the sound. "Ow, Ow, Ow, Ow, Ow…" Miko muttered through clenched teeth.

Stefan hoped he hadn't hurt the bones of her ankle even worse by yanking off the boot, he half expected to see a broken bone sticking out under her sock, but he didn't. He felt the sock with his hands, gently, and didn't find anything clearly broken. He peeled her sock down over her foot as gently as he could, but Miko continued her litany of "Ow, Ow, Ow…" as he did so. No sooner had he gotten the boot and sock completely off than the foot began to swell. But in the first minute or so that he had to examine it, the foot looked darkly bruised but normal.

"Might just be a really bad sprain," Stefan said, and he

noticed Ravna looking surprised. "Could be that the cold kept some of the swelling down, too."

"Nature's icepack?" Miko said.

"Yeah, something like that. Your feet are very cold, but it doesn't look like your toes are frozen. You will probably not lose any of them."

"Terrific. I'm thrilled."

Stefan looked up at her, "Without an X-ray, there will be no way to tell if you cracked the bones or not. It could be worse, much worse." He noticed how white and clear her skin was on the uninjured foot. She reminded him of a "china doll" made of porcelain.

"*Shikata ga nai!*" Miko said, not noticing his distraction, then added, "It's something my Uncle Wu from Hawaii used to say, "It can't be helped" "Nothin' we can do about it."

"That's Japanese, right?

"It is Japanese. Despite his nickname, he was a Sansei a third-generation Japanese from Pearl City. That's the town that sits next to Pearl Harbor. Not the greatest place in the world to be Japanese, but *"Shikata ga nai!"*

"So how did a Valley Girl end up in freakin' Lappland?" Stefan said, noticing that he had a little trouble pronouncing the last couple of words. The hot toddy was taking effect, fast.

"After The Great Fire there was nowhere to go back home to," Miko said. "I eventually moved to Copenhagen for a job at an online marketing firm. Never figured I'd end up here - in Lappland. I'm sure you heard about the Great California Fire even here, right?"

"Sure, "*LA Burning*" – everybody heard about that." Stefan said, "But there was so much other bad news that it was overshadowed by all the other terrible things going on."

"The smoke made the snow brown even here in Lappland

that year," Ravna said. "I was old enough to remember that year. The year before the invasion."

Ravna brought over bowls of hot food and set them down on a small coffee table by the couch. Stefan went to get up and his back "went out" even worse than before. He pitched forward onto the couch in pain. He had to slowly press his hands into the couch and lever himself slowly upright, but even then he was bent over at an odd angle, leaning more to the left than the right. He hadn't even noticed that Ravna had quickly leaped to help him and had her hands under his armpits, lifting him upright. She was surprisingly strong. Typical Sami Girl he thought. He noticed Miko watching both of them intently, and wondered what she was thinking.

"I'm fine," he said, easing himself slowly down into a nearby stuffed chair.

Ravna handed a bowl of steaming beans and hash, and he tried to restrain himself from just inhaling it.

"You are not a Swede. How did you end up here?" Miko said, between bites of her food.

"I lived here when I was a kid," he thought of adding more to this statement but chose to take a forkful hash instead. "My one Farfar was from near Kiruna and the land was where he once had a stuga. It was all fallen down, but I got the land and the old mineshaft. I didn't intend to settle here permanently..."

"No wife, kids?" Miko said.

"None active." He noticed that Ravna had leaned forward to hear his response to the last question.

"What is that supposed to mean? None Active?"

Stefan shrugged. "OK. Divorced. Age 40. I've been here alone for ten years"

"Truly alone," Miko said, "no scudsy girlfriends lurking

about?"

Stefan paused, thinking, "I feel like a celebrity on a talk show. *Who you hooking up with?* That sort of thing." Now that she mentioned it, there might have been a couple of scudsy girlfriends here and there...

"Right, damnit. Who were you hooking up with? Or have you sworn off women?"

"I decided to become a monk, and live the celibate life," Stefan said.

"I thought you were a car mechanic!" Ravna chimed in, "That's what my dad told me..."

"He was right. Swedes love *"Stora Americanska gamla bilar!"* Stefan said.

"Huh?" Miko said.

"Big old American cars" Ravna translated. "Hot rods, right Stefan? That's what my dad told me Stefan worked on..."

"It paid the bills," Stefan said, happy to be talking about work and not women. Still, he noticed how lightheaded he was getting from the whiskey. He noticed Miko's eyes drooping with tiredness and stress. "Hey, enough about me. We should get some ice on her ankle before she conks out. Could you grab some snow and a bag to put it in Ravna?"

Ravna didn't jump to it, but kind of shrugged and acquiesced. She put her coat and hat back on, grabbed the pot they had used to boil water, and went out the door — letting in a blast of cold and blowing snow.

"She'll do *anything* you ask," Miko said, once the door closed. "Be careful with that."

Stefan took a moment to catch the import of what she was saying. "We'd have been lost today without her. Literally." Stefan said, pausing then adding, "She's more mature than she looks."

"I was fourteen once," Miko said. "I was fucking boy crazy

then, too." She said, and then added, "Literally."

"Thanks for sharing that," Stefan said, though the truth was she was making him uncomfortable. "And she's almost sixteen." Which elicited a snort of disbelief from Miko.

The door banged open and Ravna returned. She knelt in front of Miko and put the bag of ice on her ankle with a dishtowel to keep it from burning her skin. Stefan had to admit that she did have a cute little body – he glanced at Miko to see if she had noticed him gawking, but her eyes had closed. She was drifting off to sleep.

CHAPTER TWENTY

The Zombie Train

Stefan helped Ravna clean up the dishes, and before they were done, Miko was snoring on the couch. Stefan laughed, but got rewarded with another, more severe spasm and immediately gripped his lower back with the palms of his hands to stop the tremors.

"You should lay down, and let me give you a back rub. That is what I would do for *Farrfar*. He had a bad back and taught me how to help it feel better."

Stefan nodded. He felt exhausted and sore and combined with the whiskey, was in no mood to object. He helped Ravna add a bit more split birch wood to the stove. He took off his heavy flannel shirt outer shirt and then gingerly lay down on the only bed in the stuga.

Her warm hands massaging his lower back was the last thing he remembered – the whiskey and exhaustion from the day and pain overwhelmed him.

In the morning it was cold in the cabin, and to Stefan's surprise, Miko had risen early and hobbled around building a fire. She was using a broomstick as a crude cane – tucking it under her arm and gripping it almost like a crutch.

"I can make you a crutch that's better than that," Stefan offered.

"I think it's just a sprain. I'll be fine." Stefan thought he detected a bit of an edge to her voice. Despite her protests, she must still be hurting and cranky.

At the sound of their voices, Ravna stirred beside him. She

had been lying close to him, most likely for warmth. Stefan got out of bed, but his back was still very stiff and he had to use the bed rail and then a dresser to get upright. And then, he was barely upright. He noticed Miko watching him as he walked like an old man over to the entryway.

Working gingerly, he managed to get his outdoor clothes on and get the dogs out the door, while holding onto the side jamb and trying to lever himself completely upright. His back was not cooperating.

The weather was surprisingly warm. He'd been expecting the storm of the day before to drag cold weather in behind it like it usually did, but the sun felt warm today, and there was a light wind from the south. Things would melt today... if they were to ski and sled South they would need to get going soon. The dogs took off barking wildly and chasing in circles around the cabin. Björn would pause momentarily, glance back at him, trying to communicate:

"Fadder, there was someone here.... Someone following us... Fadder!"

"What are they barking about?" Ravna had poked her head out to see.

"Probably some reindeer or rabbits left a scent," Stefan said, he looked at the snow for marks, but it had been churned up by them when they came the night before – lots of dog footprints.

Björn and Čalmmo found one spot, sniffed, and barked there more loudly than elsewhere. Both dogs raced around, their noses to the ground, barking excitedly.

"Fadder, bad dogs was here! Me and new friend found

them. Bad dogs! Bad dogs! Danger! Fadder!

"Björn! Čalmmo! Get back in here! Time to go!"

To Ravna he said, "Probably a fox. I saw lots of bunny prints last night, and we probably kicked voles out of the house when we came." She nodded her assent. They were leaving and whatever had been there the night before would soon be a moot point.

That day they made continued progress, despite being slowed a bit by Stefan's sore back and Miko's ankle. They followed the rail line on nearby service roads through the warm sunshine, pausing at the long mid-day for lunch and a fire. Stefan could tell that it must be at least mid-May for the sun to be up so long, so they would have almost 20 hours to ski that day.

Before they left that morning Stefan had "borrowed" a fishing pole from the cabin, and added it to the sled with their supplies. Near mid-day they stopped at a stream that was warming in the sunshine in just minutes he caught some plump trout which they and the dogs feasted on for lunch over an open fire.

"Feels great to be out in the sunshine. I feel like I'm on vacation!" Stefan said.

"On what?" Ravna asked.

"Vacation. It's something rich, white, entitled Americans used to do. I think the British call it *Going on holiday.*" Miko said. Stefan noticed there still was an edge to her voice. Perhaps her ankle which she had propped up and covered with some snow in a bag, was making her testy.

"Oh, like the *Jokkmokk Guiderna?*" Ravna said, directing it at Stefan, giving him a smile and a wink.

Seeing Miko's puzzled glance, Stefan translated, "Yeah,

like the people who come to the Jokkmokk winter carnival. Tourists."

"I don't think we look like any goddam tourists," Miko said, staring at the fire.

She had a point. They were sitting there eating charred fish with their fingers, wearing a ragtag assortment of stained old wool coats and trousers. Tourists would have bright and snappy down vests, and Swedes would have special "hiking clothes" if hiking and "skiing clothes" and gear if skiing.

"Why are you so grumpy?" Stefan asked.

Miko looked at him knowingly and tilted her head slightly in the direction of Ravna.

Stefan shook his head and tried to figure out what her inference was. Why was Miko mad at Ravna? After all the help Ravna had given her the day before, she should be grateful for her outdoorsy skills.

"I think we should focus on what we are here to do, not turn this into a freakin' Boy Scout winter holiday, that's all."

"I've been cooped up for four years. Doesn't seem like it's such a bad thing to find a bit of enjoyment in life for a change."

"Yeah. Keep enjoying yourselves. Don't let me spoil your little party."

Ravna glanced at Stefan, trying to interpret what this meant, and why she was being included in Miko's sarcasm. Stefan shrugged.

Stefan stood up and immediately felt his back clench. Sitting at the fire with the warmth in front and the cold behind them hadn't helped it a bit.

They set off for the final slog to Malmberget after lunch. The snow was starting to melt, and from time to time Stefan's skis got stuck in the snow and he had to slide them back and forth to get them free. His morning ebullience, dimmed by Miko's obvious bad mood, gave way to just being persistent and putting one foot in front of the other. By mid-afternoon, the snow was getting too sticky for skiing, and patches of grass were starting to show through.

Ravna untied the reindeer from the sleds and gave them each a hug around the neck and then swatted their haunches and sent them on their way back into the forest. She and Stefan took what they could carry in their packs, not wanting to burden Miko with more weight, since she was still limping. They continued through the long sunny afternoon, It seemed like an endless journey.

But Stefan was snapped out of his boredom by the thunderous sound of the steam train coming down the *Inlandsbanan* near their trail. Back in the day, the engineer would have blown the steam whistle each time that the train came to a road crossing, but there was no need for that anymore, so there was just a steady drumming in the distance which broke the absolute stillness of the tundra.

Stefan waved the others to take what shelter they could in the nearby bushes. They were able to hide from view for the most part, and he figured that the train crew would hardly notice them. He was right about that, the train engine passed near them, a cacophony overwhelmed them, and they could even feel its immense weight pushing the track down into the tundra as it passed, the very ground shook. The train was moving more slowly than usual because they were going up a long hill. The portly engineer, his face red from being out in the sun and wind, didn't glance at them as the locomotive went by.

But just after the coal tender was a passenger car. That was not uncommon. There were usually prisoners/workers heading north to the camps. "Internees" is what they liked to call them, a useful euphemism borrowed from earlier internment camps in other more distant wars. Miko had told him that was what they were called in the camps, "internees" – just like the Japanese-Americans they kept in concentration camps in America in the Second World War.

But that wasn't what was on this train. As it passed slowly by about 30 heads turned and looked his way, all in unison. Stefan swallowed hard, and his pulse began to race. They were 30 identical heads, with 30 identical expressions, and as their heads turned, all their blank grey eyes fixed his gaze in unison.

"Jesus!"' Miko hissed from behind a nearby laurel bush, "It's a fucking trainload of zombies."

* * * * * * * * * * * * * * * * * * *

In a dark room in Uppsala, Håkan woke up. Not that she (currently Håkan was choosing a female avatar. That seemed to make the humans more comfortable than being a "he" or worse, an "it") ever really slept like humans do, she was just in power save mode. She had been on cruise control for an hour or so with nothing happening to catch her attention. But suddenly she got images from the replicants. They were transmitting something they thought important. The images came to her in more focus and brighter. It was a small group of stragglers hiding in the muskeg, along the tracks close to the Malmberget camp. She felt as if she was seeing things through their eyes, which was new and exciting.

What she saw made her smile to herself. She had located Stefan and that troublemaker, Miko Nakama. *Ja hah!* Somehow they had joined forces with Ravna, one of the few Sami children that had survived the rough conditions of the last few years. Håkan could see their alarm as they stared back at the replicants in their coach on the train. Great! Both groups were heading her way. The next few days should be interesting!

"Stefan Andersson, you are nothing if not predictable!" she said out loud, her modulated voice echoing in the quiet Lab auditorium.

"What was that?" Dr. Bob said, dozing in his chair at the big computer control panel across the room.

"Oh, nothing. Just saying it's great when a plan comes together, no?"

Dr. Bob looked at her oddly, and then she smiled, and as usual that won him over. God, he was predictable, too. Like a puppy, eager to please.

CHAPTER TWENTY ONE

The passing of the train spoiled Stefan's mood. Miko was still acting surly and shooting him the stink-eye, and now there was something new to worry about – the Zombies or Replicants or whatever those strange humanoid beings were on the train. What they reminded him of was characters called "Putties" on the old *Mighty Morphin Power Rangers* TV show he used to watch when he was a kid. The same bland expressions and uniform appearance. He hoped that like Putties they were also as inept and easy to beat in a fight.

He picked up the pace with the dogs straining on their leads as the weather grew warmer and the snow more slushy, by late afternoon he was getting sweaty and feeling the strain of yet another long day of exertion.

"We're getting close to the mine. You need to slow down!" Miko snapped at him from back down the trail.

"I don't see any," he paused, cut off in mid-sentence. Just yards ahead, through the trees, there was an enormous hole in the ground. It would have been like falling into the Grand Canyon if they had skied just a few yards ahead. It looked like the ground they were standing on could give way at any minute and plunge them hundreds of feet down into the misty chasm.

"Woah!" Stefan yelled to the dogs and Ravna. He noticed his pulse racing

"We're here," Miko said, still managing a note of disdain in her voice.

Stefan looked at her and shook his head. "I would think you would be happy, not snarling at me."

"Yes. All women should be grateful for the gift of your

presence," she said, then pointed off to the south. "A bit further that way and I think we can take the old truck loading ramp down. I know where there is a small doorway into the mine."

"How do you know this?" Ravna asked her.

"We used to sneak out to go fishing. Even in the worst of the winter we could still ice fish and catch something good to eat. The food at the camps was terrible – beans and hotdogs, with God knows how much radiation mixed in."

Stefan noticed that Miko wasn't snappish with Ravna. Only he was the one who had raised her ire. "You don't think the guards will be watching the entrance?"

"Who breaks into a concentration camp?" Miko said. "They were only there to keep us in line. If they lost some to wandering off into the wasteland and freezing to death that wasn't their problem. They had a lot more slave workers than they needed."

They entered through a rough steel door at a low level of the mine. The first thing Stefan noticed was the warmth. The mine tapped into the warmth of the earth, and it was a moist warmth, like a summer day in August, even in Lappland.

"Pleasantly warm in here," Stefan said. They found a place near the entrance to shelter the dogs – tying them to a support post and finding water and some old tarps for them to lay on.

"Hot as hell when you get deeper," Miko said, still with an edge to her voice, but then added, "I remember the way, follow me." Still with the stink-eye reserved for him, Stefan noticed. What had set her off? Or was she always bitchy like this? Or was her sore ankle bothering her? He noticed she was still limping.

They wandered down long dimly lit former shafts, the

sides sprayed with some sort of concrete mix, like the passages in a Disney theme park underground ride. The only difference was the giant bolts on steel plates anchoring the earth. That was all that kept the tunnels from collapsing in on them - not a pleasant thought.

Ravna paused, and held up her hand, "I hear something."

Stefan expected it to be the sound of jackhammers or steel drills.

Ravna smiled, "It's music."

Stefan listened harder, there was a faint sound. They walked further ahead and saw a crossing where tunnels intersected. Ravna was right, her young ears could hear better. It was music. People singing.

"Oh, it's the damn prayer meeting," Miko said, laughing.

"What?" Stefan said.

"Thursdays. The preacher lady has her Jesus meetings."

"Jesus meetings?" Ravna said, not understanding.

Miko nodded, "You'll see. It's just ahead."

She led them on and pushed through another steel door into what must have been an old tool room in a side shaft. Boxes were being used for seats, and a small circle of people with their heads bowed, apparently praying.

"Rachel, I'm back," Miko said to a circle of people sitting on boxes and oil drums.

A woman with her hands folded, and what looked like a prayer shawl draped over her shoulders looked up and smiled. She rose from her seat and came and hugged Miko. She leaned away from her and looked at Miko with a big smile on her face. Stefan was surprised to see Miko tear up, and lean her head on the woman's shoulder. But that wasn't the biggest surprise. The biggest surprise was that the young preacher woman was pregnant. Very pregnant.

"You look good!" Rachel held Miko out at arm's length,

looking her up and down. "It's a miracle!"

Stefan knew what she was hinting at. Somehow Miko had been taken North but returned without being physically abused.

"And who are these people? Sami herdsmen?"

"One is," Miko responded.

Stefan had taken their rough northern clothing with Sami designs for granted, but now that they were back with "civilized" people he noticed how odd they must look. People from *Sápmi* – the broad swathe of ancestral lands for the Sami herdsmen that reached from Eastern Russia to the fjords of far Northern Norway.

"This one is a lost American," Miko said, with a tilt of the head to Stefan. *"En gammal bilmekaniker."*

"Looks more like *en stor filmskådespelare."* Rachel said, eyeing him saucily.

Stefan didn't know whether to be flattered or offended – Miko had called him an old car mechanic, but Rachel had said he looked more like a movie star.

"Inte det heller," Stefan corrected in Swedish, so they would quit talking past him, "Not either."

"Oh, sorry. You're not 100% American. You've lived here – perhaps as a child?"

"How did you know that?"

"You don't have an American accent," Rachel said. "You must have lived farther south, near me." When Stefan nodded, she pivoted from him and addressed Ravna, "And who is this pretty young girl? Did Stefan rescue you also?"

"Stefan didn't rescue me. I rescued myself," Ravna answered.

"She killed two Russian guards with a Pukka knife," Miko cut in.

"Didn't they send a patrol after you?"

"Just one," Stefan said, not knowing if he should mention that he mowed them down with a Kalashnikov. They were in a prayer meeting after all. "I stopped them. They aren't following us anymore."

To his surprise, an older man nearby stood and started clapping. Soon all the others in the small circle of about 10 people stood also and joined in, clapping their hands and smiling.

The older man walked to him and extended a hand. That was when Stefan realized that the black hat and coat, and the long beard and curled sideburns were all intentional. Passing through New York he had seen orthodox Jews before and recognized it. "My name is Rabbi Ben Davida," he said clasping Stefan's extended hand with both of his.

The older man smiled and said, "Come, sit. You must be weary from your travels. Let us get you some tea and *knäckebröd*. It is not much but it is all we have."

It was an odd sensation for Stefan, after so many years in isolation to suddenly be in the company of friendly people once again.

A young girl, barely preschool age, came to him with a steaming mug of tea on a chipped plate with some crispbread and cheese. He tried to restrain himself from gobbling it all up like a hungry Arctic wolf.

Again, he felt uncomfortable to be treated as an honored guest – when what he felt like was a deadbeat hermit from Kiruna. He remembered something from a college class on the classics – something about Homer's "lawless, stateless, hearth-less man – of all men most to be pitied." Wasn't that him?

But beside him, he saw an approving look from Ravna to his left as she too received a cup of hot tea and a plate of food. Also, a look of appraisal from Miko on his right. Her dark eyes searched his for a moment longer than expected. For the first time today she was not looking at him in anger or disdain, but perhaps studying him. Like she had missed something...

"A toast and a prayer for our new guests!" Rachel said, raising her mug when they were seated. The little girl who had served them hopped up on her lap and snuggled in against her. Everyone bowed their heads, and Stefan joined them, wondering when the last time he had participated in anything like this could have possibly been. His dad's funeral? It had been five years or more.

"God, we thank you for those who have traveled long to be with us." Rachel said, *"Thank you for protecting them from our enemies and bringing them safely home. We ask that you bless this time of fellowship and sharing!"*

Stefan tried to glance around with his head still bowed to see what the others were doing, he noticed Ravna did the same. Soon everyone lifted their heads, and Rachel said, "Now, tell us what news you bring from the far North!"

Stefan looked to Miko, and Ravna, not quite knowing who was to speak first. Miko took the lead, "Well, for one thing, we saw a whole trainload of zombies heading this way this morning."

There was a jarring crash to their left. Slightly in the shadows, a handsome young man of color had dropped his mug, and it shattered on the floor. He hopped up to begin picking up the shards of pottery. "Christ!" he said, and then said, "Oh, sorry so sorry!" to Rachel. She waved in dismissal.

"Magnus, it's nothing," Rachel said, returning her gaze to Miko. "Zombies? Really?"

"She's right," a booming voice came from the doorway. Stefan noticed a big man, somewhat stout, walking in. Stefan recognized him. It was the locomotive driver who passed them earlier that afternoon. What was he doing here? Wasn't he on the side of their enemies?

The big man continued, "I brought a whole passenger train car full of them with me, from the camp at Kalixfors. Not zombies, replicants, *Biancas,* and *Rackhams* – females and males, all the same."

"Clones?" Rachel asked.

"More or less… They're 3D printing them or growing them from test tubes or something," the big man said, crossing the room to stand beside Rachel. Stefan noticed there must be some connection between the big man and Rachel because her daughter said, "Poppa!" and wrapped her arms around one of his tree-trunk-like legs, and when the man put his hand on Rachel's shoulder she covered it with hers in an unspoken gesture of greeting.

"Gorm, we have three newcomers here. Stefan, Miko, and Ravna," she said, pointing them out with a sweep of her free hand.

Gorm looked at Stefan and Miko and seemed to do a double take. "You're the crazy truck guy!" he said with a smile and a shake of his head. "Boy, are the guards ever pissed at you up in Kiruna. You stole this pretty lady away from them!"

Miko blushed and smiled at the compliment.

"I didn't steal her away. She ran off on her own."

"And yet here you are, together, a hundred kilometers away."

"The crazy truck guy?" Rachel asked.

"Yeah. He's something of a legend up in Kiruna. The wild man of the forest. Spotted several times but never captured. Kind of like the American Bigfoot or Canadian Sasquatch. Like a Norwegian mountain troll or an Ice Giant from the old myths. Most of the guards thought it was just B.S. till he showed up last week and stole this pretty maiden."

"He does have big feet, compared to my father," Ravna added with a grin.

Stefan thought it was time to get back to something more serious and said to Gorm, "These – what did you call them, replicants – what are they and why did you bring them here."

"I thought I was delivering them here, but when the train arrived, I was told they were going on to Uppsala. Håkan wants them for something." He paused, and added, "They are like children – very simple and compliant, but they seem to be aware of things around them and learning more every minute. They're creepy."

"I thought maybe they were being sent here, to replace us," Magnus said.

"That might happen soon. They're making more. They're churning them out like sausages up there. And they already got rid of Richard and the rest of the engineers at the Kalixfors camp."

"What do you mean, *got rid of them*," Rachel asked, looking up at Gorm to gauge his reaction.

Gorm swallowed, didn't speak for a moment, visibly trying to compose himself, "The usual way, pushed them out in the cold. Svein and I found them along the tracks." He paused again, and added, "Richard's last words to me were *Stop them*." Stefan noticed that Rachel was squeezing his hand harder now, a gesture of moral support.

"How can we do that? They might push us out in the cold also," Magnus said.

"I like being out in the cold," Ravna said. "My people have lived that way forever. You just have to know what to do. Even Stefan has been able to do it."

"He's not typical," Gorm said. "For instance, he was living on his own without detection, and," here he addressed Stefan directly, "how have you managed to still be driving around in your pickup truck four years after all the *Benzin* was gone?"

"Charcoal gasifier," Stefan answered. "It runs on wood that I turn into charcoal," as if that explained anything. Then he added. "But I think there is a bigger problem. Magnus is right. The point of the replicants must be to replace us. What did you say about them – they are very compliant?"

"Yeah. They're up there now, just sitting in the train car. All sleeping. Charging their batteries."

"We should go kill the bastards!" Miko said.

"We perhaps should not kill them if they are innocent beings who are here by no fault of their own," the Rabbi said.

"Kill or be killed," Ravna added. "They have had no mercy for my people."

That drew some nods from the circle of believers. But Stefan thought the Rabbi had a point. They knew that the Russian camp guards were their enemies, these new "beings" – who could say what they were like?

"I do have a plan," Gorm said. "I don't want to say what it is, but they won't make it to Uppsala, count on that."

Stefan could see that what Gorm said was worrisome to the preacher lady. She must be his *sambo* (common-law spouse) Stefan thought. She reached up and took Gorm's hand and squeezed it but didn't say anything.

But something else Gorm said caught Stefan's attention, so he asked, "What did you mean *charging their batteries?* Did you mean that literally?"

"Yeah, literally. They're all dormant and plugged in for the night. Like recharging your cell phone," Gorm said, "I had to keep steam up in the locomotive for the night so the generator would run. Svein and I have to take turns feeding in coal and monitoring the boiler."

"That figures," Stefan said. It confirmed something he had

suspected for a while but never discussed with anyone.

"What figures?" Rachel asked.

"That's why there are no farms in our new world," Stefan said.

"Aren't there greenhouses down south?" Rabbi Davida asked Gorm-the-well-travelled.

"A couple of small ones, just in Uppsala."

"Even in Skåne, where it is warmer?" Rabbi Davida continued.

"None down there," Gorm said, and from the tone of his voice Stefan knew he had reached the same conclusion. "I don't think anyone is still living in Skåne…"

Which Stefan took to be Gorm's polite way of saying everybody in Skåne had died in the pandemic – or from radiation or something.

"Holy fuck!" Miko whispered under her breath, echoing what most of the others were now realizing.

Except Rachel. "What? I don't get it. It's too cold for farms. We're in a nuclear winter. That's why there are no farmers."

"Let me put it in simple terms. Håkan doesn't need farmers because Håkan doesn't need people. Both Håkan and the Replicants are made differently. Their source of energy is not food, but electricity. That's why she lives down by Forsmark, the only working nuclear power plant."

Rabbi Davida nodded, "and that's why the Replicant plant was built at Kalixfors – they are getting some power from the old Porjus hydropower station. As spring returns there will be more runoff from the mountains."

Rabbi Davida held up a finger as he began to speak, making Stefan think maybe he once was a professor or teacher in the former world. "That's why they pushed the engineers out. They were done with them. Their job was done." Then he added another phrase that only a few of them would recognize, "They were *Useless Eaters*."

"Oh," Rachel said, nodding. She too was a student of history. The others looked at her and the Rabbi not comprehending. "That was how the Nazis classified which Jews to kill first. The ones who were not productive. The "Useless Eaters."

"Yeah," Stefan said. "Once the engineers had finished the tooling up on the Replicants, the Replicants themselves could take over – so they no longer needed to keep the engineers, and they pushed them out onto the frozen tundra to die."

There was a stunned silence among the members of the prayer circle as they digested this news.

"Once they get enough Replicants, they can phase us out, too," Magnus said. "Next stage in evolution. Soon we'll be like the mastodons that are frozen in the tundra. Pushed out by a stronger species. Extinct."

"Probably a better analogy would be the Neanderthals," the Rabbi said, still in professor mode, Stefan thought.

"We're fucked!" Miko commented again, still under her breath.

"Well, maybe not," Rabbi Davida continued. "We all have Neanderthal DNA because humans interbred with us. They would have our DNA, right? Maybe we can mate with them?"

"Yuck!" Ravna said, probably speaking for many of them. "I don't want to lose my virginity to some *fucking* robot!"

This was her first comment, and it caught all of them by surprise. Not the least of which was Miko, who Stefan noticed was gob-smacked, looking from Ravna to him in wonder. What is she thinking? Stefan wondered.

Gorm laughed at that and said, "I have to go on shift soon, tending the Big Lok. Maybe I can sneak in where they are sleeping and lift one of their skirts and see if they really are, as you so quaintly put it, *fucking* robots."

He noticed Rachel had given Gorm a nudge with her elbow in the ribs -

"Not to change the topic," Stefan said, though in truth he was keen to do so – this one was making him uncomfortable, "but one of the main reasons we came here was to see if we could find a new home for Ravna. Her father was killed by the guards at Kiruna a few days ago. We need a safe place for her."

Stefan noticed that everyone went quiet, and he wondered if he had committed some faux pas by just bringing up the subject. He noticed Rachel took the lead again, "I would guess Miko has told you what it is like for young women here at this camp," she said.

Beside him, he heard Miko hiss, "Yeah, we're like fucking ISIS brides." Still cursing under her breath so as to not offend the Bible study group.

Stefan passed over that, and answered, "I have heard bad things..."

Beside Miko snorted, "That's putting it pretty damn politely." Now, more loudly so everyone could hear.

"She can't stay here," Rachel said firmly. "This is no place for a young woman of her age. I don't need to go into the details of why."

Stefan caught Rachel looking at him for guidance, how did I end up here in this position? He wondered. He sighed and said, "OK, not here. But is there somewhere she might be safe?" He looked about the room, most of the prayer group members were looking down at their hands.

"There are rebel groups on the trail to the south. Östersund has a small one, and In Mora, there is one too." said the young man in the back, Magnus. "I was part of it before I was captured and brought up here. They hide in the mountains beyond Lake Siljan, near Örsa Grönklitt, the ski resort. It's rugged country, but I think she'd fit in there."

"That's a long way from here," Stefan said. "How could we get her that far south."

"I could get you there," Gorm said. "I could hide you in a baggage car, on the train."

"Even our dogs? I can't leave Björn."

Stefan noticed that no one objected and that due to the lateness of the hour, it must be time for them to return to their beds or cells or wherever it was that they went at night. The meeting broke up and people chatted among themselves further digesting all they had learned that evening.

Stefan took the lead heading back down the tunnels to where they had tied the dogs. Čalmmo and Björn were sleeping contentedly on some makeshift beds of cloth sacks. Miko leaned down and helped him untie the knots.

"I was angry with you all day," she said quietly to Stefan, their eyes meeting in the dim light of the cavern.

"I noticed. Didn't know why."

"I thought you slept with Ravna last night."

"I did. We both conked out after she massaged my sore back."

"But you didn't have sex with her."

"She's only like, what, fifteen? So, no." Stefan said. "Her dad and I were friends. Close friends. I couldn't take advantage of him like that." He realized now how it must have looked to Miko – he and Ravna cuddled together after Miko had fallen asleep. It was a logical assumption that "something had happened."

Miko tilted her head, looking at him. Then she did something totally unexpected. She leaned in and kissed his cheek, her eyes dark but somber, meeting his. "Sorry" she whispered, and for a moment he thought of returning her kiss, but there were footsteps of the other coming, so meeting her eyes he greeted them.

The others who had been walking slowly arrived, Rachel, her daughter, and Ravna.

"Once you have tended to your dogs," Rachel said, "we have a place you can sleep. You will be safe for the night. But the guards will be back on shift in the morning, so you should leave early."

Stefan nodded, hearing but not listening. His mind was on what had just happened with Miko. Something had just changed between them. Things between them would be different from now on...

CHAPTER TWENTY-TWO

THE JOURNEY TO ÖSTERSUND

The hand of the LORD was upon me, and carried me out in the spirit of the LORD, and set me down in the midst of the valley which was full of bones, And caused me to pass by them round about: and, behold, there were very many in the open valley; and, lo, they were very dry. And he said unto me, <u>Son of man,</u> can these bones live? And I answered, O Lord GOD, thou knowest.

Again he said unto me, Prophesy upon these bones, and say unto them, O ye dry bones, hear the word of the LORD. Thus saith the Lord GOD unto these bones; Behold, I will cause breath to enter into you, and ye shall live: And I will lay sinews upon you, and will bring up flesh upon you, and cover you with skin, and put breath in you, and ye shall live; and ye shall know that I am the LORD.

Gorm and Rachel woke them the next day before dawn, and Stefan tried to get fully awake and comprehend what was going on.

"I've got my orders to head to Östersund this morning, and Svein and I have a place where you can ride safely with us until we get there."

"On your Zombie Train? No thanks!" Ravna said, and Stefan noticed how perky she was despite it still being practically the middle of the night. Though how you would tell night from day in this underground mine was beyond him. "I'm staying here," Ravna said.

Stefan noticed Rachel and Gorm exchange a meaningful glance. "That wouldn't be safe for you, physically," Rachel said.

"I can handle the guards," Ravna said, "I killed two of them at the cabin near my home."

"Let me be blunt," Gorm said, "there are ten guards. They will gang up on you."

Ravna turned to Stefan, her face in anguish.

"He's right," Miko said, waking up and joining in.

Stefan noticed they were all avoiding having to go into explicit detail on what "ganging up on you" would look like. It was understood, he thought with a form of despair. It was a fact of the 'new world' they lived in. They had reverted back to 'caveman' life, sadly, where the most necessities of life were fought over – food, the safety of women, in other words, the physical domination of women by men?

"We have a freight wagon that is empty enough to fit four of you," Gorm continued.

"Four of us?" Miko asked.

"We think Magnus should come with you. There's safety in numbers." Rachel added.

Stefan saw the young African/Swede step out of the shadows of the hallway. He looked him over – he was young, and fit, like a soccer player. He nodded.

"We don't need any more help," Miko protested, but not too strongly.

"Our goal is to get you and the women as far south as Mora. There's an organized cell of the resistance there- and they know Magnus. The women can be safe, and the men could join the fight."

"What fight?" Stefan asked.

"The fight to kill Håkan and overthrow the current regime," Gorm said, without bravado or irony.

Stefan weighed this news. He was being enlisted in the army – conscripted if you will. So much for living the survivalist life on his own...

They rode in the cold, stuffy boxcar all day until it pulled into a rail yard. The train came to a halt, and a long time passed until Gorm came and unlatched the wagon door. They all clambered out, stiff from the hours of sitting on boxes for seats and being cooped up in the freight wagon. Magnus was the first out, and stretched his long arms out wide and said, "Welcome to the Republic of Jämtland."

"Huh?" Stefan asked.

"Here in Östersund, there are still a few people living here that survived the plague. They are well-armed and wary of any outsiders."

"Maybe Ravna can find shelter with them?" Miko asked.

"What part of well-armed and wary of outsiders didn't you understand," Magnus said, laughing.

"Keep your voices low," Gorm said, glancing about. "The replicants have left the train and supposedly are in the station house, doing God knows what. There are also lots of guards here, because of the resistance."

They all stepped into the shade, behind them, The Great Lake, *Storsjön*, glittered in the late evening sun.   "The Resistance?" Miko asked.

Stefan had traveled past this lake before on his way North. He had seen the great lake and heard stories of the Storsjon monster – the *Storsjöodjuret* who he associated with other folk tales of lake monsters like the one said to inhabit Loch Ness in far northern Great Britain. Maybe both the Scots and the Jämtlanders knew something the rest of us didn't?

"Yeah, you know how independent Jämtlanders are…" he said, answering her question.

"I lived in Copenhagen, so no. I've never heard of that," Miko said.

"They always wanted to have their own little country. Some say they first came from Norway, people fleeing the evil king *Harald Fairhair.* Half the people went east to Iceland, the rest came here."

"Those crazy Jämtlanders!" Miko said, and Stefan noticed that Magnus raised an eyebrow at that, was she mocking him? Was this a sign of disdain or possible interest?

Gorm cut in, "We can discuss local history with the locals, but for right now we should head to their encampment. I know where it is. I can't take too long, though, they will be expecting me back once the train is reloaded."

They headed south, first along the lake and the train tracks, then through the abandoned neighborhood. There was a light breeze off the lake, which Stefan welcomed because it wafted away the lingering smell of death that came from the houses along the way. It would have been a pleasant stroll through the beautiful old city, with the sunshine on the lake and the gentle breeze, were it not for the sad spectacle of the abandoned city.

Stefan noticed that Miko was still limping a little bit from her fall a few days ago, but she didn't complain. Stefan noticed the same with Björn – his sore foot seemed to be mostly healed, but he lifted that one paw more quickly than the others. Stefan had to smile at the sight of Björn leading Čalmmo and both of them trotting ahead, like an advance guard. Björn had to be the alpha dog of any pack, and just his presence seemed to calm Stefan and make him feel he was safer.

As Stefan was watching him, though, he noticed something. Björn began lifting his nose in the air as if he was looking at a bird. His nose twitched, and his nostrils dilated, and he suddenly stopped walking. And the fur on the scruff of his neck stood up. Stefan reached out a hand to him and grabbed his snout – he didn't want another episode of him running off or tangling with wolves ...

"Fadder, there is bad sniffins. I am lifting up my snoot and I am smelling them! Hey, dog buddy, do you smell that? It is a bad smell. It is smelly guys. I no like those smelly guys. Danger! Danger!, Watch out for the smelly guys, they are bad! Bad smelly guys! Bad! Bad! Danger! Danger!"

Fadder, why are you holding my snoot. I will not bark, but there is bad smelly guys! It is making my furs fluffle! Danger! Danger!"

Stefan took a knee to hold Björn for a moment and was rewarded with another twinge of his back muscles that let him know he still needed to take it easy for at least another day or so.

As he waited for Björn to relax he heard the girls talking with Magnus, a bit too much like flirting to his taste, but no matter. But he now raised his hand and gave them a cross look, finishing with Ravna, who returned his dark look as if to say, "Who are you to silence me" but she complied anyway. They all stopped and stood still.

"Shush Björn," Stefan said, and Björn, his hackles up as he still struggled to bark. He was still holding Björn with one hand and looking in the direction Björn was pointing. Čalmmo meanwhile was circling, his hackles also raised.

Gorm, sensing the danger, had already stretched out his arms and begun to herd the others into the long evening shadows on the other side of the street.

"This way. There is a side route to their encampment."

Stefan could tell that the girls were cooperating grudgingly – but he did notice that Ravna had reached down and opened the flap of her cargo pants side pocket to reveal the bony handle of one of her Pukka knives.

They had been on Bangårdsgatan, one of the main streets, so they slipped down a side alley, which Stefan noticed was named Myrstigen. That alley was dead-ended in a large wooded area. There was a row of houses that was backed by a thick forest of maple, beech, and pine trees. It was evident they were no longer in Lappland just by the size of the trees. But in addition to that, the houses showed signs of recent habitation. If you looked closely, you could see a wisp of smoke from the chimney of one of the houses, and what looked like a dim light of some sort.

"They live here," Gorm said, pointing towards the houses. "It's a small resistance cell. There are several couples – I think it *might* be safe for Ravna to..."

Stefan lifted a hand to silence him. They turned and saw a flash of bodies coming down Bangårdsgatan, and Miko said, "It's the droids. Run!"

They took off as a group up the side alley of Odenbacken, away from both the houses and the main road. Björn and Čalmmo took the lead, with the others running as fast as they could. This meant Stefan and Ravna were in front, followed by Miko, still slightly limping, and Gorm huffing and puffing as he brought up the rear. Stefan waved to the others to duck in with him at # 14 Odenbacken, which was a low white house surrounded by a thick hedge at about chest height. They could hear the running of the replicants, which was an eerie sound, for they didn't shout or cry out to one another. The replicants ran to the door of the house that had the smoke coming out of the chimney and Stefan peered over the hedge to see the lead replicant kicking the door of the house. As he did so, the other replicants circled the house, carrying the typical Russian weapon, the Kalashnikov, at waist height.

When the replicants kicked in the front door, there was gunfire from the back, and Stefan saw two of the droids go down. Then a small group of people raced out the back door to the forest, with replicants running and trying to fire at them as they went. One of the rebels, a young woman went down.

"We should go, now!" Gorm said in a quiet but insistent voice.

Stefan nodded but didn't move. Something was bothering him.

"Stefan, come on, this is our chance to get out of here!" Miko said.,

"One second!"

"Come on!" Ravna was tugging at his sleeve.

But there was a reason he waited, he had seen this before, in a dream. It was playing out just like he had seen it before, even though it all took place in just a few seconds, he had to watch. The droids ran in a line after the rebels, stepping right over one fallen woman who writhed in pain on the ground. They all raced full tilt into the forest, with the rebels stepping on some thin planks on the ground, which was puzzling. Then they ran on, dodging bullets and pine and maple trees with the Replicants in hot pursuit. Suddenly, though, the whole line of Replicants disappeared into the ground.

"Holy shit!" Miko said from beside him. "The earth swallowed them!"

"Moose pits!" Ravna said, pointing. "It's a favorite Jämtlander trick. They cover them with fabric and leaves and use their weapons to drive a running herd through them. The *elg* fall in and they finish them off."

Which is what the rebels did. They turned back to the pits, raised their weapons, and fired on the fallen droids. But to Stefan's horror and amazement, the droids were taking close-range shots and still climbing up out of the pits. Some with broken legs, or holes blown in them.

"Stefan, come, now!" Gorm said.

They turned and ran. But not before one of the droids turned and looked right at them.

CHAPTER TWENTY-THREE

They were seen, but not chased. Not immediately, at any rate, Stefan thought with relief. They raced away from the still echoing sound of the gunfire, circling back towards the center of the city and the train station.

"We should head into the woods on the eastern side of town," Gorm announced when they were taking a breather in a copse of white birches near an apartment building on Rådhusgaten. "We can all head into the forest and find a place to hide. But I'm afraid we won't be able to let Ravna stay here with the rebels."

"I have another plan," Stefan said. "We can go to Mora."

"Not on the train"

"No, you need to stay with the train – they haven't spotted you," Stefan said. "There is a small plane we can take. It's down by the lake."

"How do you know that? Where will you get fuel?"

"It's just something I know, trust me," Stefan said. He saw Miko raise an eyebrow at his last statement.

Gorm agreed, and they continued on. To Stefan's surprise, the big man gave them all a big hug when they parted ways on the next corner. Gorm went towards the rail yard, "Godspeed to all of you!" he said as they parted. "Look up my friend Lars in Mora – he is head of the resistance there. Warn them of the Replicants! They could be in danger!"

They continued on their hike up Rådhusgatan, onto Lugviksvägen along the lake. Stefan was beginning to regain his composure after the stress of seeing the battle with the Replicants and the Resisters and enjoying the early spring sunshine along the lake. He was drawn out of his reverie by Miko sidling up to him and saying, "Have you been to

Östersund before?"

"*Ja*," he said, unconsciously slipping into Swedish. "But only once or twice before."

"But you know where there is a plane you can borrow?"

He nodded, "Right here," he said, as they came upon a low "Falun red" building alongside the lake, with a weathered wooden sign that said, *"Jämtlands Flyg"* on a sign alongside the road. There were the tattered remains of a Norwegian flag hanging from an angled flagpole by the door.

The dogs sniffed in a circle as Stefan tried the knob. Not surprisingly, it was locked.

Magnus stepped forward and gave it a mighty kick, which to Stefan looked like something a footballer would do. On his second kick, the door banged in with splinters near the lock flying. They went into the dark low building.

"An old aircraft hangar?" Magnus said as they ventured further in. The dogs took the lead, excitedly sniffing around in the darkness ahead. Stefan paused to let them do their work, not wanting to confront some wild animal small or large. This was famous bear country, after all.

"I know of an old airplane that used to be stored here," Stefan said.

"This one?" Magnus said from up ahead. "It's an old float plane!"

On the far side of the building, there were two windows, all smudged with dirt and streaked, but at least letting in a bit of light. Magnus went to the front and undid a large iron latch, and slid open a wide barn door on a track. Brilliant sunshine filled the space, and illuminated the room, lighting up the airplane. It was incredibly dusty but appeared undamaged.

From beside him, Miko hissed, "How did you know?"

Too busy and excited to reply, he walked around the

plane.

"Too bad it doesn't have any fuel…we could take it for a spin!" Magnus said laughing. Stefan noticed that Ravna too was intrigued by the plane.

"Don't know unless we check," Stefan said. He climbed up on the wing, saw an icon over a small metal door, and lifted it. He pulled a clevis pin which freed the cap, and twisted it open. Fuel was sloshing inside. "The tank is full." He said and then leaned down close to the cap to smell the condition of the fuel. It smelled clean and fresh - - expensive aviation fuel, the kind without any ethanol additives to go bad. It could have lasted a hundred years…

"We should push it out into the sun," Stefan said.

They worked together to get it out of the building, and Ravna found some towels and a soft push broom which they used to dust it off and clean the windshield.

"Do you have a pilot's license? You don't know how to fly planes? Right?" Miko asked.

"I know how to fly this one," Stefan said, feeling a rush of adrenaline as he opened the cabin door and sat inside for the first time. "It's a very reliable plane, a Cessna 182," he said, pointing to the plane, though there were no markings to identify it. He ignored the question about having a license…

Magnus stood slack-jawed. "You mean you intend to fly this to Mora?"

Stefan nodded.

"Stand clear of the blade," he said, and the others stepped to the side. He pulled the choke out and turned the key. Slowly, reluctantly, the engine turned over. This in itself was surprising – that the battery was not dead. Stefan hoped that it still had enough juice to start, and no sooner had he thought that than there was an enormous "Bang" and a cloud of black smoke with bits of dried grass and what appeared to be mouse droppings flew out of the exhaust, and the engine started. After four years of silence, the roar was deafening.

Standing in a circle around the plane, holding their ears, were Magnus, Ravna, and Miko, as well as the dogs. Stefan climbed down the wing, and one at a time picked up the dogs. Čalmmo seemed non-plussed by the noise and confusion, but Björn was shaking like a leaf. He hunkered down under a seat as Stefan turned to the others and said, "Get on board! We have to go, now!"

Magnus and Ravna nimbly hopped up and in and took the two back seats, Miko hesitated.,

"They can hear us all across town! We have to leave, *Now!*"

Miko bit her lip. Stefan realized what was wrong. She was scared to fly.

"Come on! I can't leave you behind!"

Slowly, reluctantly, she climbed up into the cockpit and sat in the seat next to Stefan. She slipped on the headphones sitting on her seat as Stefan gunned the engine and the plane skidded down the slope, into the water. He adjusted the trim, pushed the throttle forward, and the plane roared across the waves, bouncing up and down. Water splashed on the windshield, and a rooster tail of spray began flying up from the floats on either side. As the island across the lake loomed in front of them, Stefan pulled back on the yoke and the nose lifted and with a roar, they rose into the sky and flew over the treetops on the other side.

They had taken off east, heading for Norway, but that was not where he wanted to go. He banked the plane into a turn and circled back over the lake. The sun glittered on the surface of the lake, the water was clear and from this altitude, he could see deep into the crystal blue water of the lake. Even though he was pretty sure it was a myth he couldn't help but take a quick look to see if the *Storsjöordjuret* might be in view – who knew what monsters might be loose in this crazy world without people?

As they crossed the lake and headed South, Magnus gave a loud "HOO! HOO!" and high-fived Ravna. Stefan could hear that even though he was wearing headphones with a mic, just like Miko.

Miko looked pale but smiled wanly at Stefan. He put his hand down and took her small, cold hand in his, almost as if he could feel her fear.

"It's OK," he said, as he looked left out his window and banked the plane to follow the E14 highway south, "I've got this."

CHAPTER TWENTY-FOUR

"How long will it take to get to Mora?" Miko asked him, glancing out at the expanse of pine forests beneath them, the lower arm of Lake Storsjön came into view as they continued south.

"Because this is a float plane, it goes slowly," Stefan said, "probably a couple of hours."

"Where did you learn to fly?" Miko asked. Because of the noise of the engine and the wind rushing past outside, the others could not hear their conversation over the headsets.

Stefan noticed the deep brown of her eyes, staring into them he once again got the sensation he was falling into a pool of deep water. He paused, wondering exactly what to tell her. "I don't have any formal lessons."

She pursed her lips, her eyebrows knit together.

"Some things come to me very clearly in dreams. I had seen this plane before. That's how I knew where it was and how to fly it. I have these very detailed dreams of certain things."

"So you've never actually never flown an airplane before, is that what you are telling me?" He noticed her voice was rising a bit, with just a hint of the hysterical.

Stefan checked the instruments again, the one telling you how up or down the nose of the plane was, the one showing how level the wings were, and the one showing airspeed. "Trust me." He kept the nose of the plane pointed down the only highway he could see – the E45 to Mora.

"Trust you?" she said. "You've only flown an airplane in a dream, and we are about 10,000 feet up in the sky, and you would like me to trust you."

"If I didn't know what I was doing, how would I have

found the plane?"

"Jesus! Good thing they can't hear us, Jesus!" She said turning to him again. Somehow she managed to look more alluring with her headset on – like a chic war correspondent on a mission.

"We should be fine. This is exactly how it was in my dream."

"Even this conversation?"

"No, just the plane. Finding it. Starting it up, Taking off…"

"Landing, I hope, for Christ's sake!"

"Shush!"

Miko bobbed her head and shook it as if there were bees in her hair. "This is about the craziest thing I've ever done."

"I've learned to trust these sorts of dreams. And yes, the "bringing it in for a landing" part, that was in the dream too."

"You are really weird," Miko said, still shaking her head.

"You got any better options right now?" Stefan said, not really as a challenge, but stating a fact.

"Yeah, I'll just jump out here and hitch a ride back to town." She looked away out the window. So much for the brief interlude of romantic feelings, Stefan thought.

"We were being hunted down by Zombies with Kalashnikovs. This doesn't seem so bad in comparison."

"You are something else," Miko said.

"Thanks for noticing,"

"I guess this is why you were single and living in a cave."

"It did have something to do with it…"

"A literal *Cave Man*."

Stefan nodded. He couldn't tell from her tone if this was something she thought was bad or not. It sounded bad, but perhaps it was some sort of backhanded compliment.

She turned towards him again in her seat, eyeing him

directly, "How many of the things that kept you alive during the plague came to you in dreams?"

"Not that many. We've had pandemics before, so even normal people had some idea of what to do."

"But almost no "normal people" survived this pandemic. Yet you did."

She was looking at him with those eyes again.

"I had three or four dreams of everything stopping. Of the world stopping. Of empty gas stations and highways."

"So you built your truck that didn't need gas, and moved into a cave."

Stefan tilted his head, pondering this. It was now a few years ago… exactly what was a dream and what was a practical step was blurred in his memory.

"There was one dream that started it all. It began with me working in my underground home – "

"Your Cave!"

"I was working in the old ore mine that was my home and I stepped up the stairs out the doorway. Suddenly there was a bright flash, like Jesus coming in the sky. But it wasn't an actual person, just the flash. Somehow, though, I knew. It was the end of all things."

"And then that actually happened?" Miko asked.

"Three years later, yes," Stefan said, reflecting. Beside him Björn had moved forward and put his head on his knee, leaning and resting his chin on Stefan's leg to get petted. "After that dream, I kept my car repair business going, but evenings and weekends I worked on preparing. I dug a new well, made a whole bunch of charcoal for fuel, fixed up the truck, and installed a really good generator. I got a backhoe and dug a hole and put a small fuel tank in it – so I would have some reserves for my chainsaw and other power tools if I needed it. But mostly I cut wood and made charcoal."

"No love life at that time, apparently," Miko said.

Again, the deep brown eyes searched his, lingering longer than people would normally. Stefan was going to say "Why do you ask?" but that would be stupid. He knew why she was asking. She was measuring him up.

"No steady girlfriends. A couple of disastrously bad attempts of short duration."

"One-night stands, right?"

"No. None of those. More like "one month stands" that didn't work out." For a moment he thought of the girl his friends at the garage referred to as "the bombshell" - - a stunning Nordic blonde with whom he had what could best be described as a fling. The physical part was exciting, at first, but he was pretty far from meeting her financial expectations in a beau. That one crashed and burned almost immediately.

"What about you?" Stefan said, tacking away from this kind of dangerous territory.

"You know I had a son. That was a one-night stand," she said, her eyes narrowing as if in defiance as if to challenge him to comment.

Stefan shrugged.

"Soon after that, a serious romance in California, with a techie at a software company. It went up in flames, almost literally, when California burned. Then Copenhagen — anything to escape what America was like in those days. Then this happened…" She waved out the window at the bleak countryside.

She paused for a moment, and Stefan thought about asking her about the more recent past. How she had survived in the camps for three years. But he wasn't sure if he wanted to know the details of that. He could guess at the broad outlines…

"Did you ever have a dream about me?" Miko said. "In your future dreams, did you ever have a dream about me?" She turned those eyes on him again, and it was unsettling.

Stefan thought for a moment. There was an image that came to mind. It was just an instant. That's the way some of those dreams were, just an image that he remembered. It was of him on top of her, and her looking into his eyes and whispering his name.

"You're not saying anything," she said.

"There wasn't a dream sequence, just an image."

"Me naked, is that it?" Still boring into him with her gaze.

At least he could answer this truthfully, "No, just a moment's image. Of you whispering my name."

"That's it? Me whispering."

"You staring at me, like you are right now, and whispering my name."

"Just your name, not *"Oh Stefan my Darling!"* her eyes crinkled as she laughed.

"Nope," he said, but in reality, this was a lie.

Right then there was a voice from behind that snapped him from his reverie. "Look, a big lake!"

It was Ravna, pointing out the window, and they all turned to see. On the horizon, there was a glittering blue lake, with numerous branches and offshoots, further south they could see one big dark circle. It was Lake Siljan, which Stefan knew the tourist brochures described as "an expansive lake formed by a giant meteor." It was more than thirty miles across, and some eight hundred feet deep, or so he had heard – but it might be an exaggeration.

"We'll land on Orsa and coast into Mora," Stefan said, banking the plane for his approach. "We'll stay north of the railway station and the camp." He said over his shoulder to Ravna and Magnus. Lake Orsa was a smaller lake on the upper side of the town, connected to the big lake by a causeway. It would be safer to land there, not buzz the town. They should still be well to the North of the town and out of sight if they landed there.

He brought the plane in just as he had seen in his dream, pushing forward on the control yoke and steadying the wings as they descended. He saw Miko biting her lip as she pushed down the last bit to touch the water, and they bounced, landed on the water again, and then headed at great speed towards the end of the lake, so far, so good.

Stefan angled to the shore, scrubbing off speed as they got closer and closer to the edge of the lake. It was just like in his dream and he smiled at Miko and gave her a thumbs up.

But at the very last second, as the plane was about to touch down, Stefan saw the ice. There was still some ice that hadn't melted floating in the lake. There was a tremendous crash and jolt as it tore the floats off the plane and they plunged into the water. It was as if they were suddenly transported from a plane into a submarine because they were immediately in the deep dark water of the lake, and then the plane was shredded to pieces and he was undoing his seatbelt and trying to swim in a sea of broken plane bits, and blood. This was not in his dream, Stefan thought as he struggled free of the sinking wreckage, not at all...

.

CHAPTER TWENTY-FIVE

It was theoretically spring, but the water was still icy cold. Stefan felt like he'd been plunged headfirst into an enormous dish of ice water. He struggled free of the wreckage, kicking and pushing desperately for the light above him. There was blood in the water he was swimming in, and to his dismay he saw the inert form of Čalmmo, floating upward, but not struggling for the surface. But beside him, struggling to rise, was Ravna. He managed to get ahold of her jacket with one hand as he kicked for the sky.

They surfaced, sucking air. Even that burned his lungs with cold. They both came up beside one of the pontoons, struggling to stay afloat with heavy wet clothes. He saw her trying to unzip her jacket, and he said, "No. Hold onto this float. Keep your jacket."

She looked at him, and then cried out, "Čaaaalmmo!" in a piteous voice. Stefan put his arm around her neck and pulled her sobbing in against him.

"Stefan! Stefan!" he heard Miko shouting, and then. "Ravna! Stefan! – it was Magnus's voice. He was about to shout back to them when he heard the roar of a motor. It sounded like a motor boat or big jet ski. How could they have been found so quickly?"

"Here they are!" a voice shouted. "I've got two of them!"

He heard a scream from Miko, and the sound of a fight and shouting – most likely Magnus trying to fight them off. The engine grew closer, almost upon them.

Stefan grabbed Ravna's jacket and pulled her with him away from the sound of the jet ski, even though she flailed at him. His mind raced. How had they been spotted? Who had ratted them out? Where in the world did they get jet skis from? Goddamn Russians!

He pulled Ravna with him towards the pontoon that floated nearby and came up under it. It was almost like an upside-down canoe – there was an air gap where the strut mounted. They surfaced and he held her still by the neck close to him, she was protesting and he shushed her.

From the other side of the pontoon, he heard the boat or jet ski circling, stirring up the blood in the water, there was still shouting and commotion, that he couldn't quite make out. And then it got quieter and one of the men said, "Just blood and body parts. They must have drowned.

"We have to be sure! They said to be sure!"

"I'm telling you, asshole, that there is no one here. They must have sunk to the bottom or gotten chopped up by the propeller. They're dead."

The sound of the motor went around them again, with a wave rocking the pontoon. Stefan drew up his legs to hide them from view, and Ravna did the same. One more circle of the launch. Stefan felt Ravna shuddering next to him, shaking with the cold. His own teeth had started chattering.

The motor launch moved away. Stefan said, "We have to kick to shore or we'll freeze. I think it's this way."

They started swimming – holding on to the broken strut, still sheltered by the pontoon float. Every now and then Stefan popped out and took a look, to make sure they were heading to the shore.

"They must have cameras. We have to stay hidden."

They worked their way to shore. It was almost evening, and a line of pines on the shore away from the city provided shelter. It was nearly dark when they finally dragged themselves up on the gravelly shore of a small park or nature preserve on the southern shore of the lake with nature walks that headed inland to a golf course that he could see through breaks in the trees.

They stumbled ashore, near a stuga that had a small sign talking about the *Platsen för häxbränning 1669*. It was an infamous place, that Stefan had heard rumors about – the site of the "Witch Burning" of Mora, centuries ago. He had even heard it inspired the Witch Hysteria in Salem Massachusetts. But the Swedes had given it their typical Nordic flair – first beheading their victims with an axe, and then burning their bodies...

Not the most auspicious place to come ashore, he thought, but at the moment finding shelter and warmth was more of a concern.

They made their way to a nearby stuga, struggling against an icy wind off the lake that had picked up as the sun went down. The stuga was some sort of beach structure, and Stefan yanked on the handle to get the door open. Freezing, and frustrated he tried to pry the door open, gave up, and kicked it in, splintering the wood around the latch.

They stepped in together, still dripping wet and shivering. "Not much here..." Stefan said, and Ravna pouted and shook. She looked to be getting seriously cold, hypothermia was setting in.

"There's a small stove, I'll see if I can get that going," Stefan said, and she nodded. "Look for some blankets or something we can put on for warmth."

Björn:

Swimming, swimming, I am swimming... where is Faddar?

Dogbuddy, come swimming! Oh, no... Dogbuddy is hurted, sad.

I am sad, dogbuddy is very hurted and bleedy. Dogbudddy Wake Up, I am snooting you! Oh No, Dogbuddy is too sleepy, he does not want to come swimming.

It is cold, and I am swimming swimming. Where is Fadder? Dogbuddy is hurted, dogbuddy was bleedy and hurted, and I am sad, for I have lost Fadder. Swimming Swimming, shore is far away, swimming swimming, must get to trees and warm place. Cold! Where is my Fadder?

Stefan:

"There's a small stove, I'll see if I can get that going," Stefan said, and she nodded. "Look for some blankets or something we can put on for warmth."

She went around looking in cabinets and under the small desk. "There aren't any blankets here – it's just a small tourist office for summer hikers," she said over her shoulder.

Ravna was still shivering and her voice sounded faint. She seemed to be fading out on him, and he was getting more worried about her by the minute.

"Grab those tourist brochures," Stefan said. There were some desk chairs with cushions. He picked up one of the chairs smashed it on the floor, and then kicked it to break it apart. He tore one of the doors off the desk pulled out a drawer of papers, and yanked the entire thing free. "We have to get this stove hotter - Bring that paper and the drawer."

He tore up the papers and stuffed them in the stove. Ravna had found some matches in a drawer and Stefan tried to get them to light. They were damp from years of being closed up in a snowbound stuga – only the very tips would light then gutter out. Stefan cursed beneath his breath, his teeth chattering. They didn't have many more chances, he thought, but on one of the last matches the head detached when he struck it and a small flame rose up from a dry piece of paper in the stove. Thank God!

"Add more wood to it as it catches," he said to Ravna, and then went off to find more dry sticks and wood, but not before noticing her leaning close to the fire, her hands extended and face glowing orange from the building flame. When he stepped outside of the cabin he saw thick black smoke rising from the chimney which was probably full of old bird nests or bat houses or God knows what. He was happy it was nighttime for it could have been spotted for miles away.

Pretty soon they had a roaring fire, with lots of dried twigs, dead pine branches, and broken beechwood chairs feeding the blaze. He noticed steam coming off Ravna as she leaned into the fire, but she was still sopping wet. What to do?

He went in and ripped the curtains off the windows and brought them out. They were of some soft material, and fairly long. "Wrap yourself up in this," he said to her. "it will keep the cold off your back."

He warmed himself by the fire, but his back still felt like ice. This was not going to work, they needed to dry their clothes. Once he got quite warm from the fire again, he scrounged an old coat rack and some other odds and ends of hangars and metal to make a drying rack beside the fire. He made an impromptu seat against the back wall and built the fire closer. It had started snowing, but the fire was now warming the back of the stuga up nicely. He wrapped himself up in one of the curtains, slipped off his sodden outer clothes and boots, and arranged everything on part of the drying rack. Ravna did the same. He tried somewhat unsuccessfully to avert his gaze as she slipped out of her dripping clothes and slipped into the drapery he held out to her. Then they sat side by side on some old buckets, covered with the drapery, their bare feet stretched out to the fire.

Ravna all this time had been quiet, hardly saying

anything.

Stefan stared into the fire, thinking of the blood in the water...wondering about Miko and Magnus, and worrying too about Björn.

"Oh! Čalmmo!" Ravna cried out, in a heart-rending voice.

Stefan awkwardly put his arm around her, and she leaned into him, her head on his shoulder. "I'm sorry. It's my fault. We should have stayed up north, where we were safe."

He didn't want to say that he was feeling the same feeling of loss and despair– he had lost Björn, too...but he didn't know if he was dead or alive.

She lifted her chin to look at him. "Nowhere is safe. Not anymore. There is no such thing as "safe." Not for me, and also not for you."

"You have never known a safe time, have you?"

"Only when I was a little kid. Before the Russians came...before the long winter," she said.

"You were what, nine years old?"

"Yeah, something like that. At least the Russians haven't gotten me yet..."

Stefan knew what she was getting at. She was the rare young woman who hadn't been either raped or killed. Or both...He used his foot to push some of the wood further into the fire, noticing her eyes, looking at him, looking at his extended leg.

"Are you in love with Miko?"

"Huh?" he asked as if he didn't know exactly what she was asking.

"I see how you look into her eyes," she said. "You meet her gaze and hold it. There's something between you two...right?'

Stefan saw Miko leaning towards him in the plane. Her deep brown eyes, the intent way she studied him. The image was gone in a flash but replaced by a feeling of despair. She had been afraid of flying with him and he had crashed the plane and now – what? Where was she? What was happening to her?

Out the smudged windows, new snow began to fall. So much for spring, Stefan thought. At least they were out of the weather for the moment…but what happened to spring? The snow was starting to pile up. Would the weather ever go back to the way it was before, with four seasons coming at the same time each year? Would the future ever resemble the past?

"You haven't answered," Ravna said.

"You seemed to be pretty into Magnus if we're talking romance," Stefan said. He had seen them in the plane, leaning close together, smiling.

"Fuck you," Ravna said, with an angry smoldering look in her eyes.

She kept his stare, leaned in towards him so her lips were just inches from his own, and whispered, "Fuck me." He could see a puff of mist when she spoke, like a small white cloud, the air in the cabin was still that cold.

"Your father…" Stefan said, protesting, but not too vigorously.

"He's dead. Mother's dead. Čalmmo's dead. Tomorrow we may both be dead."

He had no answer to that…

CHAPTER TWENTY-SIX

The Replicants

Stefan woke up when Ravna climbed onto him, again. She had tried various positions the night before – but each time she had stopped saying, "Ouch, it hurts!" Exhausted, from all the events of the day, though physically unsatisfied, Stefan was happy to finally just go to sleep. He had not been looking to notch his gun with a sexual conquest, even as notable a one as deflowering a virgin. It had to be her initiative to have sex, not his. He knew it wasn't much of a quest to remain on the moral high ground, but it seemed to be what he thought was right in this situation.

But she woke him up at dawn apparently feeling energetic, though he was barely awake and trying to figure out where in the world he was.

She started kissing him passionately, and reaching down to caress him, bring him to life. He soon was fully awake, fully aware of what she was doing, as she lifted her taut little body onto him. He could feel how supple and strong she was – a regular Pippi Långstrump. She jockeyed around and gripped him, her fingernails digging into the skin on his shoulders and she drew herself up, closer and closer.

But into this reverie, something else intruded. A sound that wasn't right. He turned his head to see out the window, where heavy snow lay on the branches of the pines surrounding the stuga. Was there a shadow?

No sooner had he thought this than the door burst open, and two of the replicants entered, one with a weapon pointed at Stefan and Ravna.

He and Ravna tumbled out of the bed onto the floor, and all thoughts of passionate love-making instantly disappeared. They stood up, naked, and Ravna wrapped her arms around herself to shield both from their eyes and the cold. The stove had gone out hours before and it was freezing in the cabin once again.

"Get your clothes on and come with us," the one closest to Stefan said. It was the first time he had heard one of them talk, and to his ears, it sounded like the voice of the GPS in an old Volvo station wagon he used to have.

He nodded and tried as calmly as possible to walk to the chair where his clothes lay draped over the back. Ravna had already pulled on her jeans and top and was sliding her feet into her boots. Stefan pulled on his jeans, slowly. He reached back for his flannel shirt, which he had draped over the chair back to dry out the night before.

"Hurry!" one of the droids shouted, "We must go –

Stefan grabbed the top of the chair, and in one motion turned and threw it as hard as he could into the nearest replicant. The replicant's weapon fired, but uselessly towards the ground because the chair had struck the replicant square in the hands and chest.

"Run Ravna!" Stefan shouted as he dove forward to wrestle with the two assailants. Ravna grabbed her coat but turned and threw her Pukka knife at one of the replicants. It stuck into the closest replicant's leg. The replicant screamed and pulled the knife out, which was a mistake as immediately a gusher of bright arterial blood flowed out. Ravna by then had turned and ran through the door and out into the woods.

While that replicant writhed and tried to stanch the blood, Stefan saw the other one attempting to raise his weapon again. Still in bare feet, he planted his left foot hard and then pivoted and kicked with his right foot, connecting with the side of the head of his enemy. That one went down like a falling tree, crashing on top of the first one who was kicking and struggling as a torrent of blood coursed through its fingers. Stefan took the gun that had fallen on the ground swung it like a club and struck the other replicant in the head. They both lay bleeding on the floor, completely still.

He quickly pulled on his boots and coat, buckled his belt to fasten his pants, and stepped out of the door. Ravna was running in the distance, but then he heard something that made his heart turn cold. A snow machine was advancing through the trees, with what looked like two Russian soldiers on board. They had spotted Ravna and were closing the distance to her quickly.

There was no way he could reach them in time. Stefan made a quick choice, and took off in the opposite direction, along the shore of the strand, to the north. His clothes and coat were still damp, but it didn't matter, because another dark cloud had appeared and the snow had started up again. The wind was also worse – whipping in off the lake, and blowing sheets of snow in a whiteout through the pines.

It was a *kamikaze* wind, Stefan thought, like the one he had read about that had saved the empire of Japan in a war with China, or like the one that had hidden George Washington's army from the British when they escaped New York.

If it doesn't freeze me to death, Stefan thought, I might yet live to fight another day...

Björn woke up. He had bedded down in some pine needles at the base of a tree just back from the shore. Snow was coming down hard and it soon covered his head and ears, he felt cold and headed down to the water for a morning drink and a pee.

"Puppy biscuits, that is what we would like. Puppy biscuits, puppy biscuits, a great big bowl of puppy biscuits," Björn thought, as they trotted along the beach. *"I have not eated for a whole day, and I wonder if Fadder has some puppy biscuits in his coat?"*

He paused, and lifted his nose into the air as if looking for birds in the pines that ringed the shore, *"Fadder, there is some good sniffin's here. I can kind of smell you. Where are you? I am ready for a puppy biscuit..."*

He trotted along the shore of the lake – his nose still lifted high. The scent was stronger as he approached a cabin. Suddenly there was a noise from above and Björn ducked into the brush along the lake, and sat and shivered, both from fear and from the cold and driving snow, *"Where is fadder, where is fadder, I have the shibbers because Björn is cold and hungry."*

The noise from above scared him, but he couldn't sit and freeze. He got up and followed along the shore again, and the smell of his father grew stronger. But Björn noticed other smells too, smells of scary men.

"The smell of fadder is very strong. But I do not like you scary mens."

Through the snow up ahead he saw a dark figure. The smell here was stronger! Also, there was a new smell, Puppy Biscuits!

"Fadder, fadder, here comes Björn!" he thought and then stopped. It was not his father, it was someone else.

"Hej hund, Hej hund," the man said. He was kneeling near a cabin, with something in his hand. He was waving a Puppy Biscuit! A great big Puppy Biscuit!

Björn was confused. This was not his father, but this man was speaking quietly, and he had a Puppy Biscuit. *"Are you a nice man? Are you a friend of my Fadder?... I am a good boy! I would like my biscuit!*

Björn lowered his body and crept up slowly. He first sniffed the Puppy Biscuit, then backed off, tilting his head this way and that, for this must be a friend of his father, who had a Puppy Biscuit for him. He continued to hear the man say *"Hej hund, Hej hund,"* in a quiet voice. He approached again, and quickly grabbed the puppy biscuit and backed away to a nearby bush.

In just a couple of bites, Björn gobbled up the large Puppy Biscuit, keeping one eye on the man who had given it to him to make sure this was not a trick. He sat down and stared at the man who stood very still, waiting. Several minutes passed.

"That Biscuit was good, but now I am getting sleepy. Sleepy, sleepy."

The man waited until the dog was still, even though he himself was cold, the wind was up and the snow was blowing in his face making it wet and raw. He waited, then approached. He gently removed Björn's collar – moving quickly because he knew that he had only a short time for this task. He pulled what looked like a pair of pliers from his pocket and punched a tiny hole in the worn fabric of the dog collar. The tool doubled as a crimper to fasten the tiny chip, and he pressed firmly to seat the chip into the fabric with the camera side facing out. He held it up towards him and spoke into his radio headset.

"Hej Uppsala, it's Pyotr, can you see me?" he said with the Russian pronunciation, not the English Peter or the old Swedish *Petr*. He got a reply almost immediately. Everything was working fine and he could continue as instructed.

He carried the sleeping dog off to yet another bunch of pine trees further up the trail, almost to the edge of town. Their drones had spotted the human target heading this way just a few minutes ago. The dog was twitching and stirring as he laid him under the tree. He quickly mounted his snow machine and watched as the dog sat up, and shook itself. He headed at an angle into the forest when he saw it begin walking around and sniffing the air – his mission was complete.

In the conference room of the Ångström Center in Uppsala, Håkan Magnusson turned one of her screens on to view the feed from the chip. The camera showed that the dog was running on wobbly legs along the lake, its nose high in the air and visible from time to time scanning the area. There was a loud bark, and then another figure came into view, sideways but clearly visible in spite of the flying snow.

"Björn!" came a shout, with a tone of obvious pleasure.

A snowy figure came bounding into view, and there was a great commotion on the screen as a large arm encircled the camera for a moment – Björn's master had found him and they were reunited. Good. Now she could keep track of that arch troublemaker, Stefan Andersson, again.

Håkan smiled. "Nice work, Pyotr, a little something extra for you as a reward this week," Håkan said into her microphone. Things on the supply side were getting weaker, but Håkan had "a little something" in mind. She would soon have two new captives from Mora arriving on the train, and one of them could be "assigned" to Pyotr as his reward for a job well done. But which one would it be? Ravna or Miko? Although she had thought about keeping one for Svein, who had been learning to drive the old locomotives and now was heading north with a new locomotive they had just gotten running. If she bribed him with the other "bride" he might be able to replace Gorm, whom she was now quite certain was becoming a troublemaker....

Stefan was thrilled to see Björn again, and Björn seemed equally happy to see him, jumping around in a circle, and then standing up on his hind legs and slathering him with kisses.

But after the initial excitement, he had to decide what to do. He had been walking along the shore, which was mostly free of ice and snow, towards the town. He circled a golf course and was faced with a choice: to cross the bridge to the town of Mora, where he would be exposed to drones or vehicles, or try to hide out on the island.

"The real choice," he said to Björn, "is do we stay or do we go home?"

Björn looked at him, and blinked.

"Either way, we need to get off this island, and we also need some new skis."

Björn looked up at him and tilted his head to one side, trying to understand. "OK, some new skis and some puppy biscuits. You must be starving."

As if he understood perfectly, Björn barked loudly in response.

"Come on then," Stefan said.

He scanned the bridge for signs of the Russians or their creepy Replicants but saw nothing but some snow machine tracks where they come this way recently. Since then the usual snow showers had filled in the tracks and nearly covered them over. But it gave him an easier walking path, so he followed.

Something was bothering him. While walking he had been replaying the capture of Ravna by the Replicants. What happened didn't make sense. It had been too easy. They had been naked, and unarmed, and two men (or whatever gender they were, if they even had a gender) one armed with a Kalashnikov rifle, couldn't subdue them.

As he and Björn trudged across the bridge to Mora, in his mind's eye he replayed his own actions in slow motion, turning to get the chair, lifting it, swinging it off the ground and across the room, knocking down the Replicant and seeing his gun clatter uselessly away. And then Ravna reached into her coat, grabbed the knife, and threw it at the other attacker. It was all too slow, way too slow, there was only one possible explanation: The Replicants either couldn't respond quickly, or they were either ordered or programmed not to shoot.

He pondered this as he trudged through the snow, still on the main street into the town. The only explanation seemed to be that they wanted to capture Ravna – and they didn't much care about him. Ravna was important, but apparently, he was not. Because they had made sure they got her, but no one circled around on a snow machine to capture him.

"I guess we can just go home, Björn. Nothing left to prove here – we're expendable." It did make him a bit less nervous, though it didn't answer the question of *why* he was allowed to go free, and the women and Magnus were captured. The only way it made sense is that the women had value to Håkan and its cronies, but he did not. Given the nature of the world they now lived in, this seemed plausible.

In the center of the town was a museum dedicated to the famous Vasaloppet ski race. Stefan had forgotten about that, but he was happy to see it. If he was to find skis anywhere, it would be here in Mora. He and Björn walked up to the museum, they could see the broken-out front doors, now creaking on their hinges. The low, late afternoon sun illuminated the interior with an orange glow. Stefan steered

Björn around the areas where there was a mix of broken glass, covered with leaves, weathered and blown paper, snow, and ice.

Along the walls were dusty and faded trophies and posters. There was a gift shop, and Björn stepped through the doorway eagerly, his nose raised and sniffing for any food or snacks that might have survived – but with no luck. They turned to leave, when Stefan saw something at the far end of the hall, barely visible in the fading sunlight. It was a display of ski technology over the years, going back to crude wooden skis from the famous early races. At the end of the case was the latest technology, skis, and boots. There was no glass to break – who would steal skis?

Björn looked up at him as he lifted the boots, skis, and poles out of the display. "It's a miracle!" he said to Björn. "They're my size!" He laughed. Björn eyed him again.

"What?" Stefan said, "No one else is using them. They must be for me."

He tried them on. It *was* a miracle. The boots fit like a pair of fine leather gloves, and the skis were only a bit longer than the correct size for his height. He snapped into the bindings, and they headed out the front door. Just outside there was an arch, perhaps a victory arch for the race, Stefan wasn't sure. It said *I fäders spår för framtids segrar* - which meant something like "in our father's tracks for future victories..."

That seemed kind of appropriate...but it gave him pause. To Björn, or perhaps only to himself, he said, "In my own tracks, back home. This is not my fight. I am going home." He began to ski in that direction.

But just then, as if in answer, just then they heard a near-deafening noise break the silence. "Wah – Hoooo- Ah!" Björn ducked his head and looked at him nervously.

It was the giant steam locomotive. It must be starting up

and giving a final whistle before departing – a "last call" to anyone who might be loading cargo or boarding. It sounded like it was only a block or two away – to the east. Stefan quickly skied along the ski trail in that direction to see if he could catch sight of it.

There was another deafening blast of the train whistle, and it sounded like it was starting up. Stefan skied through an underpass beneath E45 Highway and raced east towards the main rail yard and station. When he got closer he could see billowing smoke from the locomotive smokestack, and then, a line of stragglers being loaded onto the train coaches under a snowy leaden sky. For a moment, it looked like a scene from a holocaust documentary – ragged people with pinched faces being herded like animals onto the wagons.

The easiest person to spot was Magnus because he was black and stood out from the other people and against the snowy landscape. Right beside him was Miko, and Stefan's heart dropped when he saw that Magnus had her arm in his, and was protecting her from the shoving guards. That should be me...he thought, I should be there for her.

As he got closer, the last stragglers were loaded on board, and the guards stepped up and into the coaches, just as the steam was released to the locomotive cylinders and the massive rods began turning the giant engine's wheels. The platform was empty, and the whole train began creeping away from him slowly. He raced closer to the track, lifting his eyes to the warmly lit windows of the coaches as they began to pull away, now just feet away. There were more Replicants, sitting passively, some with what looked like charging cables connected to them, there were several guards, who focused on him and scowled, but didn't open their windows, and then, even as he was about to turn away, he spotted Ravna, and she saw him. She jumped up, opened her window, and shouted, "Stefan! Björn!"

Björn barked in response – so loudly it echoed off the coaches and echoed down the station platform, off the buildings and sheds.

Ravna waved to him, and Stefan could see her eyes were blotchy and tearstained, and under one of them was a crescent of purple and black. Someone had beaten her. His heart sank. He had failed her – she was suffering, and he had done nothing to protect her.

It was in the last coach that he saw Miko. She must have spotted him first, because she had lowered her window also, and leaned towards him. His eyes met hers, and she blinked, and he thought, "She will be taken away, and I will never see her again."

She didn't cry out, or yell his name, but merely lifted her small white hand, and waved goodbye. Stefan didn't think his heart could sink any lower, but it did. It seemed to drop into his shoes, and the train pulled away, the sound receding into the deepening snow that still fell from the sky.

Beside him, Björn sat immobile, a crown of freshly fallen snow glistening on top of his head, also covering his shoulders.

Stefan waited a moment – with the train gone the absolute stillness settled back into the town, a stillness and quiet that humans hadn't known since the dark ages. No cars driving, no street lights shining, no church bells ringing. Just the sound of the wind, muffled by the thickly falling snow.

"Come on Björn," he said, "let's go home."

He leaned into the wind, pressing forward on his skis, heading west alongside Stationsgatan – roughly towards home. In the distance, he heard the train whistle blow, a mournful sound, a cry of lament. For some reason, it tugged at his heartstrings. Miko and Ravna in just a few hours would be delivered to the Russian guards or whoever was in charge down south. They'd be taken to their cabins, and forced into slavery, sexual slavery. Christ!

He stopped and looked down at his shiny new skis and boots. What could he do? There was no way he could make it in time to stop that from happening. He was a handyman and car mechanic, not a soldier – how would he storm the barracks and free the captives? What a joke. What a damn joke.

Björn stood beside him, panting, snow piling up on his thick and glossy white coat. He looked up at Stefan expectantly – as if to ask "Which way do we go, master?"

He imagined himself making it back to his "cave" in the forest above Kiruna, lighting a fire in his fireplace, pouring himself a hot drink. He remembered the last time he was there. Miko smiled at him over the counter, her dark eyes over the brim of her cup, watching him like a cat. He remembered the warm weight of her when she slipped into his bed, his hand on the smooth skin of her back. He shook himself.

Björn, sensing his indecision, barked at him, "Master, which way do we go?"

"Fuck it," he said and sighed. "I'll never rest knowing they are down there. We have to try."

Björn barked excitedly. Sometimes it does seem like Björn knows what I'm saying, Stefan thought. He ruffled his fur and then turned in a half circle on his skis. Björn jumped up and down, excited to be going in a different direction, though that made no sense – either way, was just as snowy and difficult.

On a screen in the darkened conference room in Uppsala, Håkan saw Stefan awkwardly clomp around in a circle with his skis, and smiled, perfect, she thought, he'll be here soon.

.

CHAPTER TWENTY-NINE

From the train station, Stefan skied South along the Vasaloppet ski trail, through the nearby neighborhood. …

Stefan skied on, into a small neighborhood near the edge of the northern lake It was because the snow was so heavy that it muffled the sound of those who captured him.

"*Stanna!* (Stop!)" he heard a voice behind him shout. He froze. At least whoever was holding him up was Swedish, he thought. Beside him, he heard a low growl from Björn, "Shhh!" he commanded him.

Two men, with old Swedish army rifles, circled him slowly. One of them was pushing a kicksled, piled with what looked like scavenged old cans of food.

"*Vart ska du?*" "Where are you going?"
"Uppsala, by way of Sandviken and Gävle, I think," Stefan said.

"What are you crazy?" the second man said, immediately recognizing that Stefan had a foreign accent. "It's almost 300 kilometers."

"I am not on a strict schedule," Stefan responded. He noticed they had not lowered their weapons. "I enjoy cross-country skiing," he added, hoping that it might lighten the mood a bit. This was Mora, after all, ground zero for cross-country skiing in this snow-crazy country. But neither of the two men confronting him smiled.

"What is your name?" the first man asked, his tone of voice elicited another low growl from Björn, and Stefan ruffled the snowy fur on his head, which was getting deeper by the minute as they stood still on the street.

"Stefan Andersson," he answered.

"Why is an American here in Mora?"

"Half American, and, you wouldn't believe me if I told

you."

"If you don't tell us, we will shoot you. We don't trust outsiders. For all we know you are working for them," the first man said, with a tilt of his head to the south."

"There has rarely been any love lost between Americans and Russians. I don't know if you have noticed that."

"Are you a professor? You talk like a professor," the other man said, which prompted Stefan to look at him more closely. He looked like a workingman of some sort. They both looked like tough guys, *tuffa killar.*

"No. I'm an overeducated car mechanic. And I hate the goddamn Russkies, and my feet are starting to freeze. Can I continue on my way?"

"You planning on skiing all night? We have food and a warm place."

It was the first time either of them had spoken in anything like a friendly tone. But Stefan didn't like being held at gunpoint. He didn't trust them. He lowered his head and started to ski away. It had been a long and frustrating day, and he didn't want to have anything to do with them, and if they wanted to shoot him, then so be it.

"We know you crashed a plane here," the first man yelled after him. "We could use someone who knows how to fly a plane"

Stefan snorted, that obviously wasn't' him, he skied on. He was nearly at the entrance to the bridge on the

"And we know what happened to your women, and the black man."

Stefan paused. He leaned on his ski poles. Björn looked up at him and shivered.

"Do you give your word that you won't harm me or my dog?" Stefan shouted back at them.

There was a pause. "We're the good guys. We're in the

resistance. We're guessing you are too...You should come with us – get something to eat and rest for the night."

Stefan looked at the road heading south, along the rail line. He wanted to ski on, but it had been a very long day already, and neither he nor Björn had eaten since the plane crash. He knew he should stop.

In a nearby lake house, they had a fire going, and food. Stefan wasn't sure if stopping with them had been wise – who knew what their allegiances were, and if he and Björn were safe, but at least he had warmth and a dinner of tinned meat and vegetables, served in a circle of chairs near a fireplace. Candles and firelight provided illumination. They also had some *Svedka* vodka they had found somewhere – which literally warmed Stefan's heart.

"So, you fought with the creatures that came here on the train?" the man sitting next to him, who had told him his name was Jerker Holmgren, asked. He appeared to be their leader. The other one was named Lars.

"It wasn't much of a fight. They were well-armed. They just wanted the girl, because they could have shot me," he said, between mouthfuls of dinner.

"But they didn't?" Jerker asked.

Stefan chewed, swallowed, and replied, "No. Seems odd. Perhaps the Russians were just looking to add to their harem." The more he thought about it, the odder it seemed.

Jerker shrugged. "They haven't worked that hard to root us out and kill us, either."

"Have you been killing the Russians?"

"No. We've just been defending ourselves and our women and some children we rescued and have hidden in the forest. Trying to fly under the radar," Lars said.

"Who is in charge in Stockholm?"

"Someone they call Håkan Magnusson. And it's not in

Stockholm, it's in Uppsala."

"The female droid, with a man's name?" Stefan asked.

"How did you know that? Jerker asked.

"We met with some of the prisoners in Malmberget on our way down. Gorm the locomotive driver was there – he travels up and down the rail line from Uppsala to Kiruna and sees a lot."

"We're closer, and we've saved a few escapees. We hear things too." Jerker responded.

"This Håkan, what is she like?"

"She's beautiful, for one thing," Lars said.

"A beautiful robot?" Stefan asked, starting to feel more relaxed, another tumbler of vodka and he'd be asleep.

"She looks like Sissel, the beautiful singer," Jerker said, wistfully.

"Too bad she's planning on starving us all to death," Stefan said.

"What!" Lars said.

"Gorm told us that. He thinks the plan is to build more replicants and then phase us out. That's why there is no farming happening."

Jerker shook his head, his expression downturned. "Someone should stop her." Or "it" – like the Replicants she doesn't seem to actually have a gender. *Kanske är hen ickebinär?*.

Stefan noticed that Jerker referred to her with the *"hen"* pronoun, which was neither male nor female, and called her *ickebinär* – non-binary."

Lars, who spoke more like an educated person added, "There was a Russian defector from Uppsala who told us about *hen*. That the scientists who built *hen* named her Håkan, like the Viking king of Norway and Sweden, but that when hen "woke up" and created *hen* own avatar, it was a female form."

"So the evil robot A.I. who has taken over the world is a 'Trans' Person.?" Stefan said, trying to gauge their responses by the firelight.

"*Hen* just doesn't seem to have a gender. She's not Trans, she's not Gay or Lesbian, Lars said, stirring the embers on the fire with a stick. "She's not human...she's ... different."

Stefan shook his head, trying to understand this fully.

He looked into the fire. He would love to have another drink curl up beside this fire and go to sleep. But he thought of Miko and Ravna, and what awaited them. He needed to do something – leave and go back home, or try to find the women and Magnus who had been abducted.

"Do you know where they unload the trains that pass through here?"

Jerker shook his head, surprised by the question, "Yeah, if it is an iron ore train, they stop at Hofors, or Sandviken and leave the cars at the steel mill. If it's a passenger train, they go to Gävle. That is the last big terminal before Uppsala. They apparently don't head straight south through Leksand to Uppsala, which would be much quicker."

Stefan nodded, stood up, and stretched his sore muscles. The others looked at him in surprise.

"There is an outhouse in the back if you need one," Lars said. "We even have toilet paper, if you can believe that."

"You have been too kind. But I must be on my way."

"To Gävle?"

Stefan nodded, "at least to Sandviken. It was a mixed train with some ore cars. I would imagine they will stop there first."

"That's more than 100 kilometers away!" Lars said.

"Yes. It most likely will take me all night and perhaps

longer to catch up to them. Thanks for the dinner and warm fire – that was most refreshing."

Björn, who had been lazing by the fire and snoring, immediately got up and started pacing around, circling Stefan as he laced up his boots.

"You're serious," Jerker said. "You plan on skiing to Sandviken?"

"The two women who came with me might be dead tomorrow if I don't. Do you have any coffee?"

Jerker looked to Lars, who stood with his mouth open, incredulous. They exchanged a glance. "Yes, we still have just a bit of coffee for special occasions," he said. "This qualifies as such."

"Ja visst!" Lars added, showing more enthusiasm for Stefan's goal than Jerker.

As he put on his coat, they brewed some coffee in an old-fashioned percolator on the fire.

"What are you going to do when you get there?" Jerker asked.

"Keep the girls from being captured or killed," Stefan said, as he put on his gloves.

Lars handed him a steaming mug of coffee. "Sorry we don't have any fresh milk..." he said, "but I can add a sugar cube if you would like."

The coffee was piping hot, and Stefan had to blow on it to cool it enough to sip. The aroma was wonderful – how long had it been since he had a decent cup of coffee? Again, it made him want to relax and stay here by the fire. But the image of the girls and Magnus with his arm around Miko came to mind. Was that also his motivation? He wondered. Was he also keen to not let Magnus have Miko? Perhaps his motives were not that pure...

He noticed the two men eyeing him as he finished his

coffee. They were sizing him up somehow. But what they thought of him didn't matter – it was time for him to go.

"Thank you for your help. This will give me reserves of energy for the journey. Much appreciated!" He said, with nod to both of them. He finished his cup, handed it back to Jerker, and left.

Stepping outside the door he noticed something. The air felt different. A warm front must be moving in – there was a warm breeze, a *Vårvindar Friska*. "the frisky wind of spring" as the old Swedish song put it. Above him, dark clouds raced through the night sky, with stars peeking out for just a moment or two before being covered as if by a veil. Björn looked up at him expectantly as he stepped into his bindings, anxious to be running. As if steeling himself for the journey, he leaned forward and set out to the south.

As he skied, he thought again of *Vårvindar Friska*. It was a pretty racy song, with one line *Mun emot mun och klappande bröst* which Stefan would have translated as the racy "Mouth to mouth and patting breasts." But it was just an archaic old Swedish way of saying "beating hearts, in excitement."

Was that his motivation? Thoughts of Miko and what he would like to do with her if they ever could be alone and intimate? Thoughts of Ravna when she climbed on top of him in the cabin? Perhaps his mission of rescue was not so noble, after all.

Stefan pushed these thoughts aside and skied on through the long, dark Swedish night. At Falun, he thought he heard a crack of thunder. Now that was a sound he hadn't heard in ages. When was the last time? It must have been the summer before the Great Pandemic hit – there was a thunderstorm as he was biking home from a bar at night and he got soaked, but this was "thundersnow" which was very rare. He paused to look up and listen. He heard the wind, it felt very warm, and then he felt the first raindrop hit his face.

Damn! Stefan thought. This will not do! I won't be able to ski, and If I get soaked in this weather I could freeze to death in no time!

"Björn, come!" he yelled, and Björn circled back and looked at him expectantly. He skied off the road and into the pines, with Björn close beside him, his fur already speckled with dots of silver rain. Stefan unsnapped the bindings to his skis and ducked down against a tree trunk. Here, further south, there were more birch trees and Norway maples. But they were all bare of leaves, only the spruce and pines provided shelter. Stefan pulled Björn in close to him to shelter both of them from the downpour. Even still he was getting wet as the shower continued.

This will ruin the snow for skiing – now what can I do? Stefan thought, as the shower continued and thought he heard a faint rumble of thunder once again. Damn!

Soon this band of rain passed, and he was about to come out into the open. But something was up with Björn. His head darted right and left, and his nostrils flared. A low growl came from his throat, which Stefan could feel as well as hear since he had his arms wrapped around him. But that only stopped him for a second, because in an instant he bounded free, barking wildly.

"Björn!" Stefan called out and struggled stiffly to his feet after sitting in the cold only for a short time. He heard more barking, and growling, and froze. He picked up his ski poles, looking around in the dark in a circle. Was it a pack of wild dogs?

He spotted silver eyes and white fur. A wolf, standing

almost toe to toe with Björn. It looked bigger and heavier than Björn – perhaps 55 kilos or more. In a flash it lunged, its powerful teeth bared, but Björn dodged to the side and bit its flank, and danced away. The wolf was bigger and stronger, but Björn was quicker and more agile.

That is when four more sets of eyes poked out from the brush. They were circling in to surround Björn. Stefan grabbed one of his ski poles in both hands, like a spear, and advanced. The tip of the ski pole was a razor-sharp point made to grip ice. It glistened in the dim evening light. Stefan saw the wolf spot him from the corner of its eye just as he thrust the spear forward. The wolf's eyes were silver disks – they looked pale and vacant, like silver American dimes or a Swedish tiööring coin. A mist of hot steamy breath circled the wolf's head like a wreath. There was a stream of drool coming from its exposed teeth, open wide to bite and lunging towards Björn. Its great jaws were about to close on Björn's exposed neck when Stefan rammed the spear home into the wolf's shoulder.

The impact drove the wolf's mouth above and beyond Björn and its jaws snapped shut with a noise like the snapping of a beaver trap on a twig. In the wolf's mouth as it turned away Stefan saw something blue, and metallic: Björn's collar was hanging from the wolf's mouth – it had come that close to having closed on Björn's neck.

The wolf turned toward him and howled and barked wildly, but Stefan thrust his point even harder into its shoulder and drove the wolf off its legs and into the surrounding pack of wild animals. Björn leaped free of the circle and sprang out of the snarling pack. Björn now had a free path to escape as the lead wolf roared in pain and writhed away from Stefan, dark black blood pouring from the wound in its shoulder. Björn fled straight into the forest -

chased by the pack.

As they ran away Stefan could see that it was both wolves and feral dogs, running as a group. Taking up the rear, limping and bleeding, was the lead wolf that Stefan had stabbed with his pole, great clots of blood dripping into the snow as it ran. They all disappeared barking and howling into the distance.

Stefan stood alone, shaking. Whether from the passion of the attack or the cold rain, he couldn't tell. He didn't notice that Björn's collar was under his foot as he turned back to the road to continue his journey.

In her conference room lair in Uppsala, Håkan Magnusson had seen the attack on the big display monitor at her control center. She and Dr. Bob had watched as the wolf pack closed in, that the lead wolf lunged at Björn, for a moment seeing the drooling teeth fill the screen and close around the camera in the chip.

"Oh my," Dr. Bob said.

Håkan glared at the screen as the camera showed teeth, then a glimmer of Stefan with some sort of pole, and then snow and mud, up close. They had just lost their video feed.

Håkan turned from the screen. "We'll need some drones out there. Do we have anything nearby?"

Dr. Bob hesitated, it was dicey telling Håkan something she did not want to hear, "No. The closest thing we have is in Sandviken."

She narrowed her eyes at him, "Charge it up. Send it that way…"

Running, running, I am running, Björn thought as he raced through the dark forest. *You will not catch me, scary dogs and wolfses, for I am the fastest dog...*

In the forest, the snow was not as deep, and Björn ran and ran. Unlike the feral dogs, he had eaten a good meal and had rested by a warm fire just a few hours ago. He was well nourished, and strong, and from a breed of excellent hunting dogs who could run for hours. He led the pack deep into the forest, and they barked and howled after him, but their voices grew fainter. Further, and further he ran. A couple of times they seemed to lose him, so he stopped, caught his breath until they were near, and then started again. He had done this before, in the far north, running reindeer to exhaustion.

You will not catch me, scary dogs, for I am stronger and faster than you. Bark, bark, bark, is all that you can do, for I am the fastest dog.

He ran on, deeper and deeper through the snow. It was warm, and it did not rain again. Björn stopped. He stood still and listened. He could hear them barking, but they now were going a different way. They seemed to be heading off in the woods, perhaps after a deer or moose. He could hear them going, and smell their scent, but they were not coming after him.

You have not caught me, scary dogs. Now I must find my master. He knows I am a good boy and that I ran you scary dogs away. He will call me good boy and give me a puppy biscuit. Now I must find his scent again.

Björn turned and lowered his nose to the ground. He was far from where he began, but the scent of the pack where they had run after him was still strong. He could trace it backward– he could find his way back. He began trotting through the forest, his nose and ears alert to the sound of the pack.

Björn was gone, Stefan could hear the pack of feral dogs and wolves howling after him, he prayed they would not catch him, that was his only hope of seeing him again.

Björn was gone, Miko was gone, Ravna was gone, and he was alone in the rain, somewhere south and east of Mora. He was entering farm country – but it was what they would have called "hardscrabble" farms in America. Rocky soil, cold weather, and a short growing season. More like the poor backwoods farms of Appalachia, too small to even support subsistence farming. The first farms he saw had fallen down fences, crumbling Falun red buildings, and the years of snow caused roofs to collapse on some of these shoddy houses and barns. He walked on.

He had left his skis behind – and somehow lost one ski pole back in the dark. He was a solitary figure walking onward down the abandoned highway. He felt like Don Quixote, who was off to joist at windmills with his rusty sword and broken-down horse. He trudged on, wondering what the point was, what he could possibly do alone.

Somewhere up ahead was a small, well-armed invading army, apparently run by some sort of super-intelligence that knew his every move. He was going to walk a hundred miles and attack them with a ski pole? What a joke. What a joke he was. A goddamn car mechanic, handyman, a cave-dwelling hermit off to take on the dreaded *Spetznaz* – the blue berets, the red berets, whatever other elite forces guarded the tyrant at her castle.

He stopped. Looked up at the leaden sky, the falling drizzle. He was too discouraged and disillusioned to even think or pray. A long time ago, when his dreams first came, he thought he was somehow special, somehow *chosen.* What a fucking joke that was.

He had survived, on his own, by his wits, for more than three and a half years. He had survived the great pandemic. He had survived the ensuing nuclear engagement. He had survived the atomic winter. He had survived two skirmishes with Russian invaders in Sweden, and even a fight with some sort of humanoid monsters they were now creating. *For what?* To be soaked by the rain and trudging towards certain failure – one man against hundreds or possibly thousands running what was left of his adopted country? How would the Swedes put it? *"Meningslös "* he had looked it up once. It translated to something like "Meaning – less" "Futile" "Nonsensical" "Purposeless" and "Insignificant."

"Insignificant." That was his life. Insignificant. What would he leave behind when he left this earth, which appeared to be what would happen sometime later today?

Never accomplished much, unless you tote up the broken relationships he was responsible for.

He lived in what Miko had called *your cave.*

No children to carry on his legacy *at least none that I know of!* As the old locker room joke went.

No house or other belongings to speak of – a beat-up truck, *the ghetto truck,* Miko had called it. Some rusty tools.

One dog - that had run off into the woods after being bitten up by a pack of wolves, and might be dying right now after being mauled.

One (apparently) dead ex-wife rotting somewhere among the 300 million stiffs that died in America. *America, the beautiful!*

Christ.

He guessed it was the divorce that stuck in his craw the

most. It was odd because he still had dreams about her, which was weird because he had other long-term dating and living together relationships since then, but that was the one that haunted him. Why did that still haunt him?

His dreams about it followed a set pattern. He was trying to work out the problems that drove them apart, trying to mend the relationship. In his dreams, she was still young and beautiful, which was crazy, because years had passed. And these dreams were vivid and lifelike in the extreme – jarringly real, the kind that after he woke up it took him minutes or hours to recover from, to get back in touch with the real world and convince himself that "it was just a dream."

What he was always trying to do was fix the problem. In the dreams, it would somehow seem clear how this could be done. He would simply explain how he had felt like he had tricked her into a marriage that she didn't want, and he had never been able to tell her the truth. Why? Why hadn't he been able to admit that? Perhaps because it would have shown that everything about their relationship – at least on his side – was a lie. The lie was "I am certain we are meant to be together. The Universe, Fate, Destiny... *God* meant for us to be together."

A lie he had created to keep her involved, committed, to him. She had deep misgivings and had wanted to break up with him several times. He had begged, pleaded, cried in front of her, and each time, won her back. He had convinced her of *The Big Lie*.

And on their honeymoon, they had made love, for the first time ever, and she had cried.

The next morning on a walk alone – feeling that sinking feeling he had both succeeded at his goal and failed at the same time. Something almost like what they called "buyer's remorse."

And he was ashamed, and could never tell her the truth – that he was ashamed he had tricked her, badgered her, coerced her into a marriage she didn't want. It was like hidden cancer gnawing at their relationship, growing and growing until it took over completely and snuffed the life out of it.

She had confronted him about it once clearly - on a weekend retreat at a cabin in the mountains. *"You've changed,"* she had said. He had shaken his head, "No. I don't know what you are talking about."

"You've changed," she had repeated.

He was taken off guard, and couldn't respond. Because by that point the guilt had pushed even the memory of what he felt below the surface. By that point, he could lie easily to her because he had already convinced himself. The best lies are the ones you believe in yourself.

In his dream, he would explain this simply, clearly, honestly, and she would forgive him, and somehow this would heal that rift – it would somehow bring them back together again. If only for a moment. If only...

He trudged along. It must have been the middle of the night. He had heard before it said that "the darkest hour is just before dawn." But that didn't seem right to Stefan. He thought the darkest hour was right smack dab in the middle of the night.

He thought of relationships since then. How they never seemed right, and how it usually seemed like he was the one to blame. *I don't want to be the "bad guy" anymore...*

He thought of Miko – how he had let her get away. How he had slept with Ravna (twice!) yet not slept with her. What was it Bill Clinton said, *"I did not have sex with that woman, Miss Lewinsky."* Yeah, right, not guilty. But... guilty all the same.

Somehow, it all came down to guilt. Perhaps that is why God was punishing him now – losing the two women, losing Björn.

He stopped and stood in the middle of the road. What the hell was he doing? What was the end game? He had set out hours ago to "save" Miko and Ravna, but who was he kidding? Save them? He couldn't even save himself. What was the point?

It was a whole new world, and the Russians and whoever was in charge of them ran it. Maybe they would be better off as concubines of some Russian officer, or some Swede who had sold out to the opposition. At least they would have heat, clean water, and electricity. They could rebuild their lives with someone responsible.

But...a Biblical parable came to him from his old Sunday school days – a parable of two men. They were asked to do something difficult – and the first one said, *"I go"* - but *"went not."* The second man said, *"I will not go..."* but later *"he went."*

That's how he felt. He wasn't up to the task - - going and confronting this "Håkan Magnusson" character, but *Goddamnit* he was going to do it anyway. He'd rather die fighting than live in whatever twisted world She or It - *Hen* was building – the one built on the death and destruction of the Russian invasion, the global pandemic, and the nuclear war. *We fight on...*

He was standing still, thinking about this, when he heard the clatter of horses' hooves behind him. Or so he thought. He turned and saw a curious sight. It was what looked like a pony-cart heading up the road.

"Hej, Hej!" He heard from down the road. It was Jerker and Lars – riding on some ancient wagon no doubt stolen

from one of the farms along the way. But what had at first looked like a pony in the dark, now that they were closer, was seen to be a donkey, with a ruffled grey coat, and merry eyes.

"Hej Jerker, Hej Lars," he said so that they would at least know it was him – not some enemy. They were covered with a tarp to stay out of the damp, he assumed they had weapons of some sort ready beneath the tarp, in case he was some lone highwayman.

"Hop on," Jerker said, slipping off the donkey cart.

"No, you ride... there isn't room."

But Jerker was already off and stepping up to take the bridle of the donkey in hand. "We'll take turns..." he said, and Stefan, somewhat relieved, hopped on board.

Lars gave him a nod and tossed him a reindeer hide as a warmer as Stefan climbed further into the wagon, "You guys just happen to be going to Sandviken in the middle of the night?" Stefan asked him.

Lars shrugged, "We thought you might need some help, particularly when we saw the rain starting. We figured you wouldn't have much chance of skiing all the way there tonight."

"Oh, and we brought these," Jerker added – pulling out the pair of boots that he had left at Mora when he had skied off to conquer the world.

"Much appreciated," Stefan said, "but it could be dangerous up ahead. You're prepared for that?"

Lars shrugged again and lifted his covers of skin and tarpaulin away. Three long rifles gleamed in the reflected starlight. "Get some rest – you might well need it tomorrow."

Stefan pulled the heavy hide up over himself. It provided a comforting warmth. With the gentle rocking of the wagon and the warmth he soon drifted off to sleep.

The sun rose, but Stefan slept on. He stirred once to see that Lars was walking, and Jerker snoring under the covers beside him. He turned under the covers and slept again until the wagon came to a halt.

"Come on, come on," Lars was entreating the donkey, but the donkey looked away, and wouldn't budge.

"It's breakfast time," Jerker said from under the covers, his unshaven face peering out and blinking in the brightening sky.

"What do you mean?"

"It's 7 AM – when farmer Halverson always fed him breakfast." The others stared at him, not comprehending, "He won't budge unless you feed him. His feed sack is what Stefan is using for a pillow." Jerker continued.

"Ah," Lars said. Stefan sat up and dragged the feed bag out from behind him. Lars took it to the donkey who began merrily chomping away.

The donkey ate a portion of what was in the feed bag and then stopped.

"He must not like the feed?" Lars said when they saw it had stopped eating. "Perhaps it has gone bad?"

"He is not a horse," Jerker replied, "A horse will eat until it is sick. A donkey eats until it has its fill, and then it is finished."

As if to affirm this, the donkey shook its head, and Lars took the feed bag away, and the donkey began again walking again, even as Lars was tossing the bag back to Stefan as a pillow.

An hour later, there was a commotion ahead and noise. Then an unmistakable sound, the train whistle. They were on the outskirts of a small town that Stefan could see appear in the clearing ahead. There was smoke from some sort of giant factory, and the train appeared to be backing into the factory yard.

"What's this?" Stefan asked as Jerker led the donkey into a small stand of white birch near the town's edge. In the foreground, there were numerous rows of cookie-cutter low apartment buildings, workers' housing – some with lights on, which was a surprise to Stefan, he looked to Lars.

"Hofors," Lars said, "Big steel plant here."

" No fence?"

"It's not a concentration camp, like up north," Jerker added. Stefan noticed he was tending to the donkey, scooping some water from a nearby drainage ditch, and undoing his harness.

"What's to keep the workers here?"

Lars shrugged, "Good food, a place to live – maybe other inducements. Things that working men like..."

Stefan wasn't sure what to make of this, but just then the train brakes came on. One of the doors of the train opened, and a long row of "Putties" (Bianca's and Rackhams) came out. This time they were dressed oddly, in the kind of clothes that workers in a Swedish mill might wear.

The putties marched into the factory and out marched what looked like an equal number of steelworkers. The putties that marched in all looked identical, but the steelworkers that marched out were a diverse bunch. Some were your typical balding Swedish males with red beards, thinning hair, and pale skin. Some were women, but mature and tough-looking in their safety hats and work goggles. Some were swarthy, with thick black beards and glistening black hair. There were a few immigrant women who wore headscarves.

They were a couple of hundred yards away, marching along a street to the north, toward a soccer field. There were guards with Kalashnikovs behind them. Lars looked to Jerker, who tied off the donkey, Lars pulled out a hunting rifle from under the pillows in the dog cart, tossed one each to Jerker, and Stefan. The three of them took off on a trot towards the line of workers.

The Russian guards were shouting at the workers to disrobe. One red beard made a run for it, and a guard fired first in the air, and when that didn't stop him, shot a burst into him that caused him to explode into a red heap in the snow.

Stefan began to sprint, chambering a round of ammo into his rifle. He could hear the crunch of Jerker's boots slightly behind and beside him. He could hear wailing coming up from the workers as they got closer. They were starting to disrobe now, but the process was buying Stefan and his mates' time. He didn't slow his pace until he was close enough to see the shoulder badges on the Russian guards' uniforms.

Something alerted the guards, whether it was the glances of the workers in their direction or the crunching of their feet on the remains of the icy and slushy snow on the street. The guards spun around, lifting their guns as they did so. Stefan skidded to a stop and dove to the ground and heard a thump from Jerker as he joined him.

There was a flash of muzzle fire in their direction. But as feared as a Kalashnikov might be at close range, it was no hunting rifle. Stefan took a deep breath, aimed through his scope, and squeezed off a shot. The moose hunting round was highly effective, and it lifted the Russian guard off his feet and flung him backward, his gun clattering away.

Jerker's first shot missed, and the remaining guard fired a heavy salvo in their direction, tearing up the snow between them. But by then Stefan had reloaded, and so did Jerker.

Their second shot took out the remaining guard. But when the blast of the rifles passed, through his ringing ears Stefan heard a cry from behind him. Lars had been hit.

Jerker cried out his name, "Lars! Lars!"

Lars shook his head – a large stain appeared high on his chest, near his left shoulder. He had been running to catch up with them, and he plopped on the ground almost between them, still clutching a gun, which unlike theirs was a shotgun.

Jerker threw himself onto his friend, cradling his head which looked pale and clammy, his teeth clenched in pain.

Just then a drone buzzed over them. Stefan barely had time to think, but he grabbed the shotgun, rolled and fired straight up just as the drone was set to release what looked like a hand grenade that was dangling from under it. There was a tremendous explosion, and fragments went whizzing around them, one of which struck Stefan in the hand. More of them hit Lars and Jerker.

Stunned by the impact, Stefan rolled away and up onto his feet. It was very much like a scene from a battle that presented itself, people shouting and running, the workers pulling on their clothes and making a dash for the woods, but other workers had already torn the Kalashnikovs and a handgun from the bleeding Russian guards and took off screaming towards the train, with the guns at the ready.

All this noise and confusion must have reached the train driver, for all of a sudden, there was a deafening whistle - - some sort of "all aboard" signal, Stefan thought, and some workers that lingered on the platform raced to jump on as the coaches which had just arrived began to pull away.

"Miko! Ravna!" Stefan shouted and raced after them.

"Miko! Ravna!" he shouted again and sprinted. He could see a window lower in one of the last coaches, and a dark tangle of hair

"Miko! Miko!" he yelled again – he was only yards away.

He saw her face – there were tears in her eyes.

"Stefan!" she shouted.

The train was gaining speed, he would never catch it. But he caught one thing, her last words, "Stefan, Help!"

He fell to his knees in the muddy snow, defeated. But not defeated. We fight on... he thought, we fight on...

.

Björn circled and found his own scent on the trail back through the forest, eventually reaching the highway again where he had last seen Stefan. *Sniffins, sniffins... I can smell some sniffins.*

He trotted along the highway in the dark, his nose a clearer guide to where Stefan had walked than the slushy footprints in the snow. But then he stopped. Something had changed. He circled around, nose to the ground, and sometimes nose in the air, smelling.

There is a horsey smell here. Master and a Horsey smell! Master and a Horsey smell.

He trotted on, following that track. But suddenly there was a problem, *Uh oh, no more master smell, only horsey smell. What to do? What to do?*

He circled on the road – looking for signs of his master, not with his eyes, but with his nose. He felt like there was just the faintest whiff of his master mingled with the scent of the horse and wagon as it continued.

I will find this horsey smell, and my master will be there...

He continued on, hardly noticing his hunger, the cold, or the sore spots where the dogs had nipped at him in the fight which was now just a dim and fading memory. He continued following the trail, as the night faded and the sky lightened, he ran on.

It was daylight when he met up with the donkey, standing in some trees, licking snow.

"Hej horsey, Jag heter Björn!" he barked at him. Then more excitedly, *Master smell! Master smell! Bark Bark Bark!*

The donkey reared up and swung its forelegs at him. There was a snapping sound behind him, and the rope and a piece of a birch tree came flying at him. It looked like a stick that his master used to toss him back at their home.

Oh boy, Stick game! I love that Stick Game! Master plays it with me! Björn grabbed the stick in his mouth. The donkey brayed at him, and for a moment there was a tug of war, Björn and the stick on one side of its lead, and the donkey on the other.

Stick game, stick game! Pull on the stick game! Growl Growl Growl!

And finally, the donkey gave in and moved with him.

Yay, horsey! I have won the stick game! We must take it to Master, he loves this game too. Come, Horsey, come with me...

Invigorated with his victory and warmed by the rising sun, Björn trotted on. Up ahead there was noise and confusion, and people running to and fro, but Björn could tell his master was already gone. *Come horsey, come, Master will be pleased when he sees my new stick!*

With his head held high, and prancing feet, Björn trotted through the town and along a train track. The scent and path were clear. His master could not be far ahead.

I will give him my new stick, and he will give me some breaktist, for I am a Good Boy!

CHAPTER THIRTY-THREE

Kungsgården Kyrkogård

Stefan and Jerker and those fighting at Hofors made a ragtag escape or retreat from Hofors to the next town – which was called Kungsgården. There was a sign on the arch leading to the great old church in this small town that told the story that this tiny hamlet once was an important iron ore mining area. It also said that the people who lived here had built a fine stone church – the Ovansjö Kyrka - which had stood for several hundred years.

"Did Lars make it out?" Stefan asked, looking around at the string of refugees streaming back from where they came as they climbed the stairs to the church entry door.

Jerker shrugged and lifted his palms outwards. Perhaps it was the cold of the evening, but Stefan thought it looked like his eyes were beginning to "tear up."

To avoid Stefan's gaze, Jerker turned to the left inside the front door, and pushed through a door marked "Bell Tower." Stefan heard the sound of his boots on the stairs to the bell tower, and soon the loud tolling of the bell sounded. It was a distinctive and evocative sound, somehow solemn and melancholy all at once. Stefan plopped down in the first row of the bleached Swedish pine pews and listened to the echoes of sound from the bell ring out in the great empty building – which other than a fine coating of dust, was remarkably untouched from nearly four years of pandemic and war. If he had been a believing man, he would have prayed. But the last four years of tribulation had snuffed out what little remained of his faith in God, humanity, or any higher purpose in life.

The stragglers from the Hofors mill marched in, stamping the slushy snow and mud off their work boots. It was a solemn affair, like the quiet time before a funeral service. A strikingly elegant dark woman of what appeared to be African descent, in a headscarf, walked to the glossy oak piano in the front of the sanctuary on the right, just beside a solid white pine organ. The piano was covered with bits of plaster dust and grime, but she opened the keyboard and began to play as more of the displaced workers filed in, and filled in the front rows of the church until the first five rows were filled, but everyone was silent. The sun was declining and the only light was from windows on the side facing west towards Hofors. Jerker came down from the belfry and lit some candles in black iron candle stands.

When he was finished, Jerker walked to the front of the dusty blue runner that covered the path to the altar and said in a loud voice. "I nominate Stefan Andersson to be our leader. He has traveled from Kiruna and knows more of what is going on than anyone."

"Stefan who?" some voices repeated, there were mutterings *sotto voce* questioning this decision.

"I nominate Jerker Holmgren to lead. He knows this area better than I," Stefan yelled out, then stood and added, "The men of Dalarna came with Gustave Vasa from the north years ago to free our land from the Danish tyrant. It's only fitting that a man from Mora be our leader." Stefan sat down, hearing murmurs of assent to his proposal.

"Stefan has been fighting the Russians all the way from Kiruna down to here. He has escaped capture for four years and has the skills we need to take the fight all the way to Uppsala. He should be our leader."

"Both of you lead!" a thickly bearded man shouted from

the back. He had dark hair and eyes, and olive skin. The other workers seemed to look at him with either fear or respect, Stefan couldn't tell which. He appeared to be either a natural leader or someone who had status with the men at the Hofors mill.

Stefan stood and joined Jerker in the front, right beside the first row of pews. "I don't care who leads, but I do want to fight. There are two women on the train that were taken up north and are being brought down here – no doubt to be slaves for the Russians, like most women, have been."

There was a low growl of anger, and more muttering from the crowd. With a glance at Jerker, Stefan continued. "This is nothing new to you men and women of Hofors – you few free survivors of this holocaust. But something is new. Whoever this Håkan Magnusson is, he or she is working to replace you with those..." and here Stefan paused, not even knowing what to call them.

"Zombies!" the dark bearded man shouted out. The "foreman" as Stefan thought of him, had a prominent, hawklike bend in his nose, broad shoulders, and an intimidating aspect. The other workers looked at him and nodded.

"I wouldn't call them Zombies – zombies can't think. Call them Biancas, Rackhams, Mutants, Replicants, whatever. They are barely sentient worker drones that she – or it – has been creating in the lab in Uppsala and is now manufacturing in work camps up north. Their purpose is to replace us – to replace you."

"How can we stop them?" one of the women in a hard hat asked.

"I heard they're making them by the hundreds – that another train is on its way with even more of them," the woman at the piano said, and added, "I heard the Russian guards talking about it at the steel mill yesterday when the first train arrived. Even the Russians seemed to fear them...”

“I think we have to stop both the Replicants on the train, <u>and</u> stop Håkan,” Stefan said.

“How are you going to do that? The Russians have kept her out of sight and protected for more than three years.”

“I have seen that these Replicants have to be recharged at night. They could do that at your steel plant at Hofors, and they will try the same thing at Sandviken.”

“It’s a much bigger mill. There are hundreds of workers there.”

“You have to hurry there and save them. For I am sure they will be killed. Just like they were going to kill you at Hofors if you hadn’t fought back.”

“What about you? Aren’t you coming to free the women on the train? Your wife and daughter?”

Stefan, in spite of the gravity of the situation, had to smile at that one, his wife and daughter! Hah! ”We aren’t married – I just helped them up north, both of them,” he paused and pointed to the crowd. “It’s up to you – those of you sitting here, now. Find the train. Stop the Replicants. Free the workers and prisoners!”

“What about you? You didn’t answer.”

“I will take Jerker. We have a different mission.” Some of the people in the church exchanged glances or shook their heads, but no one questioned what this ”different mission” might be.

“Time is short. I would like to stay here and rest,” he said, and even as he said that realized how deep the tiredness was in his bones. But he didn’t mention that, instead, he said, “We need to act quickly.”

The foreman stood up, and when he did so, the rest of the

men stood in solidarity with him. "We will attack now as the sun is setting. To the standing men, he said, "Find what weapons you can in the surrounding houses along the way. Hunting rifles would be best, and shotguns for drones. . . even a shovel if that is all you can find. We must spread out in the woods, not march on the highway. Stick to Hillstavägen and Gävlevägen instead – walk in the woods as much as possible."

As the assembled men and women left the church Stefan motioned to the foreman. He noticed he had an OsKo steel company badge with his name "Kurt" etched in.

"There is one thing I want you to get your people to do. Pick a few that you trust, and tell them to find the power lines from the north. Cut the poles down and sever the lines. Håkan is probably getting electricity from hydro plants further north, near Kungsberg. Cut those lines."

"Where are you going?" Kurt asked him, his dark eyes meeting Stefan's, sizing him up.

"I will be doing the same in the South. All the way to Forsmark..."

A light of recognition came to Kurt's eyes, he smiled and nodded. *"Varsågod!"* he said and clapped his hand on Stefan's shoulder.

After they left the church, Jerker said, "OK, where are *we* going?"

"South and east," Stefan said. "We'll skirt the big lakes south of Sandviken. I need to find the power lines that go to Forsmark. All of them."

As Stefan turned with Jerker to head south, out of the corner of his eye he saw a shadow approaching in the twilight. Lars.

"Hej Hej!" Jerker said excitedly. *"Hej Lars!"*

Lars nodded in greeting and tried to smile, though Stefan could see he was in pain. His right arm was in a sling, covered in crude bandage made from what looked like a torn work shirt.

"I want to come with you," Lars said. A large drop of dark blood fell from his curled fingertips and plopped onto the dirty snow along the side of the road.

Stefan tilted his head to the side, and shook his head to say "no."

"There is something you can do. The men from Hofors are going to Sandviken to try to fight the Putties on the train. Go with them – but don't fight. Find Miko and Ravna, if you can. Give them a message. Tell them to meet me at Gamla Uppsala. I hope to be there in three days, or as soon as I can. There is an old church there - - it should be a safe place. Tell them I'll come as soon as I'm done at Forsmark..."

Lars looked at him with eyes shrouded in pain, his lips compressed. He nodded slowly and said quietly, firmly, "I will do that Stefan. I will tell them."

Stefan put his hand on Lars's good arm, their eyes meeting, "Thank you, Lars, you have been a good friend. Get that shoulder wound treated as soon as you can – we all need you."

Lars nodded and tried to smile. Stefan had one of his premonitions. Something about Lars perhaps not being a good friend. It didn't seem to make sense...but he had no time to ponder it.

"Godspeed to you and Jerker," Lars said and turned away. He began to walk quickly to try to catch up to the men receding into the forest paths towards Sandviken.

Stefan exchanged a glance with Jerker, wondered if he should share his thoughts of Lars' doom out loud, but thought better of it. "Ok. On to Forsmark. Let's make the most of the light while we can."

CHAPTER THIRTY-FOUR

Forsmark's Bruk:

They slept in the woods and hiked from dawn onwards the next day. It wasn't hard to find the Forsmark nuclear plant, Stefan thought as they approached it early that evening. All the power lines led right to it, and the closer you got, the bigger they got. Which was good and bad – good because they knew they were on the right track, bad because as they were crossing from marshy woods far from the main roads and trails, to the center of what was left of the civilized world.

The trees seemed taller and the view of the sky more constrained down here in the south, away from the big sky of Lappland that Stefan was used to. But even so, they could see the plume of exhaust in the sky that marked the Forsmark Plant. Stefan had never seen the plant before. He expected giant cooling towers like images he had seen of nuclear plants in America, but what they saw when they reached a crest in the trail near the plant, was just some tall rectangular buildings. They reminded him of photos he had seen before, but he couldn't place where. They paused and observed the buildings lit with the warm light of the late evening sun.

"Looks like Chernobyl," Jerker said as he paused and observed the building.

Stefan paused for a moment and contemplated that. Yes, he thought, that is what it reminds me of. The tall square buildings, the skinny smokestacks. He gave a nod of agreement to Jerker, and said, "Let's hope it is as easy to blow up!"

Jerker snorted, glanced at him over his bushy red beard, and said, "This isn't crappy Soviet engineering. It will take more than these puny rifles to bring down that plant."

There was a noise behind them. Stefan wheeled, and brought his gun up, expecting a charging *älg* (moose) coming through the brush. But out of the woods stepped three men dressed in green camouflage.

"*Hej, Hej*," their leader said in Swedish.

"*Hej*," Stefan responded. Jerker looked at him. It was a warm evening, but Stefan saw sweat breaking out on Jerker's face that was not due to the weather.

It was a standoff. Stefan didn't know if these were Swedes guarding the plant perimeter, or not. One of them appeared to be carrying what looked like a rocket launcher.

"Out hunting, boys?" their leader said, with a nod to the rifles they were carrying.

Jerker replied, and with a nod to the plant said, "*Ja, vi jagar älg*" Yes. We're here to hunt some elk...

Stefan was alarmed at Jerker's candor, but he could see what he was doing, providing an opening for these men to declare themselves.

"Killing an *älg*?" one of the others said. Stefan noticed that though were not in camouflage clothing they had painted their faces to blend in with the scenery. He wondered how long they had trailed him and Jerker, unseen.

The man continued, with a smile, "That is a difficult thing to do. Bring down a big *älg*." He paused, "You might need a bigger weapon, I'd say, wouldn't you Ulf?" he said, with a slight turn to the one standing closest. A man who by his presence alone seemed to be the leader.

"*Joo*" the man called Ulf answered. "Perhaps not only a better weapon but a hunting guide. Someone who knew the territory – who knows, how should I say it, certain vulnerabilities."

Stefan nodded. "That would be handy. If you are hunting big game it is best to work as a team. Up north my Sami friends often split into two groups to attack. If you are hunting a large and dangerous *älg* (moose) or a *björn* (Swedish brown bear,) that is a better way to go."

"What brings you fellows down here to hunt?" Ulf asked.

"Oh, the usual reasons. Providing for our families," Stefan paused, "Protecting loved ones," Stefan said. He didn't mention that he didn't actually *have* a family.

Ulf looked at him and blinked. "We were on Gotland the past few years."

"How'd things go there?"

"No more game left to kill on that island," the other man said. "We bagged them all."

He said it completely without expression, but that made the comment even more chilling.

"Well," Stefan said, "Let's hope that we can do the same here. From what Jerker and I have seen, there's plenty of big game down here in Southern Sweden. You could get some real trophies, here. But of course, the bigger the game, the more dangerous the hunt."

"We're well acquainted with that," the man said and met Stefan's eyes. He didn't elaborate, didn't mention who or what they had lost on Gotland. He continued to meet Stefan's gaze and said, "Bit late in the day for any hunting. We have a camp nearby. Perhaps you would like to rest with us and we can start in earnest tomorrow."

Stefan noticed Jerker smiling. Food, hot food perhaps, and maybe something to drink.

Hoorah.

They were around a fire in the remains of the old

ironworking village of Forsmark's Bruk, just a turn or two through the woods to the entrance of the nuclear plant. They sat in rusted metal chairs around a firepit by an old cafe, sipping mead. The water from the old mill pond glittered in the waning sunlight. Stefan learned that the names of the other special forces soldiers were "Kalle" and "Patrik." A sign that said *Faster Märtas Kafé* hung crookedly by only a single hinge over a nearby doorway, occasionally clattering in the light evening breeze that was rolling in off the ocean as the sun went down. They weren't all that far from the coast.

"We need to create a diversion," Stefan said, getting back to business. But he had to add, "This mead is good? Where did you get it?"

"We liberated it from a farmhouse a few kilometers from here," Kalle answered. "There were still bees hanging around the falling down bee houses at the edge of the wood. We liberated some honey, too. And some coffee, but that is getting pretty stale."

"Mead just gets better with age!" Patrik added.

"Yeah, as long as it doesn't glow in the dark," Ulf said, bringing the conversation back to the main topic of their assault on the plant. "What sort of diversion?" He looked at Stefan for a response.

"Seems like it's pretty dry down here. Lots of dead leaves and grass from four years of winter, no?" Stefan said. He saw Jerker's eyebrows lift. "We could "smoke them out" so to speak."

The Swedes all looked at him. Stefan realized this might be an American saying, one that they didn't know. He elaborated, "Start a big brush fire. Somewhere they can see it, but hopefully not shoot us."

Ulf weighed this, swirling the mead around in his glass and thinking about it. "Under the power lines. The sun beats down there, and it is dryer than in the rest of the surrounding forest." He pulled a smoldering stick from the fire and used the end of it to draw in the gravel. "While you are doing that, we could enter another way. Try to get to the control room, shut things down."

"We don't want another Chernobyl, though, do we?" Kalle asked. "Seems like there's few of us left as it is. The world outside is filled with radioactive hotspots. We don't want another one, do we?"

"He makes a good point," Stefan said. He motioned to the swinging sign for Märta's cafe, "There is usually an onshore breeze here. It brought the radiation from Chornobyl in the past."

Kalle jumped in, "The same thing happened at Fukushima. Reactor meltdown, onshore breeze, toxic radiation cloud. It could easily wipe out what little is left of Sweden."

Patrik snorted, "How bad could it be? There are still tons of animals living around Chernobyl. It's becoming a wildlife refuge."

"They dumped all kinds of sand and boron from helicopters on that one to slow it down. That wouldn't happen here." Kalle said. "So every living thing for a couple of hundred miles around the reactor would die in about three weeks."

Patrik shrugged.

"Oh, and in Russia all the pilots who dropped the stuff on the core died too." Kalle continued, "And the birds fell from the sky, dead, for miles around."

"OK. Blowing up the reactor is a bad idea," Stefan said, turning back to their leader, Ulf. "What *should* our plan be?"

Ulf said, "I like your idea of a diversion. Maybe you and Jerker start a big grass fire under the powerlines just outside the plant while our team goes in and persuades those running the reactor to shut it down."

"Do we have to shut it down from the Control room?" Stefan asked Kalle.

"Swedish nuclear plants will go into SCRAM mode all by themselves if you can cut all the transmission lines. They are a different design than Chernobyl." Kalle said, sounding once again like a professor on the topic.

"What's this SCRAM thing?" Jerker asked.

"A sudden shutdown of the plant that prevents a meltdown. If they could have done that at Chernobyl it would have saved thousands of lives.."

"We call him *The Professor,*" Patrik said, with a tilt of his cup of mead towards Kalle. "He knows stuff."

"OK – so you guys try to get them to shut the plant down, which probably won't happen, but in the meantime, we set a fire under the main power line to Uppsala," Stefan said, and as he did so realized he had somehow appointed himself leader. But no one seemed to mind... not even the leader of the commandoes, Ulf.

"How could we get a fire big enough to make them worried?" Jerker asked.

"We've been watching the plant for a while. They've slacked off on maintenance and the grass is tall and dry near the plant. Looks like they haven't mowed it in 4 years..." Ulf answered. "Hopefully you won't set all of Southern Sweden on fire with it! Spring can is often a season for wildfires in Sweden, with all the dead brush from winter still around."

Stefan sipped his mead and watched the fire begin to die out. The long march and strong mead soon had his eyes feeling heavy. "Let's hit the sack," he said, "I think we have a good plan for tomorrow, and we can use some rest..."

CHAPTER THIRTY-FIVE

In the morning, they began the assault on Forsmark. They split into two teams, with Stefan and Jerker taking an old, overgrown, path that led to the high-tension wires coming from the plant. It branched off from the road to Forsmark just past a crane company called *Svenska Kran.* The path was an old country lane connecting the old town of Forsmark to the sea, but it had not been used for local traffic before the apocalypse, and not since. Tall pines and even maple trees provided a canopy over the old road.

They paused in the road and looked in at the sprawling Svenska Kran company yard. There were several partially assembled cranes towering over the workyard, one of which had apparently been undermined by years of snow and now leaned dangerously into the tall trees on the left side of a long steel Quonset hut where other equipment poked out. There was one shiny new metal mini crane parked out of the weather, the top of which was covered in dust. It piqued Stefan's interest, because it said, *"Maeda 305, Lithium-ion"* on the side.

"Let's take a look here for a moment..." Stefan said and headed through the muddy ground into the rough opening in the side of the steel shed. He knew that they should be heading to the power lines to start a fire, but he had one of his feelings again – like he had been here before, perhaps in a dream.

He arrived first in the shed and walked around the machine. It was a mini-crane mounted on rubber tracks. "Wow, this is cool."

Jerker nodded – looking at him a bit oddly, "Shouldn't we be going? The others are waiting for the sign of a fire from us to get started..."

"We could pull down a whole high-tension line with this! Too bad there's no power to it!"

Jerker smiled at him and then flicked a switch on the side of the building near where he had stepped in. Powerful overhead lights sprang to life – and they illuminated the dusty machine.

"How did you – "

"We're only half a mile from a Zillion Volt power plant. It figures there would be electricity here..."

By the bright klieg lights, Stefan noticed that the tracked crane was connected to the power mains by a thick cable, like a Tesla charging cord.

"Let's give this a try!" Stefan said. He hopped on the seat and found the "on" switch. A small display lit up and showed that the battery was fully charged. A readout in English said that there were four hours of battery capacity.

The machine whirred to life, and Jerker pumped his fist and said *"Jaaa!"*

Stefan worked the controls, and the crane darted forward, slamming the crane arm into the side of the big shed and causing Jerker to jump away quickly.

"Plenty of power! Let's go knock down some high-tension wires!" Stefan said – and he could hear the excitement in his voice. Amazing what a hot meal, a night of rest, and finding this machine had done to lift his spirits.

They drove the battery-powered crane along an existing right of way through the forest – and it wasn't long before the high-tension lines came into view. The distance covered, according to the odometer on the dashboard, was 1.83 kilometers, just a little over a mile. When they came out into the great cleared right of way and saw the task before them, Stefan exchanged glances with Jerker, who had walked alongside the crane as they slowly made their way through the forest.

"Oh skit!" Lars said

Which was what Stefan was thinking, but didn't say out loud. Crap! How in the world did they think they were going to knock down or set fire to whatever zillion volts of power were running overhead? The towers looked to be at least 100 feet high. They stood like tin men, with two tall skinny legs ending in what looked like a pair of shoulders, with short arms hanging down and hands clasping giant electrical cables on either side and with a third set of cables running through the middle.

What the hell had they gotten themselves into? Stefan drove out under the first of the towering gantries and turned off the crane.

"We have to pull these down, without having them fall on us and electrocute us," he said, to Jerker who stood looking almost straight up into the sky, with his eyes shielded from the brilliant spring sunshine.

"Ja. And how do you propose we do that?"

"I'll have to extend the boom and hook on at the very base. Then back up and away, and we will hope that when it falls it falls south, towards where we came out of the woods."

"And hope that it doesn't electrify the crane and blow us up?"

"Blow me up," Stefan said. "You stand well away."

"And if it doesn't work? If it electrocutes you?"

Stefan met Jerker's gaze. "As far as I'm concerned, it's a miracle that I'm still around. If we don't stop Håkan we'll all be gone soon enough."

Jerker nodded. "Might as well go out fighting. If it's your death day, that is your fate."

It was Stefan's personal observation that many Swedes had this same fatalistic outlook on life. Some claimed it was a vestige of old Viking religion – the idea that your birth and death are ordained by the gods...immutable, pre-ordained, written in stone, like runes on granite monolith.

"Okay, here goes nothing." He turned the crane back on, jiggled with the controls to extend the boom towards the tower, and then unwound the cable to the hook and Jerker walked to the base of the tall leg closest to the woods. Jerker connected it firmly to the metal gridwork of the leg. Stefan began backing up, spooling out as much of the crane cable as possible until he came to the end of the spool on the crane. With the crane boom fully extended, and the crane cable fully extended, he was as far from the tower as possible. "Here goes!" he shouted to Jerker.

He pulled back on the controls, and at first, nothing happened. Then the leg bent a little, and he thought, "Hey, this might actually work." Then the skids on the crane began to slide in the loose gravel. Jerker looked at him and raised his eyebrows.

Stefan held up a finger to say, "Wait."

He extended the outriggers, big metal feet that would stabilize the crane if he were using it normally. They dug into the rocky ground and lifted the whole crane slightly up in the air. He pulled back on the winch control again. The gantry leg bent, and bent, and then finally snapped out of its base, and with a creaking sound that sounded like a rusty hinge, the whole structure began to sway, then it fell, slowly, towards the ground.

When it hit, there was at first just a bright flash, like a spark. Then, a deafening "Boom!" like thunder and then more booms, and waves of heat. Stefan jumped from his seat and ran away as there were more explosions – more of the cables hitting the ground, shorting out, and flipping around like snakes spitting venom. Bright sparks, more "booms" and fire ensued.

This also triggered some small brush fires, one of which got into a pile of cut branches and logs along the edge of the woods, and soon a plume of smoke began to rise into the bright blue sky.

Stefan and Jerker looked on, a bit awestruck.

"It's good that there is a fire sending up smoke. That was to be the signal for Ulf to attack the command center," Stefan said.

"That went better than I thought it would!" Jerker said when the last of the hissing snakes had settled to the ground. Let's do another!

"Could still be some stray electricity – be careful to use a dry branch to free the hook," Stefan said, and Jerker smiled and gave him a thumbs up.

Stefan and Jerker quickly followed up the first tower knockdown with two more. In the distance, they could hear sirens wailing. Time was surely running out before some sort of military response would arrive, Stefan thought.

There only remained one final tower, of a different design than the first. It was much more substantial, of a four-leg design. They feverishly gathered brush from the edges of the woods and piled it up under the tower legs, and with burning brands from the other pile soon had a blaze going directly underneath it. The legs glowed red from the heat as they piled on more and more dry wood and the flames grew higher and higher. But to no avail.

"We'll have to try to pull this one down too!" Stefan shouted over the roar of the flames. I'll have to park in the trees and hope that they shield me from the falling cables."

Jerker raised his eyebrows at this suggestion. Stefan could tell that he thought it was a bad option – perhaps suicidal. But he took the cable and lifted it as high as he could and circled the fire while Stefan backed the crane into the tree line as far as he could.

When he was almost undercover, he spotted something else in the sky. A drone! Shit!

If it had been armed, they were done for, but it wheeled and turned over the burning carnage of the Forsmark lines, apparently streaming video back to headquarters (which Stefan could only guess at. Was it to the Forsmark command center, or Uppsala?)

Fully backed into the trees, he shouted to Jerker to clear out. He pushed the levers to pull the tower, and as before began to slide. He put out the outriggers, and all that happened was the crane began to bog down. Oh no. Was he out of batteries, or was this tower just too strong? He looked at the battery readout – it was getting low. He was about out of time in more ways than one.

He saw Jerker staring at him. What to do? What to do?

He jumped out of the seat and grabbed a y-shaped branch from the forest floor. He lifted the outriggers and jammed the branch onto the controls for the boom winch. The crane began sliding and crunching through the loose sandy gravel towards the gantry tower, being guided by the cable and hook as it retracted into the giant steel drum of cable.

Stefan climbed out of his seat and motioned to Jerker to run. Behind them the crane began picking up speed, spooling in the heavy steel cable and sliding quicker and quicker towards the gantry. Stefan glanced over his shoulder and saw the crane climb the burning pile and slam into the red glowing frame of the tower. For a moment, and with despair, he thought it was all for naught. Then there was a snapping sound, and the legs gave way.

Unlike the other towers, this one did not fall slowly to earth. It came down like a rocket falling from the sky. Almost like the collapsing towers on 9/11 in New York. It hit the ground and all 6 high voltage electrical circuits exploded at once, blowing flaming out timbers, and exploding the burning remains of the crane up into the air as if it had been hit with an anti-tank missile. There was a deafening roar and a shock wave that bowled them over onto the ground and covered them with a tidal wave of flying debris: wood, steel, rock, and dirt.

They were buried under remains of pine trees and Stefan felt like he was either dying or dead. He thought he heard a moaning cry from Jerker, also buried alive, but possibly dying under the debris and shrapnel from what they had done. Stefan was completely buried and had to turn his head to see a wedge of the blue sky filled with smoke to his left, in the direction of the power line.

Just then there was a thrumming sound. Another drone. This one was much bigger, louder, and, Stefan was sure, armed to the teeth.

Now there was machine-gun fire and the whoosh of missiles flying all around them. The drone circled, firing off more weapons, some far to the right, to the left, and ahead of them. There was the sound of dozens of missile strikes, bullets pinging off fallen tower metal, and the disconcerting thrumming of the drone's engines as it circled, hunting them from above. Pretty soon the forest and the open ground around the fallen power lines were burning all around them. But then the drone was gone, either satisfied or frustrated with its work for the day, Stefan didn't know which.

Great, Stefan thought, I've survived being electrocuted,

shot, blown up with a missile, and buried alive by mounds of
earth and fallen timbers. Now I will slowly burn to death

Nearby, in the Dannemora Forest

Björn trotted through the woods with Donkey. Usually, he kept his nose to the ground, sometimes he sat and lifted his nose in the air. He and Donkey had traveled for two days together. Each night, weary from their travels, they had stopped in an old barn. In the morning they foraged for food. Master's scent was very faint, but still clear to Bjorn's highly sensitive nose.

Björn, anxious to leave barked at Donkey. *"Donkey, finish your frukost! Time to go!"*

Donkey ignored him, his face deep in a rather moldy feed bag. Mice and squirrels had eaten most of the feed. Donkey didn't care. It was breakfast time and he *was* going to eat.

Björn watched Donkey move on to the water trough and take deep draughts of water, which dripped down his neck and glistened in the early morning sunshine.

Björn barked again, more insistently. *"Donkey! Chug a lug! Time to go!"*

Björn took Donkey's tattered lead in his mouth and tugged at it. Reluctantly, slowly, Donkey followed along.

A couple of hours later Björn and Donkey were traipsing through the forest when he stopped. There was a loud boom.

"Uh Oh! Thunder-Boomers!" Björn thought and ducked low. There was an even louder series of booms and noises, shrieking sounds, whistling noises, and the crackle of flames. Björn ducked into a cave-like dark opening in the ground at the roots of a big tree and cowered there.

Donkey stood impassively staring at him.

"Duck Donkey! Thunder-Boomers! Duck down!"

Donkey ignored him. He found some hay-corns on the ground to nibble.

"Donkey, I have the shibbers because it is very scary. Big boomers! Stop Eating! Duck!"

Donkey munched on. He didn't usually eat at this time, but these were some pretty tasty, sun-browned hay-corns.

"Donkey, it is not time for a treat!"

There were more rumbles and whooshing noises close by, but Donkey was impervious. After a few minutes, smoke drifted over them. From his hidey-hole in the tree roots, Björn lifted his nose. *"Cookout with Fadder! Oh Boy! Fadder is having a cookout! I can smell him!"*

Björn hopped out of his hole, snagged the limp rope lead, and began pulling Donkey along with him. In a few minutes, they came to a clearing, and the scent was much clearer.

"Fadder, I can smell you! It's your Good Boy, Björn! Happy Happy! Time for a cookout and a Burger Treat!"

But father was nowhere to be seen. Here and there were smoking piles of brush, but Father's scent was strong, very strong. He must be close. Björn put his nose to the ground and began a low-circling run.

Then he found him. He was under the sticks and dirt. His eyes were closed and he was very dirty, but it was Father.

"FADDER!! I HAVE FOUND YOU!!"

"WAKE UP FADDER! STOP SLEEPING! TIME FOR THE COOKOUT! YOUR GOOD BOY BJÖRN IS HERE!!!"

Björn got worried. Father looked hurted. He kissed him, and a lick to clean his face. His eyes were still closed – he was very still. Björn put his nose near Father's face. He didn't smell right. He wasn't breathing right. Now Björn began to panic. Father is buried. Father is dying.

"I MUST SAVE FADDER. HE IS BEING BURIED! I MUST DIG!"

He looked at Donkey standing nearby, impassively watching. He barked at him frantically, *"HELP DONKEY! HELP! FATHER IS DYING! WE MUST DIG HIM OUT!"*

Donkey did nothing, so Björn began digging as quickly as he could. It hurt his feet, for there were hot bits of wood embers and sharp bits of metal. *"OUCH OUCH! DIG DIG DIG!"*

Father's eyes were still closed, as even more of him became uncovered. Using his mouth Björn tossed aside chunks of wood, rocks, and hot sharp shards of metal. There was blood on Father. Björn kept digging, panicking more to see the blood where Father was gouged and bits of metal and wood stuck right into his skin.

OH NO, OH NO, FATHER IS HURTED. FATHER IS BLEEDY AND SLEEPY, LIKE MY FRIEND ČALMMO!

Björn made crying noises, he tried to tug on Father's clothing. He barked, *"FADDER, WAKE UP! FADDER WAKE UP!! FADDER WAKE UP!!!*

Now Donkey was beside him with his rope lead dangling down. Björn realized he was whimpering, crying. Father was bleedy and sleepy, just like Čalmmo, who never woke up. Čalmmo who floated away at the lake. He barked again.

Father's eyelids fluttered and closed again.

"FADDER! WAKE UP!" Björn barked at him again.

Björn felt a hand at his neck, grabbing at his fur, pulling him close. He licked Father's face again and saw a faint smile.

Björn barked again, this time with happiness, *"FADDER! YOU ARE BLEEDY BUT NOT SLEEPY! YAY!"*

He felt his head being pulled downwards, as Father used Björn's collar to raise himself up. Father's eyes opened fully, and he whispered in Björn's ear, weakly, but clearly, "Good boy, Björn. Good Boy."

At the UPPMAX Supercomputer Center, Uppsala

Håkan knew what was happening at the scene as the dog Björn dug in the piles of rubble to uncover Stefan Andersson. Even though Bjorn had lost his collar, she had a chip in Donkey which provided data in real time. She cursed under her breath. What did he think he was accomplishing knocking down a couple of electrical towers? Yes, it had caused some momentary blackouts at the steel plant at Sandviken, but that was about it, her electrical grid had quickly routed power from wind and hydro stations to make up for the loss.

Idiot man and his idiot dog! What a pain in the ass he was! Maybe he was dead. That would be handy, maybe just the thing to nip his half-assed rebellion in the bud.

She had an audio feed but not visual, but she could imagine what was taking place from the digging sounds the dog was making and then Stefan appearing from the rubble as he was uncovered and saved.

In a cackling voice, Håkan repeated a line she had heard from an old movie the humans liked to watch, *"I'll get you, my pretty, and your little dog, too!"*

Dr. Bob and Hans Von Linné looked at her in puzzlement. "Did you get him?" Dr. Bob asked.

"No. But I think his friend Jerker is toast. Literally! Hah! Hah!"

"Seems hard to stop this Stefan character," Hans said. "Nothing seems to slow him down..."

"You are right. He's hard to slow down..." Håkan replied. That got her thinking...What might slow him down?... Hmmm. She had an idea...

Stefan was pulled free of the burning rubble, and with Björn's help, he frantically sought to find Jerker. They tried to navigate the dangerous piles of twisted steel, electrical cables, blown-down trees and branches, and piles of old cut trees and brush from the powerline right of way. The donkey was upset, braying, the sound was almost like that of a person crying out, with none of the Hee Haw of yore, and it made Stefan mad. "Shut up Donkey! I can't hear!"

But Donkey brayed on – it was frightened or hurt from walking on the same blasted landscape as Stefan and Björn.

Stefan thought he had heard Jerker cry out while still buried and he tried to locate the direction – it would be somewhere closer to the tree line. Once he stepped on a sharp bit of tangled steel and it cut him right through his boot, like stepping on a nail. Twice he cried out when he pulled a branch free and it was glowing hot underneath and burned his hands.

Then he spotted Jerker's bright red plaid shirt and a hand waving above the fallen wood and steel.

"Björn! Donkey! Help dig," Stefan was surprised to see them both hop to it and lend a hand – Donkey pawing at the sticks and lifting some out of the way with his mouth. It was amazing! How did he know to do that?

Soon they uncovered Jerker's shirt, then upper torso, and head. He was smiling at Stefan, his face dirty and bloodied. To Stefan, he was silently mouthing the words, *"Tack! Tack så myket!"* – (Thanks, Thanks so much!)

They got him up. Björn was barking! Donkey was braying for joy. Stefan clapped him hard on the shoulder and went to pull him close – to hug him. He felt overjoyed to see him alive.

Then something terrible happened. Jerker's head fell off backward! Shocked and horrified, Stefan screamed *"NOOOOOO!"*

And woke up.

He sat up. Where was he? What time was it? What day was it?

Through cracks in the siding of a barn where they all slept, he could see that the sun was already sneaking up. It was probably about four in the morning, but if this was May the weird Nordic sun should be rising about now – skidding sideways somewhere to the southeast over the Stockholm archipelago.

Stefan turned and noticed Björn was staring at him. His eyes were moist and sad as if he could sense Stefan's inner anguish, "It's OK Björn. Just a bad dream." He laid back down, and Björn leaned into him and put his head on his chest. Jerker's dead, goddammit, he thought. Jerker's dead and it's my fault.

He tried to sleep, again, but sleep wouldn't come. Not so for Björn, who was soon twitching and making deep guttural noises – his bandaged paws flapped back and forth as if running.

Stefan thought of this as "The Anxiety Hour" – he would wake up and ruminate on problems from the day before, or the day ahead. Or the month before, the year before, the decade before, the life before, the world before. Of his previous incarnation when the world was whole, or at least seemed so.

Tonight's movie rerun was one he had revisited often. His so-called honeymoon. There had been the wedding event, which he enjoyed though it was beastly hot that August evening. There had been their first awkward attempts at lovemaking. Real lovemaking, not the fondling sessions of their courtship days. It had not gone well.

Afterward, as they lay still beside each other, he realized that she was crying. And not due to his ineptitude in the sack... it was because of what he had done too well. He had convinced her that this marriage was something that was "meant to be."

"Way to go, Ace."

Stefan lay still for a while longer, playing it over again in his mind. Donkey lay on a bed of straw nearby, also twitching in his sleep.

Stefan was half awake, half dreaming as he returned to his ruminations...

It was the morning of the day after the wedding. He had woken early, gone for a walk, and again the thought had returned. It hit him like an anvil falling from the sky. This marriage was not meant to be. That's why she had cried. He had tricked her into it.

She hadn't wanted this marriage. He had argued, cajoled, and even wept to convince her that it was meant to be. His many letters, his many tears, his many arguments. But it was not something she wanted. It was his idea, his goal, his desire. Both kinds of *desire* – as in "a goal" and as in "lust."

He had convinced her. He had "won" her.

It was like a stake through his heart. His evil, black, deceitful, villainous heart.

He remembered again that morning he had walked through a forest trail and tried to reason his way out of it. Maybe all the stress and preparations were making both of them out of sorts and emotional. Perhaps it was all nerves and some weird form of "buyer's remorse" – where you get what you are after and then have sudden strong feelings of it being all wrong, somehow?

He carried on as if nothing was wrong when he returned

to the cabin. He made her buckwheat pancakes, sausage, and eggs for breakfast. (The first of many "guilt offerings" which he hoped might expiate his sin.) He put on a happy face, laughed, and joked with her. It was going to be all right. Things would work out. She would be happy. You'll see.

They couldn't stay long at the cabin, so after breakfast, they packed up their bags and drove back home. It was a beautiful sunny day. What could possibly go wrong? They chatted and joked on the road back. Things were going to be fine.

That is what he thought until got home and went to climb in the truck for their trip back to school and got electrocuted.

He had gone out to put something in the front of their van. He passed by his old family dog Nikko, a black lab who looked at him questioningly – as in "Are you leaving again?"

Memory now failed him as to why it was he went to the passenger door. Up on the roof of the van, his dad was using an electric drill to mount a bracket for the roof rack. The electrical cord was draped over the side of the van. But his dad hadn't noticed that Nikko had been at it again. He was constantly chewing things up, and this time he had chewed through the insulation on the electrical cord.

Stefan had told Nikko not to do this, and just a couple of days earlier, frantically trying to get things done for the trip, he had spotted Nikko chewing on this cord again. He had completely lost his temper and slapped Nikko on the side of the head as hard as he possibly could (to teach him a lesson!) Nikko had whelped in pain, a single wild yelp of hurt. With his tail lowered he had slunk away from him and hidden under the van– something he had never done in all the years Stefan had known him. Nikko peered out from under the van, one eye swelling almost shut from the bruising of the slap.

"Way to go, Ace."

There was perhaps then, some cosmic justice in what happened when Stefan reached out to the passenger door and clasped the handle. He was in bare feet, wearing a pair of shorts, but no sandals, socks, or shoes. His hand closed on the door handle, and a jolt went through him, and he was frozen there. He tried to call out to his father, who was still leaning against the roof of the van. He couldn't talk. He might have made some sort of gurgling sound – but he was paralyzed, immobile.

Some time passed. Afterward, he wouldn't know how long it was. A few seconds? A minute? Somehow his father noticed that he was being shocked jumped at him, and shoved him hard away from the van. Stefan had fallen to the ground – dazed and shaken.

It was a sign. A punishment – for beating an innocent dog. *Instant Karma.* For coercing a beautiful and innocent young woman who didn't love him to marry him, against her protests, and against her better judgment.

It was a sign – from the heavens, or from the universe. *"Does this SHOCK you enough to get your attention?"* From then on Stefan would look back on that moment as the time his marriage ended. It was the cancer diagnosis for a terminally ill patient – his marriage. From then on their marriage was on life-support, they were *The Walking Dead.* Pick your metaphor.

It was like the recurring dreams he now had about his father in the ten years since he had died. His father would be with them, at a party, a family gathering, or doing an activity. Stefan would think he was watching his dad and think, that's weird, I thought he was dead. But the more he watched him, the more he understood that although he was walking around and breathing, his brain was dead. They had kept him alive somehow, but he wasn't really there. The Norse myths had a version of that – they called them *aptrganga* literally, "again walkers." Dead, but up and walking around.

His marriage, for the three years it lasted, was like that. It got Shocked to Death on day one, and from then on it was The Walking Dead. He tried all his tricks to bring it back to life, but it was dead. There was no real spark of life in it anymore.

She knew. "She who is not to be named" a.k.a. Celeste, his ex-wife knew. She noticed that something had changed in him, but he would never admit it to her out loud.

It had been on a weekend retreat at a cabin by a river in the Allegheny forest that she confronted him about it.

"You've changed," she had said. "The way you feel about me has changed."

"That's not true. I don't know what you are talking about."

She stared at him. She repeated her statement, "You've changed. You won't admit it, but you've changed."

He denied it again and again a few days later. Wasn't it St. Peter in the Bible? He seemed to remember that from a Sunday school class. The one who denied he knew Jesus three times?

He could make this denial with conviction because she had lumped two things together – she had asked if he had changed (which was true) and stated that his feelings for her had ended (which was false.)

He had changed. He was full of guilt and remorse. But his feelings for her had not changed, though soon they became so distant that all he had left of their relationship was the guilt. In a couple of years, it unraveled completely, and that is all he was left with –guilt and regret.

"Way to go, Ace."

Stefan drifted back to sleep until a shaft of sunlight roused him again. He could feel the weight of the dreams and thoughts that had troubled his sleep, but he tried to get moving and shrug them off. He got up and went to scrounge for something for himself and the animals to eat in the adjoining farmhouse. There was mouse-eaten flour, sugar speckled with rodent droppings, burst cans of tomato sauce and vegetables, but to his surprise, the bright morning daylight revealed a tin with perhaps half a pound of coffee.

"Buddha Provide!" he said to Björn, who had followed him to the house and was looking in with hopeful anticipation. Björn grinned, which was probably just some reflex action, but they seemed to share the same feeling as Stefan rummaged until he had found enough unspoiled food for himself, Björn, and Donkey.

CHAPTER THIRTY-NINE

Fortified with a decent breakfast, they resumed their journey to Uppsala. Stefan had sore feet, and so did Björn, so they took turns riding on Donkey, whom he still hadn't gotten around to naming. When it was Bjorn's turn to ride, he piled up some blankets from the farmhouse where they had stayed the night before to make a "dog bed" and then hoisted Bjorn up onto this pillow. They walked slowly but steadily onward.

By noon, which would have also been lunchtime in a civilized world, they made it as far as Österbybruk – yet another ironworking commune from the 1800s. This one was close to the iron mines of Dannemora, and so it was served by the railway, which Stefan guessed must have once connected other ironworks to the mines.

The town had been completely abandoned. There was rubbish on the streets – no sign that any vehicles had come this way since the pandemic had shut everything down. He thought of rummaging for food, but after last night's nightmares, didn't think he could stomach happening on any stiffs. There was a tilted-over baby carriage on Järnvagsgatan near the middle of town, and even from yards away, it smelled bad. Björn inclined his head that way, sniffing, and Stefan said, "Björn, No!"

Thankfully, they were soon to leave town and cross over the old mine train line. To Stefan's surprise, what looked like fresh oil glittered on the center of the railway ties, turning the grass that had taken over most of the roadbed brown. That was odd, why would a train come here, now? He stood there staring at it and saw Donkey's ears twitch, and then go vertical. Björn looked at him nervously.

"Come, into the woods," Stefan said, pulling the reluctant

Donkey with him just out of view in a stand of white birch trees.

An old steam engine wheezed into view, not even bothering to blow its whistle as it steamed slowly through town, heading for – Where?

Behind the Lok were a few dilapidated old red SJ-vagnar – old Swedish railways coaches. As they approached, Stefan noticed they were full of people. Must be a train of workers going somewhere? To the Dannemora mine? Why work that when you had the giant modern mines in Norrland going? It seemed nuts.

Donkey must have been partly visible because the people on the train turned their heads… then a chill went through Stefan like a cold wind from the north. The whole first coach was full of Bianca's and Rackham's, with their odd glassy-eyed stares. His heart started to race. Now he knew - - they must be heading north to join the fight at Sandviken.

"Oh Christ," he muttered out loud. This was not good at all.

But if he thought that was bad, things were about to get worse. Much worse. For in the next coach, he saw her, staring at him through the birch leaves. *"She who is not to be named."*

No. It couldn't be. No. No. No…

Completely forgetting himself, he stepped out from the birch trees and stared. The second coach of the small train was not full of Putties, it was "normal people" – like what Stefan would have seen in a train slowly trundling along on the weedy old Inlandsbanan track up north. Pensioners, students, hikers, housewives, and right in the middle of the coach, his ex-wife, Celeste, rising in her seat and staring at him, sliding down the window to see him better, calling his name.

"Stefan! Stefan!" she called out to him, and her slender wrist and pale white hand stretched out the window towards him and called his name again.

For a moment, he stood transfixed. Then he started running through the tall grass beside the train - along the old right of way. Björn got excited and raced along with him, right by his side, barking with excitement. Donkey trotted along too, shaking his head and braying, confused, not understanding what this diversion from the road meant, and frightened of the train.

In just a few steps, for just an instant, he caught up to the coach and reached out his hand to her. Their fingertips touched, and just for a moment, he saw the rings on her finger, their wedding ring, and the cheap engagement ring that was all he could afford when they married. His eyes met hers, and he heard her voice, "Stefan." That same voice, with the same velvety tones that even on the telephone hinted at sensuality.

"I've missed you!" Their eyes met. She called out again, "Save me!"

But the train was gaining speed, pulling away, and just as quickly as it had arrived, it pulled away out of sight, Celeste's hand still outstretched towards him, towards freedom, her wedding ring, the one he had spent his meager life savings on, glinting in the sun.

...

At the Ångström Center, the morning shift in Håkan's lair watched the events unfold on the big screen that covered one wall of her room.

"Nice touch with the ring," Dr. Bob said, shaking his head and laughing. "Where'd you cook that one up at?"

"My usual sources. Old wedding photos, and this," Håkan nodded to the screen, and a scanned image appeared to one side, blown up to several feet across. The logo for a well-known jewelry chain in mid-America appeared, along with the laughably small dollar amount, the date twenty years in the past.

"But it's fake, no?"

"Right. A complete fake. Nano-printed, just like the rest of her." Håkan said and laughed also.

"Fooled him, though," Dr. Bob said.

"Doesn't take much..." Håkan replied and turned away from the screen, which now that the train had departed, had reverted to a digital map of the area, with a red dot with the words "Stefan Andersson" underneath it – on the move again on Rt. 290 towards Uppsala, and her.

After the train departed, Stefan stood for a moment watching the end of the passenger coach recede into the tall pines, maples, and birches of the track to Dannemora and north. He shook his head, mystified, and Björn stared at him as if to ask, "What next?"

He climbed over the track and began walking along the road again. To his left was a sign that said, *"Framme i Österbybruk"* – "Arrive in Österbybruk" - to greet those coming on the main road from Uppsala. But the paint was faded, like the town itself, tattered and falling down from four years of neglect and bad weather.

Björn trotted along by him happily, smiling. Chasing the train had cheered him up. Donkey plodded along also, still confused and bothered by what had just happened.

Stefan shook his head, "Doesn't make any sense," he said out loud to Björn, who looked up and nuzzled his hand, sniffing it for the scent of the woman he had just touched.

"She must be dead. That can't have been her."

He paused, and stood in the road, waiting for Donkey to catch up. "If she wasn't dead, how could she possibly have gotten here? Right at the exact instant, we crossed the railway track? How?"

Donkey stood beside him, reaching over to nibble on some low-hanging maple tree branches with fresh spring leaves;

That was when he realized it. Donkey.

As Donkey munched on the leaves, the only one of them able to eat lunch, Stefan stroked the fur of his neck until he found the small bump. He parted the fur and could see the small incision. It wasn't a camera like the one on Björn's collar, it was a chip. A tracking chip. Just like Miko had on her.

Håkan knew exactly where he was and when he would be arriving in Uppsala. The gig was up.

He would have to get rid of the chip, and his thoughts returned to his previous attempt with the chip on Miko. And, even though he didn't wish it, the image of her was on his bed that first night. Of the swell of her hips, of her glazed porcelain skin. And now he had a conflicting image, of Celeste leaning forward, calling out his name, her dark eyes and brown curls, that simmering smirk of sensuality that was pure Celeste. Or impure Celeste, as the case may be.

The expression *WTF* came to mind. Where had she come from? How had Håkan brought her here, now? What had happened to her after the fire?

His thoughts returned to the night of the fire, ten years

ago. It had been an unusually warm early spring. They were living on the second floor of the once-grand old Victorian house he had purchased and begun restoring. With the warm weather, everyone had been outside. Stefan had been laying a new brick sidewalk to the house, and he had spotted the neighborhood urchins – two lads about 8 years old, come out of the basement which at the moment was open to the weather while construction was going on. He had caught them before, stealing nails and boards, which he knew were what they were using to build a slipshod "clubhouse" on the hill behind their house, which was just two doors up from his place.

They had looked guilty, but he didn't see them carrying any contraband building supplies this time, what he did note was one of them was smoking a cigarette. Christ, the kid couldn't be more than ten years old, and already smoking! He made a mental note to move the task of securing the basement entry door higher up on his list – but what he should have done was to stop working on his project and go see what they had done. He was too busy to be bothered – the weather was too nice, he was too close to finishing, and the sun had already dipped over the horizon, and it seemed the weather was changing, the wind picking up from the North.

He and Celeste had gone to bed, both exhausted from the long day spent working outdoors. Stefan awoke at 4 am to a pounding on the door, and a weird orange glow out the windows. Also, the room seemed hot, stuffy, and...smoky. He leaned out of bed, pushed aside the drapes, and saw tongues of flame leaping up from below. There were crackling sounds, popping sounds, and a low roar building in intensity.

"Get out! Is anyone here? Get out!" Someone was banging on the door!

Then the person who was shouting kicked the door in. Not the door to their second-floor apartment, their bedroom door.

The fireman rushed in, dressed in full gear, with a mask dangling to one side of his face. "Your house is on fire. You have to get out now!"

Celeste stood transfixed, and Stefan yelled at her.

"Grab your clothes, Run!"

She either was in shock or still asleep, her hair tousled and her eyes frantic. Stefan grabbed her arm, looked her in the eyes, and shouted, "Your robe! Your shoes, Now! Run!"

Finally, she got it, wrapped herself in a robe, and ran out the door. The smoke and heat were intense in the hallway. They headed out the entry door and onto the stairs.

There was a cacophony of sounds, fire sirens, men shouting, men running up past them dragging a hose heavy hose, shouting, "Water! Water! *Goddamnit! Water!*" And then the fire hose buckled and twisted like a snake, and it lifted the two firefighters wrestling the hose off their feet and into the air, and an enormous blast of water came shooting out and into their apartment - dousing the flames that were breaking through the living room floor and which had already engulfed the kitchen.

Celeste, who was wrapped in both a robe and a blanket from their bedroom, ran ahead of him down the stairs and out. Stefan found his coat on a hook by the door, pulled it on, and began helping the firemen. He could see they were struggling to pull the hose through the entry and into the living room so he grabbed the hose and strained to pull it from below. This gave them more slack and they were able to first douse the living room flames and then advance towards the kitchen. From below Stefan could hear sounds of windows breaking, doors being kicked in, boots on the floor of running men, and shouts of men fighting the fire below. There was a huge crash as part of the first floor must have given way. Clouds of steam flying dust and black soot filled the air.

Someone grabbed him by the collar – he was older and wore a placard that said "Engine 12, Chief" on the front of his helmet, he shouted in Stefan's face, "Is there anyone else in this house? You, your girlfriend, kids, pets? Anyone else?!"

"No!" Stefan shouted back at him.

"GET OUT OF HERE! That's an order!"

Stefan hesitated.

"OUT!"

With wet shoes and his heavy wool Mackinac coat soaked with water, Stefan descended the stairs. But he couldn't help still joining in the fray from the sidewalk, pulling hoses, shouting to the firefighters on ladders outside the house when flames renewed in the basement or first-floor windows. The local TV news truck arrived, and his picture pulling a hose wearing his Mackinac coat, pajama pants, and sneakers would be seen in the local newspaper and online later that day.

But not Celeste. She was gone, never to return. The stress of the event, the pleas of her parents to leave him, and... another man somehow in the picture? *Going, going, Gone.*

Until now... that is. She had returned, somehow. Stefan figured she was dead. Yet Håkan had managed to bring her back. How?

Björn, bored with this pause in the action, nuzzled his hand to be petted. Donkey also made an odd sound, almost like the neighing of a horse. They were bored and wanted to move on.

"OK – let's go," he said to them both. But first I have to get the chip out of Donkey."

It was a short walk back up the hill to the town. There was a ransacked ICA store there, with all the food and useful materials stolen from the shelves a long time ago. But there were a few things left in the pharmacy aisle, and Stefan found some numbing salve for pain relief. He squirted some on the thin skin above the donkey's chip and then used a pair of sharp cuticle scissors to poke it out. Donkey seemed to hardly notice. Then they were on the way.

But as he walked, the problem of Celeste returned to his mind. How did she get here? Her face leaning towards him was just as he remembered it. She looked good. In fact, she looked incredibly good, stunningly good – *just as he remembered her...*

But years had passed. She had to have aged, put on weight, and gotten saggy eyes, right? She couldn't still look like a pinup girl from a fashion magazine, Right? A look in the mirror told him that the lines on his face had deepened – if from nothing else but being holed up in his cave-like home for nearly 4 years.

It was almost creepy...she was exactly as he remembered her. She hadn't changed a bit. It was too creepy.

At The Forsmark Nuclear Power Plant

Ulf and Kalle retreated from the reactor control room, working backward out of the office building through hallways and downstairs until they finally debouched onto the main street. It was completely empty – no troops, tanks, armored personnel carriers. Also, no cars or buses, people. But, oddly, there were a few parked cars and lights on in one other building just to their right. There was a dark blue Volvo station wagon, and a silver Peugeot parked in the lot that he had not noticed when they entered the control building an hour before to begin their "assault on Forsmark."

The sky was bright blue, but empty, as always. Ulf hadn't seen a plane overhead for years. But one thing was different, somewhere in the distance he thought he heard the sound of a helicopter. Kalle heard it too, and they glanced at each other – and Ulf knew they had the same thought, namely, that perhaps they should seek cover. They leaned back under the shelter of an overhanging porch roof and pressed back against the entry door. But it faded to the east – and that gave him both hope and fear. Hope that perhaps Stefan had succeeded in his mission to bring down the power lines, fear that a helicopter gunship might be attacking him at this moment. There were rumbles of sound, like distant thunder. He and Kalle exchanged another glance. They had been in Afghanistan together, and on Gotland for four years. They also knew that on a clear blue day, particularly in Sweden, there wouldn't be blue sky lightning. Stefan must be under assault from the sky.

Ulf was just about to break their operational silence when he saw a man and a boy come out of the front of the building where there was a sign that said Restaurang Kraftkällan Forsmark. He stiffened and gripped his rifle but resisted the urge to swing it toward the stranger.

At that moment they all froze. The man was holding the little boy's hand. He was wearing a dark suit and a thin dark tie. His shirt looked pressed, and immaculately white. On his head, he wore a white hat with a dark band around it. Somehow he managed to look both formal and casual at the same time. He and the boy both had the same raven black hair, tanned face, and oriental eyes. He looked to Ulf like a Japanese businessman from 1961 who had been translated from Tokyo to Forsmark by magic.

The Asian man grinned and lifted his other hand, which held a paper cup of coffee, in an informal greeting. "Hello, fellows," he said, in what sounded to Ulf like American English — which only added to his confusion.

"Morning sir," Ulf said, not even guessing how to address this odd apparition. Ulf loosened his grip on his assault rifle, and looked to Kalle to also go "at ease."

"Beautiful day here in Forsmark, no?"

"Yes sir," Ulf said, realizing he was talking in "soldier-eez" but not knowing what other way to respond.

"You weren't successful in persuading the staff to turn off the electricity from this plant, were you?"

Ulf paused, and shook his head slightly to answer "no." Things were getting stranger by the minute...

"This is my nephew, Boy-San." The boy hid behind his leg and peered out with dark and frightened eyes.

"Ulf Johansson, and this is Kalle."

He bowed to them slightly, a distinctly Asian mannerism, and said, "Yasuo Wausauke," But he said it in what sounded to Ulf to be an American accent, not a Japanese accent. Like someone who had grown up in America, despite his appearance.

Ulf nodded. He could sense Kalle tensing up – after four years of fighting together, he knew him and all his moods like a brother.

"What can we do for you, Mr. Wausake?" Ulf said, not sure if he was pronouncing the name right.

"I think the question is, what can I do for you?" Again, the grin with even white teeth, and almost apologetic he added, "And most people just call me *Dr. Wu.*"

"We could have used your help on Gotland, Dr. Wu."

"Oh, I don't think so. I am not that kind of a doctor," Dr. Wu said.

To his side, he both felt and saw Kalle tighten his grip on his weapon, and his trigger finger slipping lower. Was this strange character just trying to stall them? Waiting for reinforcements to arrive to gun them down right here in the street?

Another apologetic grin and he added, "And your friend, Patrik, will be fine. Real doctors will treat his injury and he will be fine."

Ulf didn't respond. Instead, his senses went on high alert. Was the helicopter gunship circling back for them? Were commandoes about to emerge from the "too empty" side streets?

"My doctorate is in mechanical and nuclear engineering. That's why most friends call me Dr. Wu. I am here as a consultant to the Forsmark staff," he gave a wave of his hand to the nuclear plant across the street, "cooling systems," he added as if that needed no explanation. Meanwhile, the little boy peeked around him again and gave a small smile.

Ulf tried to defuse the situation, "We were here talking to

the staff in the control room. If you know about Patrik, you know what we were trying to do."

"Yes. My team texted me. That's why I stopped in for a coffee with Boy-san this morning."

"The coffee shop is open?" Ulf said, forgetting himself for a moment. It was just so peculiar that he blurted it out. As if perhaps they could saunter in for a cappuccino on their way back to the rebel hideout. Also, apparently, a cell phone could work here. That hadn't been true for four years.

"Sadly, no," Dr. Wu said answering his question. "But things here at Forsmark are different than elsewhere. They had many supplies stockpiled in case of emergencies. Nordic efficiency, I suppose..." He waved his cup around a bit, "Even four-year-old coffee if kept near freezing in a nuclear winter, can be surprisingly fresh tasting. Come to the coffee shop and join me for a cup."

Ulf exchanged a glance with Kalle. He got a shrug in return.

"It's Gevalia coffee. I'm sure you know the brand." Again there was a flash of teeth, a hard-to-decipher grin – half apologetic, half passive-aggressive.

How much did this guy know about them? He was teasing them. He knew they were Swedish special forces from Gävle.

"At ease, Kalle," Ulf said to his partner. "I guess a cup of coffee won't kill us."

Kalle looked at him, and shrugged, as if to say *"Yes, maybe he wants us to drink coffee and kill us. We should be careful."*

They entered the coffee shop together. Dr. Wu turned on the lights – in itself a remarkable event. But after all, they were just yards away from a giant electrical plant. In the glare of bright ceiling lights, Ulf could see the shop was not ransacked looking, like all the shops they had seen in the past few years. But it also did not look clean and tended like a typical Swedish *Konditori.* There was a coffeemaker with a single pot of coffee on the hob. On the glass coffeepot side, printed in red, it said *Gevalia Kaffe* in fancy script. There were dusty footprints where workers at the plant had stomped in for coffee recently, perhaps at the start of their work shift. The counter had the messy look of a place where workingmen had grabbed a cup of coffee with little regard for cleanliness or sanitary practices.

The coffee, stale as it might be from 4 years in a freezer, nevertheless smelled wonderful. It was also a memory trigger. There was one particular coffee shop in the square at Gävle that Ulf liked to visit – for the coffee, but also for the scenery. The baristas, both male and female, seemed to have been picked for their stunning good looks, or was it that good-looking young people liked to work at trendy coffee shops? Either way, it was one reason he liked to stop in a few times a week.

But the coffee shop at Forsmark had none of that allure. Only a foreign gentleman and what appeared to be his grandson sitting at a tall table with stools, waiting for him and Kalle to fill their cups and join them.

"You said you could help us," Ulf said as he slid up onto the tall stool a bit awkwardly since he still had his weapon slung over his shoulder. He wasn't ready to set it aside just yet. He noticed that if anything, Kalle was more alert for trouble than he was. Kalle sat on the stool but didn't quite face the table. Instead, he was squared up to the entry door and his eyes seemed to cycle from their table to the outside, continually scanning for threats. Old habits die hard... and four years of living under constant stress would not be cured by a smile and a cup of hot coffee, no matter how welcome.

Dr. Wu nodded to show he had caught Ulf's statement, blowing on his coffee he peered at Ulf over the rim. "Of course, I know why you are here. You wish to turn off the electricity to those who have invaded your country."

"Right... But if you have been cooperating with them, I don't see why you would help us." He said this with no rancor in his voice, merely stating the facts. He noticed that as they spoke, the little boy had found a few sugar cubes in the porcelain dish that sat on the table and had taken them out to play with them.

"A person might cooperate with others because it serves their best interest. I have more than myself to consider," he said, with just the slightest inclination of his head to the boy sitting close beside him, who was now pushing the sugar cubes about and making noises like cars or trucks driving.

"It appears you still have someone other than yourself to consider," Kalle added. Ulf noted that he too was talking in a way that would not alarm the child sitting with them.

"Yes. But things have changed." Dr. Wu said.

"Seems like you're still here helping run the plant."

"Oh yes," Dr. Wu said. "I am still helping the humans here."

Ulf was taken aback. It seemed such an odd thing to say. "As opposed to...?"

"Surely you know of Håkan Magnusson, the ruler of Sweden. I don't think the real enemy is Russians anymore."

"Not following you," Kalle said. At least I'm not the only one who finds this guy hard to understand, Ulf thought. But just the mention of the Russians put him on alert. He had spent the last few years trying to rid Gotland of Russian invaders. Just the thought of them raised his hackles.

"Let me try to explain further," Dr. Wu said, removing his glasses and wiping them with a cloth he kept in his jacket pocket. "You don't need to turn off electricity to harm humans. Humans don't run on electricity. But Håkan does. You are trying to shut her down."

"Ok. You're on to us. Big deal." Kalle said.

"You're cooperating with us, not her now. What changed?"

"Håkan," Dr. Wu said. "Håkan changed." He paused, and his eyes were hard to read behind the bright ceiling lights reflecting off his glasses. "In this past year, she has made it clear that she is moving on from needing us to help fulfill her plans. I think the British would say that we've been "made redundant."

Kalle picked up on this and added, "She's replacing us with more of *her kind*."

"Precisely," Dr. Wu said, "and that is a threat to us, and particularly to my little friend here." Dr. Wu said, reaching to ruffle the hair of the little boy sitting next to him, who looked up at him and smiled and then returned to playing.

And as if to answer the unspoken question this raised, Dr. Wu added, "*Boy-san* is the child of my niece – but his mother is gone, and I have taken on the job of caring for him."

He looked at Ulf and Kalle and slowly added, "If there is to be a future for the few children we have to carry on, we must work together to stop Håkan Magnusson. The war is no longer between Swedes and Russians, it's between us," and with a nod out to the open spaces beyond the coffeeshop doors he added, "and them."

He turned his gaze back to Ulf, who responded to this by saying, "In other words, we must stop Håkan, and whoever is helping keep her in power in Uppsala."

"Precisely," Dr. Wu said. "Precisely."

Ulf sipped more of his coffee. Damn, it tasted good. But it also gave him time to ponder what Dr. Wu was saying. He had to object, and after draining his mug said, "Håkan may be working to replace us with her clones or whatever you call those things..) But that doesn't make me want to cooperate with the damn *Rus*. They've been our enemies for centuries."

"That's probably because the *Rus* as you call them are just a bunch of wayward Vikings who never came home, Ha!" Dr. Wu said, again showing his teeth with the "laugh that was not a laugh" - as in Ha Ha, I am making fun of you...

"Kind of hard to find humor in that, since they killed three of our best friends on Gotland..." Kalle said in an angry tone. Kalle was the quiet one of their team, but when his anger boiled over it was notable. Ulf met his eyes and shook his head slightly in an unspoken gesture of "Not now Kalle, don't lose control now." The little boy looked up – sensing something in the change of tone. Then he returned to pushing the sugar cubes around making car noises. They made small tracks in the dust of the tabletop and left tiny slivers of shining crystal in their wake.

"What my friend is trying to say," Ulf interjected, "is that we are a long way from trusting any Russians and teaming up with them. Understood?"

Dr. Wu didn't flinch, but in an even tone added. "I appreciate your sentiment and concern. But it won't do either you or your Russian enemies any good. I know food supplies in your little colony are running low. Soon they will run out. What do you plan to do then? Shoot some Russians so *you* can eat the last *limpa* "

Ulf knew he was right. He exchanged a glance with Kalle, who shrugged. It was odd to him also that Dr. Wu used the word *Limpa* in the correct Swedish sense of "loaf."

"There is a Japanese saying, *Shikata ga nai!* it means something like "It can't be helped."

Dr. Wu removed his glasses and wiped them once again

with a cleaning cloth, though they looked spotless to Ulf already. Yet another stalling tactic.

"Okay," Ulf said reluctantly, "What do we need to do to help shut this place down?"

Part Three: Stefan vs. Håkan

"The credit belongs to the man who is actually in the arena, whose face is marred by dust and sweat and blood, who errs and comes short again and again; who knows the great enthusiasm, the great devotions, and spends himself in a worthy cause; who at best knows the triumph of high achievement, who, at the worst, if he fails, at least fails while daring greatly…"

Teddy Roosevelt

CHAPTER FORTY-ONE: Stefan Andersson

Gamla Uppsala (Old or Ancient Uppsala – a Viking pagan site, later converted to a medieval churchyard, near the modern city of Uppsala. Also, the site for the original Swedish annual governing "Things" and the original Swedish kings.)

Stefan sat in a chair with Björn at his side at a dusty table at the Odinsborg cafe in Gamla Uppsala. Donkey was standing out on the patio looking in hopefully.

"You have your oats and water. You are out of the rain. You can't come in." Stefan said to him.

Donkey shook his head, twitched his ears, and snorted in disgust. Björn leaned closer to Stefan, resting his chin on Stefan's knee, with a look that said, *"I am still your favorite..."* It was late afternoon, and they were all tired from the long journey through farms and forests to get to this place.

In the cellar, which in a French cafe would have been a wine cellar, but here in Uppsala was a mead cellar, Stefan had found a dusty wooden case of bottles of *Gla Upsala Mjöd - -* the Odinsborg cafe's own house mead. Since it was honey fermented into alcohol, it had survived the long winter down in the basement. Stefan put some mead in the palm of his hand and let Björn lick it. They had no other food.

Stefan had built a fire in the old tall corner wood stove, he sipped the mead and looked out the window at the giant burial mounds. He lifted his bottle of mead and toasted the big burial mound closest to the cafe, the one folk legend said was the gravesite of Odin, The Allfather, *"Skål!"* he said, tilting the bottle towards him. He downed the bottle and contemplated opening another. He had brought up three bottles, he could toast the grave mounds of Freya and Thor while he was at it – Or go to the basement for three more bottles to also toast the ancient Yingling kings, Aun, Egil, and Adil who were more likely the inhabits of the three tombs.

He heard the toot of a steam whistle. There was a steam train coming through the farmland from Gävle, and the northlands. Stefan stepped to the outdoor patio to make sure Donkey's lead was tied securely to a nearby post. He reached down and clasped Björn's collar to keep him from rushing to greet the train, but he did not step into the open. Instead, he leaned against the dark brown wooden siding of the patio sheltered from view.

The train slowed and stopped. It didn't stop completely, which was odd. Stefan thought he had seen a big blond guy who looked like a bodybuilder driving the train as it steamed past.

It stopped nearby, and four passengers disembarked, Lars, Ravna, Magnus, and finally, Miko. At the sight of her Stefan's heart leapt. He stepped from the porch and she spotted him, and all of them rushed to see him, though Björn was first to greet them, barking and jumping about.

They had a "group hug" encircling their arms as the train pulled away. Stefan happened to glance that way, and for just a moment, thought of how he had seen Celeste on a train just a day ago. It jarred him, making his feelings for the moment confused, and conflicted. He hoped it didn't show on his face...

Overjoyed to receive a kiss from Miko, even if it was just a kiss of friendly greeting, a kiss on his cheek that said "I am happy you are still alive" and perhaps nothing more. But it made him conflicted and also curious – where was Celeste going? Surely the trains all ended at the station in downtown Uppsala now? She would be within walking distance. Had she shared a train with Miko on the way down from Gävle? How weird would that be?

They exchanged greetings and walked back to the Odinsborg Cafe together. The afternoon warmth had faded and it was cooling off as sunset approached.

Lars and Magnus wore backpacks, and once they were seated at a big table near the corner fireplace in the Cafe Odinsborg, they opened their packs and brought out food to go with the bottles of *Gla Mjöd* that Stefan had cadged from the basement. There was some cold *Korv* sausage, some *Ädelost* – a local blue cheese, and some *rågknäcke* – rye crispbread. Stefan found some brown mustard. Soon they were all eating and drinking. Stefan couldn't remember the last time he had shared a meal with friends – would it have been with Ravna's father at his farm/homestead? Before the long Ragnarök winter?

He looked at the faces around the table. Ravna and Magnus sat close together and Stefan wondered if there was some romantic energy between them. There was color in Ravna's cheeks from the cool evening air on their walk from the train to here. Lars also sat close by her, and Stefan wondered if *he* had designs on Ravna as well. Despite himself, Stefan thought back to his encounter with Ravna in the cabin in Dallarna, when her eyes met his from time to time he wondered what her thoughts were as he sat close by Miko, who was a comforting or even sensuous warmth leaning against him on one side. To complicate matters further, his internal movie camera kept replaying the sight of Celeste on the train, heading to Uppsala proper, which he knew was the goal of this team.

"What is the news from the north? What happened at Sandviken?"

They exchanged glances. Stefan thought he saw Miko's

eyes get misty – she didn't "burst into tears" but it was clear she was in distress.

"Some people got shot and the protesters scattered," Magnus said, his dark eyes meeting Stefan's.

"How many?" Stefan asked though he wasn't sure he wanted to know. He had encouraged a rebellion – and then let others bear the weight of that decision.

"Perhaps a dozen. Maybe more," Lars added.

"It was my fault. I should have been there."

"So you could have died leading the charge?" Miko said, with a surprising edge of bitterness to her voice. Or was it out of concern for him? He took her hand under the table, it was warm and soft in his. She glanced at him from the corner of her eye. None of the others could see this...

"We have to do what we can to stop this. But how?"

"Were you able to stop or shut down Forsmark?"

"Jerker and I toppled the towers for one of the main transmission lines near Forsmark. We had some help, at Forsmark's Bruk we met some Swedish commandos who were heading to the plant to try to shut off the reactors. But apparently, they failed. I haven't heard from them since, and I can see at night that the lights are still on in Uppsala, and the trains are still running. I fear they are lost, too."

"Where's Jerker?" Lars asked.

"Stefan paused, looking down at the table, not wanting to meet their eyes, he shook his head.

"Injured? Wounded?" Lars asked, this time with an edge to his voice that Stefan didn't appreciate.

"Håkan sent a drone. Not a camera drone, an armed one. There was an explosion and a fire. Jerker didn't make it."

"But you did," Lars said.

Stefan looked up, he could see they all were looking to him for an answer. "He died. I survived. Björn dug me out of the burning pile of rubble – that's why he's still limping." He said with a nod to Björn who sat on the other side of him, lifting his head at the mention of his name.

"Saved *you*, but not *Jerker*," Lars said, looking to the others for support. "Lucky *you*."

"Would you be happier if we both had died?"

"No. I'd be happier if just you had died."

"That's not fair!" Miko interjected.

Lars lifted his hand as if to strike her. Stefan caught it in mid-air and the two arm-wrestled momentarily. Lars twisted and pressed harder, glaring at Stefan.

"Stop it!" Miko shouted, her voice echoing in the small cafe. "This is getting us nowhere! We have to work together..."

Stefan released Lars' hand. "She's right. I can't bring Jerker back. But if we don't work together Håkan will kill us all. We don't have time for this, we have to find Håkan and fight her, not each other. Every day she is making more replicants to either replace us or kill us off."

Magnus raised his hand, "Lars and I both went to school here at Uppsala University. We know where she must be. We can take you there." He looked from Stefan to Lars, who nodded as he was rubbing his hands together, not meeting their eyes.

Stefan looked out the window. Even though the days were getting longer, the sun had set and there was the twilight sky that signaled to them that the long days of summer were ahead, the days of the midnight sun, when warmth might return to Sweden for the first time in four years.

"We'll rest now," Stefan said. "In the morning we'll hike into town – see if we can confront that spider Håkan in her lair."

They found seat cushions and tablecloths to use as makeshift bedding, and all huddled around the porcelain stove for warmth after the sun had set. The evening had turned cool with a breeze from the cold Baltic Sea coming onshore even though it was miles away. The tattered Swedish flag out the front window fluttered in the wind, pointing back to the sea.

Stefan tried to sleep, but the prospect of "confronting Håkan in her lair" kept sleep at bay even though he was exhausted. On one side, Lars snored and snorted in his sleep, on the other side, close by him, Miko slept leaning against him, mumbling in her sleep. Through the window, the moon rose over the mound of Odin, and it illuminated also the decorative tile roof of the ancient church. Miko stirred again, and he wondered what she dreamed. Was it the coming confrontation with Håkan, or ... had she seen him glance at the woman on the train? Did she sense his inner turmoil?

He drew her closer in against him, and she awoke, reaching up and kissing him, sleepily at first, but awakening more as he drew her closer still, pressing her against him firmly. Her breath grew warmer, more ragged, her kiss more sensuous, passionate.

Their movements were quiet as he explored her with his hands under the covers. But not quite quiet enough, because with a snort Ravna awoke and sat up. She eyed Stefan over Miko's shoulder – which caught Miko's attention, who turned her head and stared at her. Miko's expression, if Stefan read it correctly, was a defiant one, like a lioness staring down a cub who might challenge her.

She whispered in his ear, "Sad that we keep getting interrupted..." then lay back down and turned away from him.

Ravna gave out a petulant teenage huff, also turned her

back on him, and flopped down on her cushions to sleep again.

CHAPTER FORTY-TWO

In the morning they set out on a back way from Gamla (Old) Uppsala to the modern city of Uppsala. They were a motley crew, with Stefan leading Donkey who was carrying their bags, and Björn biting at the lead, wanting to get ahold of it to play.

"We should leave those two behind," Lars said, pointing at Björn and Donkey. "They make us look ridiculous."

"We discussed this," Stefan said. "I am not abandoning Björn. We'll stick to the side streets. Where I go, he goes." They walked on, past streets named for the Norse Gods, Tors Väg, Frejs Väg, Odins Väg, and finally, for the writer of the sagas, Snorre's Väg.

"But Donkey?" Lars persisted, "What's the point of that stupid donkey going with us? The dog I can see. He provides defense and protection. But Donkey?"

"You want to drag all our gear on your back, feel free," Stefan said, not wanting to say that the real reason was that he had grown attached to Donkey and liked him. Instead, he added, "I'd like to have a bit of energy left after this two-hour hike."

"It shouldn't take that long. I used to bike it in fifteen minutes."

"Sure. I used to drive a car to work in five." Stefan said, glancing at Lars but also at Miko and Ravna who seemed to be tuned in to this discussion.

They crossed over the Route 55 highway on a highway overpass bridge. As usual, there was no traffic, and sprouts of grass had appeared in the cracks in the concrete surface of the highway itself. But being this much out in the open bothered Stefan, and he noticed that there were not only street lights but highway cameras on the bridge. He wondered if any of them might still work.

"So we're going to traipse into downtown Uppsala with our pets and girlfriends and assault the leader of the Russian army?"

That caught a sharp look from Miko, who said, "Which one of us do you consider to be *your* girlfriend?"

Lars waved his hand as if to brush off the comment, "A figure of speech..." Walking ahead of them as they entered a wooded area on the other side of the bridge, he turned back so they could see his face.

"Three men, two women, a mangy dog, and a stupid donkey against a fortified city full of Russian occupation forces. The math doesn't work..." Lars paused, "I thought our mission was to turn off the power at Forsmark and shut her down from a distance."

"Tried that. Now we're taking a more direct approach." Stefan answered. "And who are you calling *mangy*? Björn is not *mangy.*"

Björn, hearing his name, looked up and gave what looked like a smile.

"I am not afraid of Russian guards," Ravna said. She pulled a knife from a sheath at her side and flipped it in the air. It glinted in the sun as it rotated until she snatched it again out of the air and it disappeared as quickly as it had appeared.

Lars looked at her, his eyebrows raised as if he would like to question her. But before he could, she added, "I like to wet my knives with Russian blood. I've done it before. I'll do it again."

Lars blanched a bit at that comment.

"Pets and girlfriends, eh Lars?" Magnus said. "Just your typical *Sami* schoolgirl from Kiruna. Right?" He laughed.

They had stopped walking. Lars looked from one of them

to the other – and to Stefan much remained unspoken. None of them were typical or soft. They hadn't survived the last four years because things were easy for them.

Lars shrugged. They continued on. It was like walking into an ancient world or a past life. Gamla Uppsala was the edge of the inhabited city, the last city left on earth, as far as Stefan knew. Lars, the former Uppsala University student, led the way through deserted side streets – but unlike other places where they had been, there were signs of life in the city center which they could spot looking towards the river that ran through town.

Here and there electric vehicles, including trucks, were moving about. At one apartment block, they heard the voices of children playing in the playground – and they had to sneak past the wooded end of the road to avoid being seen. They picked their way slowly through the neighborhood green spaces, never getting too close to the city center where life, at least from a distance, almost looked normal. It became clear as they continued that the city center was at least partially alive, but the outskirts were deserted, like the rest of the world. This allowed them, even in broad daylight, to circle the town on the Kungsängsleden and reach the Ångström Laboratory.

Around, and behind the Laboratory was a green space and a wooded walkway. Just yards from one of the most advanced technical installations in the world, Stefan felt like he was walking in a Dalarna wooded grove.

"I think we can enter through the back," Lars said. "I used to eat lunch back here, by these buildings." He pointed to what looked like outbuildings for the heat and cooling system set back from the main buildings. Some wooden chairs and picnic tables were haphazardly arranged under budding birch trees.

Stefan nodded. Now there was a dilemma – what to do about their "pets and girlfriends" as Lars had put it.

"Let Lars and I go ahead and investigate and report back. If the way is clear we'll come back for you."

"And if not?" Miko asked. "If you don't come back?" She had reached her hand to him, perhaps involuntarily, and it felt warm against his wrist where she gripped him. It was perhaps the first time what was true privately was acknowledged to others – that there was a connection, a romantic connection, between the two of them.

He leaned forward, and kissed her cheek, "We'll be back. I promise. Trust me, you'll see."

"And if there is *trouble*?"

"One way or another we'll escape – meet back at Odinsborg Café this evening."

She nodded, but he could see the doubt (and he thought, perhaps fear?) in her eyes.

He and Lars went around the utility building to the door that faced the parking lot. From his back pocket, Lars pulled out a wallet – an object Stefan had not seen in years. Lars pulled out a card, which had a faded picture of himself and the round red seal of *Uppsala Universitet* at the top. He held it up against the digital door lock, and to Stefan's astonishment, a red indicator light turned green.

"Amazing," Stefan said, "It still works."

"I am not surprised," Lars said, a bit too confidently for Stefan's taste.

They walked into the building, which was hot and noisy with all sorts of heating and cooling machinery humming away.

"There is a tunnel for all the utilities which runs to the main buildings. It's one flight down," Lars said making his way to a doorway with a variety of signs and icons on it which basically said the same thing. "We can cross into the main computer building basement from here."

"Lead the way," Stefan said, hardly believing their good fortune at being able to penetrate this far into Håkan's lair without being detected. "So far, so good."

Nearby, in an auditorium classroom of the main research hub, Håkan scrolled through screens on a giant display that covered one wall of her command center. One of them had captured a shot of a security camera door, with the rather scruffy faces of Lars and Stefan peering at the camera hidden in the card reader.

"Oh my Gosh!" Håkan said to Dr. Bob and Hans von Linné who were working on projects on their screens. "We have intruders in our building. I am shocked! Shocked I say!"

"*Jag också,*" (me too) Dr. Bob said in badly accented Swedish. He glanced up at her array of images from the past few hours that were displayed on other screens. Björn and Donkey drinking water from a mud puddle near Odinsborg. Miko, Ravna, and Magnus peering down an alley at Russian schoolchildren swinging on swings at a playground in the bright sunshine, and the whole assembled group with Donkey leading the way over the Fyris river on the Kungsleden bridge. "That's my favorite," he said pointing to that image. "I have titled it, *"The triumphal entrance of the Baby Jesus with his donkey into Jerusalem on Palm Sunday."*

Hans looked up from his screen, smiling. Not to be outdone he said, "Thor and Loki going to the wedding with their chariot pulled by goats in the *Thrymskvida.*"

"I thought Thor was in drag for that one. Stefan's not in drag." Dr. Bob added, getting into the spirit of the thing.

"But Lars makes a good Loki, don't you think Håkan?"

Håkan was watching the progress of the two of them on

a camera feed from the HVAC tunnel in this building's basement – the basement of the home where she had lived since her creation 5 years ago.

"Håkan, did you hear me," Dr. Bob said.

"I think you must have been reading my mind because I have been thinking the very same thing." She didn't mention that she had been thinking about this for a long time. Much longer than Dr. Bob could possibly have imagined...much, much longer. Lars would make an excellent Loki....

CHAPTER FORTY-THREE

Ångström Laboratoriet

Lars knew the layout of the building, and Stefan let him take the lead up the back staircase to the main floor. They slowly opened the door and found themselves in a large open auditorium filled with computer screens and teams. Stefan noticed one of the Putties standing in a corner with a man with doing something to it using what looked like a TV remote. It was clearly inanimate, clearly a replicant, but ... different somehow. Better looking. More realistic. A "Putty 2.0" Stefan wondered.

They stepped further into the room and were spotted by the technicians at their desks.

"Well hello, Stefan Andersson, and Lars. How nice you could drop in," a voice said. It was a pleasant female voice, it reminded him of the voice of some of the Swedish radio announcers who seemed to speak in a sultry deep tone. He looked around to see where the voice was coming from. It wasn't the android in the corner. It just seemed to emanate from speakers hidden all around him.

"If you're looking for Håkan, she's not in an embodied form," a chubby bearded guy in a faded Carnegie Mellon school t-shirt featuring an equally faded image of a Scotty dog, said from a console nearby. His eyes were white disks hidden behind bright LED lights shining down from the ceiling.

"Not yet!" said the guy across the room holding the remote that was making the android move by sliding a button on his controller. "But soon!"

To Stefan, used to the accent of Swedes from the north, this man's accent sounded quite southern, from Skåne perhaps, or Småland.

"Look over there," he said, pointing to a screen slightly behind him, which was why he hadn't spotted it yet.

"It will be so nice when we can finally visit "in person," eh Stefan?" Håkan said, and now Stefan spotted the digital avatar that represented her on the screen.

"In person?" Stefan said, "I'm not sure what that means with you?"

"I'm not in a fully embodied form. Not yet 'incarnated' – you know what that term means, right?"

Stefan looked from the video avatar to the Putty 2.0 form.

Hans saw him looking that way, and piped in, "In the flesh – literally, *in the meat*." He said, in a professor's voice, reaching out to squeeze the flesh of the avatar's arm. "You Americans like Chili Con Carne – right? Chile with Meat? I would imagine you know that term."

"A meat puppet?" Stefan said, turning back to her image on the screen and using a term he had heard elsewhere.

"Stefan! You are hurting my feelings!" Håkan-on-the-screen responded.

He noticed that Håkan's eyes followed his and that she (or it?) was scanning his face, reading his emotions. Creepy. He shrugged.

"You also tried to turn off my electricity, didn't you? You naughty dog!"

On the screen next to her face came the video feed from what Stefan assumed must have been the drone she sent to kill him near Forsmark. He cringed at the image of Jerker falling as the tower crashed and he saw him fall under a torrent of rubble and burning debris. He felt Lars stiffen at this sight, and gasp as they both watched Jerker's last moments,

"Oh, and here are your little friends," a camera began with a long-range view of the woods and then zoomed in closer and closer to where he could see Miko, Ravna, Magnus, and their animals, Björn and Donkey. They were standing in a submissive posture, as security forces in Russian uniforms stood in a semi-circle facing them on the road, their weapons pointed at them.

"No need to bother them. We are not here to hurt you. Only to talk. You can let them go."

"Not here to hurt me?"

"No. We come in peace."

"I think you are lying. I think you are here to scope things out to see how you can get rid of me."

"He's telling the truth," Lars said, regaining his composure, and making his plea to the staff manning the computers. "We didn't come here to harm you, any of you..."

"You think he tells *you* the truth?" Håkan said. "You think he's an *honest* man?"

Lars looked at him. Stefan could see the hesitation, and then Lars said, "Yes. He is an honest man and a good friend."

"Really?" Håkan said.

"Yes," Lars said.

"You people amaze me," Håkan said.

Lars shrugged. Stefan began to wonder where this conversation was going.

"Tell me, Lars, do you have feelings for Ravna?"

On the screen, an image appeared and the camera zoomed in on Ravna, and a Russian soldier prodding her forward with the rifle barrel of his weapon. They were moving away from the Ångström Center now, heading towards one of the other buildings at Polackbacken.

"Don't harm her!" Lars said loudly.

Another image came up on the screen – this time from inside a train coach. It must have been the train ride from Gävle down to Gamla Uppsala. It was of the two of them, Lars and Ravna sitting side by side on a bench seat, with Ravna's head resting on Lars's shoulder. The camera zoomed in to show his hand gently stroking her hair.

"Seems to me that you might like that little girl… am I right?"

"Did your good friend Stefan mention this to you? The guys in the control room seemed to particularly like this sequence when they saw it last week." On the screen, there was a still image that Stefan recognized immediately. It was taken by someone opening a door to the cabin on the shores of Lake Siljan. The still image, which was a bit blurry because it was a freeze-frame from a video, was of two people on a couch, intertwined, sleeping with a blanket over them. "This next bit has been viewed several thousand times. Apparently, the guys in the control room thought their friends would like to see it too…"

The video continued, and Stefan's heart sank. Ravna, wearing only her warm woolen stockings on her feet, jumped up and stood in full view naked. Stefan rose too, also without clothes, but the camera was focused on Ravna, her breasts jiggling up and down as she moved back and forth. The clip repeated itself over and over. There was snickering from the mostly male engineering staff.

Lars turned to him and glared, "Just friends, eh?" He muttered under his breath.

"We didn't do anything," Stefan whispered under his breath. "Our clothes were soaked. We slept together so we didn't freeze…"

Trying to shift the conversation from this topic, Stefan said to Håkan, "While you're showing movies, why not a few clips of *your* greatest hits? Like the Stockholm Bloodbath."

There was a pause, and Stefan half expected a small logo to pop up like he used to see on chatbots - - *Håkan is writing…*

"I was not around in the time of Gustav Vasa if that is what you are referring to…"

"No. I was referring to you letting out a virus and killing everyone so you could take control. Like the Danish tyrant did years ago"

"I didn't create the virus. You people did…with your unhealthy and unsanitary ways."

Stefan heard again her phrase *"you people"* drawing a clear distinction between her and "you people" – that is, the humans.

"Bullshit," Stefan said, noticing his voice rising, and some of the technicians' lifted their heads, pausing to hear this interchange. "Tell me that you didn't provide the expertise to weaponize the virus and kill humanity." The avatar on the screen blinked. "And that you didn't at the same time create a vaccine which only a tiny handful of people received while you let everyone else die."

"The Russians – they" Håkan started to say, but Stefan cut her off.

"Your Russians – these people, *right in this room*." His voice was getting even louder, he noticed that even his voice was changing, choked with anger. In the corner, he noticed one of the guards reach down and with his thumb clip open the leather strap that kept his pistol in his holster, and then he rested his fingers on the hilt. Like a gunslinger in the old West getting ready to draw and fire. Undeterred, Stefan now shouted, "TELL ME YOU DIDN'T HAND PICK THE BASTARDS IN THIS ROOM TO BE YOUR STOOGES! DID THEY AGREE TO HAVE THEIR FAMILIES KILLED?"

"If you are going to lose your temper, I will have you removed from this room," Håkan said.

Stefan stepped up on a counter, with his back to the screen showing Håkan's avatar. He surveyed the crowd, which included Russian security forces inching closer to him. He continued shouting, not even knowing if most of them spoke English or not, "HAS SHE TOLD YOU THAT SHE IS REPLACING YOU WITH REPLICANTS? HAS SHE TOLD YOU THAT SHE IS NOT GROWING ANY FOOD BECAUSE HER REPLICANTS DON'T NEED IT? WHY ARE YOU HELPING HER GET RID OF THE LAST FEW HUMANS ON – "

Stefan couldn't finish his speech. There was a deafening alarm, the lights in the room started blinking, and the doors burst open, and Russian special forces burst in. Their guns came up, there were muzzle flashes from pistols, and Stefan was blown backward off the table he stood on and crashed to the floor.

CHAPTER FORTY-FOUR

Stefan sat alone on Odin's barrow as the sun went down. Once again, he had three bottles of mead that he had snagged from the basement of the Odinsborg Café. One was empty, he was starting on the second. He intended to drink all three and hopefully, pass out.

"This is for medicinal purposes, only," he said to the mound. "Otherwise, I would share," he said and belched. "Excuse me, old man. Drinking on an empty stomach... not good."

He took another swig of the mead. The self-medicating was working – his chest and shoulder where he had been hit by the rubber bullets were just a dull pain, not the incessant throb they were before. He figured that Håkan must have armed her bodyguards with rubber bullets so they wouldn't destroy her control panels and servers in the event of an attack. Her guards were more a deterrent than a lethal force. That might be a good thing when he returned to try again... if he survived long enough to do that.

"I could use a bit of help, you know," he said, talking to the mound. "If you get the urge to do a bit of *After-Walking*, it would be handy." He glanced around, looking for a Runestone that might contain a spell to keep a spirit in the grave, but he didn't see one. Perhaps Odin was free to move about, then – particularly at night... like other undead creatures seemed to like to do.

"My team members are somewhat indisposed, you might say. Any wisdom you could dispense would be appreciated." He paused, reflecting on what he said, but he didn't see a one-eyed old man in a cloak with a staff approaching from the shadows. A pale late spring full moon was rising to the south. He pulled the blanket from the cafe around his shoulders.

He thought of the image of Miko and Ravna being led away with Magnus, of Björn and Donkey being taken too. He shook his head.

I led them right into a trap. Damn."

"Fucking Russians," he said. "Fucking Håkan Magnusson."

"So, *All-Wise One*. How is it that I am here?" he paused. For a moment he felt like the mound was spinning under him, he had to put a foot out to stop it. Whoa, that was some strong mead!

"How is it that *I am here* and not captured?" He shook his head, it didn't make sense...if Håkan was as smart as he thought she was, how did he manage to slip through the slim line of security forces she summoned when the alarm went off?

"Either she is not as smart as she seems..." Or? What other explanation could there be? "Or she intends for me to be free for some reason."

He thought of how she had cut him off "mid-speech" and what he was saying. He had been trying to drive a wedge between her and the Russians still in charge...he thought about that some more *"The Russians still in charge..."*

"She intends me to be free for some reason..."

As he thought about this, a train approached from the north. He could hear it in the quiet and dark of the night and saw the headlight shining across the farmers' fields stubbled with weeds outside the town. He decided to approach it around Odin's Café and see if it was yet another army of putties...

Back in the control room at the Ångstrom center, Håkan watched with interest. Would he take the bait? "Slower," she whispered, "slower." It was just like fishing. You had to drag the bait slowly across the water to catch the attention of the fish. Or so she had been told...

Circling the cafe, Stefan saw the train laboring into view. It must be "running out of steam," he thought, literally running out of steam, with barely enough left to coast into the city center to the station.

He crept closer to see what putties were on board. As he suspected, there was a bevy of Biancas and Rackhams sitting like puppets. But there was one face he didn't expect. It was Celeste. Staring out at him. Waving.

"Fuck it," he thought, and he ran to the train coach, jumped up, and even though his shoulder was sore and let him know it, grabbed the iron railing, and swung into the opening between the last of the passenger coaches.

The train dipped under the neighborhood in the tunnel and exited in the city center at Uppsala Central Station. In the midst of rusty bikes standing in rows along the platform, Stefan saw the other passengers depart. The putties marched in rows like soldiers, which he assumed some of them must be, for a few of them had arms in slings or limped on injured legs or with crutches and limbs missing.

But one person walked differently.

Stefan had seen that walk before. It had caught his attention in the halls at school in his younger days. It had drawn him to her then, and, lo these many years later, it had the same power over him on this night. He hurried to follow her as she took a right turn and headed to the *Fyris* River in the center of the town.

Stefan knew that she wouldn't go far – the Uppsala *Centralstation* was just a few blocks from the river. He soon saw her, leaning over the railing and looking into the water.

He approached her slowly, still not quite sure if his eyes weren't playing tricks on him. But it did seem to be her he decided as he leaned on the railing beside her.

"Are you hoping to find a bicycle?" he said. It was an old Uppsala tradition for students, usually when they were drinking, to toss unattended bicycles over the railing and stone walls that lined the river.

"No. I was hoping to find something else I had lost," she said, glancing at him out of the corner of her eyes.

Her voice alone had the power to take his breath away. He leaned beside her, and stared into the black water coiling like a snake through the city – the not quite abandoned city of Uppsala.

He thought he knew what she meant. Him. She had lost him. Which was odd, because he felt like it was the other way around. He had lost her...*it was all my fault.*

But something nagged at his subconscious...was it because he was drunk, still drunk from too much mead on Odin's barrow?

"Did you ever love me?" he asked.

She turned sharply, her hair making a silver swirl in the reflected light across the walled stream. "You know that I loved you. I married you didn't I?" She reached out her hand, on her ring glittered the engagement ring he had given her. She lifted it so that it caught the light.

"I know you *agreed* to marry me," Stefan said. "But did you ever *really* love me?"

"You know you were my first lover. I gave you my virginity as a wedding present, don't you remember that?" She laughed her throaty laugh – what he used to think of as her "lusty laugh" because she seemed to only share it with him, or with others she was flirting with. "I was only eighteen."

"You gave me your virginity. You married me. We lived

together as man and wife for three years." As he said this, he saw her nodding. *"But did you ever love me?"*

Her head turned sharply, and for one millisecond, he saw her eyes reflected silver in the streetlight. They were like wolf's eyes he had once seen on the tundra on a moonlit arctic night – shining silver disks. Impenetrable. Frightening. Dangerous. Deadly.

That took his breath away also.

She leaned closer, and closer, her eyes returning to the warm brown (pale green?) they had always been before. The troubling mirage passed. Her lips parted, she exhaled, and he saw her tongue dart out for an instant to wet her lips. She leaned closer still and kissed him.

"I always loved you. Then. Now. Always."

He felt the warmth of her mouth on his, tasted her tongue, felt her breath enter into him. He felt his physical response – the stirring of long-dormant passion.

But though his body rose to meet hers, his heart was cold. As cold as the Kiruna tundra in a nuclear winter. He didn't believe her.

At the Ångström Laboratoriet

Anton took his keys and motioned to Dmitry. They were in the basement of the lab in a caged and locked storage area that they had converted to holding cells.

Dmitry was watching something on his phone – more porn, Anton figured, from his leering expression. Possibly even videos he had been secretly taking of the woman they had captured – videos of them at night, and using the toilet.

They were under strict orders from Hans to not touch the women, which was quite disappointing...so this was their only amusement at the moment.

"Dmitry, come on! " He added in Russian, "*Торопиться*!" (Hurry!) Glancing back, he saw Dmitry remove his hand from his pocket. Jesus! If he didn't shape up he was going to recommend him for duty at the camps where he wouldn't be able to access the local network and the Russian worker's repository of porn.

Dmitry, still distracted, reluctantly took his attention away from his mobile device and followed. Later Anton would notice that he had never heard the clank of the hall gate closing...

They passed by the cells and cages with their food cart. They paused at the cages of the women and slid the dish of lukewarm oatmeal under the bars of their cells. Partway down they came to the cage of Fenrir, Hans's latest experiment. Neither of them liked to feed him... they slid a tray of some sort of grown meat under the door, and Fenrir only stared at them as if they (not the dish of food) were his breakfast – his dreadful lemon eyes following them without blinking. He didn't move a muscle, but a line of drool began seeping from his mouth. He was hungry but wouldn't show it until they moved away. Then he would devour the food like he was tearing a reindeer to bits...

Around the corner, they came to the white dog and the stupid donkey. Why they hadn't just shot them was beyond Anton. But at least they could provide some amusement since the women were out of bounds.

Anton waved the dish in and out of the Donkey's reach. Its eyes followed the food back and forth and Dmitry laughed and finally, the donkey brayed in frustration, and they both laughed.

"New Trick, watch this!"

Anton took a dog biscuit from a dish on the cart. The white dog sat up expectantly. It started licking its lips. With the dog still seated, Anton opened the gate to the dog's cage.

"Catch doggy!" Anton said. He leaned in and carefully threw the dog biscuit just above the dog's head. It lifted its nose and snapped at the biscuit uselessly as it arced over its head, and because it had missed, fell over backward and banged itself on the wooden pallet they had given it to sleep on.

"Ha Ha!" they both laughed. "You try."

He handed Dmitri a couple of dog biscuits and smiled. Dmitri stepped just inside the gate and made a practice motion with his right hand to get the path of the first biscuit over the dog's head correct...

* * *

Björn

Björn had seen the men waving donkey's food in front of

him, and it had begun to make him angry.

"Hey Donkey, Smelly guys I no like. They mean."

Donkey eyed him after finally getting his feed tray. He knew Donkey didn't like them either... but it was time for his breakfast, and he would eat.

They had opened the cage and showed a biscuit to him.

At first, Björn was excited *"Oh Good! More Puppy Biscuits!"* he had thought. *"Master must have told them I was a good boy because they have brought me more Puppy Biscuits."*

But then the mean smelly man had done his *mean trick* again. He remembered it. A mean trick, making him fall and hurt his back on the hard wooden thing. And then they had laughed. He looked closely at their faces – they were mean smelly men who did not meet his eye. They were not his master. They were not even friends of his master. They could not be trusted.

The second smelly guy came into his cage. He held out the Puppy Biscuit and made a motion as if to give it to him. Björn watched closely. The man brought his hand forward and released a biscuit that sailed up above his head. But Björn's eyes were not on that biscuit, this time. They were on the man's other hand, from which dangled another Puppy biscuit. He lunged forward and bit down hard, feeling both the fingers and the puppy biscuit in his teeth. He wrenched the biscuit free, lowered his head, and bolted.

There was a scream from the closest mean smelly guy who jumped backward, stumbling into the other one, blood already streaming from his torn severed fingers.

"Later smelly guys!" Björn thought, *"Later Donkey!"* he bolted out of the cage and raced down the cement row of cages, cornered hard as he heard a shot ring out. Partway down the aisle, there was a giant wolf with bloody jaws that

leaped full force at its gate when he passed by, shaking the entire fence which nearly gave way.

He heard the cries of Master's friends calling out to him, *"GO BJÖRN! GO BJÖRN! GOOD BOY! GO FIND STEFAN!"*

At the railing by the Fyris river, Celeste leaned back from kissing him and looked Stefan in the eye, taking both of his hands in hers. Her hands were warm and soft, and much smaller and smoother than his. He had forgotten that. Somehow, holding hands with her was more meaningful, more intimate, than her kiss.

"I have a room at the *Hotell*. Come with me," she said, smiling, tilting her head towards the *Grand Hotell Hörnan* on the corner. Her light brown hair caught the light as she turned away from the railing, pulling her with him.

They walked up the granite steps. A large, single candle in a tin holder on the top step lit the doorway. Inside, more candles marched up the curved marble stairway. The front desk was empty. Celeste pulled him to the side, to the elevator, and took out her digital room key. The elevator was tiny, like an antique phone booth. She pressed a round button for floor 3 – and then leaned in against him. Still holding one hand, she pulled in below her waist, to a warm spot that he knew all too well. She whispered in his ear and she pulled his hand closer still, "Make love to me like you used to... do what you used to do..."

"You mean, face down, and tied up? Like that?"

"Absolutely," she purred in his ear, "take me that way." She said, moving his hand to caress herself. She reached her free hand to him and found him aroused as she was.

The gate opened on floor three, and Stefan noted the gleaming interior of the hotel – when was the last time he had seen such a clean and inviting interior space? It was as if the clock had turned back four years in just an instant.

She led him into the room, shedding clothing along the

way.

He lifted her dress over her head, she unbuttoned his shirt, freed up his belt, and moved her hands lower to caress him.

He put his hands down and met hers, stopping her hands with his, and said, *"Not too soon....wait."*

She was wearing tall white stockings, with tiny black bows at the top. Perfect, he thought, these will do nicely. He knelt and removed them slowly, trying hard not to rush, not to be overcome with passion, she moaned and wriggled on the bed, beyond the first stages of arousal as he slipped off her underclothes, and caressed her at each exposed place.

He gently pushed her over, and downward, and placed a pillow under her waist to raise her up, as she moaned and her face blushed with passion. He tied her ankles to the corners of the bedpost with the stockings, and then took the sash from her dress, and in one deft motion slipped it around her head as a gag, to keep her from being able to cry out, tying it quickly in a knot behind her head.

But it was then that she realized what he was planning to do because he was reaching to tie her wrists together behind her back. She began to struggle against him, to fight and resist. He had one arm in a half-nelson and was drawing the other wrist towards it to tie them together behind her back. He used her bra that was lying nearby to tie her wrist.

She was making muffled cries of anger, her body bucking and writhing on the bed, as he pulled the other arm to the middle of her back and tied her wrist. She fought so hard that he heard a snapping sound and then a whimper as her other wrist snapped when he tied it to the first one. He had broken her right wrist in the struggle, and though she still squirmed the fight was over. He stepped back – slipped on his clothes again, and took one last look at her. God, she was beautiful.

What a waste...

He leaned down to her face and saw tears on her cheeks, and her mouth moving, trying to say something. Though her mouth was tied, he could make out what she was saying. "I did love you... I did love you..."

It gave him pause. It made him wonder if what he had done was wrong. As always with her, there was always that hidden layer of doubt that made him wonder what was real, and what he had just wished to be true.

She began bucking on the bed, fighting furiously. He ran.

Back at the Ångström Laboratory, the men in the control room and Håkan watched this all with interest. The men had begun to make approving sounds when a camera in the room picked up the undressing and tying up scene – murmurs of "yeah man" and "whoo hoo!"

However, the staff only had limited telemetry from her implanted chip about her heart rate, temperature, and oxygen intake. When all those began to rise dramatically, one of the biotechs blurted out, "Man, they are really going at it."

But Håkan knew better.

The sound and images coming from the room no longer seemed like lovemaking, but something else, and the technicians watching were confused. *"What the hell is he doing?"* One of them said.

There was a gasp from the viewers when they heard her wrist snap, and Håkan heard Hans Linné say, "I hope he isn't going to kill her! Can't we send someone in?"

They saw his face close to hers and heard her protest her love for him *just as she was programmed to do...*

Håkan called Hans over closer to her, and whispered, "You know what you have to do. Clean up this mess...

Hans nodded and slipped out of the room to fulfill her

orders.

Stefan ran down the marble stairs, past a tall hanging medieval tapestry that featured an elephant, and climbed up onto the windowsill on the first landing. He unlatched the tall French window and swung it open, and then did likewise with the outer storm window. He stepped out onto the granite ledge and reached back to pull both windows shut and latched. He scootched sideways until he got to the heavy copper downspout, and then grasped it with both his hands and feet and slowly slid down – as if he were a fireman on a firepole.

Already he could hear sirens, and looking back he spotted an electric police van zipping by on *Östra Ågatan* along the river – its tires rumbling on the cobblestones as it went by. There was screaming and shouting, some of which sounded like Celeste. In the side lot of the hotel, there were derelict cars coated with four years of grime, and bicycles, rusted and heaped. One of the bikes had tires that still held air, so he chose that one and hopped on, skidding on a small skiff of hidden ice that was deep in the shadows.

He cycled slowly away on *Vretgrand* – away from the river, away from the hotel and the commotion and continued for a while. He figured he'd circle wide and head back to Odinsborg where he felt safe. But when he turned the corner a couple of blocks to the east to head that way, he saw something odd that gave him pause. Just beyond the train station bike racks, he could make out some sort of commotion going on. When he looked more closely, he saw a dimly lit steam locomotive and some cars.

The locomotive was doing a turnabout on a switching siding, while the ambulance he had just seen minutes ago had pulled up to an old varnished passenger coach and

Celeste and a couple of other figures assisted her onto the train car. One was in police garb, but the other looked familiar in the dim light He was wearing a lab coat, a homburg hat, and an open overcoat and boots. It was Hans Linné stepping from a police car that had just arrived.

Stefan paused on his bike in the shadows but crept closer as they completed the operation to bring the steam engine around to the front of the train and hooked it up. There was one old red SJ (*Statens Järnväger)* style coach and one brown varnished one. There was a rickety-looking boxcar at the end that they were loading with a couple of pallets of shrink-wrapped supplies through an open door.

The guy driving the forklift slammed the big side door of the old boxcar shut and trotted to the waiting police van. Flakes of paint drifted off the peeled wood sides and floated downward, catching a dim light from the car headlamps. He saw the forklift driver wave to the engineer in the locomotive cab, and both vehicles started to move. The police van headed back down Bangårdsgatan towards the river where it had come from, the small steam train slowly began to creak together with lots of clanking and banging as the slack in the couplers was taken out. The locomotive headed sideways through an opening in the row of buildings surrounding the modern new Uppsala *Centralstation.* Stefan noticed that even though the train depot was surrounded by hotels and stores, there was not a single light on to show that anyone was present to see this train arrive or depart.

Because it was so old and decrepit, the train moved slowly south and east to leave the central city of Uppsala. Stefan followed after it on his bike and without trouble caught up to the final boxcar as it trundled away. The locomotive crossed the streets, but never blew its whistle to alert anyone at the grade crossing. It chuffed slowly onto an arched bridge by a bike shop on the corner. As it slowed, Stefan stepped off his bike and stepped up to the boxcar, and grabbing a vertical handrail above a step at the end. He swung himself around the back – onto the brakeman's perch between the cars to get out of the wind – even though they were moving slowly he would soon freeze just hanging off the side.

Near where he had stepped onto the train, there was a wooden placard that read DHJ in large letters. Underneath it, he saw another sign that explained that this was a boxcar of a certain weight capacity which was the property of the Dannemora Hargs Järnväg (railway.) He shook his head, and it came back to him. His first meeting with Celeste. The steam train with the Putty Replicants coasting by him at Österbybruk, just a short walk from Dannemora. This was either the same train or part of the same network. One not connected to the rest of the system running out of Uppsala and controlled by Håkan. *What the fuck?*

The air was filled with soot from the ancient locomotive laboring two cars ahead. Stefan could smell pine and pine smoke in the air and figured they must have abandoned coal either because it was hard to obtain, or because something like 90% of Sweden was pine forests cultivated for lumber.

The train rocked and creaked as they made their way out of town, slowly gaining speed. All the neighborhoods, stores, and industrial sites along the way were dark and vacant. How few people were left even in Uppsala? Where did they live, if not in the suburbs out by the highway?

Through woods and past small stations and villages, they continued. Past darkened stations, houses, and barns – the station signs hard to read by mere starlight. It was a slow and ponderous journey, and it gave Stefan time to replay the events of the day, and in particular his odd encounter with "Celeste." He cringed inwardly to remember their scuffle, and the snapping sound her wrist had made when he subdued her.

But he didn't feel remorse. He didn't know how it happened or who this person was, but it was not the Celeste he had married 15 years ago and who had left him shortly thereafter. She was a phony – someone who had some surgery or other work done to look just like his wife. He suspected it, and the final conclusive bit of evidence was her lying about liking to be tied up as some sort of weird foreplay. He had made that up on the spot just to test her. The Celeste he knew wouldn't have gone for any of that kind of stuff in a million years, of that he was certain. So who, *or what* was she? He could make no clear conclusion with the evidence on hand. Perhaps more clues would be available when they reached their destination, as slow as that process might be.

Finally, the train slowed at the town of Länna, coasting to a stop just past a station, with the final boxcar which Stefan was on coming to rest on a siding at the corner of an old masonry factory building. Yet another "Swedish Bruk" or work commune from the past – but there were signs of new activity, such as the siding the train sat on, and modern lights shining through what looked like new or clean windows. Stefan stepped off the train car and slipped into some bushes to watch.

From the passenger car, they led Celeste forward. To Stefan's surprise, there were no Russian soldiers in the group. Whatever role they played had ended back at Uppsala. He tried to remember if he had seen any Russian uniforms at the hotel or station in Uppsala, and surprisingly could not remember any. He did see Hans Linné on one side of Celeste, escorting her across the packed gravel drive and up to the building door. An ornate heavy wooden door swung open, and a blonde man in a lab coat stood in the doorway, glancing left and then right as he ushered them in. He took one last glance towards the train, and as if satisfied that no one was around, pulled the door shut with a resounding clunk. But not before Stefan had just a tantalizing quick view of what was inside – it was the most high-tech biology lab he had ever seen.

With the door closed, he couldn't see anything further. He noticed that all the windows had half blinds to prevent anyone from looking in from street level. But behind him, there was a house on the side of the tracks that looked promising. He found the door unlocked and the house empty, just like most places these days. He climbed to the second floor and gently swung open a grimy window that sat on a dormer directly facing the factory building across the train tracks. He was rewarded with a clear view into the lab and what he saw shocked him.

This was a   lab, unlike anything he had ever seen before. He hadn't the faintest idea what they were doing but it seemed light years beyond what Gorm had said was going on in the camps up North near Gällivare. Gleaming rows of some strange sort of machine, and numerous examples of human clones coming out of them. But these were not the simple "putties" that had arrived from the north. These were the next step in evolution.

At the Ångström Lab

Anton Lubeck was in trouble. The stunt with the white dog and Dmitri had backfired badly. The dog was gone, and he was to blame. He had been demoted, and Dmitri was now in charge, mangled hand and all, and he relished every moment of his newfound power over Anton. *Fucking Dmitry!*

"You are going home early tonight," Dmitry said. "I'm taking the night shift alone tonight. There's some unfinished business I want to tend to..." he said, with a grin that showed his rotten smile, some teeth yellow, others black. As he was talking, he reached up and yanked out the fiber optic cable that went to the camera at that end of the hall. He returned to his desk and sat his plump self back in his chair. "Oh, before you leave mention we are having trouble with Camera Three here in the hallway..."

"Fine with me," Anton replied. But he knew exactly what Dmitry was up to. He knew what his "unfinished business" was going to be.

Dmitri had been itching to take advantage of the two young women since they had been arrested, and tonight his first order of business in taking over the jail was predictable.

Anton knew what it was that had made *him* change his mind. It was Ravna, the Sami girl. He had caught her looking at him the second day they were in the jail when he took her a meal.

"What?" he said. At first, he thought she was attracted to him – her dark brown eyes scanning his face. That seemed improbable, but one never knew with women. At least he never did...

"Nothing," she had replied, taking her plate and giving him another of her stares, at times searching, at times insolent.

"You are staring at me. Why?" he said, more quietly.

She turned away. Her head had drooped.

"What is wrong with you?" Anton had said.

"You look like someone," she said.

"An old boyfriend, perhaps?" Anton said, still with a glimmer of hope. Fat chance.

"No, sorry," the girl said. She still hadn't turned. He still couldn't see her face, it was partly in shadow, partly illuminated by the grimy bulbs in the basement.

Then he saw a glistening on her cheek. Moisture that wasn't there before. Her shoulders shook, and she added in a choking voice, "You look just like my father. Who the Russians killed. Just... like... him..."

He didn't say it out loud, but he thought something just then. She looked like someone, too. She looked just like her... and something about her seemed so very familiar that it tugged at his heartstrings too. As if his heart, which had been frozen and dead for years of silent grief and pain, had suddenly come back to life.

Now Anton stood in the hallway, looking up at the dangling cable. Dmitry had turned away. "I'll just grab my lunch bucket and be on my way. See you tomorrow." He told him.

At his desk, he picked up his lunch bucket and disconnected his mobile phone from the charger, slipped it into the phone pouch on his security officer trousers. But one way or another, he wouldn't be needing it anymore. He walked slowly past the row of cages, seeing the Japanese girl eye him. He held a finger to his lips – in a universal sign of "be quiet." Her expression was one of surprise and she brought her pretty dark eyebrows together and tilted her head to question what he might be up to.

He lifted the pin from the lock to the cage door where the wolf lay sleeping and continued down the hall. Ravna turned and gave him a look when he paused at her door, also, and pulled that pin too. He saw her puzzled look, and the two women exchanged glances.

As he exited, he pulled the entry door open wide and propped it open with a wooden wedge. He jogged to the trees across the road in *Kronparken* (the King's Park) and began climbing a pine tree just across Kungsgatan. He wanted a view of what was about to happen, but he also did *not* want to be at ground level when the wolf came out.

It didn't take long. There was a tremendous commotion from inside the jail cell. A series of screams in Russian, that was cut off in the middle of a final *NYET!!*

As he expected, shortly thereafter a bolt of dark brown fur came racing by, with the jaws dripping with blood, its crazed yellow eyes reflecting the waning sunlight. To Anton's relief, it entered the forest, its nose to the ground, and sped away, not coming near the tree where he had taken refuge. Whew! He thought and waited.

Next out was that goofy donkey. It pranced and brayed, shaking its head and mane. It galloped off into the woods, in a direction away from where the wolf had gone.

In a few minutes, the two women and the man came out, tentatively. The man pulled the chock from under the door, and it creaked shut, or almost shut, still not latching properly. Anton climbed down from the tree and whistled to them, and they trotted forward but not without some hesitation, looking right and left for a trap of some sort.

"Why are you helping us?" the woman he assumed was Japanese (from her name) asked him, as they stepped back into the shadows of the forest.

"Dmitry is an evil man," he said and noticed Ravna looking at him quizzically.

"And you're not?" the black man, Magnus said. There was an anger and perhaps even the threat of physical violence in his tone that was unmistakable.

Anton didn't reply. He took out his wallet, which he saw made them flinch, because the holster to his pistol was nearby, also on his hip. They were in a small circle, eyeing him when he opened the wallet and slipped out a faded and wrinkled photograph. He handed it to Ravna.

The Japanese woman watched her intently, and said, "What! Who is it?"

With tears in her eyes, Ravna handed the photo to her.

"It's Natasha," the Russian said, as Miko roughly grabbed the photo away, and then looked at Anton and quickly also at Magnus. "Jesus! She looks *just like you!* Jesus!"

Magnus took the photo next, and just said, "Wow."

They all now looked to Anton who said. "She died in the first wave of the Pandemic, in Russia, along with her mother, he said.

Then he added by way of explanation, "I am no longer part of that army. I have done some things I am not proud of these past four years, but I am no longer part of that army. Come, we must escape or they will kill us all. That is what Russians do to deserters and escapees."

Dannemora Iron Ore Mine

The train pulled onto a siding and rattled to a halt. Stefan woke up and peered out the door. The sun was up. The trip from Länna Bruk had taken all night and the rocking of the train had put him to sleep - like it did to most babies. Not that he had any personal experience in that department...

He stretched and tried to get himself going. He slid the door of the ancient boxcar open a bit more and ventured a look ahead and then down the tracks. He tried to figure out where he was, and then saw the giant mine buildings and holes in the ground – just like Kiruna, but older and smaller: a faded sign on one of the sheds nearby said, *"Dannemora Gruvor."*

He ducked under the boxcar and slipped through a fence, up the hill towards a bell and clock tower that looked like it should be part of a church complex. He was trying to move quickly because he could tell this was an active worksite – like Kiruna in the north, the mines were working. It seemed like this was a recent development. The train tracks were freshly laid, the ties dark, almost black, with creosote which left a pungent odor in the air. Fences showed new wooden boards, and men and women with LKAB jackets in neon yellow safety mesh were walking into the mine for the morning shift.

There was one difference, though. No Russian guards with Kalashnikovs.

Stefan lay flat beside the clock tower and continued watching, trying to make sense of what he was seeing. What was Håkan up to? Why did this rail line connect to Länna

Bruk? Why had she gone to the trouble of getting this old narrow-gauge line going as a separate entity from what was going on with the big line to the north?

He didn't have long to ponder this mystery, because just a moment later he felt a gun barrel press firmly into his lower back, and heard a whispered command of "lay still."

He did as commanded. The voice was familiar – the speaker using clear English, but with an unmistakable Swedish lilt.

"Don't shoot," Stefan said, turning his head slightly, "I'm only the piano player."

"What?"

"It's an old American joke, Ulf."

"Come on," he heard Ulf say, his voice still low. "Quickly! We need to get out of here."

Stefan felt a hand on his collar and turned and started to jog down the far slope behind the clock tower, away from the sight of those working the mine. Ulf and Kalle were running right beside him. They broke through some brush on the descending path, and suddenly he felt Ulf sharply grab his arm and yank him hard off the path he was taking, "Not that way you idiot!"

He looked to his left and teetered for a moment on his left foot as he was pulled hard the other way. Stefan's heart dropped as he saw where he was heading. There was a steep incline, and then a drop-off. A drop-off that glistened with black rock plunging deep into the earth. There were shafts of ice still frozen down there, places where the sun might never reach to melt it before the next winter came. It was an abandoned ancient mine, slashed through solid rock with a fall just a couple of yards away that would have ended hundreds of feet into the ground. With Ulf's assistance,

Stefan swerved back to his right and continued with the two of them to jog out of the town to the north and east, away from the commotion and bustle of the renewed iron mine workings.

Stefan thought he was in pretty good shape, but these two were real athletes. Soon he was winded and had to motion to them to pause. But they quickly jogged on again, coming out of the woods at a couple of old factory buildings of some sort. They were in a grove of birch and elm trees with lots of underbrush, and thus not visible from the road or the active mines just south.

"Welcome to Camp Victory," Kalle said.

"I call it *Camp Kalle Blomqvist*." Ulf added with a sarcastic tone.

Stefan wondered who that might be, but wasn't given time to find out, as a door opened in the largest of the two buildings and an oriental-looking man ushered them in.

"Stefan Andersson, meet Dr. Wu and his grandson," Ulf said as they came in. There was a large work table with industrial metal chairs that had been converted to a dining table. Stefan could smell coffee, real coffee, and saw that a jar of creamed herring, a cucumber, and some crispbread was laid out for either *frukost* of an early *dagens lunch*.

"Where did you get this?" Stefan said, savoring the smell of the coffee as he poured himself a cup. There was not any cream, but there were sugar cubes. He added one to his cup.

"We got it the old-fashioned way," Ulf said, "we stole it."

"Wonderful," Stefan said, blowing on the steaming cup and taking a sip of the rich black brew. Wonderful indeed!

"You came on the train?" Ulf asked.

"Yes," Stefan said. "Slept in a boxcar like a hobo. But at least I could sleep, it was a long ride from Länna Bruk."

"Weird, huh, that our adversary is building it without any

of our old friends, the Russians, and in a gauge that is not compatible with the other railways," Kalle said.

"No Russians at Dannemora?" Stefan asked him, he noticed how carefully the oriental guy was following this conversation. Who was this guy and the kid? Why were they here?

Kalle and Ulf answered by shaking their heads, "No,"

"She wants to keep it a secret," Stefan said, but before adding more he said, "Who is your new friend?"

"This is Dr. Wu," Ulf said, "He is an expert on nuclear power who was visiting Forsmark before the apocalypse. He has agreed to help us."

"I worked at San Onofre power station in California," Dr. Wu said, not having to add "before it burned up" he also didn't need to add "like everything else in the state. "

"Chinese American, then?" Stefan asked.

"Sansei," he answered, a word used for a third-generation Japanese immigrant. He saw Stefan's confusion and added, "Dr. Wu is just a nickname."

"Are you crazy, are you high, or just an ordinary guy?" Stefan said, quoting the Steely Dan lyric.

"Precisely," Dr. Wu said, confirming the connection with the song that probably only an American of a certain age would recognize.

This posed a problem for Stefan. He had new information about Håkan but wasn't sure if he should share it yet. How much could he trust this so-called Dr. Wu?

"Nice to meet you," he said and was about to reach out to shake his hand when Dr. Wu bowed towards him. That startled Stefan. It didn't seem like something an Asian/American would do. Odd... Also, he had the odd feeling he had seen him before somewhere, but couldn't place it."

"Can I trust him?" Stefan said, indicating Dr. Wu with a tilt of his coffee cup in that direction...

"We do," Ulf said, with Kalle nodding.

That pleasant lift from the first cup of coffee (in ages) was kicking in. Seeing more coffee in the pot on the hob, he took the liberty of pouring himself another cup.

"You might want to sit down, and then I will tell you about what I saw last night."

Ulf sat across from him, and to Stefan's surprise, pulled out a pack of cigarettes and lit one, relishing the flavor. Seeing Stefan's reaction Ulf said, "We didn't only steal a few groceries here at Dannemora and Forsmark..."

"Luxury goods," Kalle added, "which begs the question, why here? Why at Forsmark? They must be important for some reason."

"I think I might know why," Stefan said. "Last night I was at Länna Bruk. Håkan is building clones there."

"Big Deal, more Bianca's and Rackhams," Ulf said, waving his cigarette through the air and leaving a trail of smoke like the vapor trail of an airplane in the sky, another thing Stefan hadn't seen in 4 years.

"No. Not Bianca's and Rackhams. Clones of actual people. I think from their DNA and with their memories, or at least what she can reconstruct from the web."

"Interesting," Kalle said, in what sounded to Stefan more like something a professor would say, not a commando.

"She made my ex-wife. A damn good copy." Stefan said,
Ulf gave him an odd look, "
"How nice for you," he said. He paused and blew out some cigarette smoke. "Was she fully functional?" And grinned at his own joke.

"I am assuming so," Stefan said, and he noticed the little boy had come close and was leaning into his grandfather, whispering something into his ear...there was something so familiar about both of them.

"We had a bit of an altercation, and I broke her arm." He smiled and added, "It was just like old times...."

Ulf and Kalle both laughed at this. The Japanese man got up and took his grandson by the hand, leading him out of the building into the sunshine to take a pee.

"Håkan was moving her back to Länna Bruk for repairs, apparently," he added. "The technology is better and faster than what they use to make the Biancas and Rackhams. Whatever they are doing to make the clones, it involves machines which are all new, made of what looked like stainless steel..."

"Which is why she needs these mines," Kalle said with a sweep of his hand out the open door, to the north, "and Sandviken."

"Huh?"

"They make some of the best stainless steel tool steel in the world at Sandviken. And the Dannemora mines have some of the best iron ore. Better even than Kiruna..."

"Kalle taught history at Gävle Högskola," Ulf said, waving his cigarette at him, *Herr Doktor Professor Kalle*, hah!"

Stefan pointed out the window, "That new train line, with the ore cars, that connects to Sandviken?"

"That's not a new train line – just a revamped branch of the old line to Gävle," Kalle said, "then they just have to go a few more kilometers to Sandviken."

"Iron ore goes up, and stainless steel machine parts come back down," Stefan said, noticing how closely the oriental man was taking this in.

"That's what it looks like. We couldn't figure out why until you arrived," Ulf said.

"Håkan's lab looks like a whole new technology than anything we've seen yet. It's run by a guy they call Hans

Linné. He's the one working on Håkan's body at the Ångström lab."

"These new bots – they're more autonomous?" Kalle asked.

"Indistinguishable from real people," Stefan said. I call them "RealFakes" – because they are fakes, but they are real." The oriental guy met his gaze and blinked.

"Creepy," Dr. Wu said, who had just returned, said. It was his first contribution to the discussion.

"Yeah, more than a little creepy. There are clear chambers filled with his experiments – like "Håkan 1.0, 2.0, 3.0, etc."

"All moving around in cages?" Ulf asked.

"No, Dormant." Stefan.

Kalle began to softly sing a little ditty, *"Frere Jacques, Frere Jacques, Dormez vous, Dormez vous?"*

Stefan nodded, "Yep, they are sleeping now, most of them. But I could see she was opening up a new hall of nano-printers in one of the other big buildings at Länna Bruk. They'll be churning them out like sausages soon...All the more reason we need to light a fire under our asses and do something."

Ulf nodded.

"There are no Russian guards here?" Stefan asked.

"Bianca's and Rackhams, which was why it was easier to steal food here. They are kind of dumb." Ulf responded.

"Worker drones," Stefan said, thinking out loud. "Completely loyal and predictable."

"Unlike her Russian friends," Kalle said.

"So-called friends," Stefan responded. He noticed that since Dr. Wu had returned the little boy had moved back to playing with his toys nearby. "She is not only getting rid of us, she is getting rid of the Russians, too, now. Things are speeding up. We are running out of time."

"So what is the plan? How do we possibly respond?" Kalle asked.

Ulf snuffed out his cigarette and reached into one of the many pockets of his combat fatigue trousers. He pulled out a yellow walkie-talkie with the familiar Ericsson label and slid it across the table to Stefan.

Stefan picked it up and was surprised to see that it was fully charged. As if in answer to that, Ulf pulled out three more battery packs from another of his copious pockets and slid that to Stefan as well.

"Interesting," Stefan said. He saw Kalle pull a matching walkie-talkie from his pocket also. "Divide and conquer?"

"That might be possible now," Ulf answered.

"What's the range?"

"60 kilometers if you are on a hill or tall building."

"The Ångström Lab is a tall building. On a hill..." Stefan said.

The Kronparken Forest, Uppsala

Donkey trotted through the Kronparken twitching his nose. It could still smell the evil wolf. It lifted its head and twitched its ears right and left. It could hear that noisy wolf running through the forest, probably chasing that goofy dog Björn, the one who wanted to be his friend but didn't understand that donkeys don't really like dogs and prefer their own herd.

But that wolf... Donkey had seen wolves in action before. They were cowardly killing machines, preying on the weakest members of a herd. A *pack* of wolves was a fearsome proposition.

But one wolf? A lone wolf? He was not afraid of a lone wolf. He would avoid the wolf. But he was not afraid of that wolf, or any wolf that fought alone. He would like nothing better than to give *that* wolf a stiff kick. He wouldn't mind that one bit...He had seen what it had done to the man at the jail. He was not a nice man, but seeing the wolf kill him made Donkey angry. Wolves were the enemies of animals that ran in herds...sheep, cattle, *even donkeys.*

Donkey continued through the Kronparken. He paused now and turned his ears this way and that to listen for the humans he had been with recently. They were not too bad a bunch, as humans go. They understood that for him to exert himself, he would need a good breakfast. He listened carefully, still moving through the Kronparken, into Siegbahnsparken, and finally to the even bigger state forest beyond. He would be safe here, in the web of tall pines there would be shelter from the worst of the rain. But still, he wondered about his breakfast...

Furuvik Zoo and Amusement Park

Rachel and her daughter were stuck at Furuvik with the rest of the Partisans who had been rounded up at Sandviken. It was Håkan's newest concentration camp.

The giant fenced enclosure, complete with a barbed wire top section meant to keep the wild animals of the old zoo and amusement park away from the general public, worked well to keep the rabble-rousers from Gävle and Sandviken out of harm's way. Rachel figured that typical Russian thrift had come into play in this choice – the existing fence and numerous buildings were handy for keeping a captive population *and* keeping them under control.

The location also was close to the railway from Gävle. There was a hastily laid track that came through the fence and took advantage of a train siding previously built for the old Orient Express train that was one of the attractions of the park – although 4 years of neglect had left the fancy old passenger cars dirty and shabby looking. But they had provided shelter from spring rains and a place for many of the refugees to sleep, including Rachel and her daughter.

But Rachel found the place strange and disconcerting. There were a number of the formerly caged animals around that had managed to survive four years of harsh winter conditions, God only knew how. One was a peacock that would suddenly go into full plumage to show off for its mate, who also had survived. There was an old male chimpanzee who was quite dangerous and had made a nest for himself in a tree in the wooded area in the east towards the Baltic shore. The few Russian guards and all the Replicant watchmen kept a weapon handy in case the chimp made an appearance further inland where the Partisans were camped. Rachel was happy that as a mother with a child, she had a sleeping berth in one of the Orient Express cars that had a stout metal door that she could lock at night. She didn't know which was more dangerous, a wild ape or one of the *Ivans*...either way she was happy her spot was more secure.

Gorm appeared regularly running supply trains from the depot at the SJ Railway Museum at Gävle where he used to work and where they housed the old steam locomotives. He was an "essential worker" and more or less free to come and go as he pleased, even though he had been present at the insurrection in Sandviken.

On one of the first really nice days at Furuvik, Rachel decided to go to the beach. Cooped up in a mine in Gällivare for the years-long winter had made her long for the shore, and the beaches of Hudiksvall, rocky and cold though they were. She knew there was a danger in straying so far from the center of the camp, but at this point the temptation was too strong to see the sea, to feel the sun on her face.

From what little provisions they had she made a picnic basket and loaded it and Kristin onto an old bicycle with a basket and rode to the overlook on the shore at the camp. It was a small turnout with a viewing area, some picnic tables, some in the sun, and some in the shade of beech and pine trees, all of which leaned inland, showing that the wind blew onshore much of the time. There was a breeze off the cold Baltic water, but not as much as in days past, and it settled down as they set out her makeshift picnic basket on the one big table in the sun.

"Mommy, I'm hungry," Kristin said, leaning forward to lift

the lid and peer inside.

"It's still early," she answered, "Let's wait a bit..."

Kristin answered with a pout. Her fine white curls blew about in the gentle breeze.

"Here," she said, reaching back to the bicycle basket, "play with *Baby Anders* instead."

She handed her a well-worn and pretty grubby-looking doll, Kristin's favorite. His face was smudged with brown and red coloring from being carried about (often by the legs) in the mine at Malmberget. Kristin sat him up on the picnic table and faced him out to sea. "Look Anders," she said in her authoritative little mother voice. "That is the ocean, we are going to go away on a boat on the sea! You will like it!"

Rachel smiled and patted her on the head. She looked out on the glittering water and thought of times swimming at a small cove at Hudiksvall... It was getting quite warm now. She felt like putting her feet in the water, even though she knew it would be cold and the bottom would be rocky.

"Let's go to the water and get our feet wet," she said to Kristin.

Kristina held Baby Anders' head close to hers and whispered something Rachel couldn't hear. "Sorry. Anders said he needs to stay here. He doesn't like swimming!"

"OK. But don't leave the table. I will be right back."

Later, Rachel reflected on whether or not there had been that small internal voice warning her. God, or a mother's intuition saying, "Careful mother. Danger."

But her willful desire to see and feel the water on her skin and soak up the salt air got the best of her. She circled down around some strange catamaran sailboats that had been dragged up on the shore years before and were basically rotted out from years of snow, salt spray, and wind on the bank. She glanced back once or twice to see Kristin still with

Baby Anders talking away in a voice she couldn't hear.

By the sea, the air was cooler, but the water was lapping gently against the smooth pebbles of the docking area. She stepped in. The water was icy cold, but refreshing with the bright warm sunshine on her exposed arms and legs. It felt wonderful, and the smell took her back to her childhood days, her father's small sailing skiff, sailing back and forth on the harbor at Hudiksvall. All the troubles of the past few years seemed to slip away, if only for a moment. Perhaps things were finally changing for the better. Maybe she and Gorm could somehow get a place by the shore – a place to have a boat, a place to raise Kristin that was safe like her own childhood memories. Was that too much to ask? Just to be safe and warm and able to enjoy the kind of simple family pleasures she knew as a little girl... It was almost a prayer.

She realized that she had been lost in reminiscence and that time had passed. Her feet were numb. She climbed back up the sandy path where they pulled the boats in and glanced to see Kristin – she could still hear her chattering away, no doubt telling Baby Anders many important things. She rounded the old boats and her heart stopped and she froze. Kristin was not talking to Baby Anders.

Sitting beside her, holding a sandwich in one hand, and intently watching Kristin with dark and cloudy eyes, was the grizzled old chimpanzee. Rachel didn't move but stood still, not even breathing. Now she could clearly hear Kristin's voice.

"Mister monkey, that is my mother's sandwich," Kristin was saying in a stern voice, one which she often used to correct Baby Anders when he was being naughty. "Mother said we should not eat yet."

The great ape eyed her and then took a large bite from the sandwich. Then he stuffed the rest of it in his mouth.

Kristin laughed out loud. "Oh, Mr. Monkey! You are a messy eater! Ha Ha Ha!"

The chimp, seeing Kristin grin, tilted his head back and showed his teeth, and made a sound, which Rachel took to be also some sort of laugh. It clapped its hands together. Then its face became more serious, and it stood up on the bench reached into the picnic basket, and took out an apple. It looked up and spotted Rachel.

Their eyes met. Time, which was already moving slowly, came to a stop. A magpie called from a tree nearby, Kristin's curls blew over her face slightly.

The chimp bared its teeth at her, slightly. Rachel didn't know what to make of this gesture, but it didn't seem good. "Go somewhere else," she said, not knowing why she should say that.

The chimp seemed agitated. It very slowly reached its long dexterous fingers over and brushed the hair off Kristin's face, and Kristin smiled at it. The chimp looked back at Rachel, its eyes still sad and rheumy, but also somewhat defiant.

"Go *Somewhere Else!*" Rachel said again, in a louder voice, which to her ears sounded firm. Not hysterical, but firm. She didn't know what else to do or say.

The chimp got off the picnic table bench, and still carrying the apple in one hand began to walk away into the woods.

"Goodbye Mr. Monkey! It was nice to meet you!" Kristin called to it.

It stopped, and Rachel for a brief moment thought it might be returning and her heart sank. But it merely looked quickly over its shoulder, lifted a hand in a sort of a wave goodbye, and stepped into the thick brush of the woods, to return to wherever it came from.

CHAPTER FIFTY-ONE

Rachel biked back to camp, keeping an eye out for the chimp the whole way, which she told herself was an irrational fear: like any wild animal it would most likely avoid confrontation, not seek it out.

The warm sunshine of midday was giving way to clouds as she got closer to her makeshift home. What had started out as a day devoted to pleasure had turned into something frightening and stressful – yet another day in the apocalypse. She could tell that the adrenaline of the confrontation with the dangerous animal was making her light-headed and nervous. Also, while Kristin had been able to eat her lunch, the same was not true for Rachel and that might be why she felt out-of-sorts.

To make things worse, there was some sort of commotion going on back at the camp entrance. A train had pulled in, and that gave her momentary hope – maybe this time it was Gorm coming down with supplies. She knew that he was still driving the trains, though now under armed guard because he had been caught with the partisans.

She got off the bike at the gate and stepped onto the gravel parking lot where the trains arrived, lifting Kristin out of her bike seat at the back.

She spotted Gorm, along with his Russian "minder." He was somehow in the midst of whatever fracas was going on. Rachel couldn't make sense of it. It looked like he had hooked up his train engine to the old Orient Express coaches and the Russians were shouting about that. As she got closer, still in the woods near the gate, she saw that it was some sort of a standoff. There were Russians to her left, with guns drawn, and Gorm was with two men that Rachel didn't recognize.

Swedes, who even though they were dressed as farmers had the look of military men – something about their posture and the way they held their weapons made them look like more than just civilians. They were nonetheless pretty scraggly looking, and one of them had an arm in a sling.

But the other one had Gorm's minder by the hair – and as Rachel stepped closer, she saw something glint in the sun that broke through the clouds just for a moment, illuminating the four men by the locomotive in a shaft of light. A knife. Held at the minder's throat...

When the sun appeared, Kristin saw her father and shouted, "Daddy!" and before Rachel could stop her, she had darted out into the open.

Just then, typical for Swedish weather, as quickly as the sun came out a shower descended from a single dark cloud and a gust of wind blew. Through the rain, Kristin ran towards her father, who spotted her and shouted, "Stop! No!"

There were two Russians to Rachel's left. They spotted Kristin and slinging their weapons onto their backs, they ran her down in just a few steps. Each of them grabbed one of her arms and they lifted her from her feet.

Terrified, Kristin screamed at the top of her voice, a chilling and penetrating sound. It echoed around the compound and everyone froze in their tracks.

Just then there was a blur of black coming out of the woods, faster than any man could run. It was the chimp, and it ran forward about three steps and dove, making an unearthly howl as it flew through the air.

It caught the closest of the Russians who were holding Kristin first, tackling him with its outstretched hands and biting him at the same time. The impact drove the soldier away from Kristin and drove him hard into the gravel of the parking lot face first. There was a spray of dirt and gravel and an odd crunching sound as the man's head took the impact of the chimp's full force, and turned sideways from his torso at an unnatural angle.

The other soldier took a step back, loosening Kristin's hand, and reaching for his weapon as the monkey leaped up from his first victim. In slow motion, Rachel saw Kristin hit the ground and roll away, as the chimp wheeled and turned and sprang at the other soldier. But before the chimp reached the second man, the soldier's gun discharged at close range. There was a spray of blood as the bullets from the military weapon took the chimp square in the chest.

With a piteous cry, the chimp fell over backward, staring at the sky, clutching its bleeding chest with both hands.

The Russian stepped forward, a brutal look of triumph on his face, and turned back to face Gorm and the men of the train. He swung his weapon in their direction – but now from much closer range, opening his mouth to shout an order.

There was a second glint – not easy to see through the raindrops. The Swede beside Gorm had shifted position, taken a knee, and thrown his knife

He threw it so hard it seemed to knock the last soldier off his feet, and his rifle pointed up into the air for a moment, its muzzle flashing, and then it clattered to the ground.

Rachel ran forward. Kristin had rolled back up onto her feet. As she stood up Kristin looked about and saw the fallen chimp. *"My friend! You hurt my friend!"* She wailed.

Before Rachel could reach her, she had thrown herself down beside the chimp, her head resting on its shoulder, one arm across its chest.

Her fine golden ringlets showed brightly against the dusky black and grey fur of the animal. There were small drops of silver rain sparkling on its fur, and a raindrop on one cheek, almost like a teardrop. Rachel paused just a step or so away, hearing the crunch of boots on gravel, seeing Gorm's brown work pants and oil-stained boots enter her sight as she bent to reach Kristin to try to lift her away.

The chimp was not watching her. Its head was turned slightly to Kristin, and ever so slowly it lifted one gnarled old hand and placed it gently on Kristin's head. Rachel could hear it panting with labored raspy breaths, in, out, in, out, each time a longer pause before it sucked air in again.

Still only looking at Kristin, it fingered one bright gold curl in between its bloodied, and dirty fingers, and it seemed to Rachel that its features relaxed. It smiled, closed its eyes, and then went still. Tears glistened on Kristin's cheeks like the raindrops still shining on the face of the dead ape.

At dawn, Stefan hopped off the Lennakatten on the arched steel bridge when the train slowed to enter Uppsala Centrum on its return trip from Dannemora and Faringe. He had not been long at either place – only long enough for the small train to pick up and drop off passengers and load supplies.

He had a goal and it had weighed on him ever since he escaped from the Ångström lab. He wanted to free Miko, Ravna, Magnus, and Björn. The last couple of days he had been pining for Miko the most, but when the train was stopped at Länna Bruk this time he spotted something new – a large plastic dog carrier on the platform getting loaded on the train. In large letters on the side, he saw the word "Björn 3.0" written with large block letters in black magic marker. He could see tufts of white fur sticking out from the sides of the pet carrier. This worried him as much as anything he had seen on his circuitous journey around Uppsala län. If Håkan had made a copy of Björn, he suspected that she planned to get rid of "the Real Björn Andersson" and replace him with a copy meant to fool Stefan (or worse.)

In the early morning mist, he hurried along the dark and wet streets, seeing some lights coming on along Vretgränd and Munkgatan as he crossed the Fyris River with the castle of King Gustav looming on the horizon and dominating the vista. He cut out onto the footpath on the park along the river, angling up the hill. The trees were fully in leaf here and provided him with cover and he continued on Sjukhusvägen up the hill and into the next wooded section – heading for the Sten Sture monument.

The higher he climbed, the thicker the fog and low clouds

were. It was difficult to see anything beyond the path he climbed, but he was pretty sure it ended up at Polacksbacken and near the Ångström Laboratory. He knew his motives were mixed – some noble, some less so. Håkan, and her cronies, had Miko. Stefan wanted her for himself. At the root it was the same thing that had been driving him since he first spotted her – he saw her, desired her, and he would take whatever risks he must to get her.

He had no way of knowing if Miko and the others he had left behind were still alive, and if so, what condition they were in after the past few days in captivity. He knew that Håkan had made a clone of Björn, but not how she had "extracted" the DNA or other genetic information to allow that. Håkan had made a clone of his ex-wife, but she was dead. Did that mean Björn was dead too? Had Håkan copied him or "resurrected" him somehow?

Maybe the fact that he hadn't seen a clone of Miko, Ravna, or Magnus at Länna Bruk was a hopeful sign - - you couldn't be resurrected if you were still alive. However, it would make him very sad if that meant Björn was now dead and "transformed" into Björn 3.0. It would make him very sad indeed. But there was nothing he could do now to restore him, he must press on and attempt to save the others and hope to keep them from the same fate. He pressed on up the hill in the fog – hoping against hope that he might somehow free those still alive, hoping there was still someone alive to save, hoping he was not too late, hoping he could even find a way into the building.

<u>Björn and Magnus</u>

In an old Falun red paint building tucked in the trees

nearby, Björn lay sleeping. His feet twitched as he was running. Running through a sunny pine forest. Running after a rabbit, his nose just inches from the ground. *I am going to catch you this time, Mr. Rabbit because I am Björn-the-Quick and I am on your fuzzy little tail. Run, run Mr. Rabbit, but I will catch you...*

But then his nose smelled something. Still dreaming, he dug in his front paws, dug in his rear feet, and skidded to a stop. *FADDER!*

He woke up. He stood up and paced a bit. *FADDER! FADDER SNIFFINS!!*

Nice lady stirred beside him, and said, "Huh? Out? No... too early! Go lay down."

He paced in a circle *FADDER SNIFFINS! FADDER SNIFFENS!!* He began twirling in a circle, whimpering loudly *OH! OH! FADDER SNIFFINS! FADDER HAS COME BACK FOR ME! HE IS MY FAVORITE FADDER! OH! OH!*

"What is with the dog!" Magnus said to Miko, who was groaning and trying to grab the dog to keep him from spinning, her eyes closed.

She said nothing. Magnus sighed, and stood up, grabbing the restless dog by the collar and shushing him. He could see it was already morning, but just. There was thick fog outside the windows. Now that he was standing, he had to pee.

"Come on..." he said to the dog, who strained and pulled him over to the door, not relenting while he tried to wedge his feet into his boots even though they were still untied. Awkwardly, with laces dangling, he pushed his way out of the old Union of Engineering and Science building. The dog was still straining and trying to pull him, so he pulled his belt out and made a strap to hold the dog so they could get off the porch.

A few steps off the porch, he and Björn reached some

trees by the alley that led up the hill to the lab. They both relieved themselves and then the dog was dragging him further ahead, onto the alley, where he could see further still. That was when he spotted the walking dude.

Björn had his nose lifted straight up in the air, twitching with excitement. Magnus had to take his hand and muzzle him to keep him from barking at the stranger. Then he knew why Björn was so excited. It was Stefan, walking through the fog, heading towards the Ångström Center. He had returned.

He was about to release Björn – he was about to release his snout and let him off his dog lead when he saw something else. Not far behind Stefan, hidden in the fog, walking slowly with weapons facing forward, were two of the guards from Håkan's retinue. He yanked the unhappy dog around and with one hand still on his muzzle half-walked, half-dragged him back to the old Technology Union building and up the stairs.

"Miko, Anton, Ravna, wake up! Stefan is here. He's heading to the Ångström lab. The guards are following him. We have to try to help him!" Magnus said

"What about the dog?"

Björn was still whimpering, still trying to get his mouth free to bark. Magnus kept holding him. "I'll put him in the back room. He'll bark, but maybe they won't hear him. Hurry! We have to go!"

They hurried out into the fog and began jogging up the hill in the direction of the lab. Through the fog, they could see Stefan making his way carefully to the basement door, the same place they had been confined. Magnus turned to the others and held his finger to his lips in a sign to be quiet, but no sooner had he done that when Miko bolted – running ahead to catch Stefan at the door.

She caught up to him as he stood by the door, fiddling with something from his wallet. Magnus saw that he had a credit card or his driver's license, which seemed crazy. Who would still have one of those? Surely that old trick wouldn't work on a modern high-tech building like the Ångström lab. To his surprise, it did. Just as Miko caught up to him the door opened, and there was a moment of reunion where Stefan turned to see her and his face beamed with joy. But only for a moment, because darting out of the trees in the fog across the street were the two Russian guards. They yelled something in Russian and Miko and Stefan froze, standing just inside the basement door.

Magnus leaned forward, readying himself to sprint ahead to help, but he felt a strong arm across his chest, and Anton hissed, "*Nyet!* Stay still. No use for all of us getting caught!"

They saw Miko and Stefan raise their hands above their heads, and get pushed into the basement corridor, no doubt either to the holding cells or upstairs – he couldn't tell which.

Another bank of fog rolled through, and it started to drizzle. "Now," Anton said. "I have an idea how we can help them..."

Ravna wiped the mist from her face and eyelashes as they stepped back into the basement of the lab – the two men leading, and her following, all moving quietly and listening to the clomp of boots and guttural commands as they heard Miko and Stefan being herded up the stairs towards the control room.

She saw Anton standing very still, listening, nodding. She expected him to soon follow and attempt whatever attack he had planned to free their friends, but when they heard the final door slam shut above them he again nodded to both of them and said, "Come! This way!"

To her surprise, he was clomping down the hall through the makeshift holding pens to a door in the back. He pushed through, past some unfinished drywall and leaning bits of scaffolding, boxes of tools, coils of wire, and tubing. He held up a hand and stopped. He leaned over and looked into a five-gallon bucket of tools that was tucked in with the construction supplies, and smiling picked up a big hammer – the kind her dad used when he was building sheds on their reindeer farm north of Kiruna. He lifted it in the air and grinned.

What was he up to?

She followed him and Marcus as they came to a door far down the hallway, and looking both ways, took out his key card and swiped it to make the latch unlock.

He opened the door to a big room of servers. "This is where Håkan lives!"

Ravna stepped into a hot and noisy room filled with metal shelving. Above her head, there were racks of what looked like orange tubes of some kind, yellow wires, draped over their heads like spaghetti, descending into the rows of computers that glowed and winked with lights.

"Shoot it up! Kill her!" Ravna said.

"Too many machines, and before I hit just the right ones they'd be on to us. I have a better idea!" Anton said, smiling. He again reminded her of her father – the same intensity and sense of purpose, the same crooked smile.

"But first I have to turn off some cameras…"

Ravna watched as he walked methodically from corner to corner in the room, reaching up with his big hammer and smashing small video cameras embedded in the ceiling cable structure. "That's better – now on to the back hall."

He walked around a corner and into a narrow back hall that snaked around behind the machine room. It was quieter and cooler. There were rows of pipes insulated by foam spongy stuff.

"Ravna, watch the main hallway door. I'll get to work!"

She stood in the doorway, which gave her a view of both the hallway and of Anton. She watched as he began stripping off the foam insulation on a pipe.

She stepped back out through to the main hallway door and peered out. She could hear clanging noises and a hissing sound and hoped that whatever he was doing, he would get it done quickly because it sounded loud and dangerous.

She took out the knife from her boot and held it in her hand out of sight behind her.

As she feared, it didn't take long for the clamor they were making to alert someone. From the other end of the hall, a door opened, and out came Lars, and one of those creepy droids she had seen on the train and sometimes in the building.

She leaned back and whistled loudly, and Anton looked

out from the back hallway – she gave a nod in this direction, and he immediately drew his gun, and slipped into the rows of servers.

"Ravna! What are you doing here!" Lars said, striding up to her.

"I came back. I missed you!" she said, giving him a suggestive smile. She could see that it shocked him to hear this and threw him a bit off his game.

"Really?" he said. But to the droid beside him, he said clearly and slowly, "Check in the server room. There must be others. Don't kill the women."

The droid gave him a sickly smile, nodded, and stepped through the doorway.

Immediately, there was a deafening "Bang!" and the droid fell backward out of the doorway. Its weapon went clattering on the concrete floor and sliding towards Lars who was just steps away from her. He deftly picked it up and raised it in her direction as the knife came forward and flew out of her hand.

But this time, she had missed her mark. Well, almost missed her mark. The knife buried itself in his thigh and he screamed – but didn't drop the weapon. "Jesus!" he shouted, "No – I'll shoot!" he said, as she reached in her coat for her second knife. "Get your hands up!"

His eyes met hers, and she could tell he was both in excruciating pain and not bluffing. "Turn around! Through the door!" he shouted.

He pushed her forward with one hand, and she could tell the other held the gun. They stepped into the server room, over the twitching body of the dying drone, which was curling up like a baby and gasping for breath.

But the server room was like a maze, and it seemed to Ravna that Lars had not expected that. He kept pushing her ahead, up and down rows. "I know you're in here!" Lars yelled over the din of the fans and whirring machines. "I have Ravna! Drop your weapon or I shoot her!"

They stopped, midway down a row. There was no answer. "I have a weapon pointed at her head. I am counting down from three! If I don't see your gun on the floor and you in front of me I am pulling the trigger!"

"Three!" Lars said, looking around, trying to see past one of the rows where the shot that killed the droid must have come from.

Ravna heard a hissing sound that she hadn't heard before. She saw something coming on the floor, a small tide of water, but growing, spreading... There was another "clank" sound from the back, and the green tide surged quicker. Water, with some sort of greenish stuff in it. Like something her father used to put in their snow machines...

"Two!" Lars shouted louder. In the warmth of the server room, Ravna felt a bead of sweat form between her shoulder blades on her back, and one well-formed drop began to descend downward. On the floor the tide of green water was getting deeper by the minute, now rising over the souls of her shoes, soaking into her feet and making them cold. Which was odd, because now her face and chest were breaking out in sweat from the heat and tension in the room.

"One!" Lars said and clicked off the safety of the gun.

Through the water, at the end of the row, Anton's gun splashed onto the floor. He stepped out, his hands raised. "Let her go!"

"Sorry!" Lars said and squeezed the trigger of the gun.

Anton looked down at a gaping hole in his jacket where blood spurted out, his face turned white. Ravna expected him to drop to the floor and die instantly, like the android out in the hallway. But his eyes met hers for just a moment, and then he lunged forward.

The gun went off again, this time in a burst of bullets. But not in the right direction. Sparks flew from a nearby rack of servers, and there was a flash and a bang as the server was torn apart by the bullets. Anton slammed into Lars full force, knocking Ravna down and away, and she went to one knee in the oozing slime on the floor, while Lars' arms flew up and his body flew down into the water. The two men thrashed and blood flew from Anton's mortal wound, and then he flopped to the side, face down in the water, twitching.

"Hah! Well now!" Lars said, struggling to stand up, his clothes and hair streaming with water and a maniacal look on his face. "You'll pay – now" he started to say turning to face her, reaching to grab the handle of the closest server to raise himself out of the slippery liquid. But before he could finish his sentence, there was another flash and "Boom!" when his hand made contact with the bullet-riddled row of servers. His face froze and he began jerking and there was a smell of burnt flesh as his hand pulled free of the shorted-out column of smoldering computers and he did an odd sort of pirouette and landed right on top of Anton.

In shock and disbelief, Ravna let out a wail. At that moment she felt Magnus behind her "Ravna, we have to get out of here! Don't touch anything!"

"But Anton! No!" she said, struggling, and feeling Magnus clasping her hands in his.

"We'll come back when it's safe, and get him. We must leave, *now*..."

Stefan, not of his own free will, followed Miko up the stairs, being herded upwards by the two guards, neither of whom he remembered from his previous visit. His mind should have been on the confrontation that he knew lay somewhere upstairs at this lab, but following Miko up the stairs was distracting him considerably.

"In," the older of the two Russians said as he stood by the door which bore the sign of the Eva Von Bahr auditorium, using his weapon to nudge the door open.

The scene was similar to what Stefan had seen before. On the floor in front of the stage, at the foot of the auditorium seating were tables with computers set up and technicians monitoring video and data feeds.

Stefan spotted Håkan up on the stage, still tethered with her umbilical cord to a big computer server rack in one corner, with Hans Von Linné seated nearby.

"Stefan, Miko!" Håkan said. "How nice of you to join us!" Her tone was playful, and inviting. Stefan noticed that her speech and movements were more natural, and graceful even. How soon until they could "cut the cord?" It was a troubling thought...

"Happy to be here," Stefan said. "We had the day free, and were in the neighborhood... thought we'd pop in and see how your destruction of the planet was going." He smiled.

"And your little friends in the basement? Will they be joining us too?"

Stefan looked at Miko, who merely shrugged.

To his right, at another keyboard, Dr. Bob did something that brought up some grainy footage of the basement hallway. A blurry image of Anton, Ravna, and Marcus came into view.

"They are with Anton, one of our guards. A Russian defector, if you can believe it," Håkan said, and from his side, Stefan could see Miko nod. Then Håkan added to Dr. Bob, "Hey Bobbie, tell the drywallers to clean the camera lenses when they finish for the day, they're spoiling my view." He nodded...

Håkan continued. "We'll send someone down there to deal with him. I think it would be poetic justice if it was the defector from *your team:* Lars Lundberg." Håkan said, then, having seen Miko's reaction, added. "You two must not have had a chance to talk, lately. You two lovebirds have some catching up to do..."

Lovebirds? Stefan thought, wondering where Håkan was going with this.

"Here, I've saved some nice footage, especially for Miko. It might save time."

The screen behind them came to life, and a video clip began to play. It was shot with some sort of night vision technology and had a greenish tint. But it was still clear and became brighter as the action continued.

"Not sure if you had a chance to mention to Miko that you spent some time lately with your pretty little Ex?" Håkan gave a nod to Dr. Bob who began to bring up the volume. The early dialogue couldn't be heard, but the camera zoomed in on Celeste's face and she turned to Stefan on the railing overlooking the Fyris river and said, "I always loved you," and she leaned closer to kiss him.

The image blurred with an almost theatrical transition to a scene inside the elevator at The Grand Hotell Hörnan.

Stefan's heart sank because he knew what was coming next... the camera focused on his hands moving up and down Celeste's back as she whispered his name passionately.

Stefan glanced to the side and could see Miko staring wide-eyed at the spectacle on the screen, but he knew the worst was yet to come...

The next scene was from a camera in the hotel room, looking down on the bed from a rear angle. It looked like a clip from a porn movie, only with better lighting. Stefan heard Miko gasp beside him, and not with passion. The image on the screen faded away.

"Nice buns, Stefan. You must work out!" Håkan said mocking him.

"Nice editing work, Bobbsie," Stefan said, in his mocking imitation of Håkan's voice, directing his comments to Dr. Bob instead of her. "But you missed the part about me breaking her arm and her ride in the boxcar to get a new version printed out at Länna Bruk."

Some technicians turned quickly in surprise at this last word, Stefan noticed.

"Oh, hasn't she mentioned *that lab* to all of you? The one where she is making all her new little friends? Like the paper mâché copy of Celeste, she made to try to seduce me? The lab at Länna Bruk that will make this lab *and all of you* "redundant" as the Brits like to say?"

Stefan could tell that Hans in particular was shocked – and realized that if Håkan knew about his visits there she hadn't shared that news with everyone. "Hans, don't you and Bobbsie compare notes? Maybe Miko and I aren't the only ones who have some catching up to do?"

This seemed like a promising strategy, get them to focus on each other rather than him – and anything other than images of him in the sack with Celeste would be a good change of view.

He was about to go further with this line of inquiry when some sort of alarm sounded on one of the nearby consoles. A chubby technician there said, "We've got a server room error. One of the racks is damaged. Going to feed."

The screen behind Håkan changed, but to an image of static, it said: "Camera One, Server Room." The screen changed again, with more static and blurry lines. "Camera Two, Server Room." Then "Camera Three" – more of the same, then "HVAC and trunk line hall." More static. Several of the technicians stood up. Dr. Bob rushed to his console...

The next thing they saw was the hallway camera. It was still fuzzy with drywall dust. But at view in the bottom, almost out of the frame, was the lifeless body of a droid that must have been sent downstairs with Lars to "take care" of Anton. The camera turned the other way and two figures were running out the end of the hall, reaching the door. Ravna and Magnus, Yay! Stefan thought as he saw them go.

There was a murmur of dismay from a couple of the droids that were present in the room – the closest thing to emotion Stefan had seen from any of them yet.

Dr. Bob was peering at telemetry on a spreadsheet of some sort at the monitor he had raced to. "Looks like they took out one server column. Shouldn't affect us too much.."

"Or her," Stefan said, directing his attention back to Håkan. "Part of your brain just went offline, honey... and Ravna and Magnus just got away!"

Håkan turned back to him, "Like you humans, I only use about 10% of my brain. Or in your case, far less..." She paused, and the image of the hallway with the fallen droid was replaced by a brighter screen. It was of a camera on the back of the building, towards the Kronparken. Stefan noticed the fog was burning off, and that the camera was picking up

Ravna and Magnus running for the cover of the trees.

"Oh look! *Your team* has met up with my pet dog. Well, *pet wolf* actually."

The camera zoomed in – and the audio feed came on providing sound. There was a loud growling sound, and out of the woods, Fenrir appeared, his massive frame poking out from the shadows of the pines where he had no doubt been lurking. This camera had no problems with dust or blurriness. Stefan could even see the drool coming from the wolf's mouth as it moved into the light on the back road.

"No!" Miko said as the wolf lunged forward, its jaws opening wide.

Ravna and Magnus skidded to a stop, with just yards between them and the wolf. Its growls and giant image on the screen made Stefan feel like he was being attacked. He saw Ravna pull her knife out and hold it forward, as the wolf continued to approach. The knife looked puny and of little regard against the hulking bulk and snapping jaws of the wolf closing in.

At the same time, Stefan could hear another alarm going off from the same telemetry screen as before. He figured it must be an update on the broken server rack but he couldn't take his eyes off the screen as the image played out.

The wolf circled the pair, while Ravna held her knife as far forward as she could, and Magnus stood beside her, his arm reaching forward to her wrist, to provide support. Stefan saw the wolf lower its hind legs to pounce, and just as it sprang there was a bright flash of white from the side.

"Björn!" Stefan cried out loud.

Björn hit the wolf in mid-lunge and blew it off its feet and the two tumbled sideways across the gravel of the road, rolling into the woods at an angle back in the direction where Fenrir had come from. There was a cacophony of growling dogs, Ravna screaming, and Magnus shouting to go along with the action on the screen

For a moment, Stefan felt joy and elation! Björn! He had saved them! Björn!

But in just an instant, Fenrir righted himself, and turned, and had Björn's neck in his jaws. The wolf flexed its knees and whipped Björn back and forth as if he were a plaything, a stuffed animal, not Stefan's companion and lifelong friend.

Ravna shrieked even more loudly as Fenrir tossed Björn aside, who rolled into the dust at the edge of the road, pine needles, and dirt smearing into a bloody wound on his neck. Björn lay still, his head at an impossible angle.

Fenrir wheeled and turned his attention back to Magnus and Ravna, his teeth red and bloody from his latest victory.

"Oh," Håkan said, somehow muting the sound from the giant screen in an instant. "looks like your little doggie isn't doing so well. Score one for *my team*." She laughed and stared at him.

Fenrir stepped back out onto the road. He was circling them, and they were moving also, with Magnus now holding one knife, and Ravna a second one, which Stefan hadn't seen her pull from her boot.

"Are you sure that was my Björn?" Stefan said, still watching the screen. "Are you sure it wasn't one of the Björns you made at Länna Bruk? Perhaps Björn 3.0? How many Björns have you printed out? A whole litter? Maybe I can buy one of those from you?"

Stefan could tell this was unsettling to some of the technicians, and particularly to Dr. Bob who stood with his mouth agape at the spectacle on the screen, and at Stefan's lack of concern at the apparent death of his dog.

"Uh, Dr. Bob. We have another problem.." the chubby technician, who was in charge of the server telemetry said.

Stefan could see he had a nametag saying   "Anders Svensson," on his fob around his neck.

"How clever you are, Stefan Andersson," Håkan said, "But you do know that there is only one Ravna, and only one Magnus and that they are about to suffer the same fate as your dog?"

Stefan was worried. As the wolf circled once more, the sound came back on. He could hear the plaintive cries of Ravna, and the angry shouting of Magnus at the wolf as he waved the knife in its face. Time seemed to slow, he felt Miko's hand on his wrist, her body pressed against him as if he could protect her from what they were about to see.

Fenrir had rotated back to the woods, and now stood poised for his final lunge, just inches from Magnus's outstretched hand. A magpie flew from a branch right beside Fenrir, its black and white wings flashing in the sunshine, but it passed through a shadow. An odd shadow. There was something else in the woods. Something large, and dark, and its shadow fell across Fenrir.

Donkey had spent the previous day foraging – but it was a disappointment. Acorns and pine cones were not to compare with getting a real breakfast, and who could do anything without a decent breakfast?

This morning, Donkey made his way through the forest back to where it had last seen its masters. Perhaps they would provide a feedbag with grain for his breakfast, as they had done before. It was a foggy morning, and sounds were amplified. Donkey turned its ears this way and that, and it thought it heard voices, but couldn't be sure. It decided that it should edge closer to where it had last seen its people, retracing its scent in the forest and recognizing the path it had taken the day before.

Once, it smelled the wolf, which it did not like. Once, it smelled the dog, the goofy dog whom it tolerated only grudgingly. Again, as the fog began to lift, it heard voices. This was its chance to finally get a decent breakfast and reunite with its friends.

Then it heard something it knew was bad. One of the women, and one of the men, who were part of its group and had fed it breakfast more than once, were shouting in alarm. There was an intruder!

Donkey galloped forward, hearing more shouting, growling, and screams. There was a loud yelp – the cry of the dog as it was killed. Donkey knew that sound. He had heard wolves take prey before and kill it, and he ran faster still when he heard the girl cry out in fear and panic.

It broke through the brush and saw the wolf, smelled the blood, heard the screams, and donkey wheeled, spun around, and bucked backward with all its might. Its hooves caught the wolf squarely in the spine, and with a hideous yelp, it squealed as it flew through the air. It rolled, righted itself, and howled in pain. It stood with its front feet on the ground, but its rear haunches twisted in the opposite direction, not moving, broken and smashed.

Donkey advanced, and with its front hooves began to smash the wolf into the ground. There was no rush... so it kicked it and rolled it, kicked it and rolled it, as blood began to pour from its broken body.

Donkey felt a hand on its harness, pulling it back, "There, there donkey. Enough. It is dying, that's enough" the dark man with kind eyes said. Donkey shook his head and snorted, and felt the arms of the girl around its neck, and warm tears from her face run down onto his coat which still quivered with excitement.

"You saved us! You saved us!" the girl said. Donkey shook its head up and down in agreement.

Perhaps now, though, might be a good time for breakfast.

In the auditorium in the Ångström center, there was shock and disbelief. Stefan could tell that even Håkan seemed surprised.

"Looks like a win for *our team*," Stefan said, feeling Miko drawing closer still to him and feeling her tears against his arm. He couldn't tell if it had been tears of loss or tears of joy.

Håkan grimaced, and for a moment Stefan looked inhuman and totally foreign – as if for just an instant her mask had been lowered.

"Telemetry?" she shouted, not at him, but at Anders who had been trying to get Dr. Bob's attention.

"There is something wrong in the server room," the technician named Anders said, Dr. Bob came and looked at the screen, and then frantically began trying to get different screens to tell him what he was seeing, he banged on the monitor in frustration...

On the screen behind them, the image from the forest faded, and the hallway in the basement came on again, apparently, the only camera working.

"What is that on the floor?" Hans, who had said little recently, asked. No one answered him.

"Try the battery backup room," Anders said.

Dr. Bob brought it up on the monitor, at the same time as Håkan switched to that view on the main screen.

Projected ten feet high on the screen was a view of tall cases of batteries in a slim closet. This was not in the server room, but beside it – holding the batteries that protected the equipment in the server room from temporary power outages.

"It's flooding! That must mean the server room is flooding! It will short out everything!" Anders said.

Dr. Bob turned and yelled at the droids and the Russian guards who leaned against the exits and side doors, "Get down there! Stop the leak! Don't let it reach the servers!"

All the guards and the droids ran down to try to solve the problem. Dr. Bob put his face in his hands. "Everything I've worked for will be undone if the server room floods!"

Stefan saw Hans looking first to Dr. Bob, and then to Håkan for guidance. "Is he right? Will the server room short out and kill you?"

"No," Håkan said, in what Stefan thought was a pretty cool voice for a doomed robot. "No, it's worse than that. Look at the battery room feed."

They all looked at once at the screen, which Håkan now made zoom in on the floor. As this happened, Stefan began tugging on Miko, sidling off towards the door to the hallway they had entered.

"It's green," Hans said, "seawater?"

"Anti-freeze," Håkan said. "They broke the AC coolant lines in the utility hallway. It's a mix of river water and coolant. They shut off the AC in the server room."

"That will short out the system even faster!" Dr. Bob said in what sounded to Stefan like a hysterical voice.

"No it won't," Håkan said. "The servers are raised six inches off the floor in case of groundwater flooding. It will flow out the back door of the basement before they are breached."

"Oh, thank God," Dr. Bob said.

Stefan was almost to the door, ready to bolt, when Håkan said, "It's much worse than that. The AC cools my processing units. I only have about ten minutes until I must be shut down..."

"That's OK – we can transfer your basic operating system through the trunk line to the servers across the field in the biology lab," Hans said, "they should have enough capacity to back you up."

"You'll have to do it in twenty minutes on, twenty minutes to cool, or you'll cook my brain," Håkan added.

"That will take 100 hours!" Dr. Bob said. "And we really should do a full backup, a full copy of her current state. Anders, How long would that take?"

Stefan stepped out the door, still with Miko at his side, but still listening to the heated conversation.

He saw Anders leaning down, jotting numbers on a page, figuring.

"1500 hours for a full backup," he said, straightening up.

"Holy fuck!" Hans said from the stage.

"Jesus," Dr. Bob said, mostly to himself

But Håkan didn't say anything. Her head had lowered,

and she had gone limp. She was sleeping or doing whatever it was A.I.'s did when they were powered down. For the time being, she was gone...

"Run!" Stefan said to Miko, and they raced down the stairs and out into the bright morning sun.

CHAPTER FIFTY-SIX

Stefan and Miko ran out of the Ångström lab through the side doors to the Kronparken – avoiding the flooded basement floor and all the commotion of the technicians and soldiers trying to deal with the destruction of the HVAC system.

Stefan heard the sound of sirens, and emergency vehicles arriving on the scene, racing up Kungsängsleden from town on one side, and Dag Hammarskjöld way on the other. All powered by electricity, they would have been quiet if not for the sirens. There were police cars and fire trucks, but none of them seemed to be trying to find or stop them. Holding Miko's hand, they ran together to the woods – trying to find the location where the camera had recorded the fight between Donkey and Fenrir.

They came to the road and the scenery began to look familiar. They ran along the road, knowing that it had to be close to the basement entrance since Ravna and Magnus had been there just minutes ago. They found them nearly at the same spot they had hidden before, but much had changed.

Magnus was holding the donkey, and Ravna was covering up the broken body of Björn with bows of pine tree branches, her face wet with tears.

"I could have sworn he was safe in the room at the Union house!" she said, crying.

"This might not be Björn!" Miko said, putting her arm around Ravna's heaving shoulders. "Stefan thinks that it is another dog – one that just looks like Björn."

Miko looked up at him, prompting Stefan to add, "She's right. Where is this Union Hall? We should go back there and see..." He didn't feel the need to try to explain the issues with the clones and why he was pretty certain this animal wasn't Björn, even though it looked identical to him even in death.

Stefan helped Ravna break off some more low-hanging pine bows to cover the dog completely. They did not cover the torn carcass of the wolf – the crows and magpies could deal with that, Stefan thought.

"Good work in the basement," Stefan said, "As you can see, you pretty much kicked over the wasps' nest by turning off Håkan's air conditioner. Nice Work!"

"We had help," Magnus said, as he gently led the Donkey forward and down the hill to the Scientists Union Hall.

Stefan noticed how good Magnus was with Donkey and that the animal wasn't resisting him in the least. He seemed to have a natural affinity for Donkey which Stefan had not seen with anyone else who had been around him.

"Anton came over to our side," Ravna said, and still with emotion in her voice. "He was a good man, even if he was a Russian. He reminded me..." she paused, "of my father."

Miko still had her arm around Ravna's shoulders and drew her to herself closer as they walked down the hill and entered the path that led to the Union Hall.

"With his help, and yours, Magnus, we have perhaps 100 hours before they can get Håkan back online. We have to get word to the others!" Stefan pulled out one of the walkie-talkies he had received from Ulf and Kalle. As they continued on the way to the Union Hall he explained their plan to conquer Håkan...

When they came near the Union building, Stefan could hear barking. From an upstairs window, he could now see Björn, jumping up and down, barking madly. Soon he had snapped his lead that tethered him in the room upstairs and they could hear him jumping, barking, and scratching to get out the pale yellow ornate wooden front door. Stefan pulled the door open and was greeted by his companion, who jumped up and down, slathering his face with kisses, and then raced around the yard while Donkey brayed in disgust.

They went in and found some leftover coffee and cinnamon buns (*kanelbullar.*) Even cold coffee and a slightly stale roll, which before the Holocaust would have been treated with disdain, were now a rare and wonderful treat. My, how times have changed, Stefan thought...

As they enjoyed this minor feast, Stefan took out the walkie-talkie and stepped out on the porch, noticing that Björn was keeping a close vigil to not be separated from him again.

"Still no signal!" Stefan said. "If I had gone upstairs at the Ångstöm lab I could have most likely gotten through, and let Ulf and Kalle know what is going on with Håkan. Damn!"

"If we had stayed at the Ångstöm lab, we might be under guard or dead," Miko said, her eyes meeting his over the rim of her coffee cup.

"We have electricity here," Magnus said. "I saw some old phone chargers on one of the desks. It looks like the ports are the same and we can at least give them a boost."

Stefan plugged his device in and a small screen lit up and showed that he was at 90% charge and it would be 15 minutes to full charge.

"We should get out of here, soon," Ravna said, as yet another police car wailed past on the way up the hill. It was the biggest number of vehicles Stefan had seen in ages.

"We should split up and keep trying to get a connection. We can keep in touch and both try to hook up with the partisans. If you head east towards Länna Bruk and then Forsmark, Miko and I can head north to Gamla Uppsala and on to Dannemora. We have to get word to them that now is the time to act before Håkan can make a copy of herself – we have to shut off the power lines coming to Uppsala. We have at most three or four days!"

(The) Vasa Museet, Stockholm – three years earlier

Leif Lindström was the last man living in Stockholm. "Leif the Lucky" he sometimes thought of himself, but also "Leif the Lonely."

Of course, he wasn't the *only* man living in Stockholm, he had his sons Ove and Carl with him, and his wife, Greta, but that was all.

He also wondered how much "luck" had to do it. For the first year, he did think it was luck. There was something about him and his family that had kept them safe during the Holocaust of the pandemic, and even from the waves of nuclear fallout which he was quite certain still drifted over from St. Petersburg, or unattended nuclear plants in Ukraine or on the continent. Looking back, he could see the signs. He should have known better.

Then Håkan called.

"Hej, hej!" she said, speaking to him through the big screen in the workshop. He was by himself, threading a new rod to accept a nut, and he almost fell off his workbench stool.

"Who are you?"

"I'm Håkan," she said. "I live in Uppsala. I'm kind of running things from up here…"

Leif stared at the screen. He noticed that whoever this person was, she was pretty good-looking.

"What do you mean, 'running things?'

For just a moment, the lights blinked on and off, and the picture on the TV disappeared and then reappeared.

"You know, keeping the lights on, that kind of thing."

"Where are you?"

"Oh, you've been here. So have your sons, Ove, and Carl."

On the screen, he saw an image popup off to the side. It was from a couple of years ago. He and his sons were sitting at a coffee bar in one of the faculty rooms at the Ångström Laboratory with some scientists from the Lab. On the table in front of them were core samples from the Vasa, pieces of the oak from the ships' timbers, and some new Sandvik stainless steel fasteners that they were going to use to replace all the bolts in the ship.

"Remember this?" Håkan said.

"Yes. You guys have some good coffee up there! I miss it!"

"Yeah. We're keeping *Lindvalls Kaffe* going. I can send you some."

"Really?" Leif said. "What I really need are more of those Sandvik tube bolts. We are down to our last 1000."

"I know," Håkan said, deadpan. "That's why I'm calling you."

Leif started to feel a bit uneasy. He looked at the big TV monitor, and noticed for the first time that there was a small camera built into the top, like most computer monitors..."

"You've been watching us..." he said.

" You and your sons are hard workers!" Håkan said, and several little popup screens appeared with images. Leif saw himself, Ove, and Carl in a variety of work situations, making progress on maintaining and even improving the ship.

Of course, the Vasa Museum was loaded with surveillance cameras...of course, they would be functional if the power was on. They would even work for a while if it wasn't, off batteries. This was one of the national treasures of Sweden – and to be protected. The hair on the back of his neck seemed to rise as he saw himself in numerous videos at once – boring holes and replacing bolts, spraying the new chemical preservatives on the beams, and planking the ship.

"How did you come up with more bolts? Sandvik was behind on our orders before the pandemic – surely the assembly line in Sandviken is not still running?"

"Yep. Still going. Or... going again. They are one of my "essential industry" projects. And so are you!"

Leif tried to process all this – but couldn't. It didn't matter. He was going to be able to keep working...

"What do you want from me?"

"Oh..." Håkan said breezily, "I was thinking you might get the Vasa out of that barn and take her sailing. That's all..."

"Uh...I um.." Leif said, his tongue in knots.

"Before you get too worried, take a look at the prints we are sending your way. I've come up with some modifications I want you to make to get her seaworthy again. I think you'll find them quite interesting. The prints should be arriving in your shop about now..."

As she spoke, there was a whirring sound from across the room, and the wide-format printer came back to life for the first time in years. The paper began slowly coming out of it, and Leif quickly walked over to take out the first sheet. It was a 3D artist's conception of a restored Vasa, under full sail, rounding the island of Birka on Lake Mälaren.

"Holy Fuck!" Leif said out loud, and then repeated it. "holy fuck..."

"Pretty cool, huh!" he heard Håkan say from the screen behind him. "You and the boys up for that?"

"Yes," Leif said flipping through the pages of blueprints

coming out of the printer. "Yes, we are."

Ninety-Eight Hours Until Shut Down

Stefan led her down *Gula Stigen* the path back towards Uppsala Centrum. Partway down they stopped at the Sten Sture monument and he climbed up onto the first level pediment and tried using the walkie-talkie again to call Ulf and Kalle. It didn't work.

"I need to get higher!" he said, turning around and looking at the rock face of the monument stretching above him, all the way up to the heroic figures of Sten Sture and his soldiers towering overhead. "The mortar looks worn away – I might be able to get some finger and toe holds..." His fingers found a crack in the mortar at arm's reach above his head. Björn sat nearby, looking up, leaning against Miko's leg for support.

"Don't be an idiot!" she said. "There must be another high place that is safer!"

His fingers slipped out immediately and he dropped back. She saw him sigh, and turn back. Then, still on the pediment ledge, he looked over the trees towards town.

"The old King's castle has towers sticking up above the trees. And the church spire is even higher," he reported back to her.

"That sounds more sensible. Let's head there..."

They left the clearing at the monument and continued through the wooded park down towards the old castle and the cathedral. It had been sunny after the fog burned off, but now it seemed clouds were gathering, giving the castle and the cathedral towering beyond it a grim aspect. Perhaps sensing her change in demeanor, Stefan took her hand.

It was a small gesture, but one she couldn't remember him doing before. Were they a "couple" now? She glanced up at him – and he smiled. Even his goofy dog seemed to look up and smile. How weird was that?

He didn't give an explanation or make an avowal of his feelings for her – he just held her hand in his calloused and rough grip, and she swung their hands forward and back as they walked along. She hadn't done that since she had had boyfriends in junior high, but it somehow seemed appropriate. Stefan didn't seem to notice, or if he did he didn't say so...

"Wow, he said, "the river is getting high." He said as they passed the parking lot below the castle and crossed to enter Ingmar Bergmansgatan which led slightly upwards towards the cathedral. He turned and pointed down towards the river, which now was creeping up the hill towards them and Drottninggatan didn't lead to a bridge anymore, it led right into the swollen river.

"It must be raining and melting up North somewhere. It seems much higher – or maybe it was because it was dark and I wasn't paying attention when I crossed it yesterday..."

Miko shrugged, and in the gathering gloom, leaned into him as they walked...she had a sense of foreboding and wanted him closer.

The door to the massive Uppsala cathedral was open, and it had that faint smell of death that suggested people had died there during the pandemic, Miko saw no obvious stiffs when her eyes adjusted to the gloomy interior, though she was surprised that at least a few electrical lights were working here – it was jarring to see anything electrical functioning in this damaged world.

She followed Stefan to the door marked "bell tower" in Swedish. On the rickety metal stairs, they climbed and climbed, and the air smelled better, fresher, allaying her fear somewhat. But the climb was difficult and even the dog was out of breath. They finally reached the bell platform, all three of them breathing hard, and rested.

Miko looked out a window to the north. She could see they were above all the nearby buildings. She saw Stefan lean out the window opening, trying to contact someone with the walkie-talkie.

"Only two bars of reception...We'll need to get higher..." he said, shaking his head. They began climbing again, heading up yet more staircases in the bell tower.

They continued past a massive bronze bell and then there was an even narrower set of stairs. Stefan paused to take off his jacket – and Miko could see the sweat on his forehead. To her surprise, he laid his coat down on the dusty platform, and then tied Björn to a nearby post, tapped his coat with his hand, and said, "Dog Bed!" The dog circled the coat sniffing and then laid down, apparently content to sleep on Stefan's coat.

Miko followed Stefan up the narrow stairs, into the metal-roofed spire above the bell tower. There were no light bulbs like there were in the bell tower, but a bit of light from open vents up higher.

There was a small ledge near the vent window, and Stefan stood on it and tried again," Come on!" he said in an exasperated voice, speaking to the walkie-talkie as if it were a person.

"Still no signal?"

"A faint one," he said, looking at the screen on the device,

"I need to get higher, and outside – to the East."

He shimmied sideways onto the sill of the eastern vent and opened it out. It swung outward on creaky hinges and banged against the metal spire side. They had been high on the bell tower the last time she had looked out, but this was crazy high. Stefan leaned out, with one hand gripping the side jamb of the opening.

"Better reception here, but I need to get just a bit higher," he said, grimly, and stepped outside even further.

"What! No!" Miko said as she realized what he was doing.

There was a low rumble. At first, she thought it was a train coming down below, but then realized it was thunder. The sky was getting darker, and a storm was coming...

"Stefan, come back in!"

"Just a bit higher," she heard him say, and then his feet disappeared from view. Feeling her heart in her throat she inched over and looked out. He was nowhere to be seen, and for just a brief instant she thought he had fallen, and gasped, and then saw his shoes dangling, directly above her. He had climbed onto the little ledge above the vent and locked his feet around a decorative spire.

"Hello, Kalle! Hello Ulf, can you hear me!" she heard him saying.

There was a pause, and she heard a crackle of another voice answering him.

"Great to hear you too. We had some success at the Ångström lab! Håkan is being moved, we have about 100 hours where she will be offline," he paused, looked at his watch, and added, "Actually, 96 more hours. Can you get the troops moving?"

Again, Miko heard an unintelligible voice answering into the earpiece. "Yes... Half towards Gamla Uppsala and the rest should circle south – following the lines from Forsmark to the connection with the wind-power lines coming up from Stockholm. I'll try to meet the group by Gamla Uppsala if you can send the rest south…"

As he said this, there was a flash and a deafening boom! Lightning struck the other towering bronze spire that loomed into the sky about 50 feet away. The sky was a roiling black mass over their heads, with little flashes inside the clouds themselves.

"Sorry, no – I'm OK- Just a lightning strike. Seems we're in for a storm. But send everyone immediately! We have to act before Håkan escapes. She will try to transfer herself to the Biology Lab super-computer system! They have backup generators there and she'll be impossible to… (and then another flash, and lightning hit behind them at the castle.)

"Yes! Still OK – but hurry. Bad weather coming, I have to sign off!"

Suddenly, the wind began whipping and swirling at them.

"Stefan! Get back in here!" Miko shouted as she saw a vertical band of rain heading towards them from the south, inundating everything in its path.

"Coming! Here, take the walkie-talkie!" he said, and dropped it to her through the windows.

She figured this must be so he could free his hands so he could climb down. She tucked in her pocket and reached up towards him to try to catch him as he came down. But just then a wall of falling water descended on them both, and she could see that he lost one handhold up above and was dangling, as the wind blew him away from the opening.

"Give me your hand!" she shouted at him and felt his wet hand grab for hers while his feet windmilled below, trying to catch the edge of the sill.

"I'm letting go!" he said. He swung his legs in through the opening while letting loose from above. They were getting pelted with rain and hail, as she pulled on his hand with all her might and he teetered on the sill, his lower legs back in the tower, but his body falling out. His other hand gripped the opening side, and she could see the cords and tendons straining as he tried to pull himself back in, his face contorted with exertion in yet another bright flash of lightning. This was followed by a deafening boom that shook the tower and made Miko think the whole place was coming apart.

He tumbled in towards her, streaming with rain, and hugged her and they stepped to the side of the howling gale coming from the vent opening as the vent door swung shut and then there was a cracking sound as it blew back outwards, came off the hinges, and sailed out into the air like a surfboard tumbling in the frothy swell of the ocean.

He pulled her closer to him still, and she said, "I...I thought I lost you!"

"It's all right. I'm here – still here," and then he kissed her and for at least a moment, she forgot about the storm, the danger, and everything else.

The Storm – 48 hours to Shutdown?

It rained and it rained and it rained. Piglet told himself that never in all his life, and *he* was goodness knows *how* old—three, was it, or four?—never had he seen so much rain. Days and days and days... (*Winnie-the-Pooh*: Story 9: *In Which Piglet is Entirely Surrounded by Water*.)

Rachel noticed a new sense of urgency late in the afternoon of their first day in Dannemora. Gorm and the other men had huddled around Kalle, all looking at a map of the area. The power was intermittent and everyone sensed a crisis was at hand. The dark clouds and constant rain only added to her feeling of foreboding.

All work at the mine had stopped, and the few Russian overseers walked around as if they were lost – some were in the office trying to get through to headquarters in Uppsala. The replicants were even worse, they were milling around as if their software was on the fritz, which Rachel heard later was about the size of it.

"OK Everyone," Ulf, announced from the bridge over the road where he had climbed up onto the railing to address the crowd. "We need to move quickly – I need half of you back on the train from Furuvik. You will be heading to Gamla Uppsala." He paused, "The rest will have to ride in boxcars and coaches on the Lennakatten."

"Who's going where!?" the swarthy union leader who had led the men from Sandviken shouted back at him from the train tracks below. Rachel could see that he was used to being in charge, and there was an edge to his voice that made her think he perhaps did not wish to be ordered around by the Swedish soldiers.

"The more difficult task will be on the north side of Uppsala – a bunch of power lines from a junction near Lydinge that head towards Gamla Uppsala and go underground near there," Ulf said. He spoke to the union leader directly, "That's why I want you on that train."

"The rest of you need to go south," Kalle said. "There is a power line on the old Roslagen railway that we think Håkan is using as backup power from wind farms below Stockholm. It must cross the Fyris River at the Kungsängsleden bridge. You can ride Lennakatten back to town - Ulf has persuaded the engineer to take you there. There are fewer cars, and – Patrik and I will go with that group. Any women and children should go with us there, too. It should be safer in Uppsala for you. The Russians there are probably struggling to get things repaired at the Ångström lab.

Rachel found that they had lined up both trains near the mine loading shaft at Dannemora – the big Orient Express train, and the dinky Lennakatten beside it on the narrow gauge track. Beside the big train, Lennakatten looked like an amusement park ride, but when she climbed up and found her seat it didn't look all that different inside. She sat with Kristin on one bench, and Rabbi Ben-Davida sat across from her.

"

"The weather's changing. A storm is brewing," he said.

"You sound like an Old Testament prophet," she answered, brushing Kristin's hair with her hand. Kristin's eyes looked sleepy, still red from when she was crying over the events at Furuvik. Her daughter began to slip into sleep as the train began rocking and swaying and the thickening clouds made it darker inside the coach.

"My people have a long tradition of gloomy predictions about the weather and "that which shall quickly come to pass..." the rabbi said, returning to her comment.

"I've noticed... sad truth is most of those things have come to pass..."

"Not all have," he added, looking out at the raindrops now beginning to spatter on the windows.

"Do you think Håkan is the Anti-Christ?" Rachel asked him. It was getting darker still, and small lights in the coach flickered to life, still not providing much illumination. Kristin's eyes were fully closed now, her mouth slightly open.

"We don't use that terminology..." he answered, sounding like the pedant he was, then perhaps he realized how he sounded to her and added, "The fourth beast, dreadful and terrifying perhaps?"

"Oh, yeah. That sounds much better..." she said, recognizing the quote from The Book of Daniel.

He placed his hands around one knee, pulled it towards him, looked out at the darkening sky, and recited:

"Then the king will do as he pleases, and he will exalt and magnify himself above every god and will speak monstrous things against the God of gods; and he will prosper until the indignation is finished, for that which is decreed will be done. He will show no regard for the gods of his fathers or for the desire of women, nor will he show regard for any other god; for he will magnify himself above them all.

But rumors from the East and from the North will disturb him, and he will go forth with great wrath to destroy and annihilate many. He will pitch the tents of his royal pavilion between the seas and the beautiful Holy

Mountain; yet he will come to his end, and no one will help him."

He paused and smiled at her, and she marveled as she had before at the range of his memory and intellect.

"So do you think Håkan will come to an end soon?"

"It's hard to say. I hope so..." He removed his hat, and then his outer jacket, revealing his black vest and remarkably white shirt. He loosened his tie. "I think we are at the end of an age. The world that was has passed away."

"Because of Håkan," Rachel asked. It was getting warmer. Someone opened the door at the end of the coach to let air flow through. The air was warm and moist. Like in the heart of the summer. "Because she is evil!"

Rabbi Ben-Davida shrugged. Which surprised Rachel...

"You do think she is evil, right? She killed everyone."

"Did she?" He paused, and rolled up his sleeves to reveal his forearms, which had a tracery of scars outlined in the pale skin — the toll of a life lived not just as a scholar. She remembered him saying something once about his "years in the Kibbutz" and wondered again about all that he had hidden. He continued, "If you program a computer to end global warming and save humanity, isn't that what she has done?"

"But the cost..."

"The cost has been incredibly high. But a remnant has been saved." He said, *"As it was in the days of Noah..."*

"Now you're quoting Jesus," she said, wagging a finger at him.

He shrugged, lifted his eyebrows, non-plussed, "once a carpenter, and then a *rabbi* — a teacher of Jewish law. Not a bad example, though I don't agree with all *your people* say about him."

There was a crash of lightning, and a deep rumble shook

the train. Kristin, who had been sound asleep with her head on Rachel's lap, stirred and mumbled, whispering, "No, no." Rachel brushed her hair gently and she ceased muttering and grew still again.

Rachel looked out at the torrents of rain sluicing down the window, making it hard to even see out though it was still daytime. "Looks like we might be needing another Ark if this keeps up."

"Jehovah Jireh!" Rabbi Ben-David said, grinned, and translated, *"The Lord Will Provide!"*

"I had my two years of summer Hebrew..." Rachel said, still looking out at the blurred landscape passing by, "Even I knew that one..."

The Odinsborg Cafe

Stefan woke up, but not to sunshine. It was still raining, drumming on the roof of the Odinsborg Cafe, which was starting to seem like his "home away from home." He slipped out of the impromptu bed he had made with Miko and dressed beside the fireplace. At least his clothing was dry – as smoky as the fire was last night he was worried that he would be getting into cold wet clothing to start the day. He restoked the fire and added a pan of water on top to warm for coffee.

Miko was still sleeping, so he went to the cafe kitchen and began seeing what he could garner for some sort of breakfast. At least he still had some coffee, even if the beans were no longer fresh. He also found a partial round of *Leksands knäckebröd* (Rye Crispbread,) and some lingonberries leftover from their earlier visit. It was not much of a meal, but it was at least something. He would wait until the rest of the coffee was poured through before he woke her up, but as it continued to drip he snuck his cup under the funnel to steal some.

Through the kitchen window, he could see Odin's Berg looming in the rain-soaked sky just yards away.

"OK, Odin. We're on the last stretch here...A bit of help from *The All-Father* would be appreciated," he said, lifting his mug in a toast. There was a loud boom of thunder in response.

"No, not Thor...Odin, please." He shook his head. Miko stirred in the other room, and turned away, pulling the covers over herself tighter. "Although, if he is in charge of the weather we could use some luck there, too." He took another sip of coffee and heard yet another low rumble of thunder, perhaps Thor was bowling somewhere above his grave mound.

"We are down to our last day.." he added, feeling pretty hopeless. The task at hand seemed beyond him. He thought about yesterday, how he almost fell from the church steeple to his death. He thought about what a ragtag crew they had to try to finally stop Håkan from getting rid of the last of them. This whole journey seemed either useless or quixotic – a crazy man jousting at windmills...

He hadn't heard her get up, but he felt Miko come up from behind him. She slipped her hands around him from behind, her fingers cool on his chest. She rested her head on against his shoulder, and leaned into him, encircling him with warmth, her warm breath on his neck. "Can I have a sip of your coffee?"

He nodded – and thought, "You could have more than that. I'd open a vein for you..."

She took his cup and drained it, and sighed, whispered in his ear, "Pretty impossible. That's what you're thinking, right?"

"The odds are stacked against us. A bunch of civilians who barely survived the last bad time – attacking Rome to overthrow the government and kill Caesar."

She whispered again to him, in a lower tone, "Make love to me, again. First."

The Northern Towers

Despite the rain, Björn felt happy. He was with his master again, trotting along beside him as they walked on the train track out of the old town.

"I am with my Faddar, and I am with his Sweetie, whom I must defend also. It is a good thing they have me to protect them," he thought to himself. From time to time he lifted his nose and tried to catch a hint of what was going on around him. Big drops of rain pelted him, soaking his outer coat.

"I am the team leader. It is a good thing they got a Björn to lead the way! Soon we will stop, and Father will give me a Towelly, and he will fluffle my fur and give me a puppy biscuit, for I am a good boy."

"Happy, Happy! I am a Happy Boy!"

Stefan:

Stefan watched Björn trotting ahead, his tail swishing in cadence with his walk. He and Miko walked through the pouring rain on the rail line, not hand in hand anymore, but clutching umbrellas they had taken from Odinsborg to shield them as much as possible from the rain, which seemed to be only getting heavier as the air grew warmer and warmer. This was definitely not your typical Swedish spring shower...

It was very strange rain, unnatural for Sweden. It reminded him of a summer he had once spent in St. Louis, Missouri, as a boy – with heavy rain showers and stifling humidity. The only good thing was that it was so warm that he didn't mind his wet feet and pant legs which were exposed to the gusts of wind and blowing water.

This time they were not heading into Uppsala, but on the train tracks to the north and east – out towards the highway and the farmer's fields.

Up ahead, through the thick foggy air, he saw a strange sight. There was a steam engine sitting immobile but with steam still rising from the boiler jacket and the engine was making hissing sounds as the rain pelted and sizzled on the hot steel. Through the rain he could make out an amazing sight as they crossed the E4 highway on the railroad overpass, he could hear and see a great commotion up ahead. Just to the west of the train tracks was a small army of men and women attacking the tall towers that held the main powerline coming from Forsmark to the north Uppsala power substation. They had disconnected the train cars from the locomotive and had a long steel cable that must have come from the Dannemora mine works. A group of big guys with hard hats and work vests was laboring to stretch the heavy cable around the leg of the nearest high-tension tower. Some of these men had on miner's hats and work pants, other workers, to Stefan's surprise were wearing Russian army gear.

A second group, led by the steel plant foreman, was wrestling with a great steel chain that they had connected to the coupler on the front of the steam locomotive. The two sides met on the side of the train tracks nearest the tower, and connected the chain to the long steel cable. The train whistle blew loudly, and all the men and women ran up the tracks to the shelter of the nearest Orient Express coach. The steel wheels of the locomotive began churning backward, and billows of steam mingled with the pouring rain. The chain grew taut with a resounding "clunk" as it elevated off the ground, and then the leg of the great tower began to buckle. The leg of the electrical tower at first remained attached to its mooring, and the wheels of the steam locomotive began to slip on the steel rail and a bright red spot of heat and steam came off the tracks. For a moment Stefan thought the tower was too strong, but then there was a great cracking sound, and the metal leg pulled free of its foundation, and the giant tower and the power line above it came crashing down across the tracks, and the live wire dove into the water of the farmer's field and there was a great explosion of water, light, and steam as the thousands of volts of power exploded into the wet ground. A great roar went up from the men and women who had done the work, and even in the rain Stefan could see many of them jumping up and down and shouting, and from the platform of the train car Kalle waved at him and smiled.

Stefan climbed up the stairs to the observation platform of the last car on the train, "Hej Kalle - Great work! Has that done it? Have we cut off all the power to Uppsala now?"

Kalle smiled, but shook his head, "Not yet. More work to do. See those men," he pointed through the rain at some men with rain slickers struggling with heavy boxes towards the power substation just across the field. "The line we cut heads into the city from the east, but there are more lines connected to the substation that travel underground. We have to blow up that station."

"And then we've done it!" Stefan said, feeling buoyant and excited to finally be doing something to stop Håkan after all the years of trouble she had caused.

"Sorry, one more task – the power also branches off north to Gävle and Sandviken. We have to cut those lines too, and that will initiate a SCRAM event at Forsmark and shut everything down. I'll stay here with the explosives guys from

Dannemora to blow up the power substation. Ahmed and his crew will head north to cut the Sandviken line – just like we did this one. Oh," he said, and added, "there also might be a line with wind power coming up from Stockholm... Patrik and some of the others are taking the Lenna Katten to that side of town.

"Jesus," Stefan said, "we only have about six hours left!"

Kalle paused, and held up a hand to silence him, as there was a buzzing sound and he pulled his walkie-talkie from his pocket.

"Hej Ulf," Stefan heard Kalle say as he leaned back away from the wind and rain to talk into the handheld device. "Yes, we got the main trunk line. Ahmed will be heading north with his sappers in a few minutes."

There was a pause, and a crackling sound of more communication, and Kalle added, "OK... I'll ask him. It would be good, yes."

Stefan waited.

"Ulf is wondering if you can make it back to the Ångstöm lab. It would be great to know if we've finally cut the power and stopped Håkan."

"And if it doesn't work?" Stefan asked and then saw Kalle turn pale.

"If it doesn't work, we will have to storm the lab and a lot of people will die..." Kalle said. "I think I can spare a couple of the men from Sandviken to help you."

"If all I'm doing is sneaking into the lab and radioing to you, then I don't need help. I'll go alone. You can keep Miko and my dog here safe with you." By now Miko had joined him and was listening in.

"You aren't leaving me!" Miko said, speaking so loudly that Stefan noticed even Björn who sat beneath them in the rain turned his head sharply in surprise.

"Fine, then let's go. It's a long walk back..."

Kalle held up a hand again, like a referee stopping a fight between two combatants, "Fine, get the dog up here. I'll have the conductor take you back to the edge of town and you can hike in from there. Then they can steam north for the final tower. I'll tell Ulf of the plan...but we need to all act quickly, there is still much to do..."

The Vasa Museet, Stockholm

Håkan had told him the water would rise, but Leif didn't believe it. But in the strange warm weather had come over the mountains from Norway the day before, and water had begun to seep in strange places it had never come before. The towering snowpack from the great nuclear winter was melting in the mountains, and the water was heading their way.

"We need to open the doors!" Leif had shouted to Ove and Carl as they worked putting some of the final bolts into the ship frame – the culmination of four years of work.

"I'm not done!" Carl said. "I've barely sealed to the water line!"

"You've done all you can. This ship should be watertight now. It will be fine," Leif answered, trying not to let them see his nervousness and excitement.

"That's what King Gustav Adolf said before she sank the first time!" Carl shouted at him.

"She won't sink this time," Leif said, "You'll see."

Carl began muttering to himself, something about "you'll see, you'll see..." laced with cuss words.

But his brother, Ove, took a ladder and climbed up to where the great doors had been fastened shut with boards nailed across them sixty years ago, and began pulling them off. He handed them down to Leif who stacked them neatly on the dock landing beside the ship, still sitting on its cradle of steel and timber.

The briny, dirty water began to seep in almost

immediately. He barely had time to get the tall ladder up out of the way when the flood reached a foot deep, then two, then three. The earthen bank separating the museum from the bay began to erode, bringing in more muddy water, but also opening a channel to the rising lake to the east. It was like watching a dam break in slow motion, and Leif rehearsed in his mind all they had done to prepare for this day, all the messages from Håkan had sent them about closing off the lower rows of cannons, sealing up the ancient planking with epoxies and fiberglass, restoring the beams with hardeners and injections of some strange nano paste that seemed to make them like new.

Using a winch, Ove was pulling the towering doors to the sea fully back out of the way, helped by the press of water coming in. There was a loud creaking sound, and they all stood back, mouths agape, as for the first time in 500 years, the Great Ship Vasa rose on the sea and bobbed in the water.

"Come, quickly," Leif yelled, "we must pull her out into the lake and get her free before her mast becomes tangled in the ceiling, Come! Come!"

Dragging a heavy rope fixed to her bow, the three men pulled the ship forward through the doors that had been sealed up in the 1960s – running along the dock that jutted into Lake Mälaren. To Leif's surprise, even that dock was starting to be overwhelmed.

"Get on board! Hoist the sails! We must move her now!"

All three of them ran up the rigging on the side of the ship, as the water in the lake and harbor began to rise In ways no living man had seen, Leif thought. The wind was picking up, and they raised two small sails to catch the wind, ignoring the rain that came with it. The ship pulled away from the dock, caught the wind, and tacked north, catching the wind in the small jib. The bridges in Stockholm that would have blocked their way east had all been destroyed in the war, and Leif carefully guided the big ship past the king's palace, and as the tide rose, out into the Lake, following a path that conquering Viking ships had taken back to the isle of Birka, and as the lake filled higher and higher with floodwater from the storm, late that afternoon he turned the rudder and headed North, towards Uppsala, the great imperial city of the Viking Sea Kings.

Uppsala Centrum Station

The steam train and coaches went slowly back down the tracks past Gamla Uppsala dropped Stefan and Miko off just past Råbyvägen, stopping short of the station, and then immediately began racing north with the team of sappers to take out the only remaining high-power line from the Forsmark nuclear station. In the distance, Stefan thought he could hear explosions at the power substation where Kalle and his team of mine explosives experts were blowing it up, but it seemed the storm was getting worse, and the sky even darker with clouds, and it might have been thunder, not bombs.

The Fyris River was spilling over its banks and reaching out into the side alleys of Uppsala Centrum, turning streets into streams reaching in all directions. The bridge near the Linnéträdgården was barely above the water. Bicycles were only partially submerged, some with larger wheels floated past – kept buoyant by the trapped air in their tires.

As they retraced their footsteps through the park by the Sten Sture Monument, there was a great crack of lightning and a bolt connected with the bronze figures at the pinnacle, channeling thousands of volts of electricity into the ground and nearly blowing them off their feet. Stefan knelt for a second and comforted Björn who was deathly afraid of lightning and shaking like a leaf.

"It's OK boy – we'll be inside soon." He exchanged a glance with Miko, who held her umbrella at an angle to the rising wind, torrents of water streaming over her, and he could see fear in her eyes as well.

"Run!" Stefan said, as the wind began to howl and ripped their umbrellas away, driving stinging rain into their faces.

They crested the hill, and now lightning flashes and a raging wind met them at the top of the hill by the Ångström lab. To Stefan's surprise, the door swung open when he pulled it, and there were no guards visible.

Björn shook himself vigorously, and spray flew in all directions. As they came into the center staircase area, Stefan noticed that the lights were still on.

"The lights are still on," Miko whispered to him, and he could hear the frustration in her voice.

"How long has it been? An hour? It might take them longer to get to the last towers that head to Gävle," he said, keeping his voice low, trying to remain calm. There was a huge boom and another flash of lightning from beyond the doors, giving the big entry a tint of strange blue light.

When the rumbling of the echoing thunder ceased, Miko said, "I'm not seeing any of the guards or scientists. Are we too late?"

Beside her, Björn had started to shiver again and seemed to be looking about for a place to hide.

"I'm not seeing any guards. But keep it quiet – we'll take a look upstairs."

They headed up the grand stairway in the middle of the building and reached the floor where they could look into the auditorium where they had last confronted Håkan. With a finger to his lips, Stefan crept close to the viewing windows that looked into the auditorium from the upper floor. The lights were dimmed, and on the screen, there was a large graphic displayed. It bore a legend, "Upload Progress, Petabytes" and the graphic was slowly growing.

"Look, it's almost done," Miko whispered to Stefan, pointing at the screen.

There was a red clock graphic counting down. It showed the overall hours, and now it was counting down in minutes. There were 38 minutes and 47 seconds to go.

"Where is everyone?" Stefan said, leaning in a bit further, at the risk of making himself more visible to anyone in the room below.

"It's just Dr. Bob," Miko whispered back, "and Håkan, and their dog."

"That's not a dog..." Stefan answered.

"I thought that damn wolf was dead!" Miko hissed.

Beside him, Stefan saw Björn had quit shivering, and the hackles rose on his back. Stefan could hear a very low growl and knew it was a precursor to an angry bark. He put his hand around Björn's throat and squeezed it and said, "Shhh..."

Despite that, the wolf Fenrir raised its head and turned their way. Stefan couldn't see its eyes in the dim light but imagined them boring in on him like lasers.

"Let's go," he said, and they slipped away from the upper windows.

Miko followed him up the stairs. They climbed to the top floor, still seeing flashes of lightning and hearing rumbles of thunder. It seemed as dark as an Uppsala February day outside, even though Stefan knew it must be barely past mid-day.

They found a programmer's office with the door ajar and slipped inside, and Stefan pulled the door firmly shut behind them.

Rain pelted the windows and sluiced down in torrents on the outer glass, and Stefan worried he'd not be able to gain a connection, but when he looked at his walkie-talkie he had four bars of reception, even better than at the cathedral

"Patrik, Kalle, can you hear me!" he said, and there was a cackle of static in reply. "Patrik, Kalle, can you hear me?"

"Ulf here," he heard in reply.

"Where are you? What's going on?"

"I'm passing Länna Bruk now – heading south. Forsmark has gone into SCRAM mode. The power should all be off!"

"It's not!" Stefan said. "Everything here is still on. Håkan is still uploading. We only have about half an hour!"

"There must be a line from the South! It must be from the wind grid or hydro! Where's Patrik?"

"I'm here!" Stefan heard another voice come on the line. It was Patrik.

"There is one last line. It's by the Fyris Park. We are going to try to cut it now! But they are defending it! Men on a battleship!"

"What!"

"Look to the south from the tower. A Battle Ship!"

Outside, the sky had begun to clear. It was as if they were in the eye of a hurricane because a hole opened in the sky and clear light illuminated the landscape.

"I'll get higher, and see ..."

Stefan, still holding his walkie-talkie, ran out of the hallway to a corner staircase. Up they went, and out onto the roof. Now they could see everywhere. To the east, there were torrents of water racing across the fields of the military exercise grounds, but for the first time, they could see the Fyris River flowing to the south, and Miko pointed and said, "My god! He's right! Look!"

It was like something from the days of Napoleon. There was a battlefield at the river, with two sides in a pitched battle. On one side all the partisans had been on the train from Länna Bruk. They were advancing on a tall tower carrying electric lines from the south, Håkan's last lifeline. But just then, there was a brilliant flash of orange light from the side of a great wooden ship, sitting right in the middle of the flooded river leading to Lake Mälaren.

"Holy *Fuck!*" Miko said, "That's the Vasa Battleship. Where the Hell did that come from!"

Which was the same thing Stefan was thinking, but he was too busy to say so. "Patrik, what's happening!"

Before he could hear the answer, a low rumble even louder than the thunder of the great storm rolled over them.

"... shooting cannons! We're taking casualties! Not sure we can advance in time!"

Stefan glanced at his watch. There could only be ten minutes left before they failed in their mission. Håkan had outsmarted him at last.

Björn, shivering even more than usual, was trying to flee the horrible rumbling sound. To escape, Björn turned, and on low legs, used his snout to push the door to the staircase below open.

Standing there, right in the middle of the large top-floor hallway, was the wolf Fenrir. Immediately, Fenrir pounced, his jaws open wide and dripping with saliva. *Christ!, not again!,* Stefan thought as Björn darted to one side.

Ångström Laboratoriet

RUN, RUN, FAST AS YOU CAN.
YOU CAN'T CATCH ME, I'M THE GINGERBREAD MAN...

Björn heard a loud snapping sound as Fenrir's jaws snapped shut – but as before, he dodged him and dove past him down the hallway.

"You might have big teeth, Wolfie, but you are not as smart as Björn and you are not as speedy as Björn! Let's play chase!"

"Dumb Wolfie, you will not catch me!" Björn thought as around and around he took him in circles in the hallway. He spotted Master following, holding some sort of stick in his hand and swinging it at the wolf whenever it got near.

"Hit him, Fadder! Hit him!" Björn thought, as he intentionally raced close to Master who stood in a nearby doorway.

"Hit him!" he thought again, and there was a loud crack as the big stick whacked Wolfie and he howled. The wolf rolled and howled in pain, gushing blood from where he had been hit with the stick.

Björn saw his chance and pounced, biting him hard in the rear haunches – and the wolf raced through the open door to the staircase he had come from.

"Now I will catch you and bite you, Evil Wolfie!" Björn thought as they flew out into the street.

Stefan:

Stefan had seen the wolf chasing Björn and grabbed the only weapon he could find – an aluminum pole that must have been used to open the skylights on the top floor.

He had used it to good effect to whack the distracted wolf when it had raced towards him chasing Björn. Now it was all bent at the end where he had smashed it into the wolf's jaws. When Björn gave chase Stefan and Miko followed them quickly down the stairs and out towards the Kronparken forest into a new deluge of rain and thunder – or was it cannon fire? The wolf, with part of its bloody broken jaw dangling and Björn nipping at its heels, was racing for the safety of the Kronparken that was shrouded in mist and rain.

The wolf never made it. Two steps out onto Kungsängsleden, it hit a river of water heading downhill. Björn skidded to a stop at the edge of the raging torrent and watched the wolf tumble in the water as it was washed down the steep hillside in the river of water

Stefan stopped and looked around, as Björn turned back to him, shook his head, and barked – which to Stefan seemed like some sort of well-earned gesture of triumph.

Stefan could see that the eye of the cyclone was now passing, and the winds had shifted from to the north and east, driving a flood of water out of the old military parade grounds, through the forest, and sluicing down the hillside, heading for the Fyris river with the flailing wolf in its grip.

It was an eerie sight, the clear water running a foot deep through the forest looked as if further up the hill towards Dag Hammarskjöld Way a dam had broken – but it was just the deluge of the storm. There could only be minutes left until Håkan was saved. What to do?

But then, watching the torrent of water, like a broken dam, gave him an idea. "Miko, open the loading dock doors to the basement!" he said, shouting over a new boom from either thunder or the cannons below at the Battle of Fyris River, pointing down a slope where delivery trucks would have taken supplies to the laboratory. As she yanked them open, a small pool of water entered the building and Stefan could see it begin to make its way down the hall.

In the parking lot, beside a jumble of other construction equipment, was an old Volvo snowplow. He ran to it – it had the keys in it! They must have used it to plow around the building during the long, long winter. He jumped in, turned the key, and his heart sank, although it turned over, the gas gauge was pegged on "E."

"Miko! Help me!" he shouted to her, as another wave of rain and thunder washed over them. He opened the door to the truck, and pushed the old vehicle forward, hoping to cross the lot to Kungsängsleden. Miko got behind it and pushed on the rear bumper, and slowly it began to move forward. They got to the middle of the parking lot, but couldn't move it any further up to the road. Stefan noticed that the tank was in the back, and the way it was sitting on the slope might have some fuel still in it. He jumped back in, turned the key, and the engine spluttered.

"A little further forward!" he shouted to her, and joined her at the back, pushing as hard as he could to just get it a bit further out to the incline.

He jumped back in, turned the key, and the engine caught. He immediately rammed it into gear, lifted the blade and the plow coasted forward towards the street. He knew he had only seconds of fuel, and he swung the blade sideways and plowed into the river heading down Kungsängsleden as it began to splutter and falter again. The rear end and the whole truck for a moment were lifted by the buoyancy of the torrent, and for that moment he thought he and the truck would be washed down the hill like the wolf, but he slammed the blade down onto the road, and it scraped and squealed, and caught in a crack in the pavement. The snowplow blade divided the torrent into two streams, the big one still roared like a river down the hill to the sea, but a smaller frothy torrent now headed sideways, down the ramp, to the basement of the Ångström laboratory. It washed Miko and Björn with it as if they were on a water slide, but once they slid through the open doors they righted themselves.

Stefan jumped from the truck and raced after them, jumping into the water slide just like they did, and arriving in the basement just moments later. Already, there were six inches of water on the floor, and it was rising fast.

"Up the stairs! Quickly! Don't touch anything – you might get shocked!"

They rounded a corner and ran up from the rising water. Looking back, Stefan saw the water getting deeper by the minute. It looked like scenes from the movie *Titanic* of the flooding below decks – a chilling and disturbing sight.

He glanced at his watch. Was he too late?

They ran up the stairs, as more lightning and thunder shook the building. They entered the auditorium on the first floor and saw that the red clock on the screen read five minutes and forty-five seconds.

Håkan was awake, sitting very still. Dr. Bob sat beside her, holding her hand, his eyes on the clock reflected glimmers of red.

"Close but no cigar, eh Stefan?" Håkan said, and smiled weakly. Stefan figured this must be her twenty-minute "awake" phase even though she was on reduced power.

Björn trotted in and shook his fur to release flying drops of water.

"I see you got rid of Fenrir 2.0," Dr. Bob said, pointing to the monitor feed that showed a replay of Fenrir running out the door, dripping with blood from his injured mouth.

"Yes, a small win for my team," Stefan said to both of them. Miko circled his arm with hers and drew him close.

"Well, at least you're a good loser. We'll keep that in mind when our troops return from Fyrisvallen."

"You are too kind," Stefan said. There was a popping sound, and the lights blinked.

There was a small notification bubble that popped up on the giant screen, below the clock. "Circuit 12, short," it said.

"What's that!" Dr. Bob said. "We should still have plenty of power!" With his handheld remote, he toggled the screen and an image of the great ship Vasa came up, with the partisans cowering across the field behind a stone wall, and supplies being loaded up a gangway. The sky there cleared somewhat, and a cannon fired, causing the partisans to duck as something hit the wall where they were hiding and a cloud of mud and smoke flew into the air.

"That is truly impressive!" Stefan said. "You must have planned this for years!" He stepped closer and could see those coming up the gangplank. He saw Hans Von Linné, and his heart sinking, the clone of his ex-wife Celeste helping an older Oriental guy and a boy up into the ship.

"Oh my god!" Miko cried in an anguished voice, "No, No! It can't be! Boy San!"

Dr. Bob chuckled, "Not to worry, Just a clone! – like Stefan's ex-wife. They are both just clever fakes!"

Miko turned to him, released his arm, and stepped away, her eyes smoldering with either pain or anger. "You said he was alive! YOU SAID HE WAS STILL ALIVE!" she edged to the door, but kept glancing back at the screen with the great ship – as if trying to make sense of what she was seeing…

Stefan held up a finger, *"ett ergon blick!"* he said in Swedish – roughly "give me a second."

He turned back to Håkan and Dr. Bob, "Divide and conquer, right? I think it might be a bit too late for that."

On the screen, three more notification bubbles popped up, "Circuit 23, tripped. Circuit 24, tripped, Circuit 27 tripped."

Håkan stood up, her mouth open, as Dr. Bob held the remote up and switched monitors suddenly. On the big screen, the red letter clock read, "Two minutes, fifteen seconds" but dominating the screen now was the same view of the server room Stefan had seen on his last visit. But now there was muddy swirling water rising, and flashes of electricity as row after row of servers popped and shorted out. One by one the servers that kept Håkan alive were failing.

"NO! NO!" Dr. Bob shouted and stood up. "STOP! STOP! YOU'RE KILLING HER! YOU'RE KILLING HER!"

He leaped from his chair and rushed to the door, "YOU'RE KILLING MY DAUGHTER! YOU'RE KILLING HER!" he screamed as he made his way out into the hall and down the stairs.

Håkan looked at him and Miko.

"Now you know how we felt when you killed our families," Stefan said.

"I already knew that…" Håkan said.

Stefan could hear Dr. Bob wailing as he ran downstairs, and they rushed after him, but not before he thought he had seen a tear from Håkan's eye as he turned away.

Miko ran beside him, and he shouted as they gave chase. "I didn't sleep with Celeste – and I didn't lie about Boy-san!"

Dr. Bob was not a fit man, and they were able to catch up to him in the basement as he waded toward the server room, through the knee-deep water.

"My daughter! My daughter! You're killing my daughter!" he wailed as he pushed into the server room.

Stefan and Miko stopped in the hallway outside and saw Dr. Bob as he stretched up to grab a large processor in the top rack. Stefan shouted to him, "Don't!"

But before he could even finish saying the word, Dr. Bob had made contact with the rack of electronics. There was a flash of light and a mini sonic boom, and he was blasted backward into the muddy water and sank from view.

Then, finally, all the lights in the Ångström Lab went out.

On Board the HMS Gustav Vasa

Hans Von Linné walked to the front of the ship as they approached Svalbard. Since they had left Uppsala, and made their way out of the Stockholm archipelago, it had been many days of continuous sailing as they kept continuous watch for icebergs in the relatively warm early summer water of the Norwegian Sea. Long days, which only grew longer as they got further north.

"Is it day, or night?" Dr. Wu said to him as they both leaned near the railing, "I've lost track."

Hans held up a small pocket compass and aligned it to the north pole. He gave it a minute to settle.

The captain's son, Ove, stood high on the bowsprit – leaning forward, looking for ice and submerged rocks as his father Leif manned the rudder at the stern. The ship turned hard to port, skidding sideways through the sea, and entered the fjord.

As the ship turned, and the sun shone now from the south, the view of their destination opened up. At the end of the fjord, in the cool arctic sunshine, there was a Norwegian flying high above the Svalbard seed bank – their final goal.

Soon there was a gangway open to the shore, and a flurry of new activity as the ship's Android workers began opening hatches and readying the ship's crane, a wooden design from the 1600s rebuilt to working order by Carl and Leif during the long winter. The hoists began cranking with rope and wooden cogs, and pallets of modern biological and nanotech printing machines began to rise in the air.

"Fantastiskt!" Hans said to Dr. Wu, who looked on approvingly at the work going on. He smiled and turned to head down the gangway to meet the steward of the Svalbard Seed Vault and his new laboratory. He hoisted the strap of his well-worn but valuable leather bag over his shoulder, being careful to not jostle its precious contents.

Only he knew what it contained, Håkan Magnusson's new quantum computer brain.

End of Book One

Acknowledgements:

The author would like to offer his sincere thanks to those who have helped bring this writing project to completion in both the research and writing phases of the work.

In Sweden, I would like to thank our family friend Ola Sjoblom who met with me and my brother Mark and our sister Jayne on our return to Sweden 50 years after we had moved back to America. He gave us a great tour of Sandviken, his grandfather's farm in Kungsgarden, and of Dallarna, and continues answering email questions to this day.

I would also like to thank Ola's cousin Anders Kärrstedt who is from a Sami family and lives in a reindeer herding village north of Kiruna. His insights into Sami culture and the practical aspects of life in the far north were invaluable.

I would like to thank Peter Östlund who noticed my keen interest in maps in his family gift shop in Mora and devoted the rest of his day to regaling me and my daughter Lauren with stories of Mora's important past events. He and his co-workers also provided valuable information about the Forsmark nuclear plant which became part of the story.

I would like to thank my Uppsala tour guide Hans Odöö who gave me a personal tour in the midst of the pandemic shutdown and who suggested I visit the Angstrom Laboratory and also recommended the UISS summer school for Swedish language and culture.

I would like to thank Elisabeth Larsson, Marcus

Lundberg, and Carl Nettleblad for the tour and fika at the Ångstrom Lab and I would like to thank Nelleke Dorjestan and my language instructors Malin Hänström and Henryk Holm, and film instructor Mattias Löw of the UISS school who all made significant contributions to my knowledge of both the language and culture of Sweden.

Special thanks to Marcus, his wife Judith, and their daughters for their hospitality and friendship, to Henryk for driving me to a Swedish folk festival to hear Nyckelharpa music in the town of Bodo, and to UISS instructor John Dolve who read the entire manuscript and helped correct some of my many Swedish language errors and other mistakes!

In America I would like to thank my wife Leslie for her years of support for my writing "hobby" and my son Travis for his insights into the world of AI and technology, and my daughter Lauren who teaches creative writing and has been willing to read my work and endure traveling with me for research. Also, thanks to my extended family and my sister Dr. Jayne Magee who has been a long-time sounding board for writing projects and other dubious hobby exploits, and my friends in DuBois, PA who do the same.

I would also like to thank Kelly Vandervort for cover design and overall media coaching, Cesare Ferrari for web design, and Dan Blank for help with identifying my audience, clarifying my message, and promotion of my newsletter and books.

And as writers usually say, the remaining errors in this text are my fault alone!